What Has Gone Before

Clariette de Artegnean, her cousins Jolfe Endarion and Deren Mumbasi, along with their new friend Ariarra Popplevensie, set out to experience the world beyond their sleepy town of Good River.

It isn't long before danger finds them!

With their new employers handicapped with a couple of severely injured members, Clari, Jolfe and Ariarra set off on their own to help their friend Mecomi rescue some children.

Having survived their first skirmishes with the perilous beasts of the wilderness, our heroes finally arrive at the city of Bridgetown...

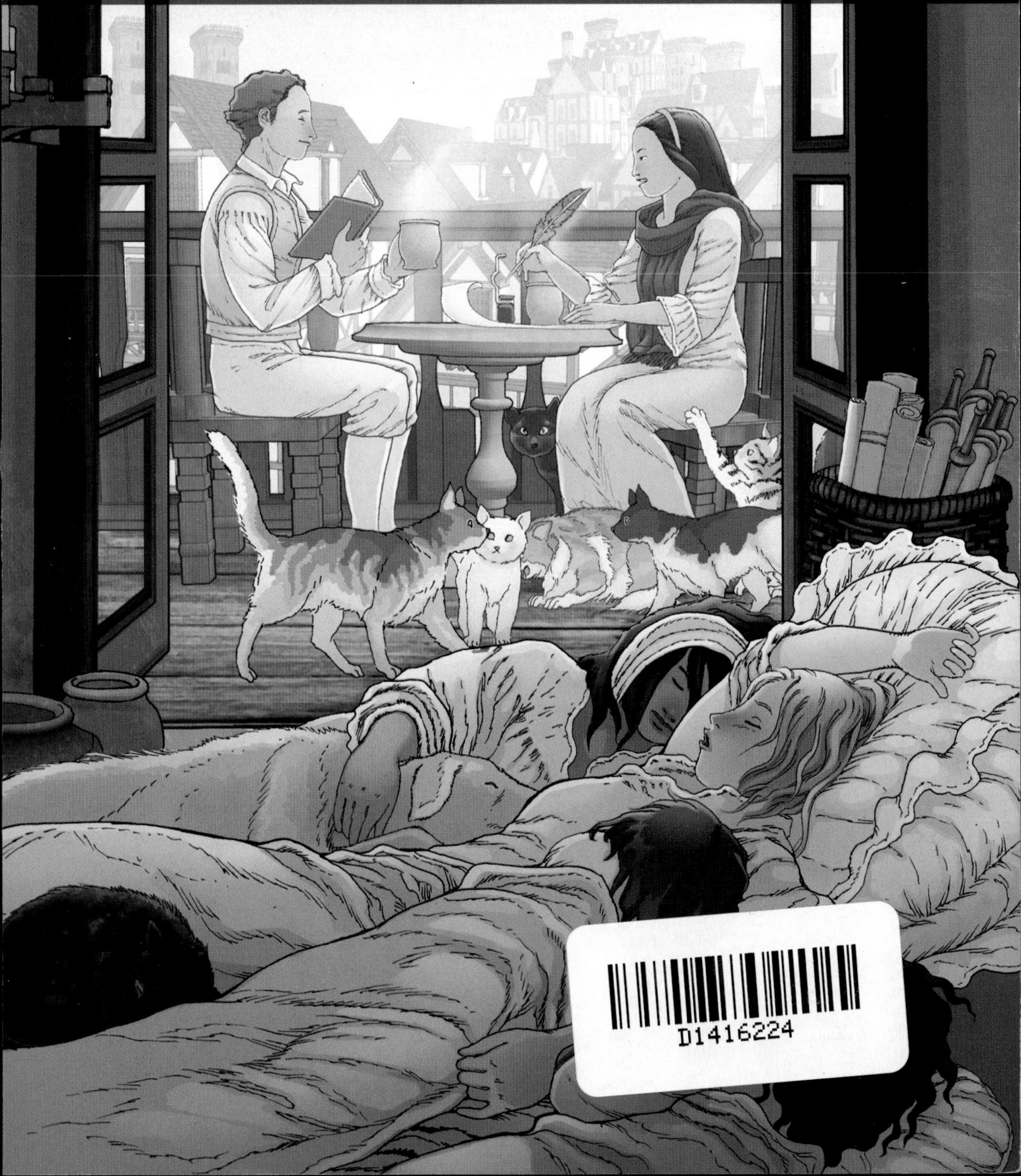

Chapter 1: The Long March

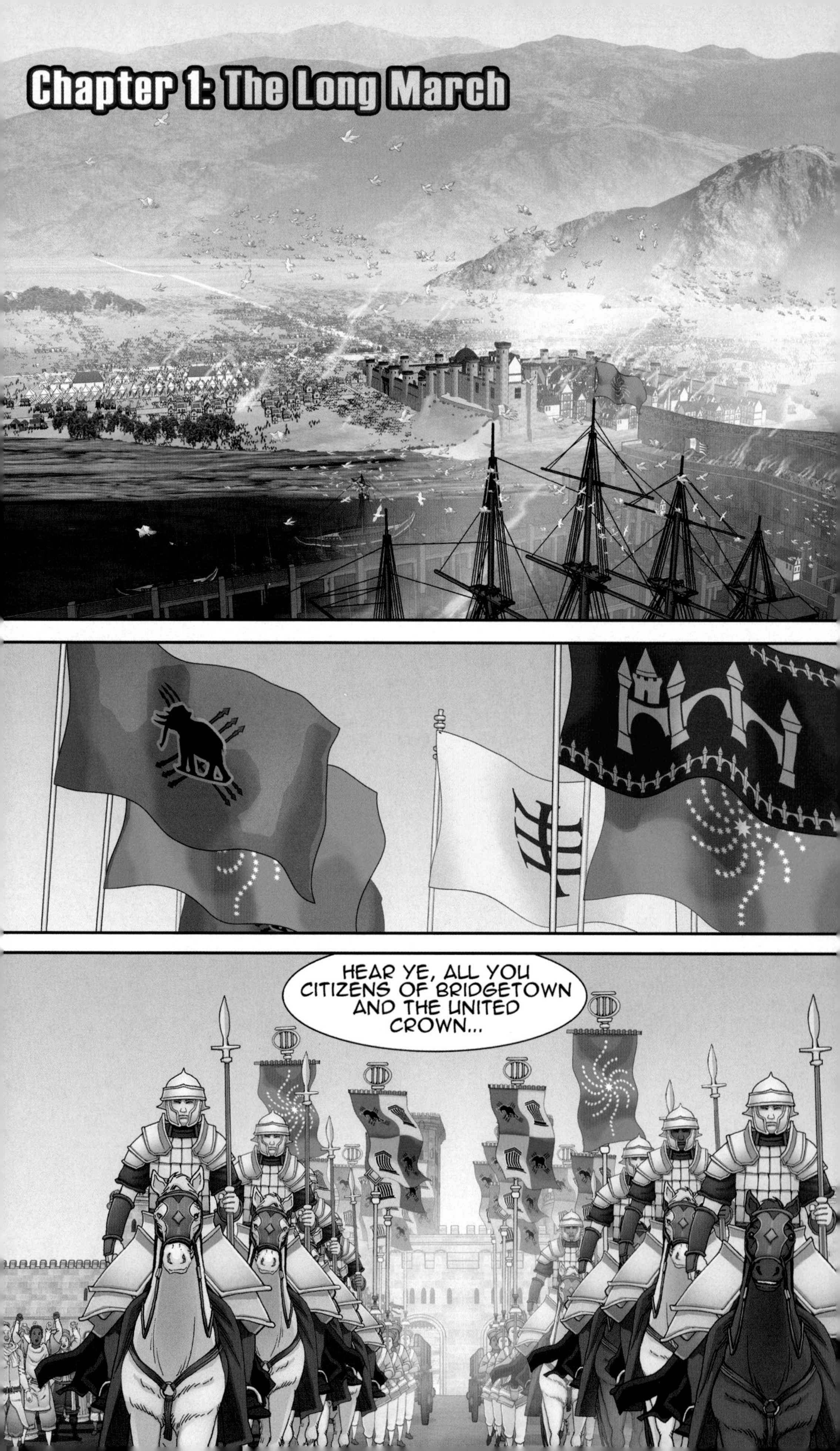
HEAR YE, ALL YOU CITIZENS OF BRIDGETOWN AND THE UNITED CROWN...

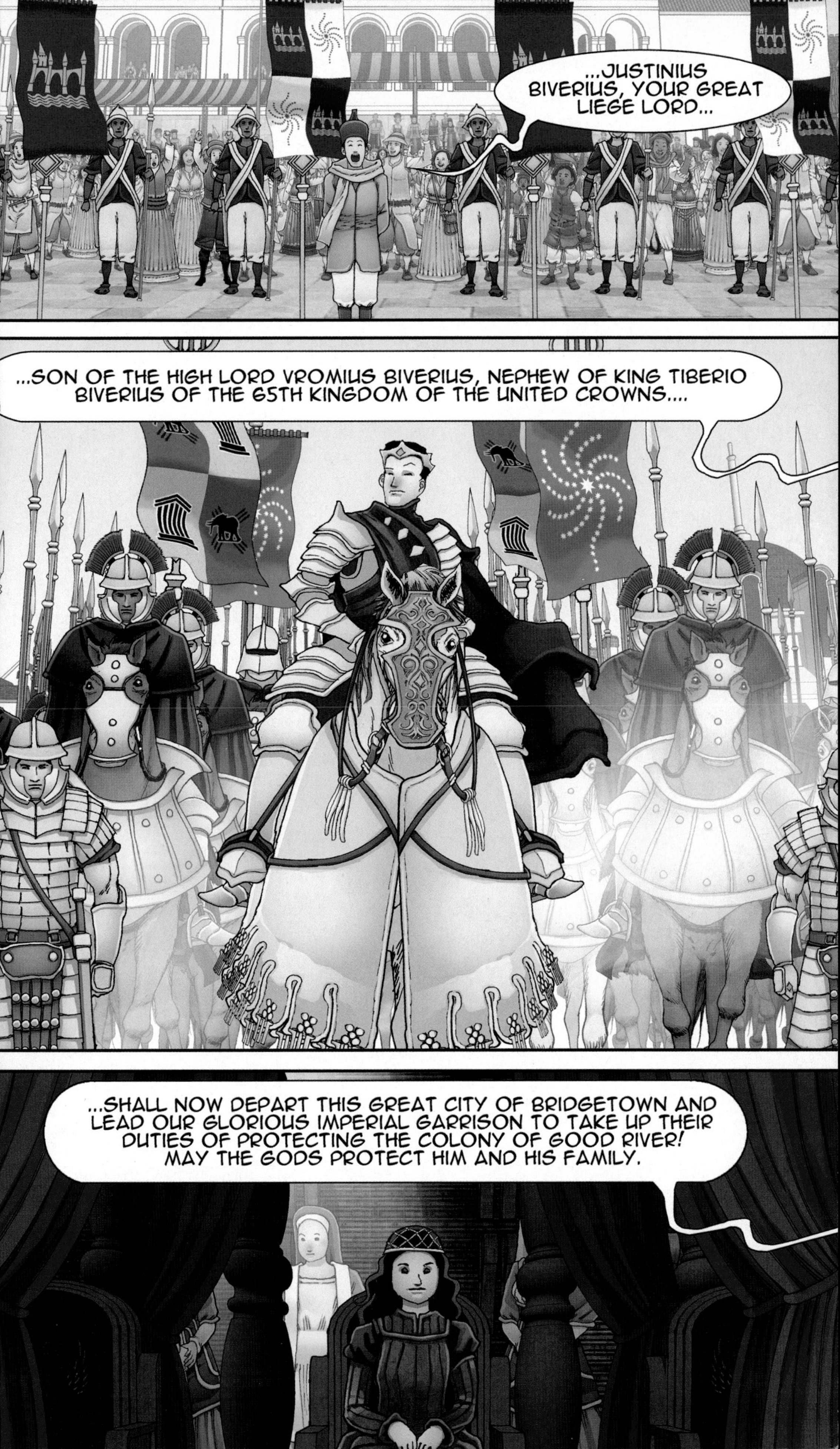
...JUSTINIUS BIVERIUS, YOUR GREAT LIEGE LORD...
...SON OF THE HIGH LORD VROMIUS BIVERIUS, NEPHEW OF KING TIBERIO BIVERIUS OF THE 65TH KINGDOM OF THE UNITED CROWNS....
...SHALL NOW DEPART THIS GREAT CITY OF BRIDGETOWN AND LEAD OUR GLORIOUS IMPERIAL GARRISON TO TAKE UP THEIR DUTIES OF PROTECTING THE COLONY OF GOOD RIVER! MAY THE GODS PROTECT HIM AND HIS FAMILY.

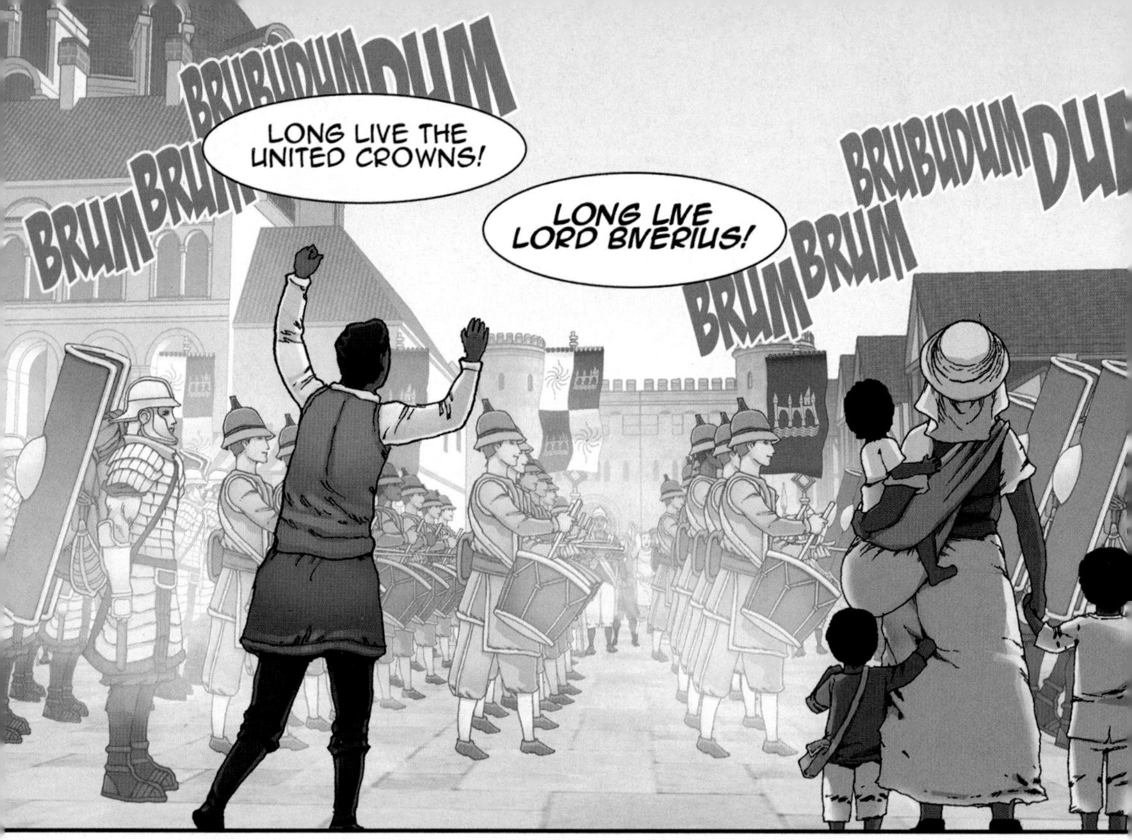
BRUMBRUM
BRUBUDUMDUM
LONG LIVE THE UNITED CROWNS!
LONG LIVE LORD BIVERIUS!
BRUMBRUM
BRUBUDUMDUM

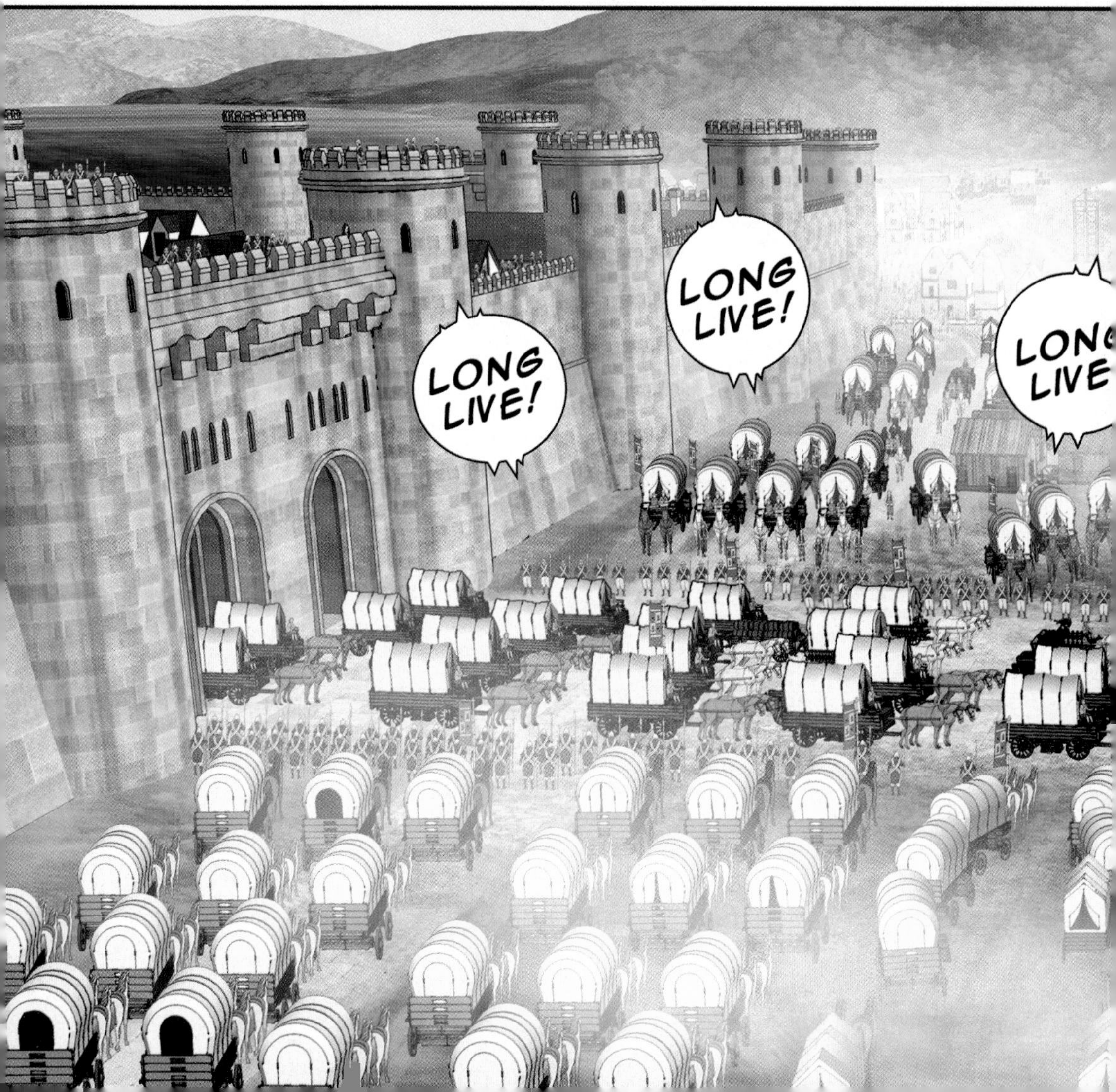
LONG LIVE!
LONG LIVE!

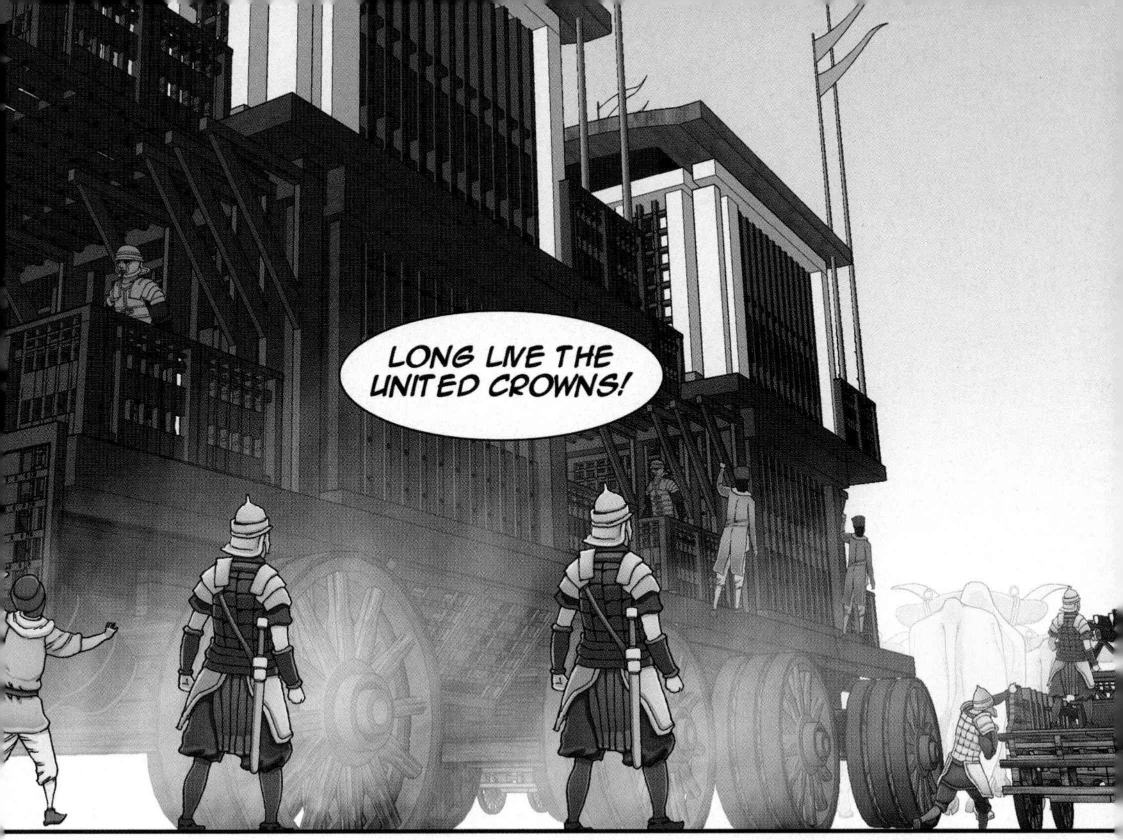
LONG LIVE THE UNITED CROWNS!

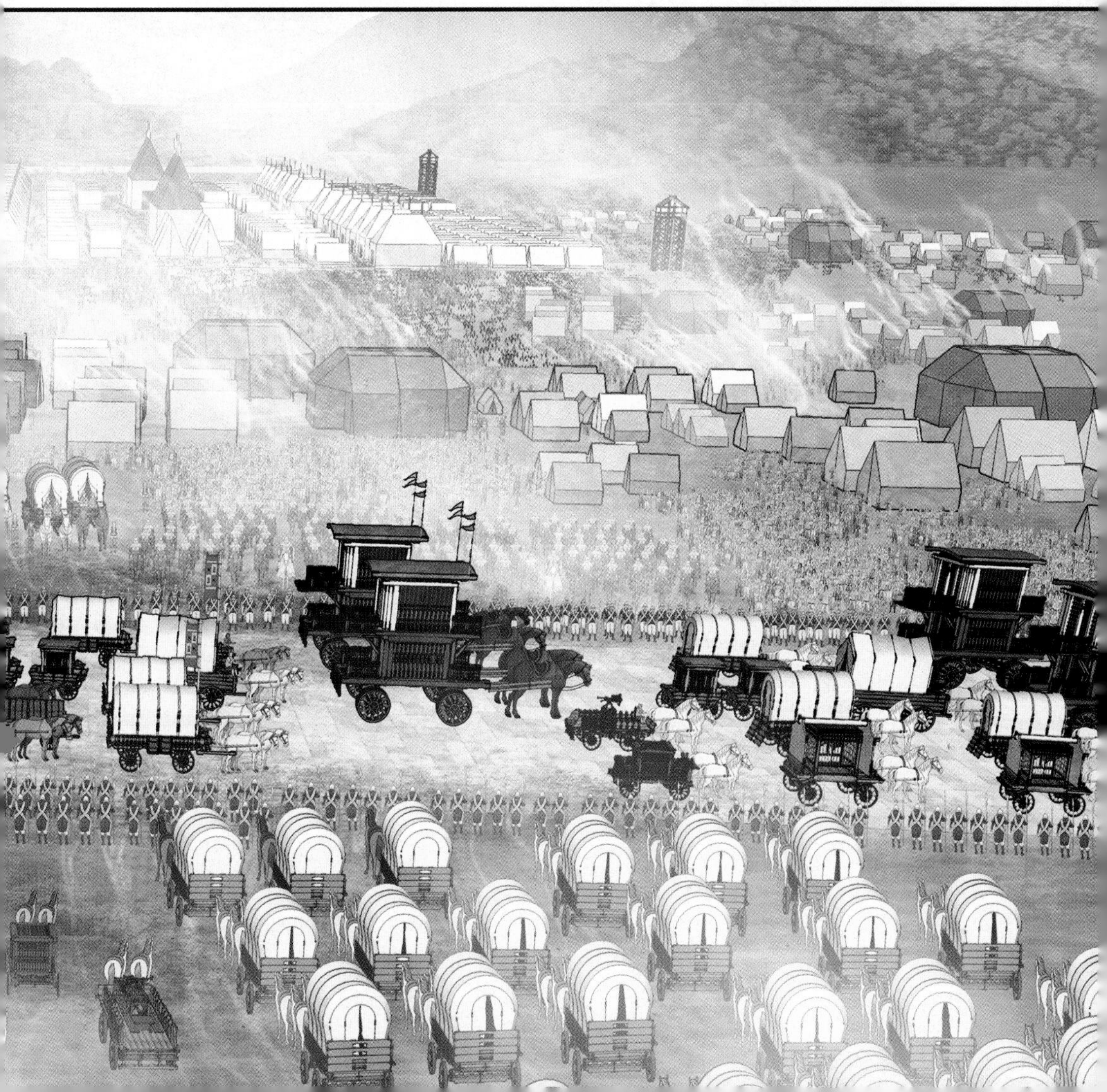

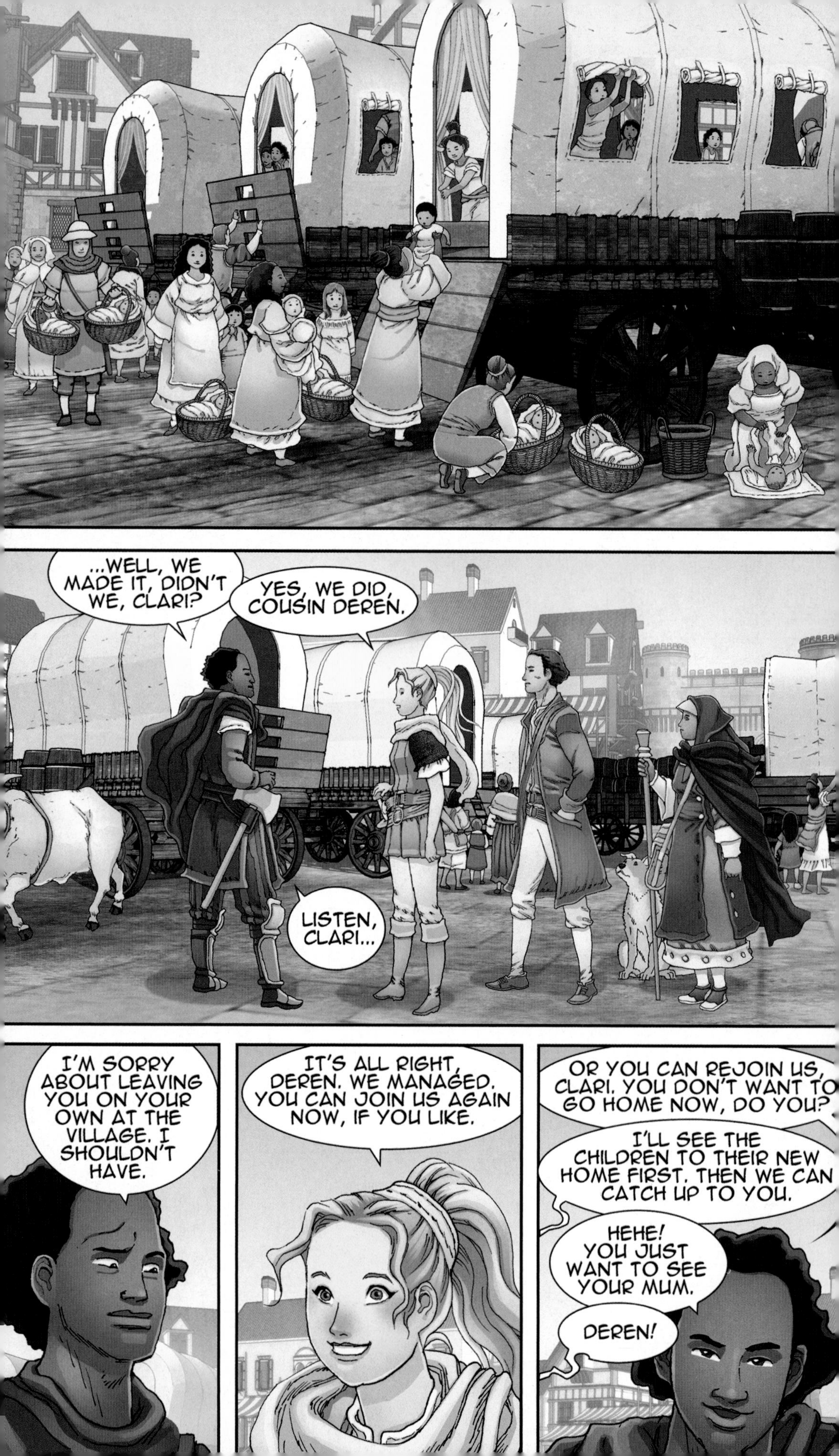
...WELL, WE MADE IT, DIDN'T WE, CLARI?
YES, WE DID, COUSIN DEREN.
LISTEN, CLARI...
I'M SORRY ABOUT LEAVING YOU ON YOUR OWN AT THE VILLAGE. I SHOULDN'T HAVE.
IT'S ALL RIGHT, DEREN. WE MANAGED. YOU CAN JOIN US AGAIN NOW, IF YOU LIKE.
OR YOU CAN REJOIN US, CLARI. YOU DON'T WANT TO GO HOME NOW, DO YOU?
I'LL SEE THE CHILDREN TO THEIR NEW HOME FIRST. THEN WE CAN CATCH UP TO YOU.
HEHE! YOU JUST WANT TO SEE YOUR MUM.
DEREN!

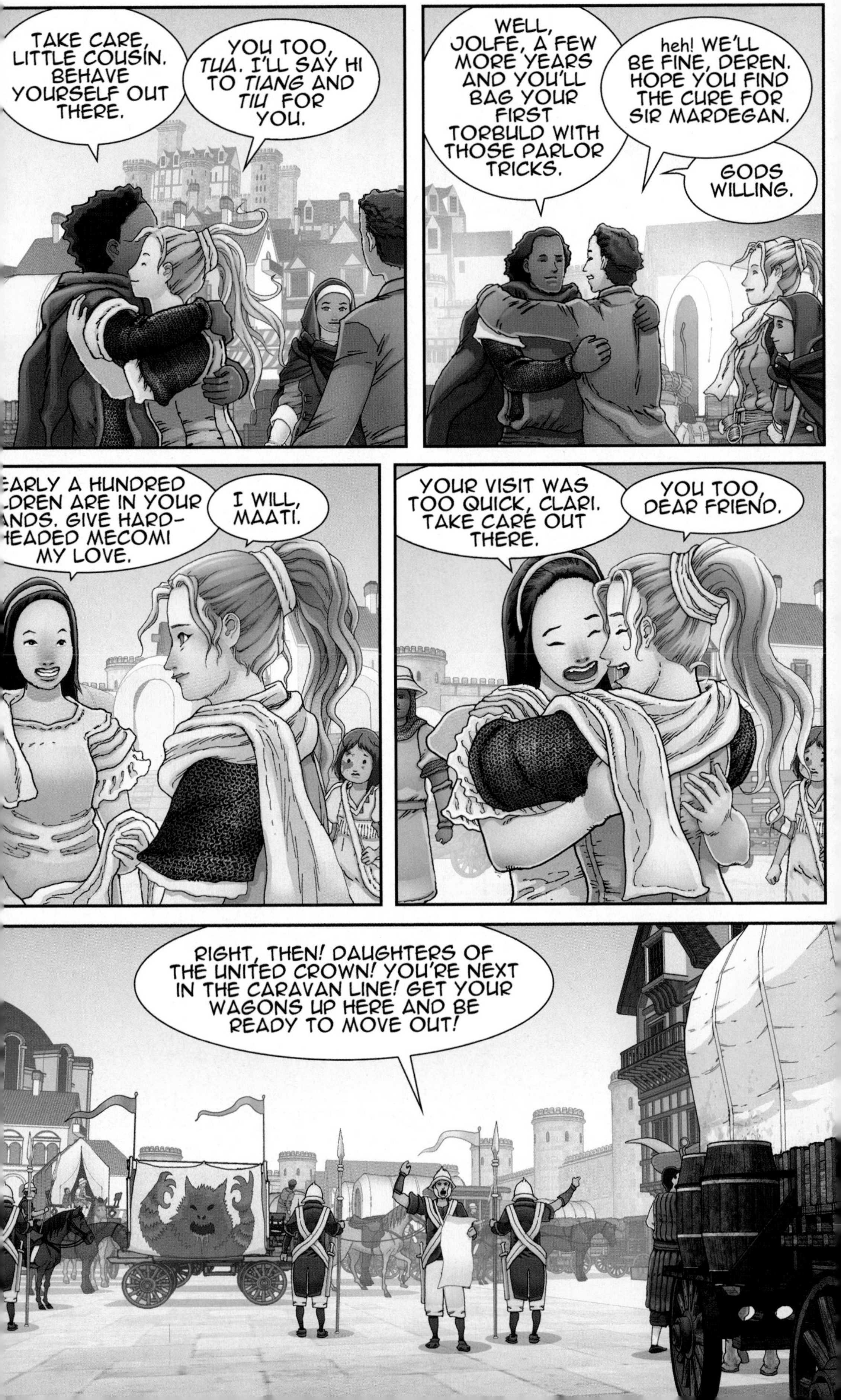

TAKE CARE, LITTLE COUSIN. BEHAVE YOURSELF OUT THERE.
YOU TOO, TUA. I'LL SAY HI TO TIANG AND TIU FOR YOU.
WELL, JOLFE, A FEW MORE YEARS AND YOU'LL BAG YOUR FIRST TORBULD WITH THOSE PARLOR TRICKS.
heh! WE'LL BE FINE, DEREN. HOPE YOU FIND THE CURE FOR SIR MARDEGAN.
GODS WILLING.
EARLY A HUNDRED LDREN ARE IN YOUR ANDS. GIVE HARD-HEADED MECOMI MY LOVE.
I WILL, MAATI.
YOUR VISIT WAS TOO QUICK, CLARI. TAKE CARE OUT THERE.
YOU TOO, DEAR FRIEND.
RIGHT, THEN! DAUGHTERS OF THE UNITED CROWN! YOU'RE NEXT IN THE CARAVAN LINE! GET YOUR WAGONS UP HERE AND BE READY TO MOVE OUT!

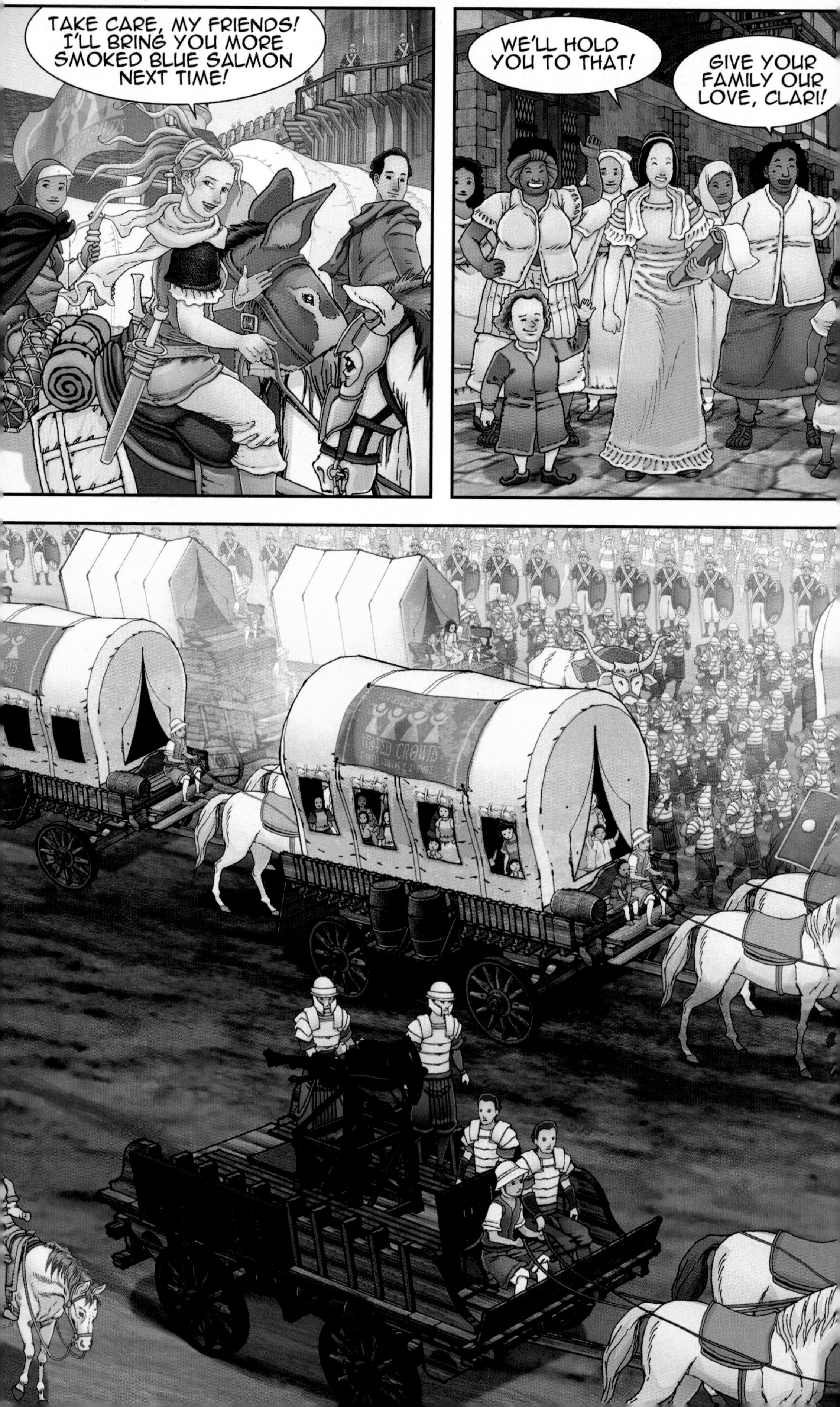
TAKE CARE, MY FRIENDS! I'LL BRING YOU MORE SMOKED BLUE SALMON NEXT TIME!
WE'LL HOLD YOU TO THAT!
GIVE YOUR FAMILY OUR LOVE, CLARI!

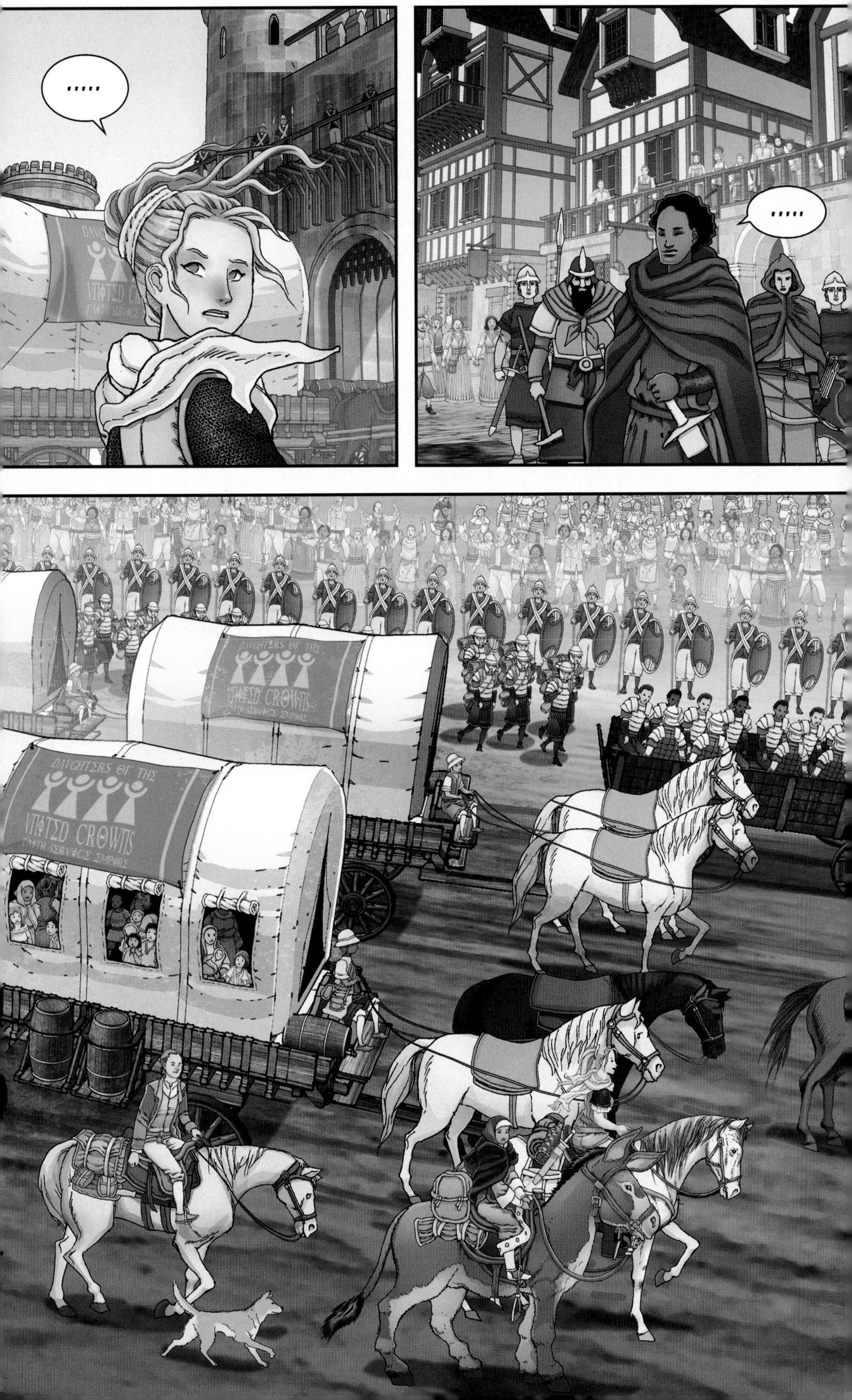
......
......
DAUGHTERS OF THE
UNITED CROWNS
FAITH SERVICE EMPIRE

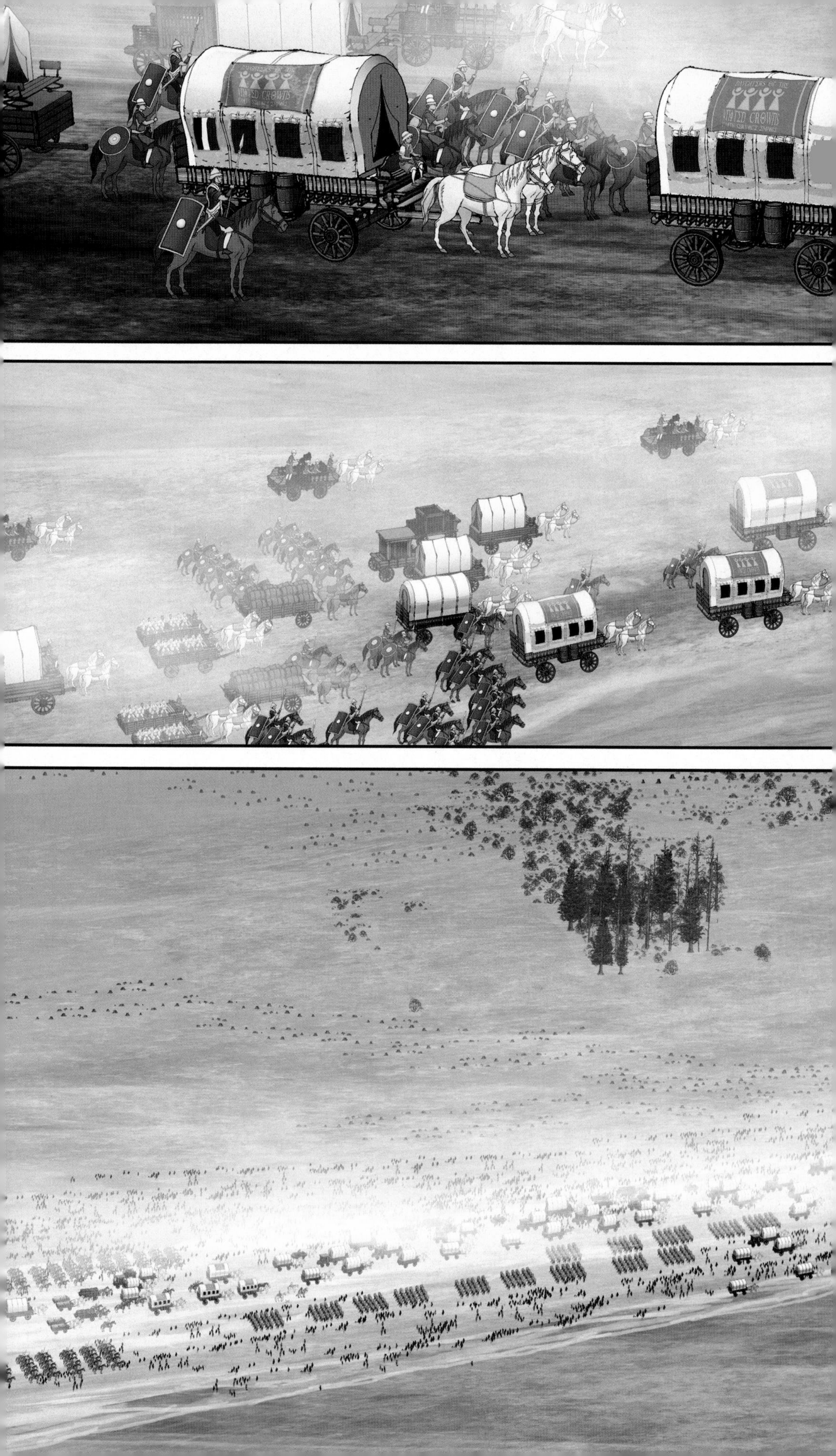

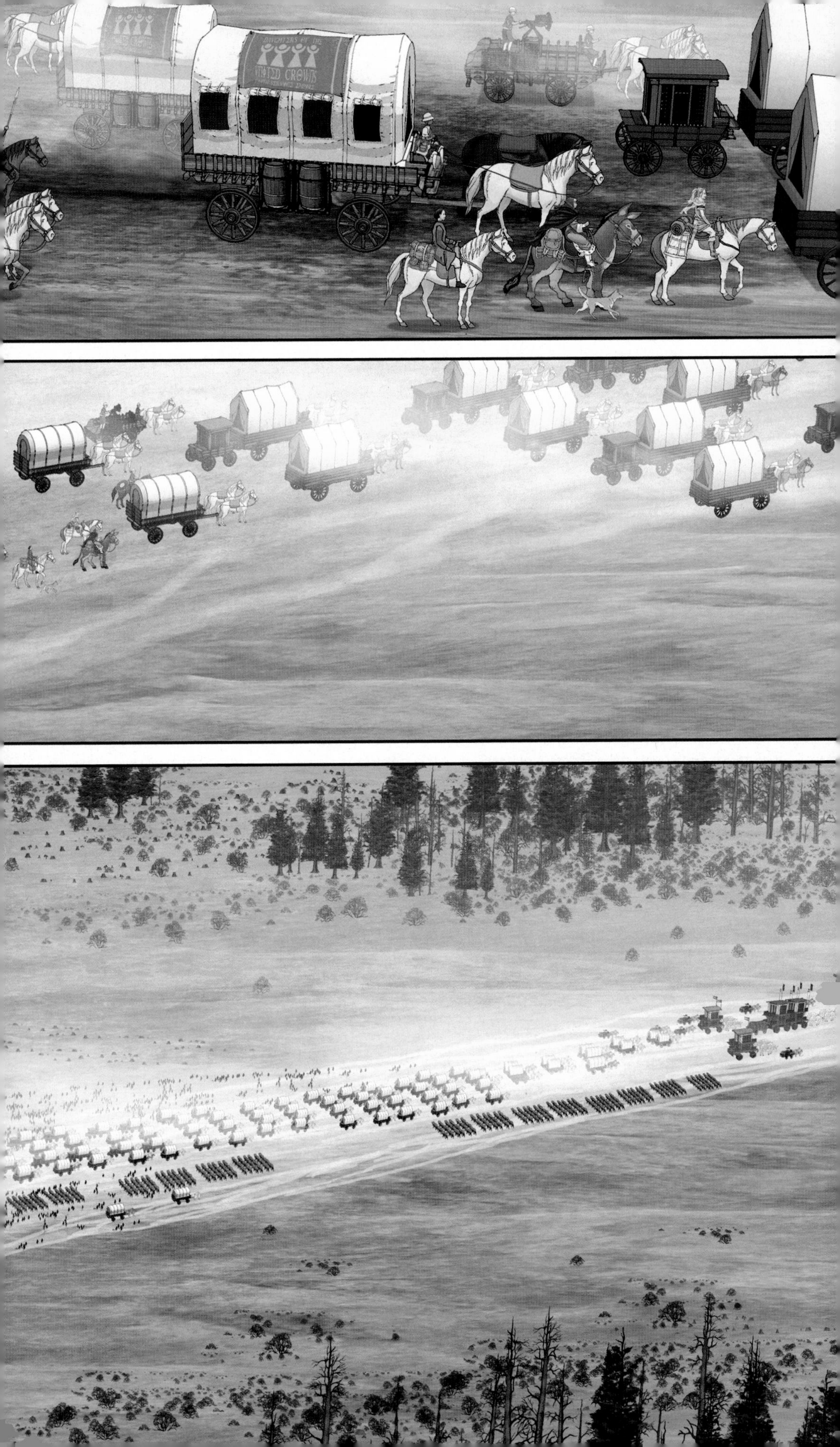
UNITED CROWNS

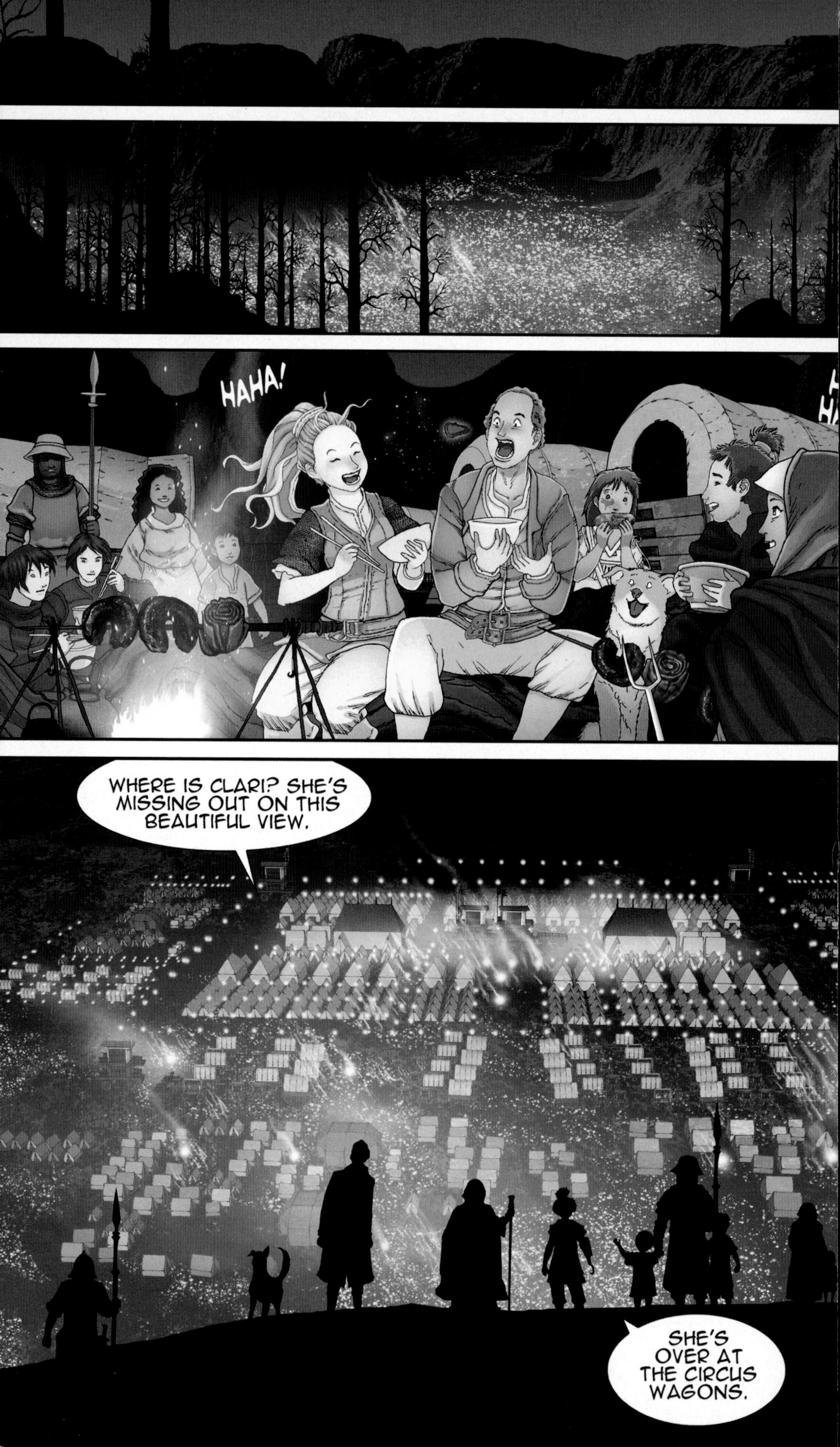
HAHA!
WHERE IS CLARI? SHE'S MISSING OUT ON THIS BEAUTIFUL VIEW.
SHE'S OVER AT THE CIRCUS WAGONS.

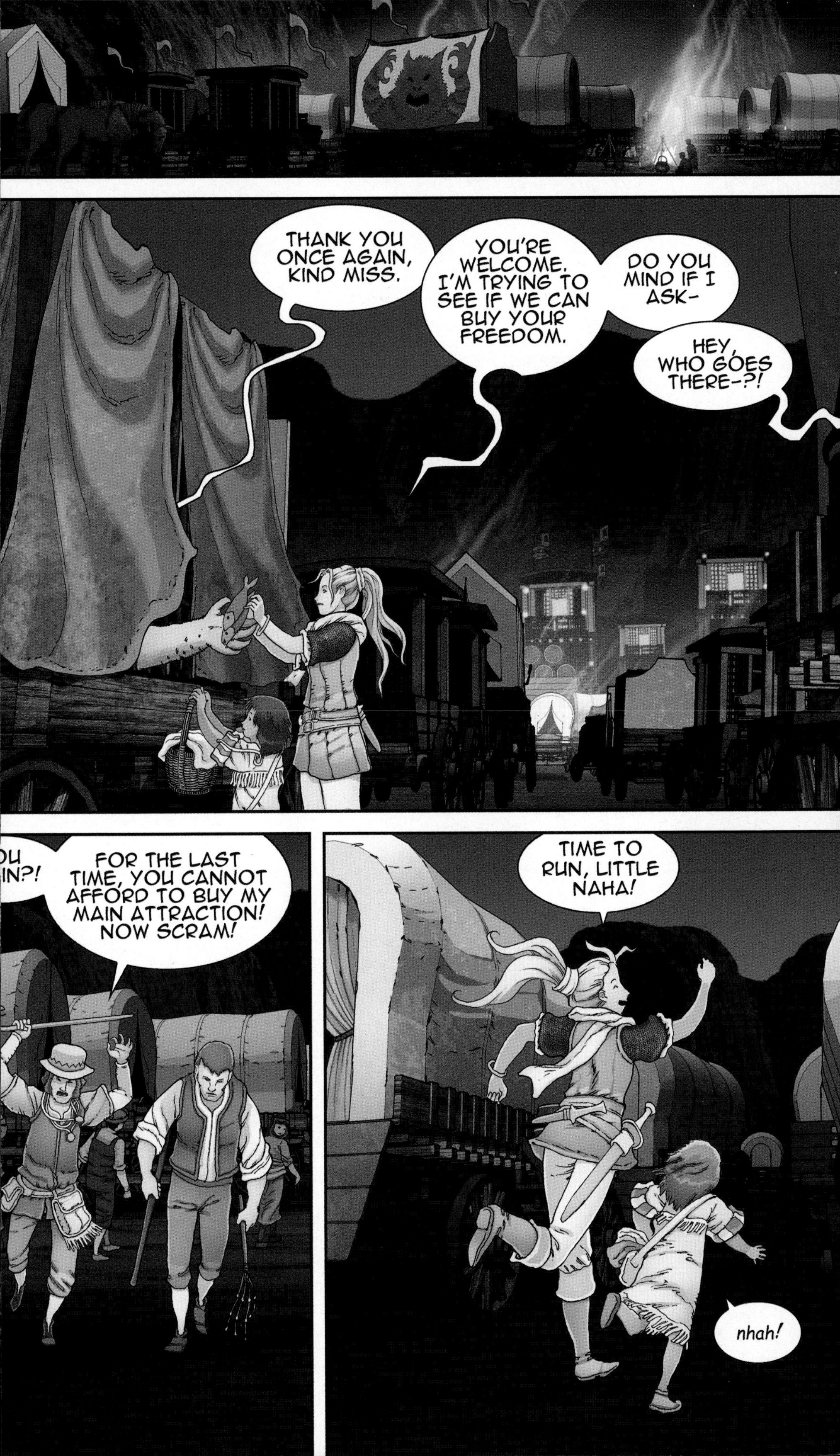
THANK YOU ONCE AGAIN, KIND MISS.
YOU'RE WELCOME. I'M TRYING TO SEE IF WE CAN BUY YOUR FREEDOM.
DO YOU MIND IF I ASK-
HEY, WHO GOES THERE-?!
FOR THE LAST TIME, YOU CANNOT AFFORD TO BUY MY MAIN ATTRACTION! NOW SCRAM!
TIME TO RUN, LITTLE NAHA!
nhah!

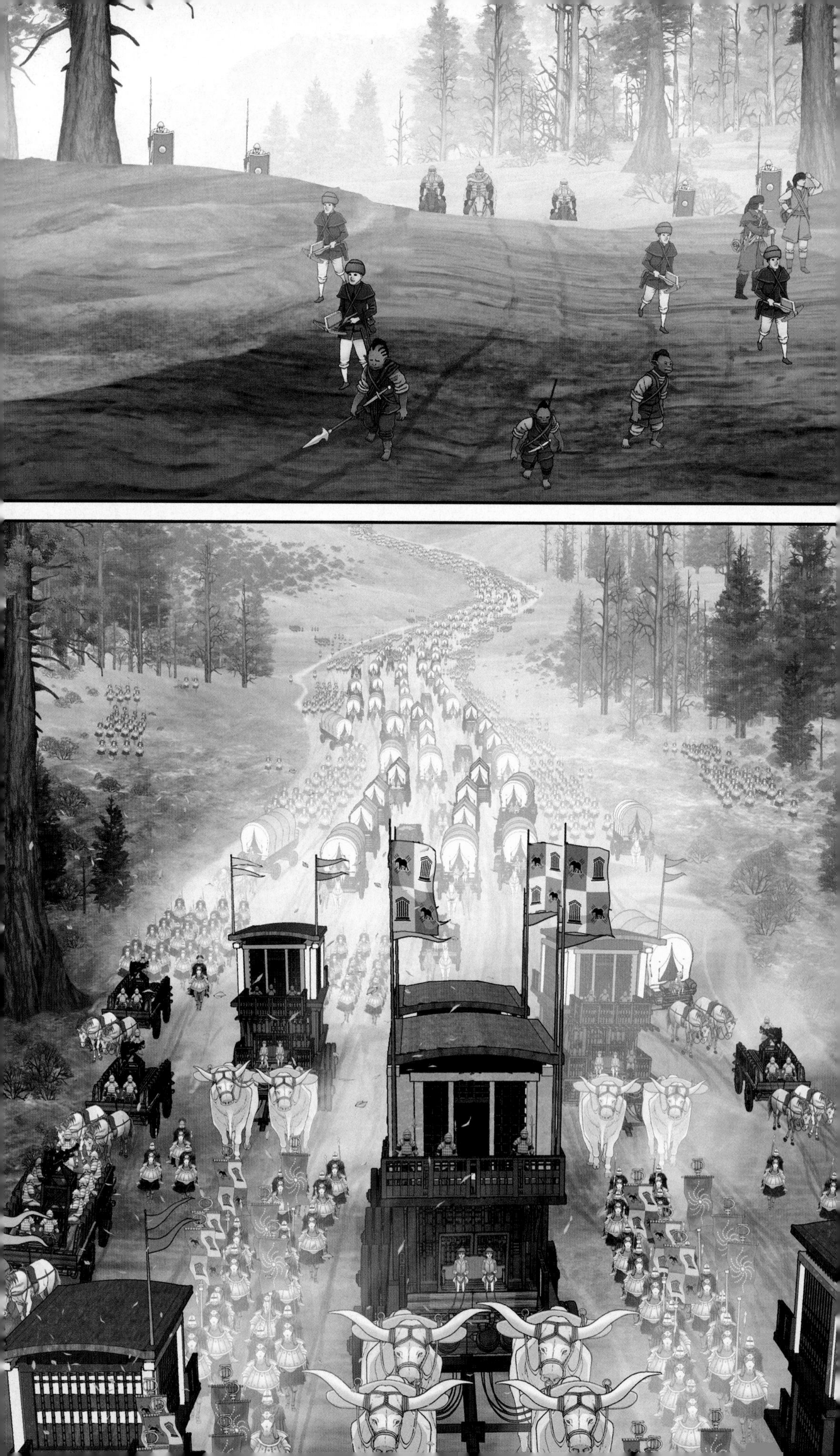

GOOD RIVER IS A SMALL [TO]WN. THIS SHOULD BE AN EASY YE[AR] [L]ONG POSTING. YOU HAVE TEN THOU[S]AND SOLDIERS AT YOUR COMMAND [AND] TWO THOUSAND MOUNTED HORSES [THIS] WILL MEAN A LOT OF HONOR [F]OR THE HOUSE OF BIVERIUS [...YOUR] FAMILY WILL BE...

...WE, THE BRIDGETOWN HONOR GUARD, HAVE BEEN ESCORTING ORPHANS TO THE VILLAGE FOR YEARS NOW.

THANK YOU FOR YOUR SERVICE.

YOU SEE, NAHA? NOTHING TO BE AFRAID OF... IT'S JUST PLENTY OF BEAUTIFUL TREES. YOU LIKE TREES, RIGHT?

.....

WROWW WROWW

N'AWRF

KRAK

?!

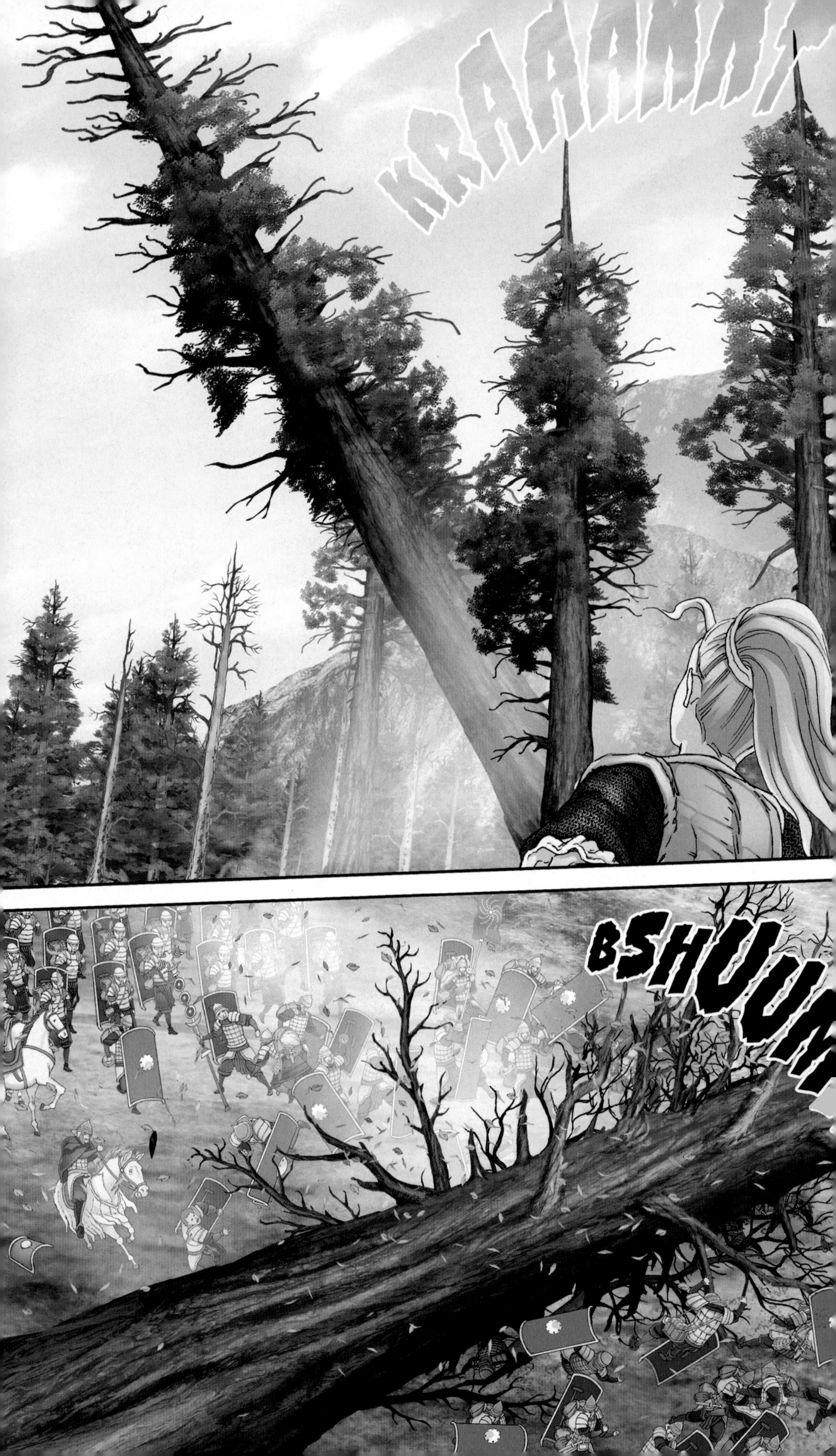
KRAAANN!
BSHUU

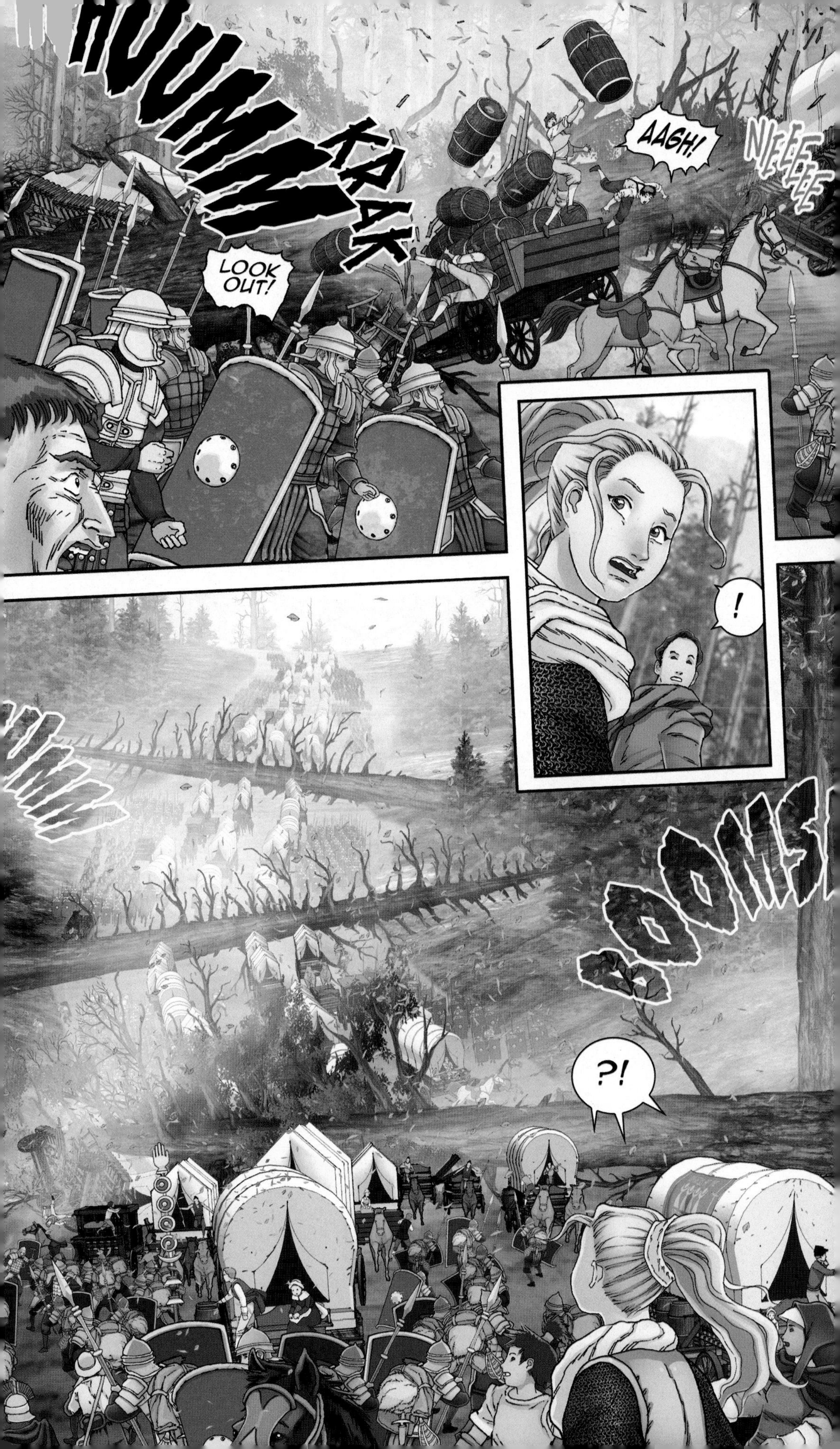
KRAK
LOOK OUT!
AAGH!
!
?!

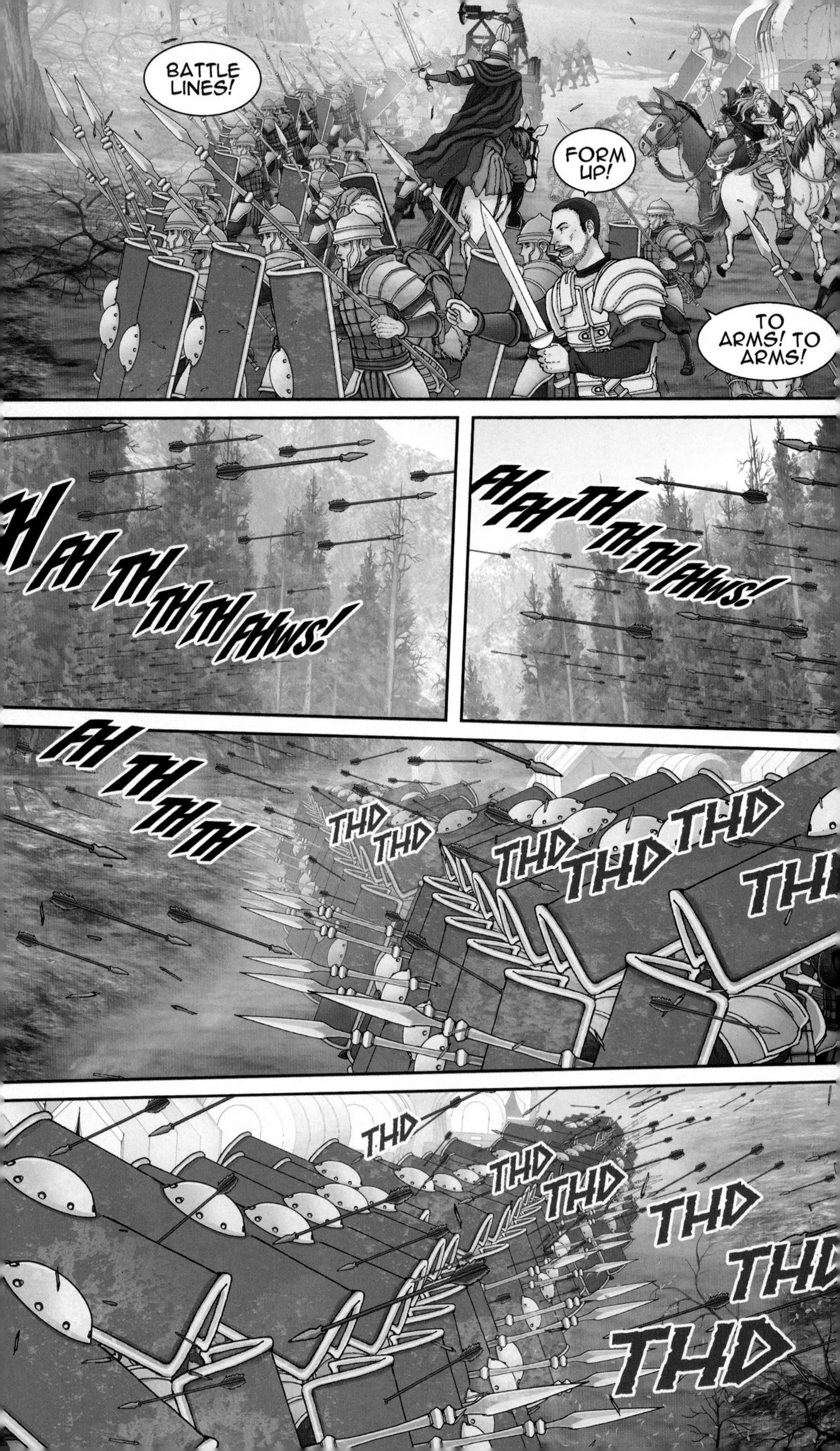
BATTLE LINES!
FORM UP!
TO ARMS! TO ARMS!
FH TH TH TH FHWS!
FH FH TH TH TH FHWS!
FH TH TH TH
THD THD
THD THD THD
THD
THD THD THD
THD
THD

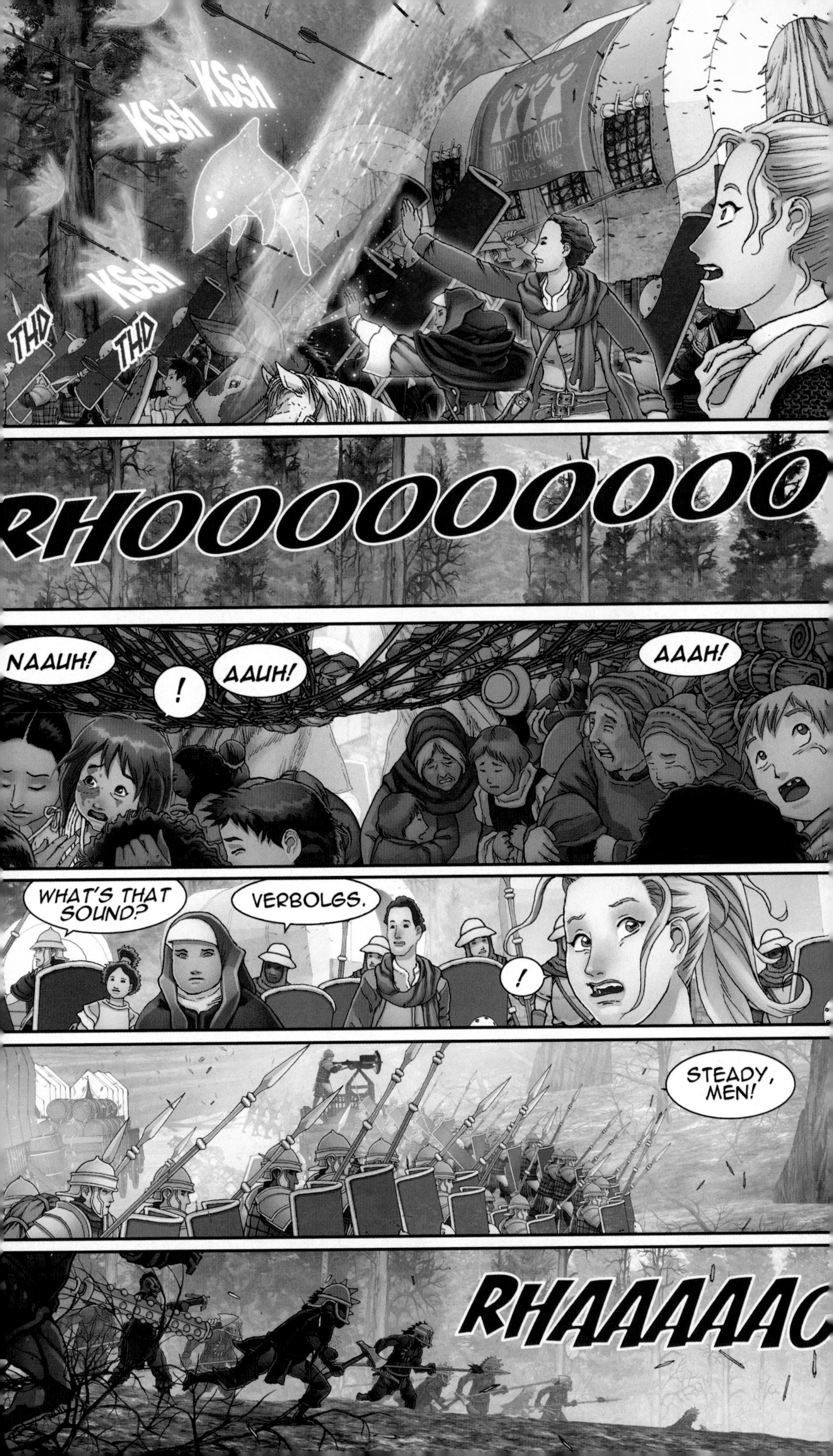
KSsh
KSsh
KSsh
THD
THD
RHOOOOOOOOOO
NAAUH!
!
AAUH!
AAAH!
WHAT'S THAT SOUND?
VERBOLGS.
!
STEADY, MEN!
RHAAAAAC

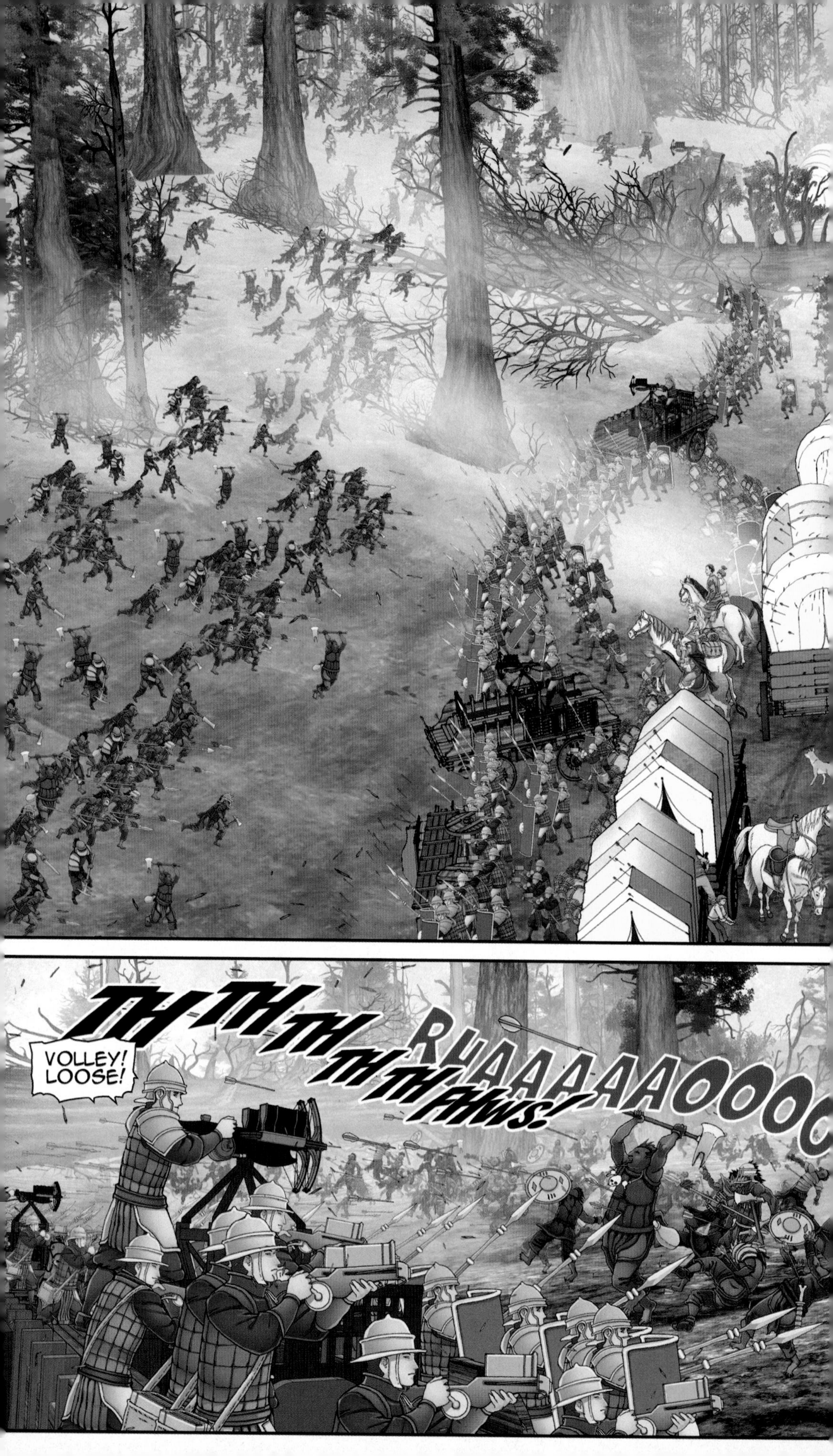

VOLLEY! LOOSE!
TH TH TH TH TH FHWS!
RUAAAAAAOOOO

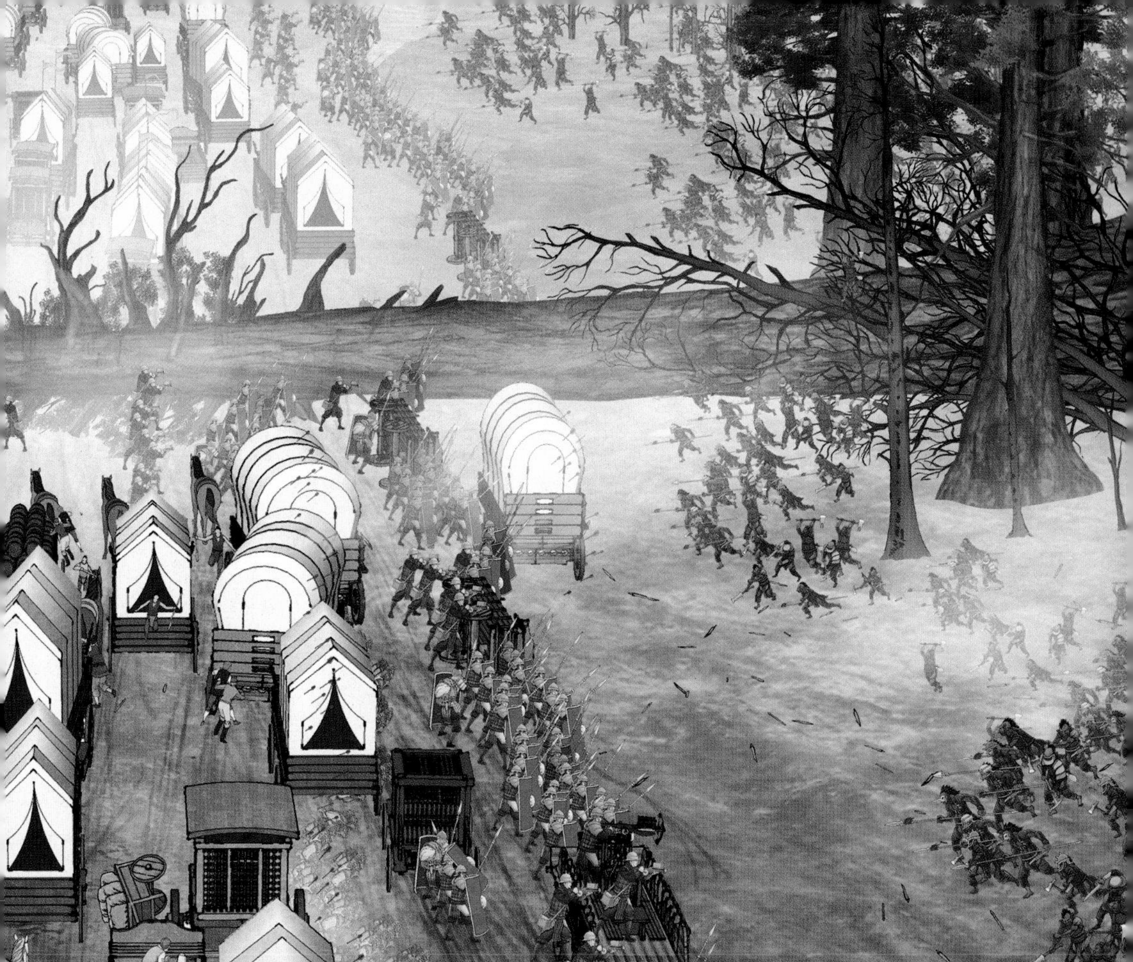

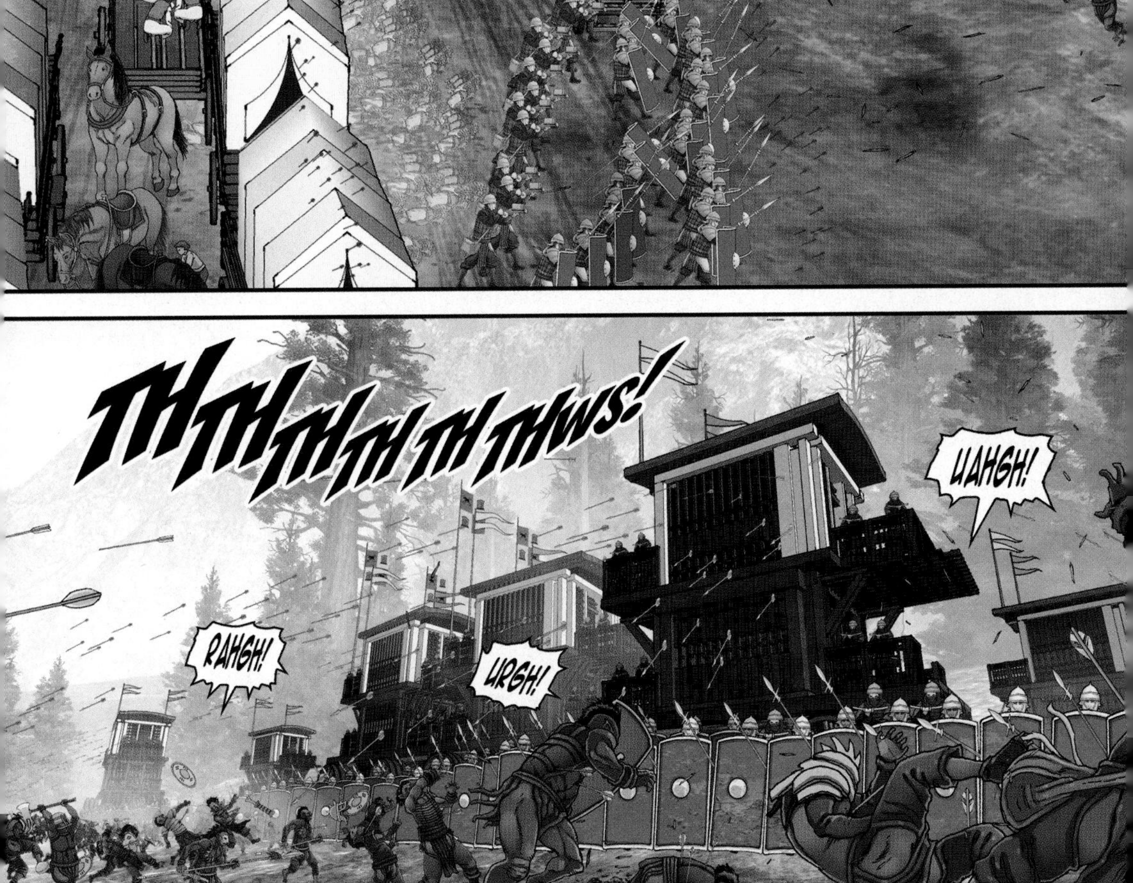
TH TH TH TH TH THWS!
UAHGH!
RAHGH!
URGH!

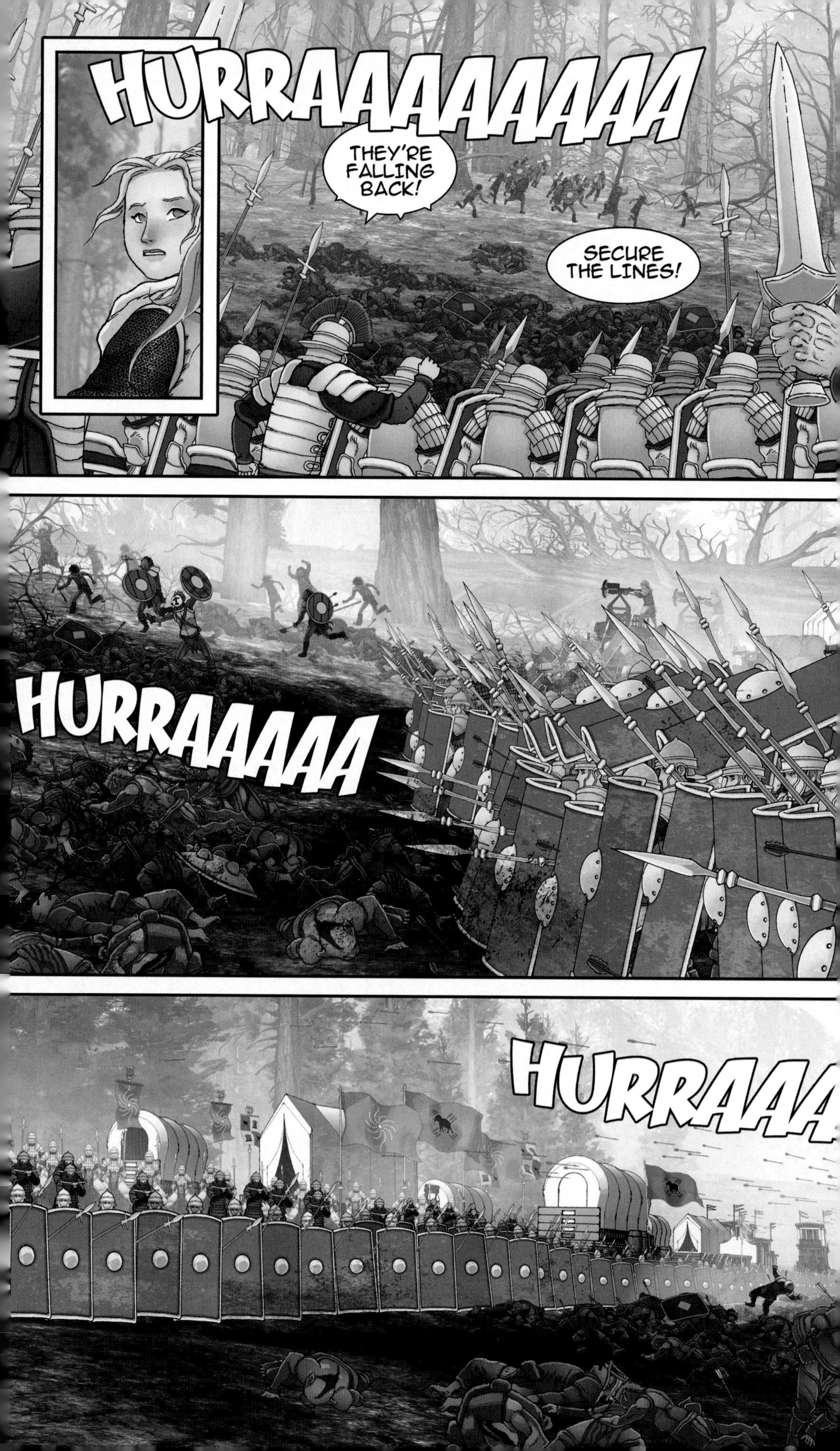
HURRAAAAAAAAA
THEY'RE FALLING BACK!
SECURE THE LINES!
HURRAAAAAA
HURRAAA

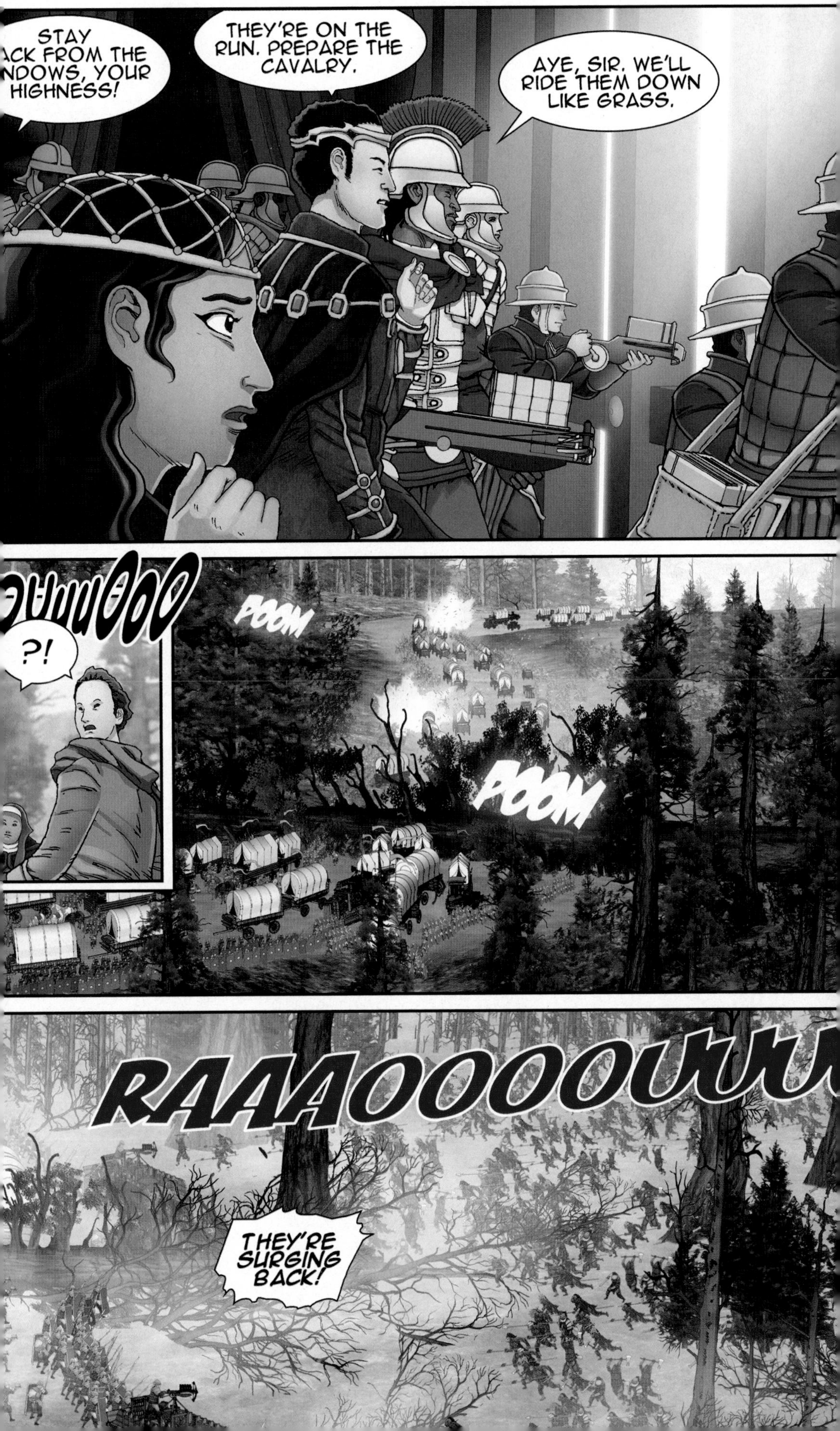
STAY
ACK FROM THE
NDOWS, YOUR
HIGHNESS!
THEY'RE ON THE RUN. PREPARE THE CAVALRY.
AYE, SIR. WE'LL RIDE THEM DOWN LIKE GRASS.
OUUUOOO
?!
POOM
POOM
RAAAOOOOUUU
THEY'RE SURGING BACK!

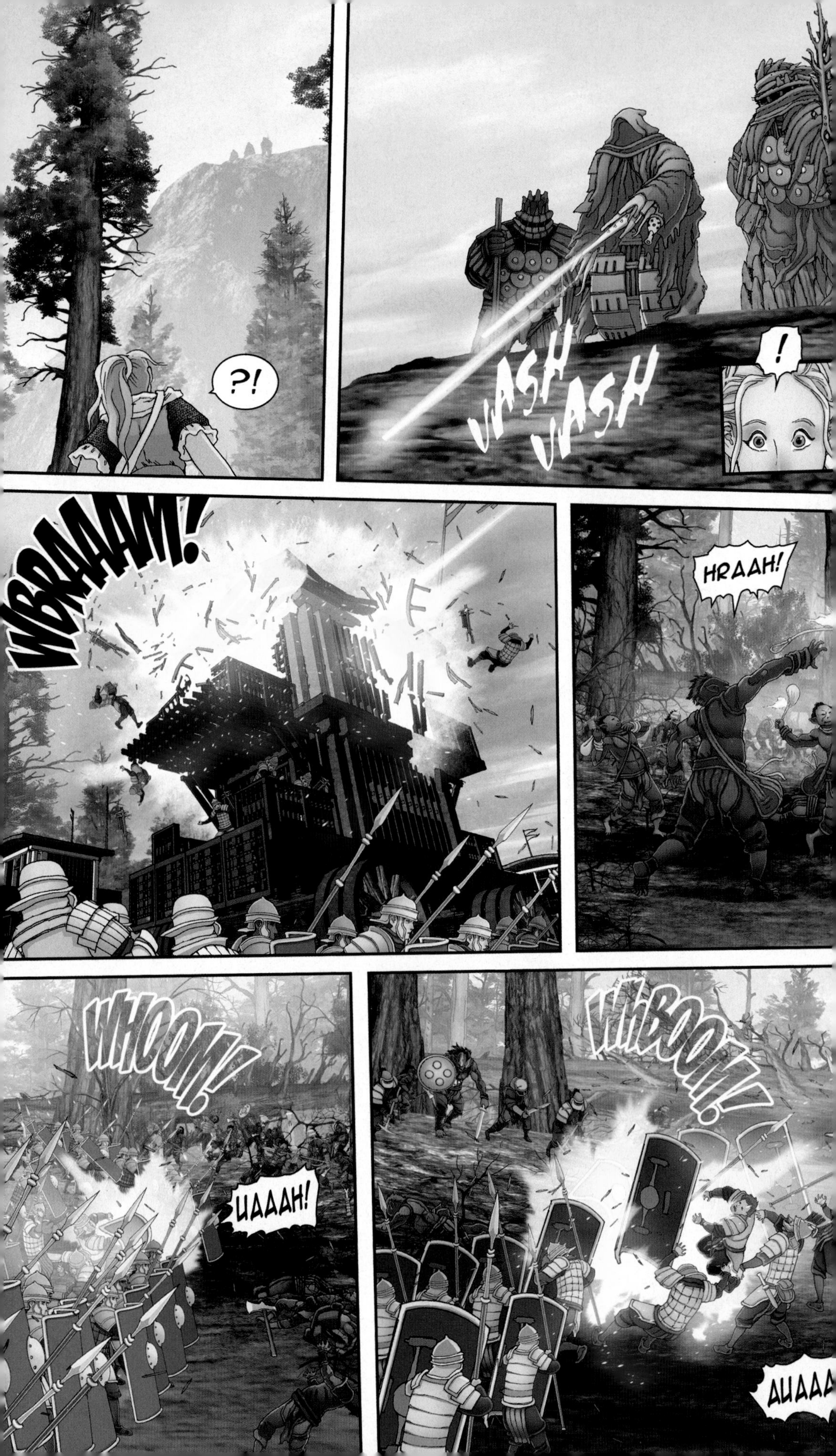
?!
VASH
VASH
!
WBRAAAM!
HRAAH!
WHOOM!
UAAAH!
WHBOOM!
AUAAA

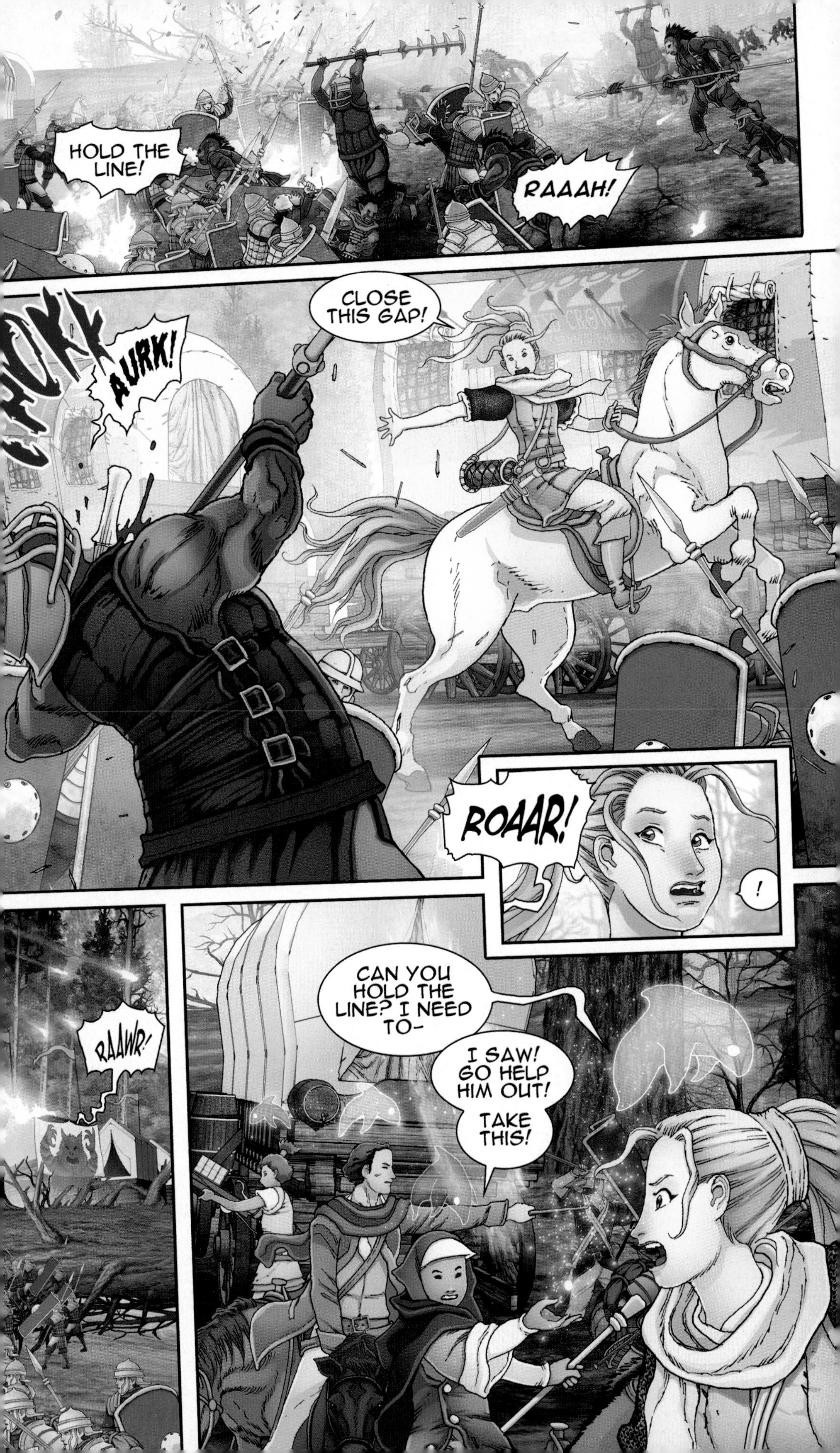
HOLD THE LINE!
RAAAH!
CHUKK
AURK!
CLOSE THIS GAP!
ROAAR!
!
RAAWR!
CAN YOU HOLD THE LINE? I NEED TO-
I SAW! GO HELP HIM OUT!
TAKE THIS!

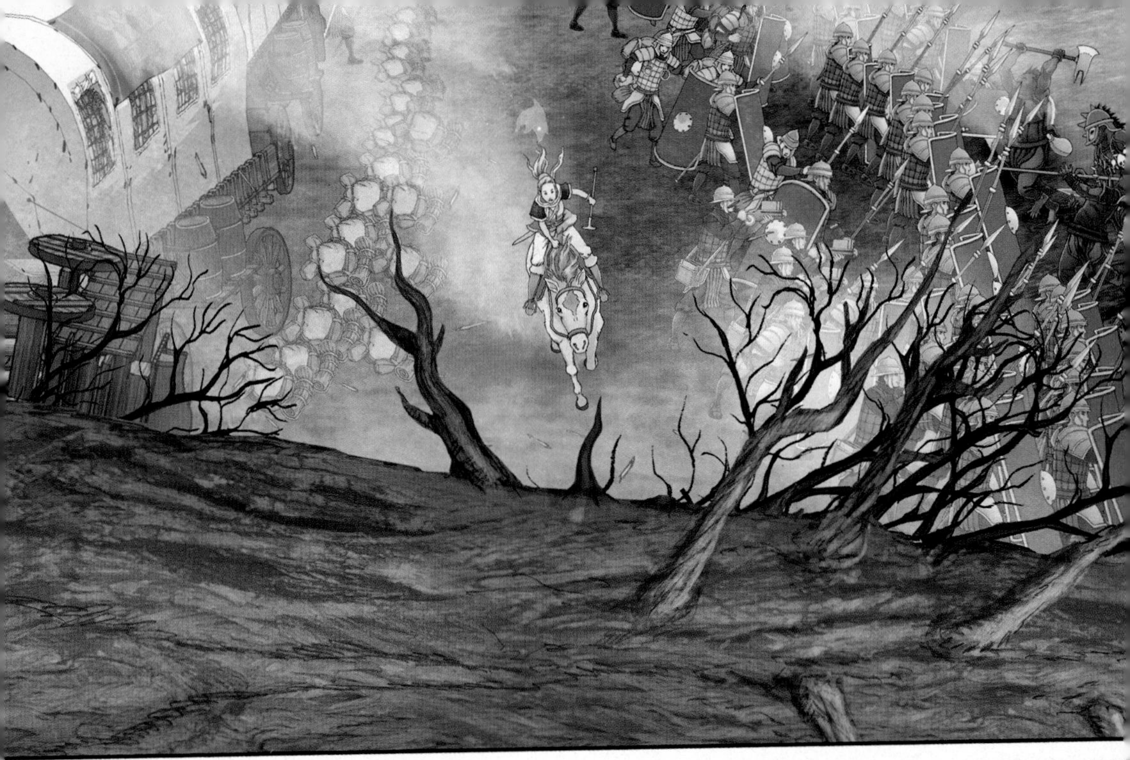

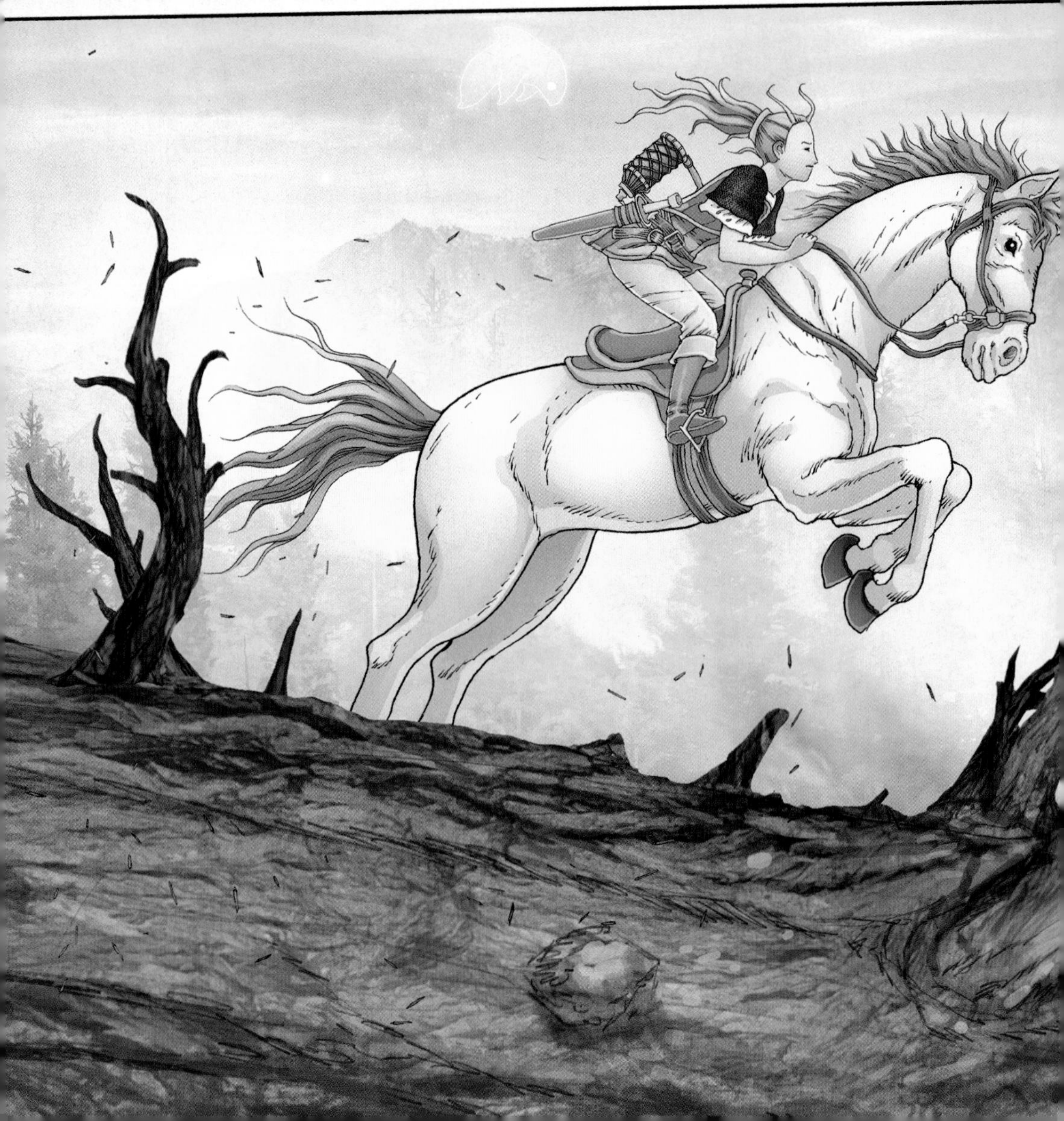

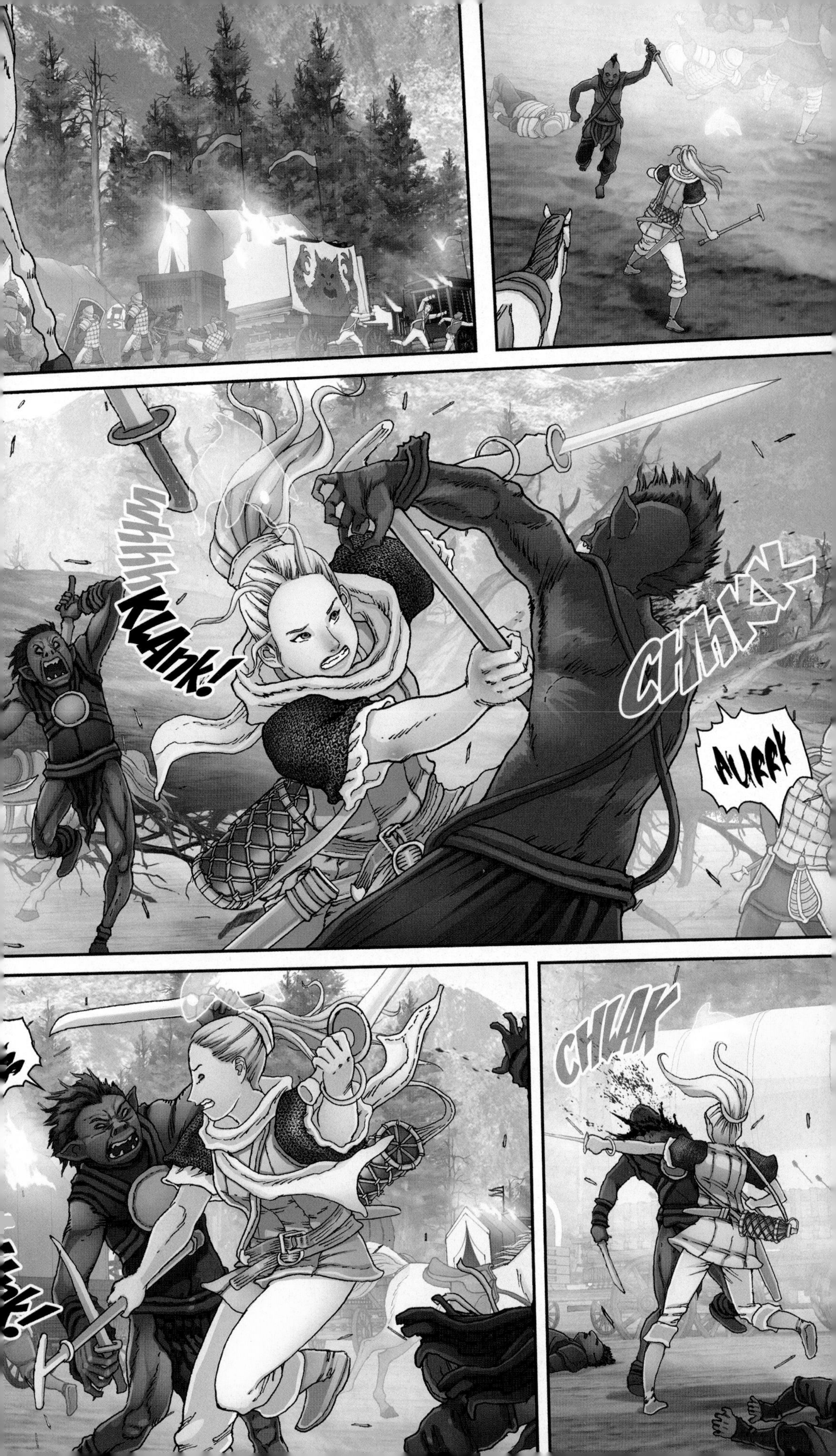
whhhKLAnk!
CHHNK!
AURRK
CHLAK

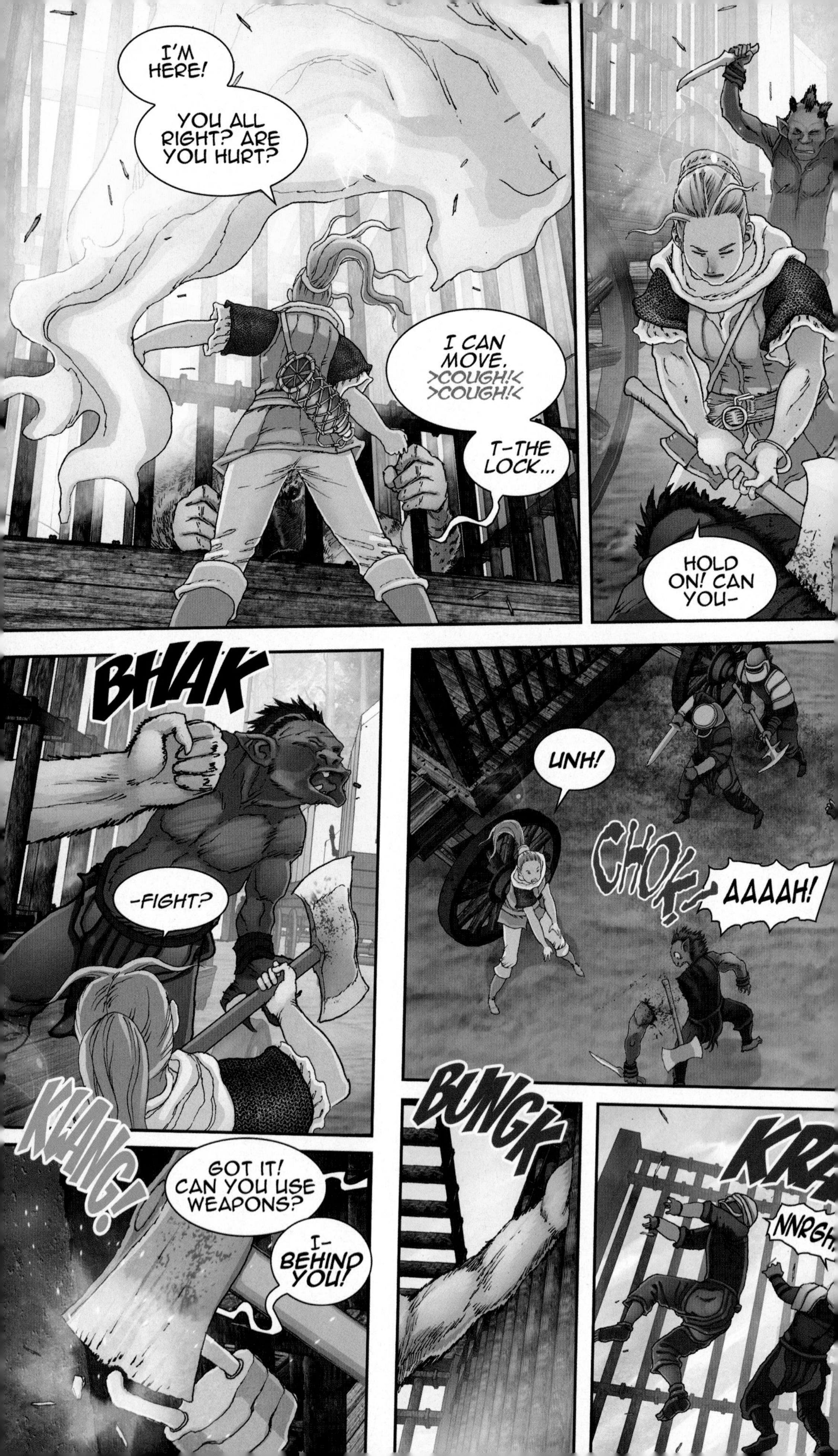
I'M HERE!
YOU ALL RIGHT? ARE YOU HURT?
I CAN MOVE. >COUGH!< >COUGH!<
T-THE LOCK...
HOLD ON! CAN YOU-
BHAK
-FIGHT?
UNH!
CHOK!
AAAAH!
KLANG!
GOT IT! CAN YOU USE WEAPONS?
I- BEHIND YOU!
BUNGK
NNRGH

HOLD THE LINE! HOLD!

I'LL TAKE THIS, THANK YOU.

WHAT THE-?!

I'LL TAKE THIS TOO, IF YOU DON'T MIND. I RECKON I EARNED ALL THIS AND MORE, REALLY.

NO! YOU-

AAAAAGH!

HGK!

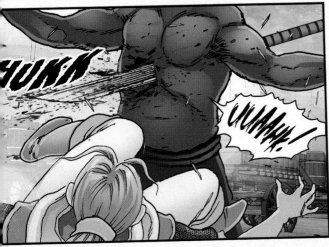

HUKK

UUHHH!

SSWOOOO

SSCHLAAAAAK

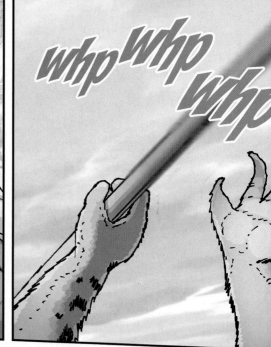

whp whp whp

SSCHLNPT

KRAAKT

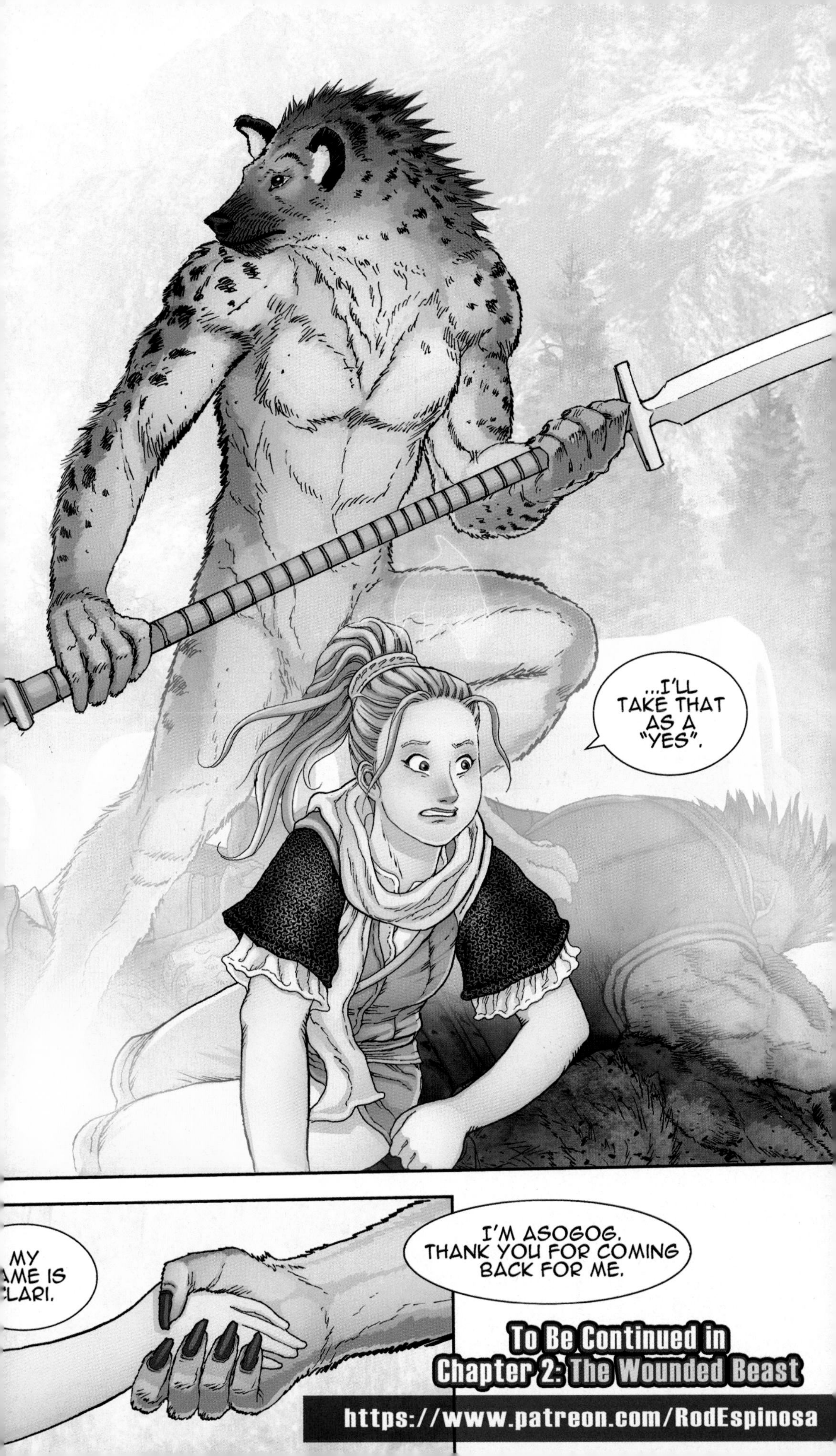
...I'LL TAKE THAT AS A "YES".
MY AME IS LARI.
I'M ASOGOG. THANK YOU FOR COMING BACK FOR ME.
To Be Continued in
Chapter 2: The Wounded Beast
https://www.patreon.com/RodEspinosa

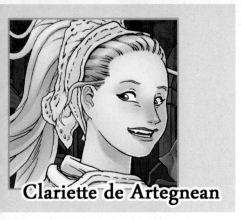

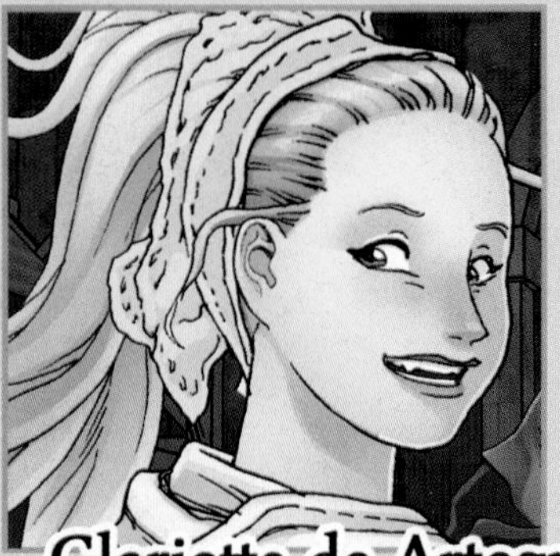
Clariette de Artegnean

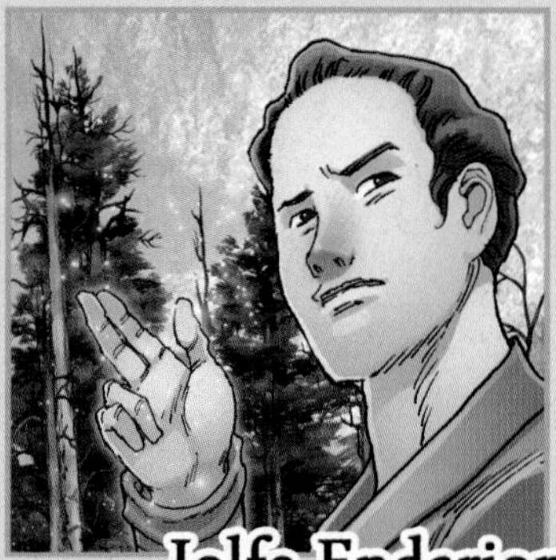
Jolfe Endarion
(related on the Mhou side)

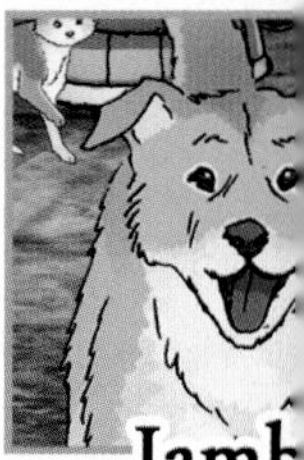
Jamb

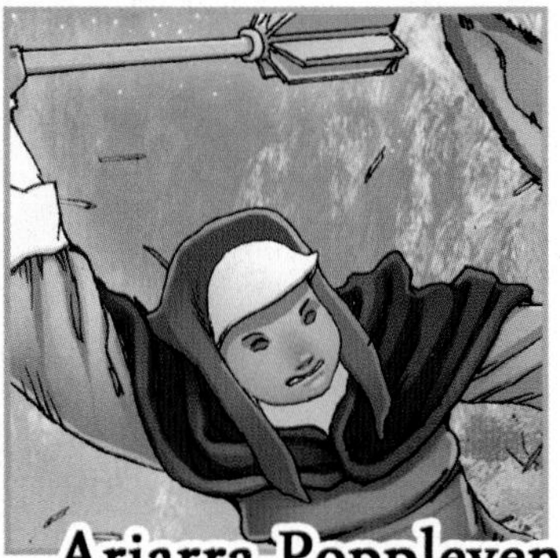
Ariarra Popplevensie

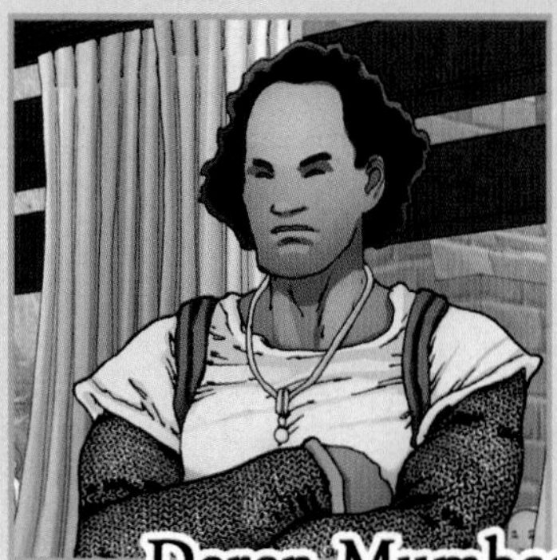
Deren Mumbasi

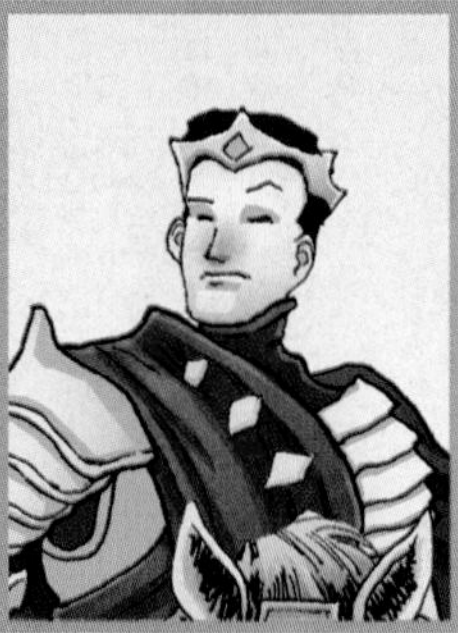
Justinius Biverius

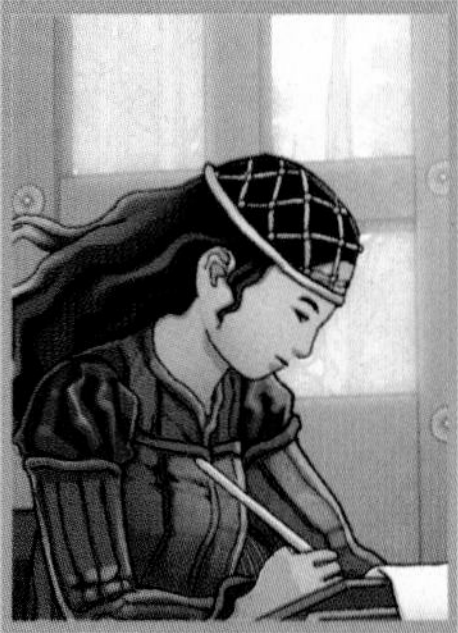
Herminia Biverius

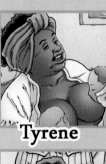

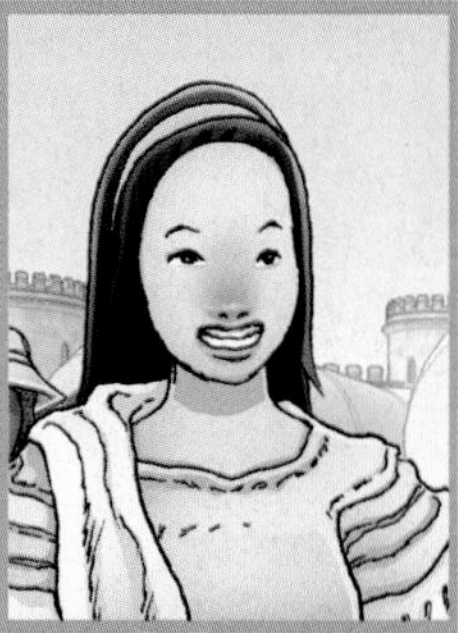
Maati

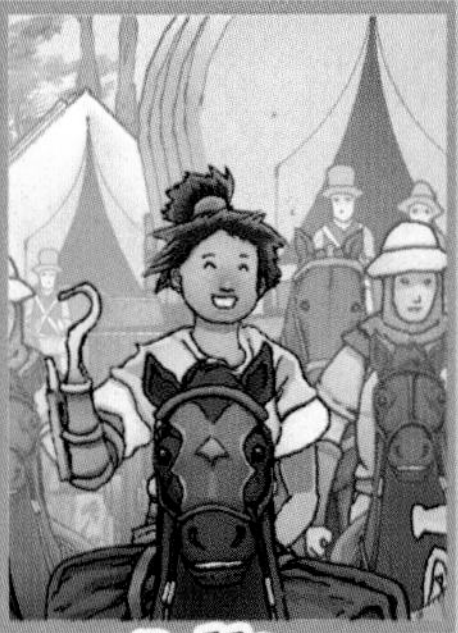
Jallia

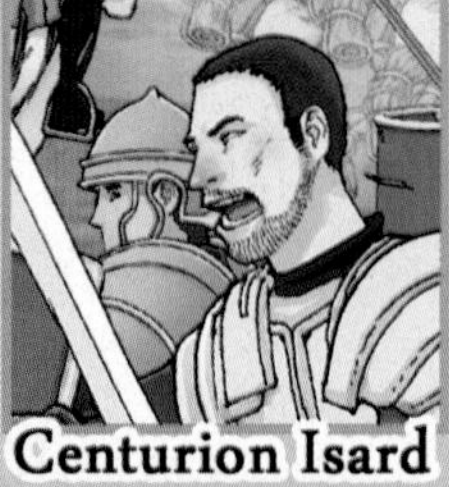
Centurion Isard

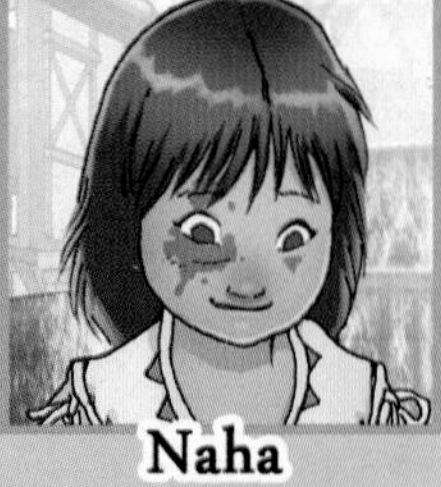
Naha

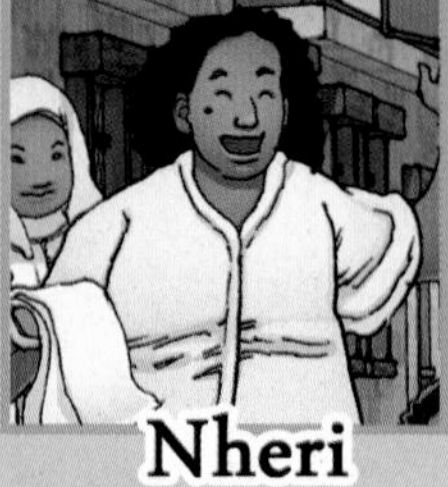
Nheri

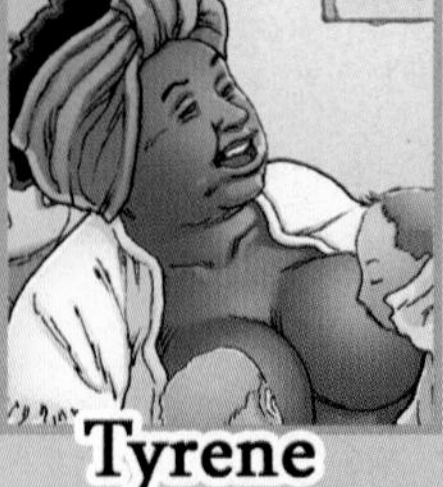
Tyrene

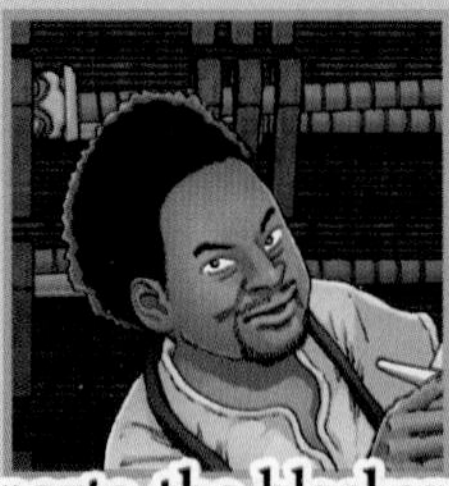
Aporto the blacksmith

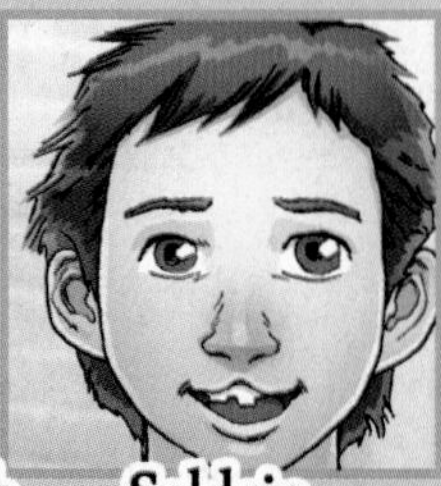
Seldric

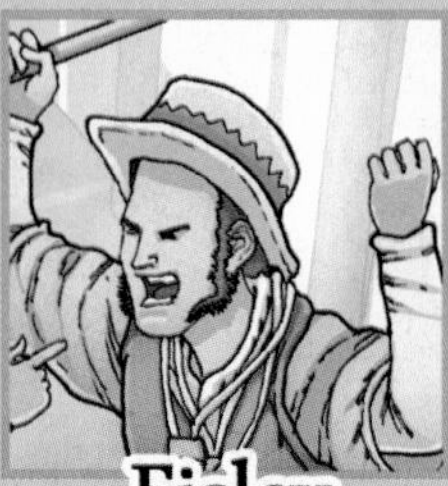
Fisley

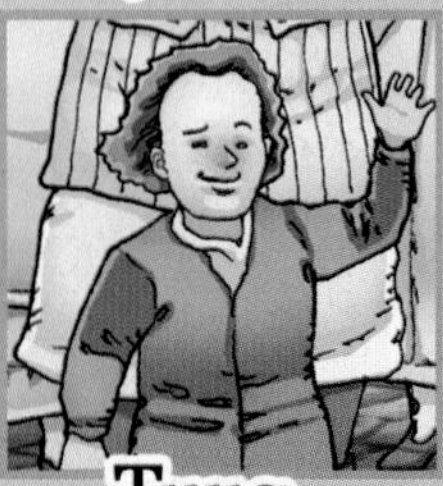
Tuug

Adventure Finders

Rod Espinosa: Artist and Author

Bryan Seaton: **Publisher/ CEO**
Shawn Gabborin: **Editor In Chief**
Jason Martin: **Publisher-Danger Zone**
Nicole D'Andria: **Marketing Director/Editor**
Jessica Lowrie: **Social Media Czar**
Danielle Davison: **Executive Administrator**
Chad Cicconi: **Adventure Posse Hireling**
Shawn Pryor: **President of Creator Relations**

tps://www.patreon.com/RodEspinosa   http://rodespinosa.deviantart.com   https://www.facebook.com/RodEspinosa.92

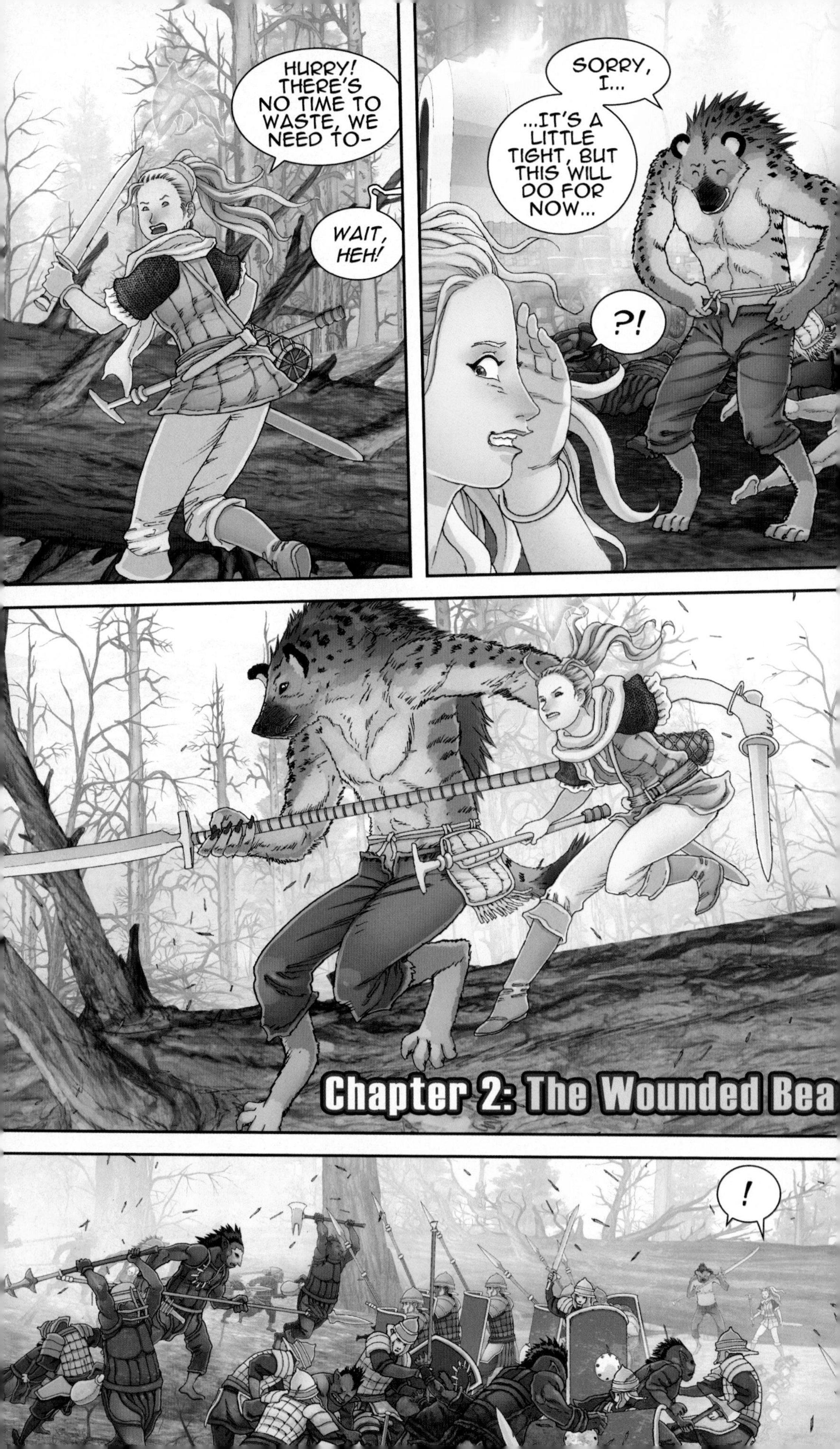
HURRY! THERE'S NO TIME TO WASTE, WE NEED TO-
WAIT, HEH!
SORRY, I...
...IT'S A LITTLE TIGHT, BUT THIS WILL DO FOR NOW...
?!
Chapter 2: The Wounded Bea
!

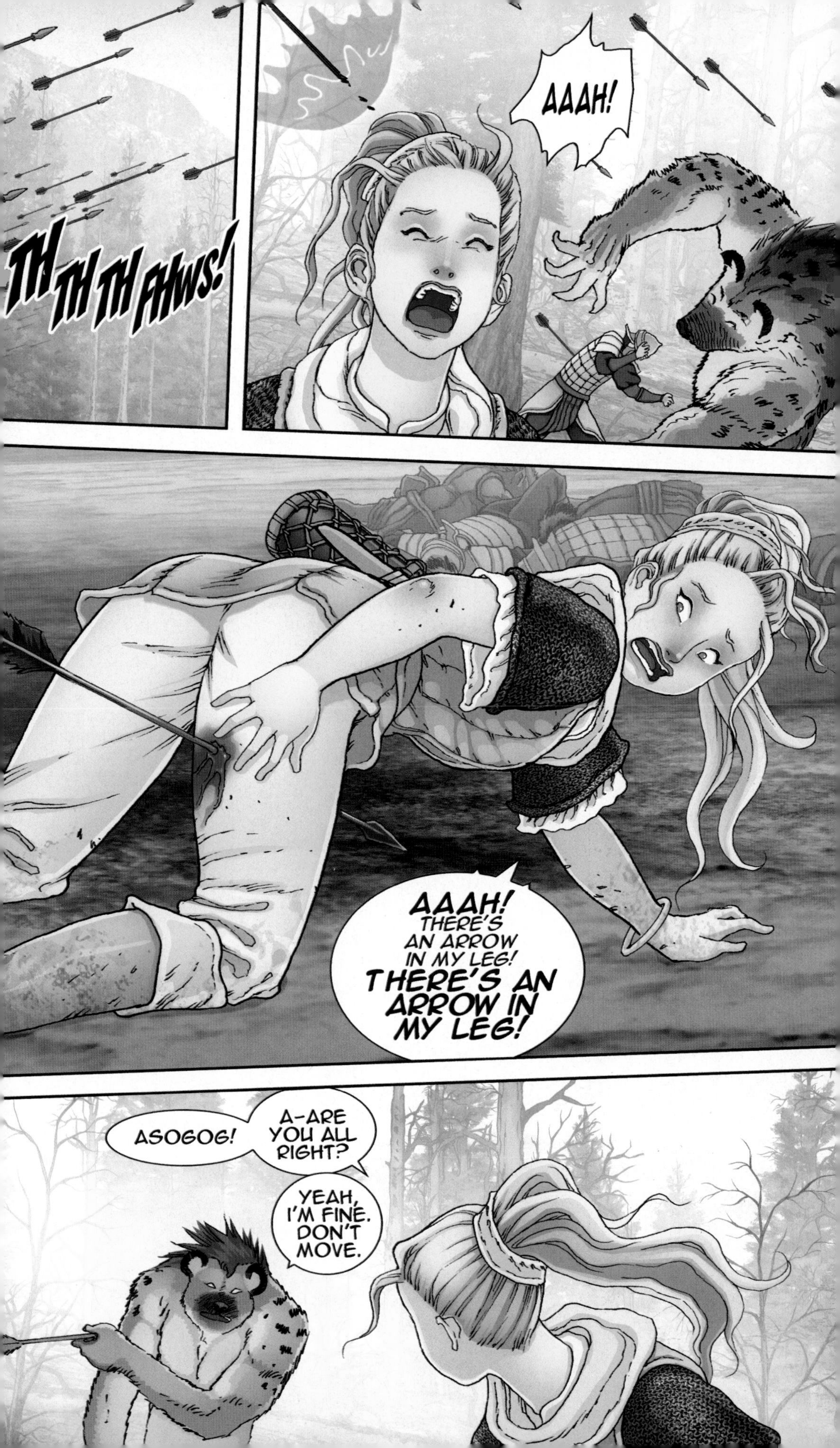

TH TH TH FHWS!
AAAH!
AAAH! THERE'S AN ARROW IN MY LEG! THERE'S AN ARROW IN MY LEG!
ASOGOG!
A-ARE YOU ALL RIGHT?
YEAH, I'M FINE. DON'T MOVE.

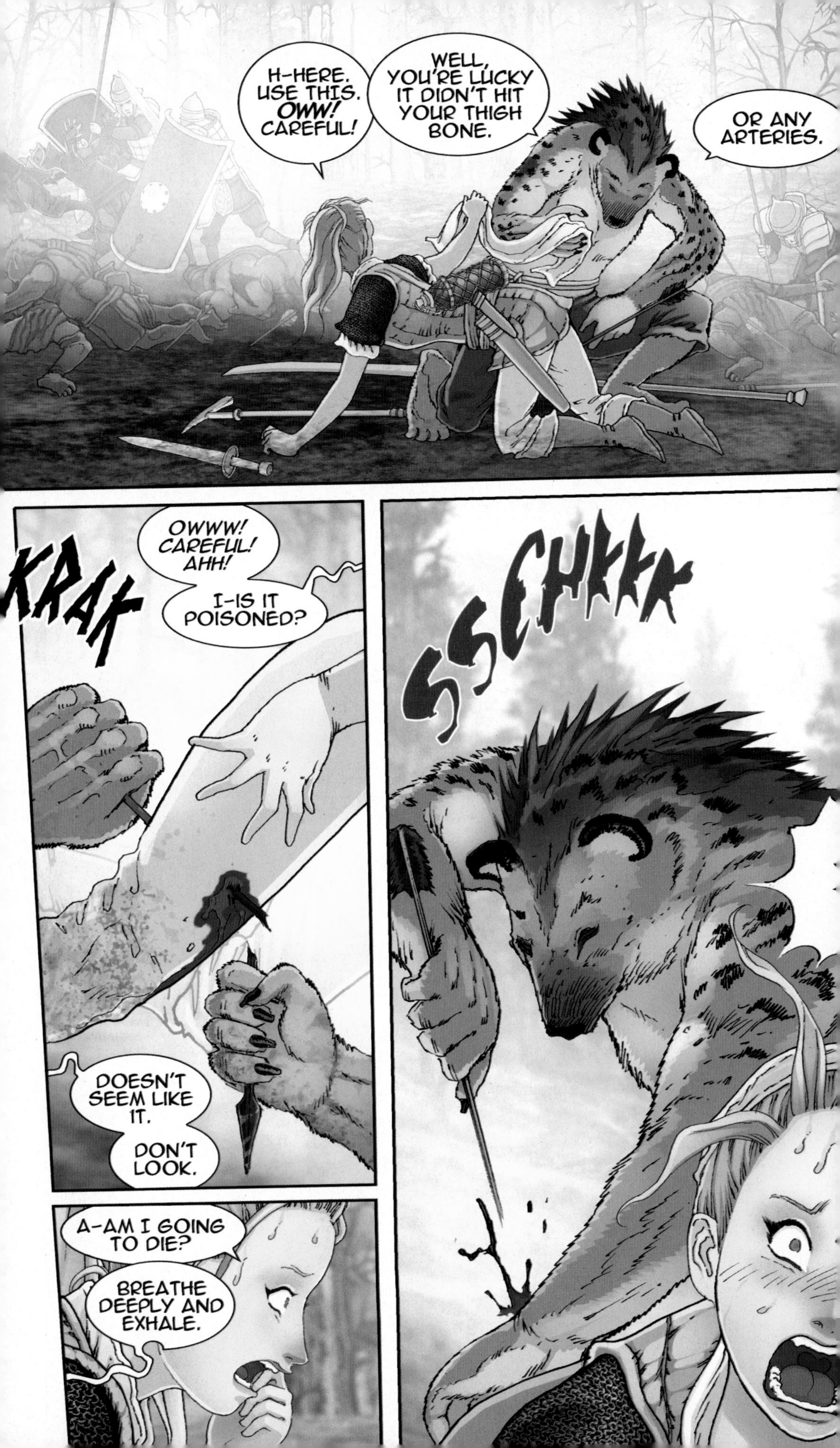
H-HERE. USE THIS. OWW! CAREFUL!
WELL, YOU'RE LUCKY IT DIDN'T HIT YOUR THIGH BONE.
OR ANY ARTERIES.
KRAK
OWWW! CAREFUL! AHH!
I-IS IT POISONED?
DOESN'T SEEM LIKE IT.
DON'T LOOK.
A-AM I GOING TO DIE?
BREATHE DEEPLY AND EXHALE.
SSCHKKK

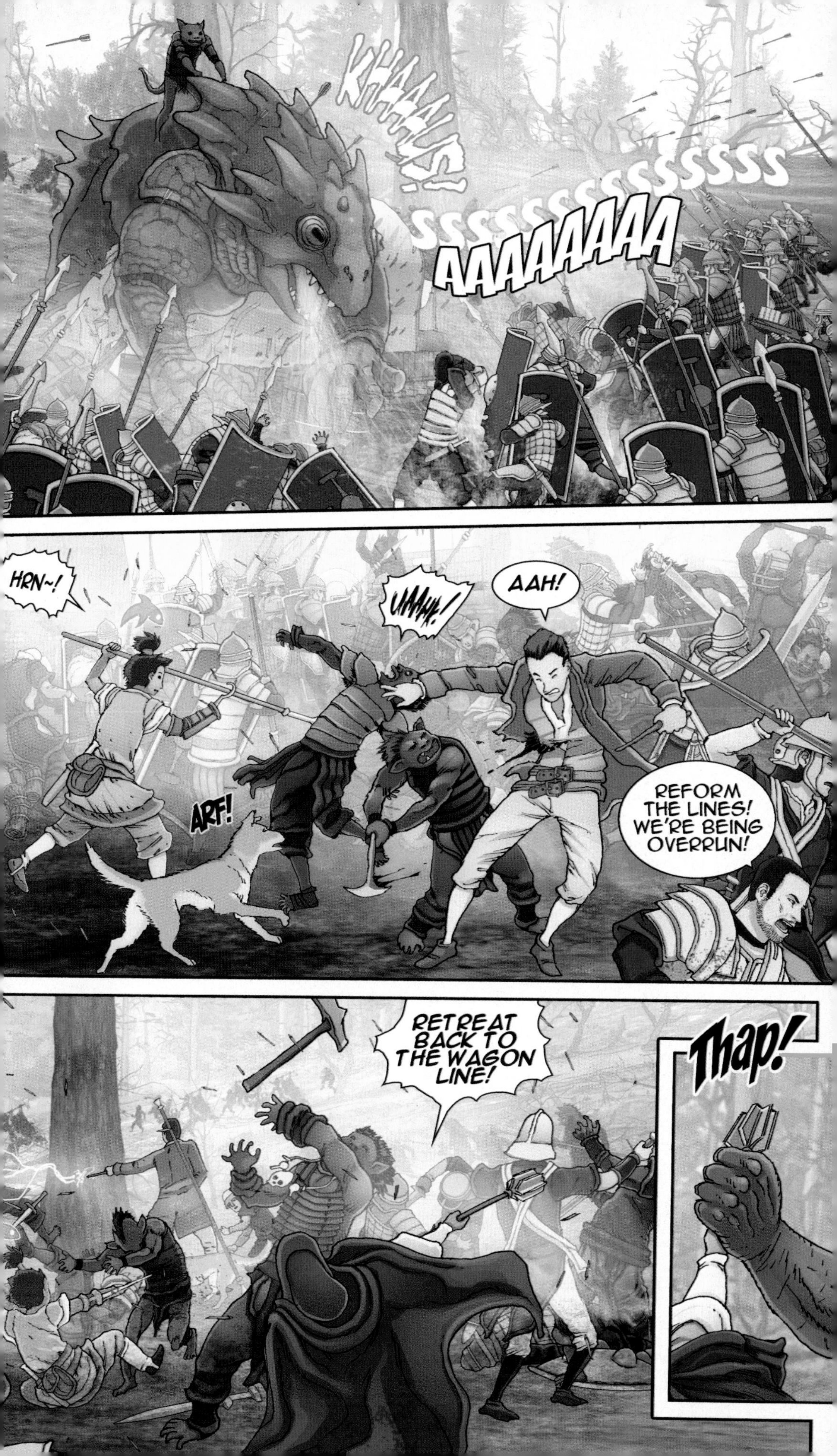
KHAAAUS!
SSSSSSSSSSSSSSS
AAAAAAAA
HRN~!
UAAAH!
AAH!
ARF!
REFORM THE LINES! WE'RE BEING OVERRUN!
RETREAT BACK TO THE WAGON LINE!
Thap!

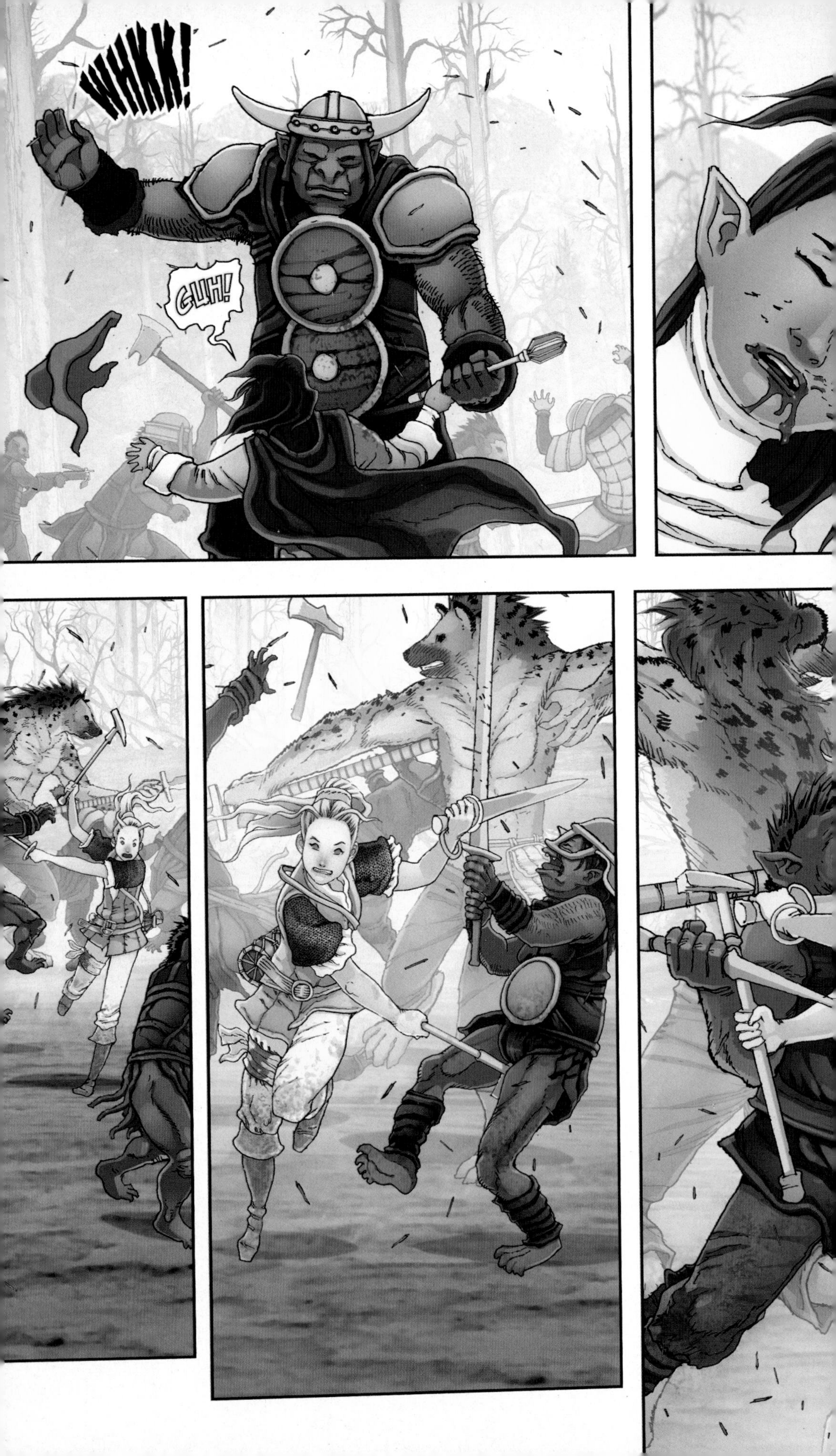
WHKK!
GUH!

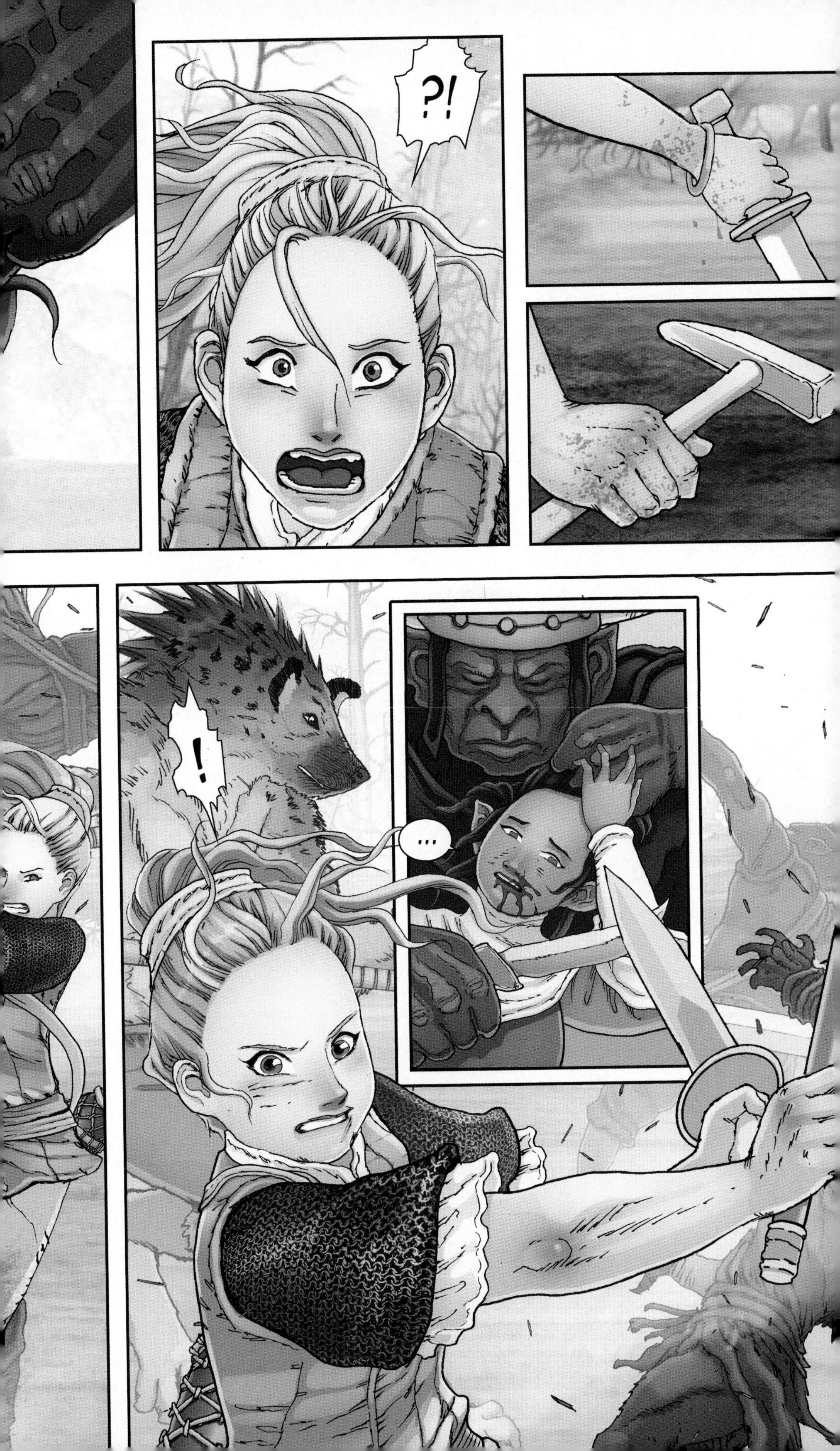
?!
!
...

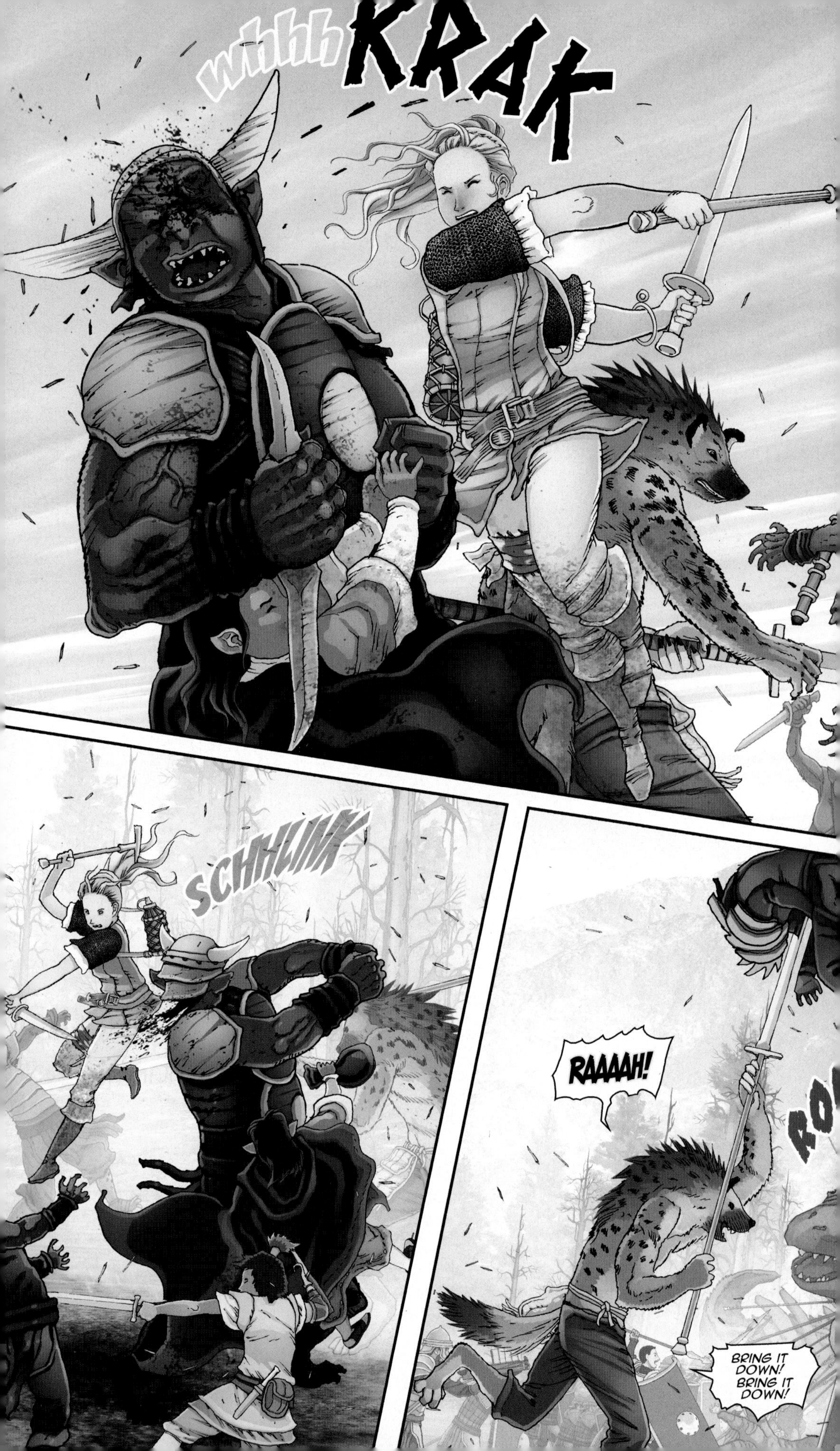
whhhh
KRAK
SCHHLINK
RAAAAH!
BRING IT DOWN! BRING IT DOWN!

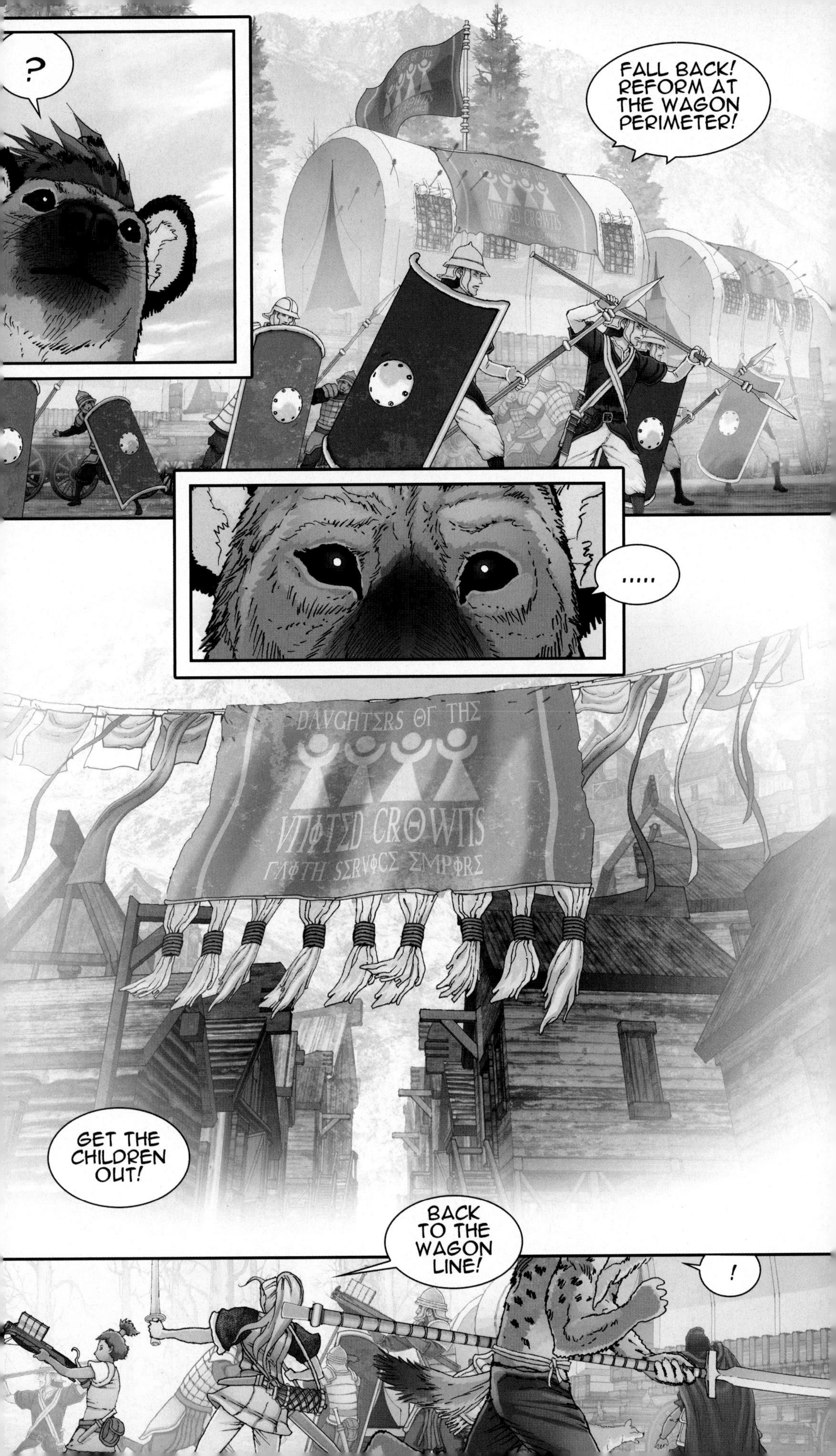
?
FALL BACK! REFORM AT THE WAGON PERIMETER!
.....
DAUGHTERS OF THE
UNITED CROWNS
FAITH SERVICE EMPIRE
GET THE CHILDREN OUT!
BACK TO THE WAGON LINE!
!

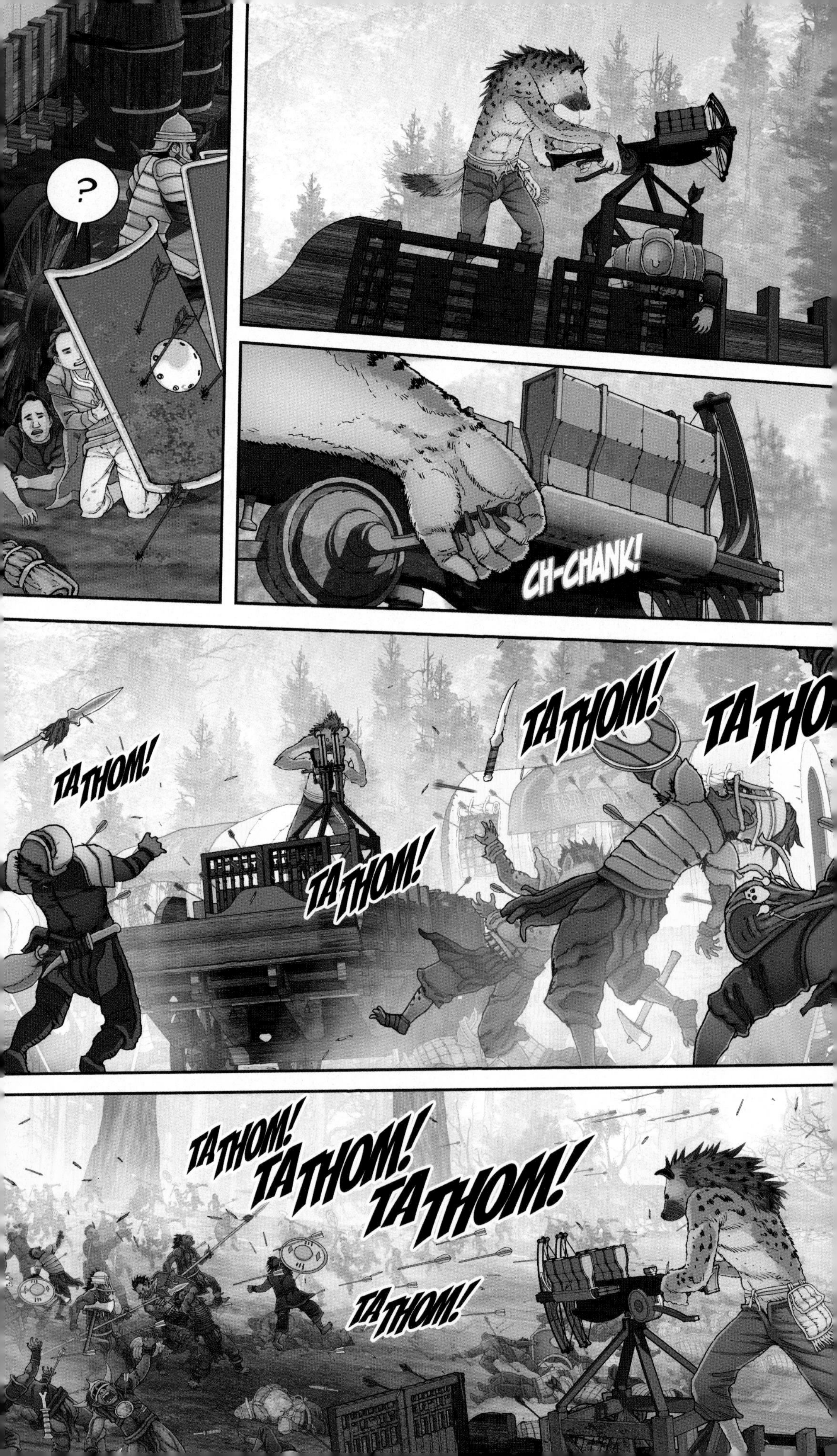
?
CH-CHANK!
TA THOM!
TA THOM!
TA THOM!
TA THO
TA THOM!
TA THOM!
TA THOM!
TA THOM!

YOU'RE THE GNAULL CLARI AND ARIARRA BEFRIENDED?

AYE, CAN YOU HAND ME THOSE BOLT CASES BEFORE I RUN OUT?

MY NAME'S JOLFE, CLARIETTE'S COUSIN. GOOD TO HAVE YOU WITH US!

I'M ASOGOG. GOOD TO MEET YOU, JOLFE.

swooohhh
swooohh

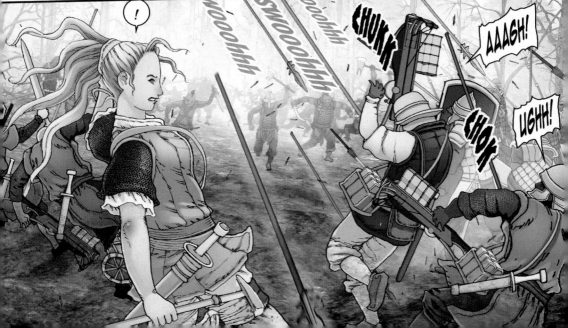

!

swoooohhh
swoooohhh
swoooohhh

CHUKK

AAAGH!

CHOK

UGHH!

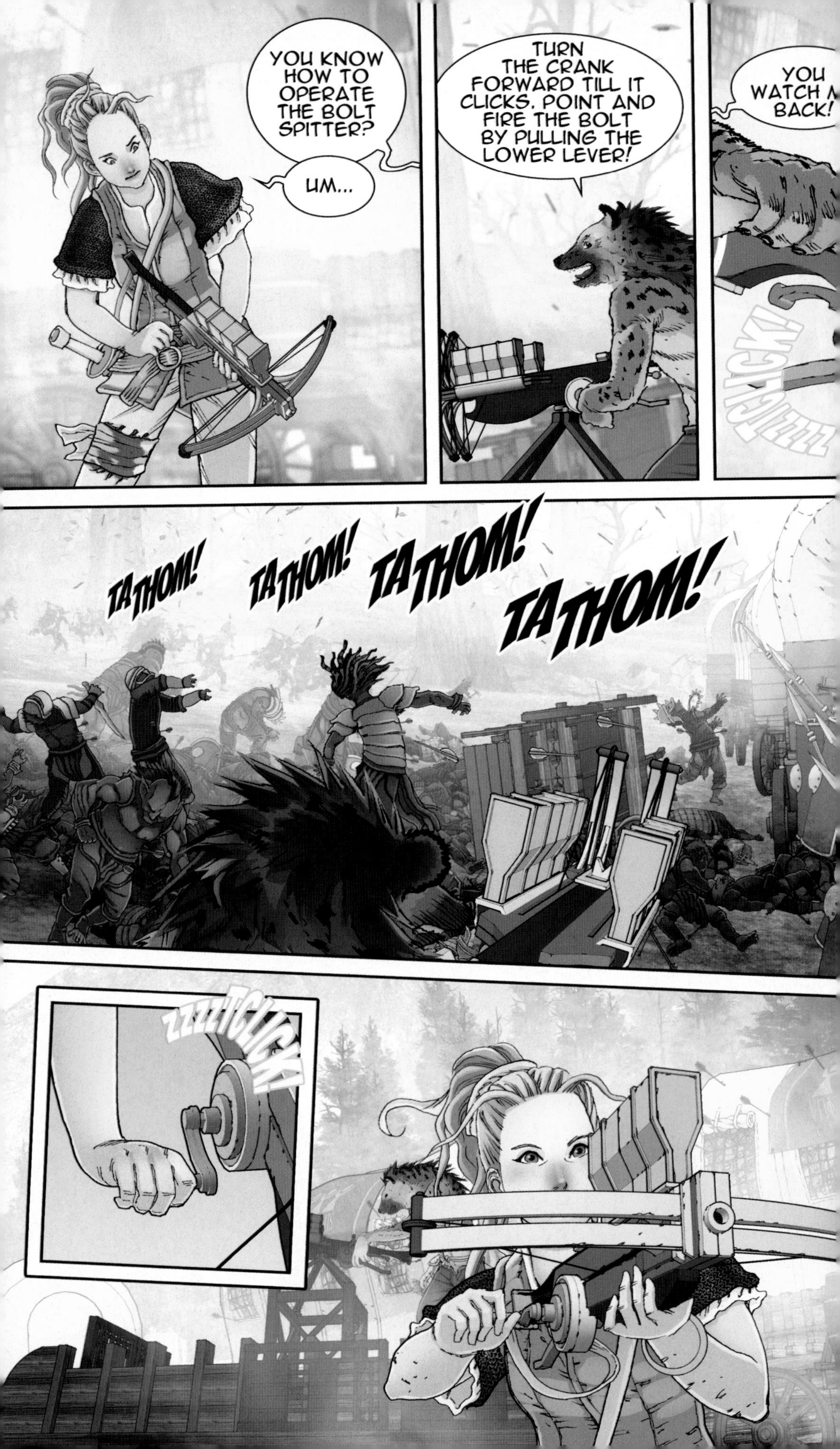
YOU KNOW HOW TO OPERATE THE BOLT SPITTER?
UM...
TURN THE CRANK FORWARD TILL IT CLICKS. POINT AND FIRE THE BOLT BY PULLING THE LOWER LEVER!
YOU WATCH M BACK!
ZZZZTCLICK!
TATHOM!
TATHOM!
TATHOM!
TATHOM!
ZZZZTCLICK!

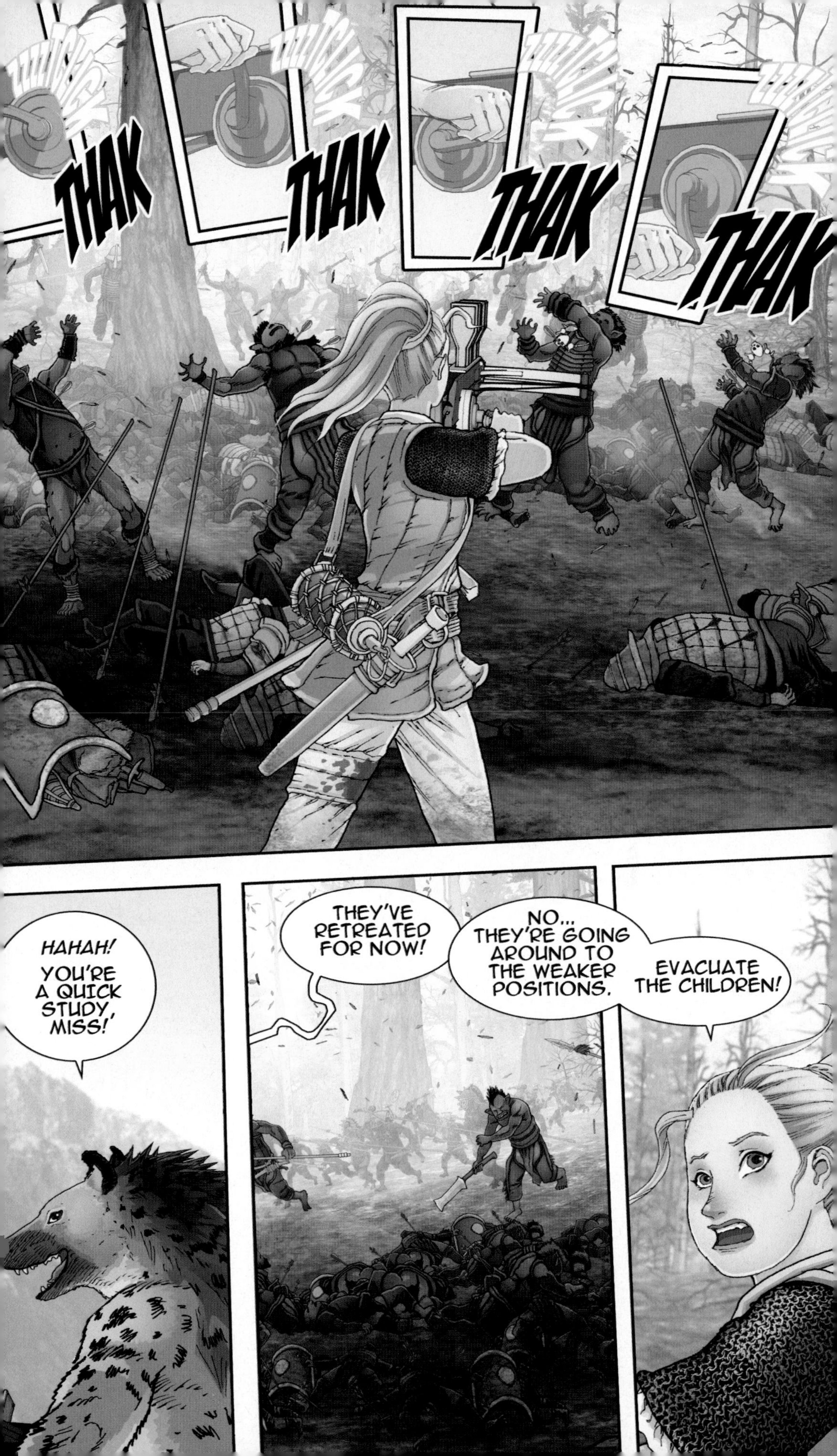
ZZZTICK
THAK
ZZZTICK
THAK
ZZZTICK
THAK
ZZZTICK
THAK
HAHAH! YOU'RE A QUICK STUDY, MISS!'
THEY'VE RETREATED FOR NOW!
NO... THEY'RE GOING AROUND TO THE WEAKER POSITIONS.
EVACUATE THE CHILDREN!

AAAA!

AAAH!

ROAAH!

CENTURION! WE CANNOT STAY OUT IN THE OPEN! WE WILL BE OVERRUN!

AYE, THEY HAVE FIRE THROWERS ON THE RIDGE, POSSIBLY AIDED BY MAJERES. I'LL GATHER MY MEN!

WE'R ALMO DON CLA

ARE THE CHILDREN ALL OUT?

AAA!

AAA!

VASH VASH

BVThBOOM!

UAAAH!

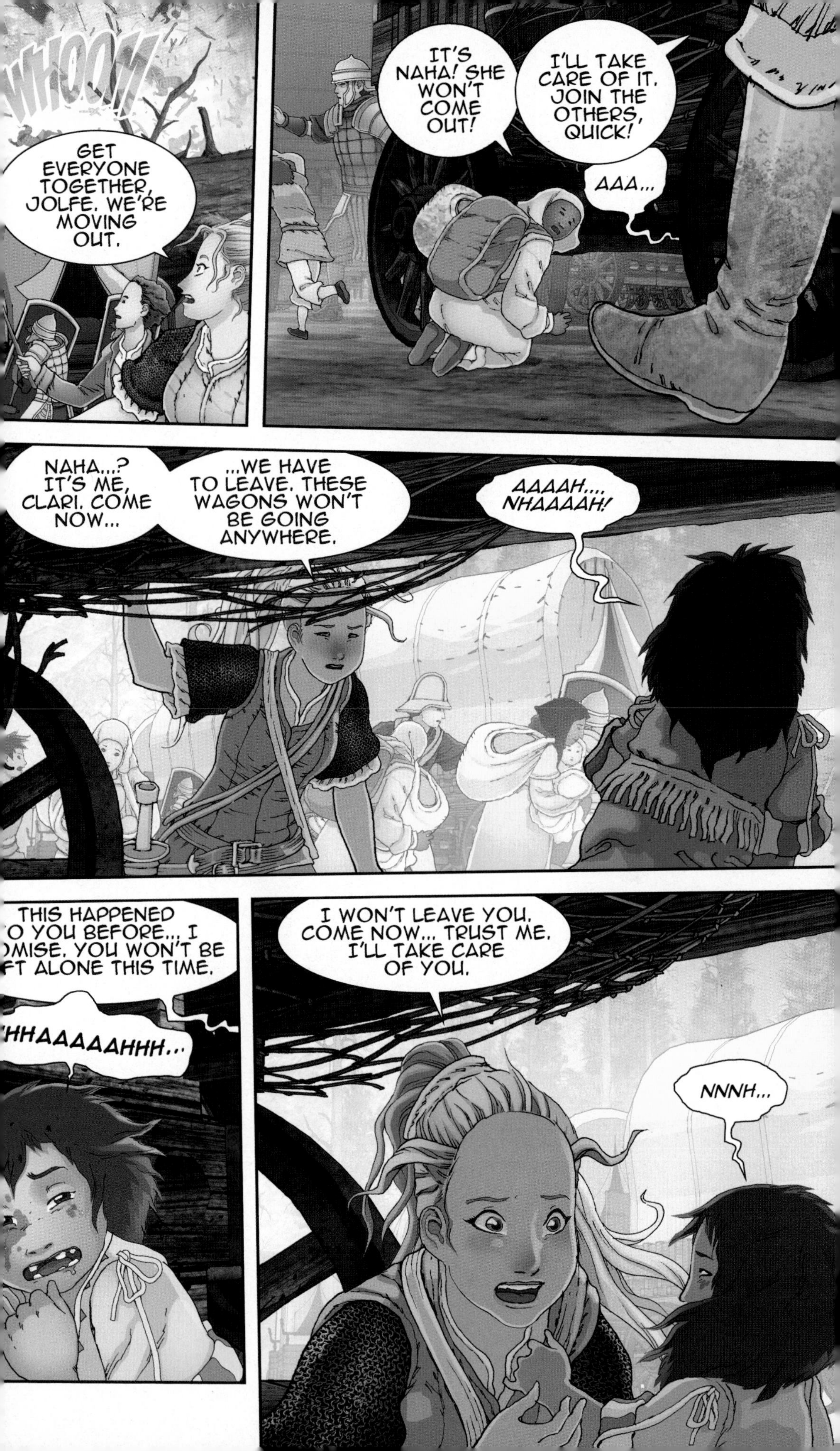
WHOOM!
GET EVERYONE TOGETHER, JOLFE. WE'RE MOVING OUT.
IT'S NAHA! SHE WON'T COME OUT!
I'LL TAKE CARE OF IT. JOIN THE OTHERS, QUICK!
AAA...
NAHA...? IT'S ME, CLARI. COME NOW...
...WE HAVE TO LEAVE. THESE WAGONS WON'T BE GOING ANYWHERE.
AAAAH.... NHAAAAAH!
THIS HAPPENED
O YOU BEFORE... I
OMISE. YOU WON'T BE
FT ALONE THIS TIME.
HHAAAAAAHHH...
I WON'T LEAVE YOU. COME NOW... TRUST ME. I'LL TAKE CARE OF YOU.
NNNH...

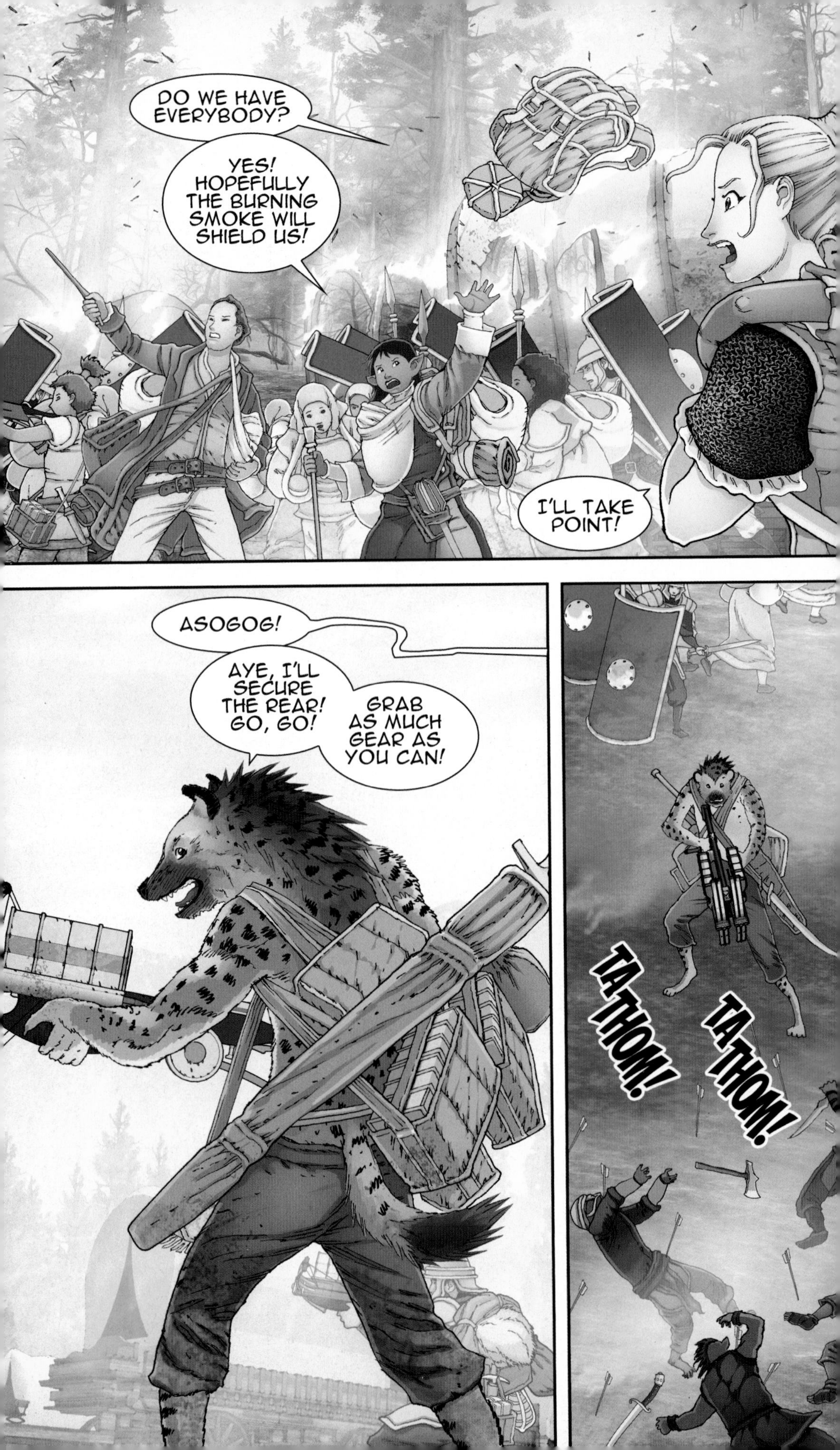
DO WE HAVE EVERYBODY?
YES! HOPEFULLY THE BURNING SMOKE WILL SHIELD US!
I'LL TAKE POINT!
ASOGOG!
AYE, I'LL SECURE THE REAR! GO, GO!
GRAB AS MUCH GEAR AS YOU CAN!
TA THOM!
TA THOM!

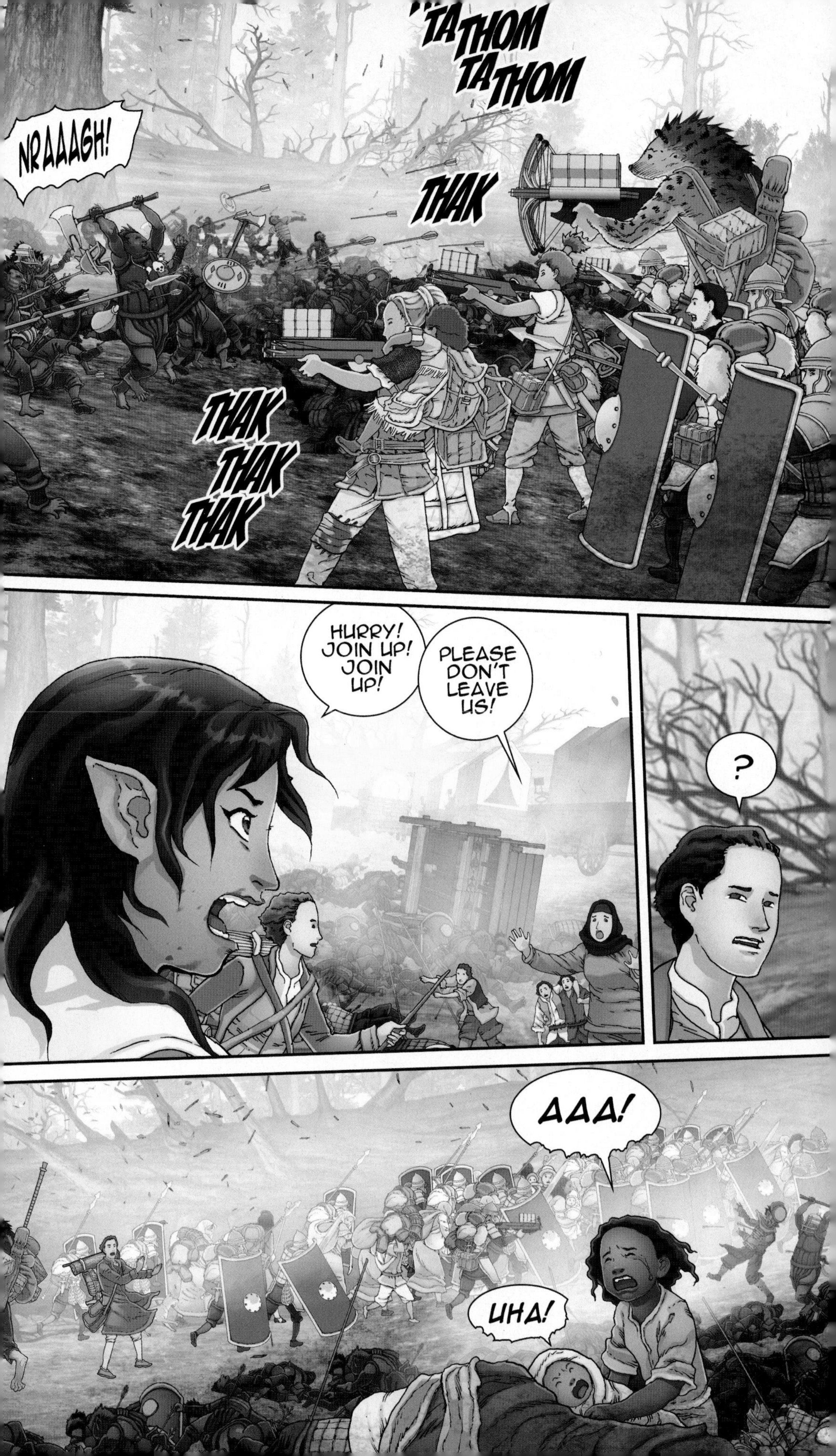
TA THOM TA THOM
NRAAAGH!
THAK
THAK THAK THAK
HURRY! JOIN UP! JOIN UP!
PLEASE DON'T LEAVE US!
?
AAA!
UHA!

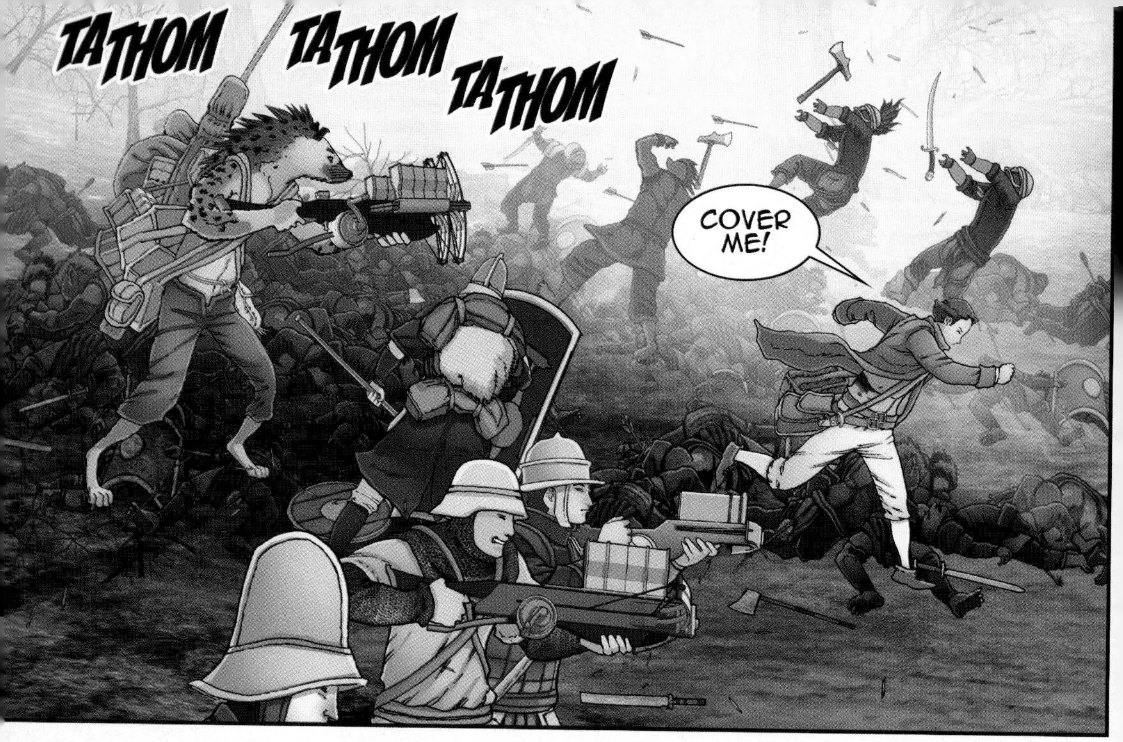
TA THOM TA THOM TA THOM
COVER ME!

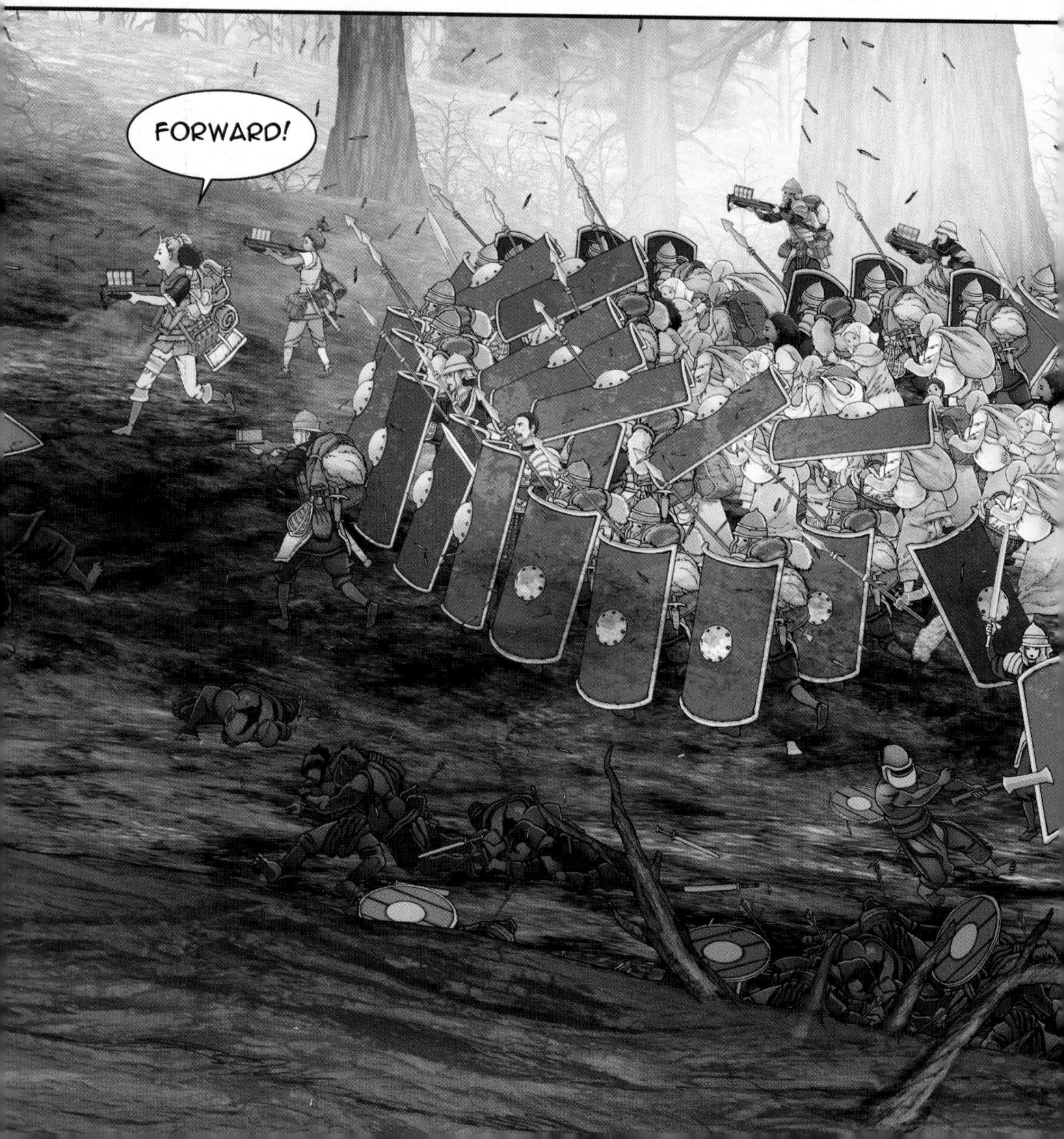
FORWARD!

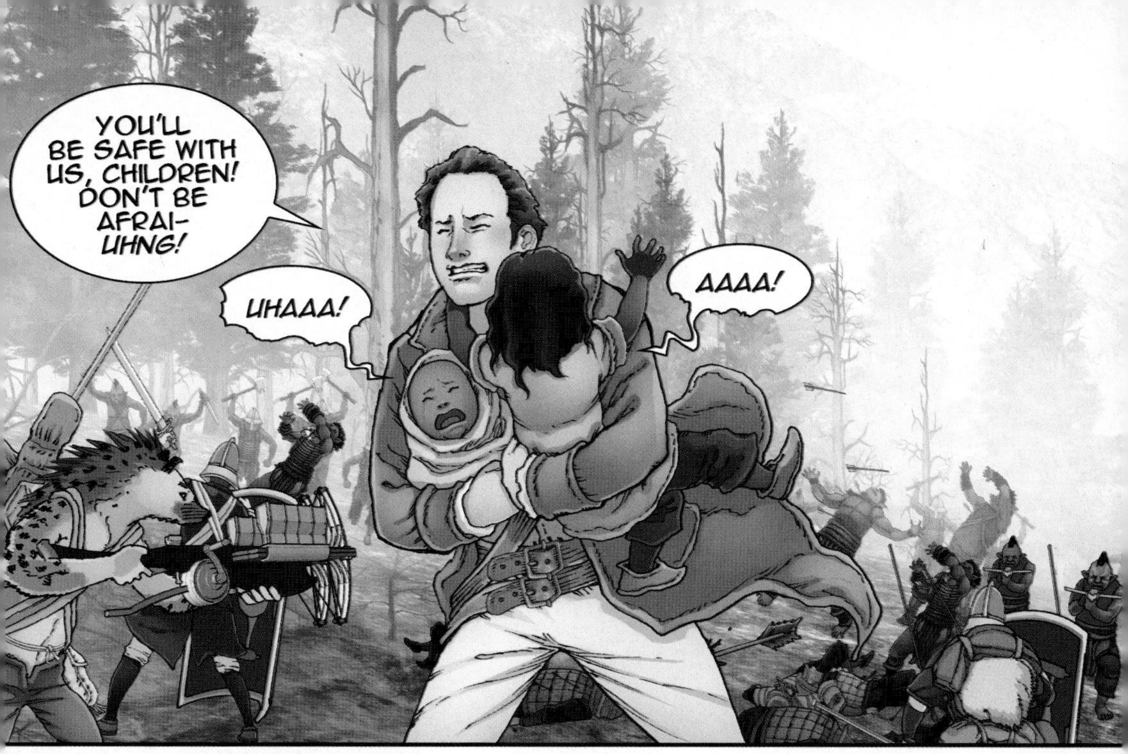

YOU'LL BE SAFE WITH US, CHILDREN! DON'T BE AFRAI-UHNG!
UHAAA!
AAAA!

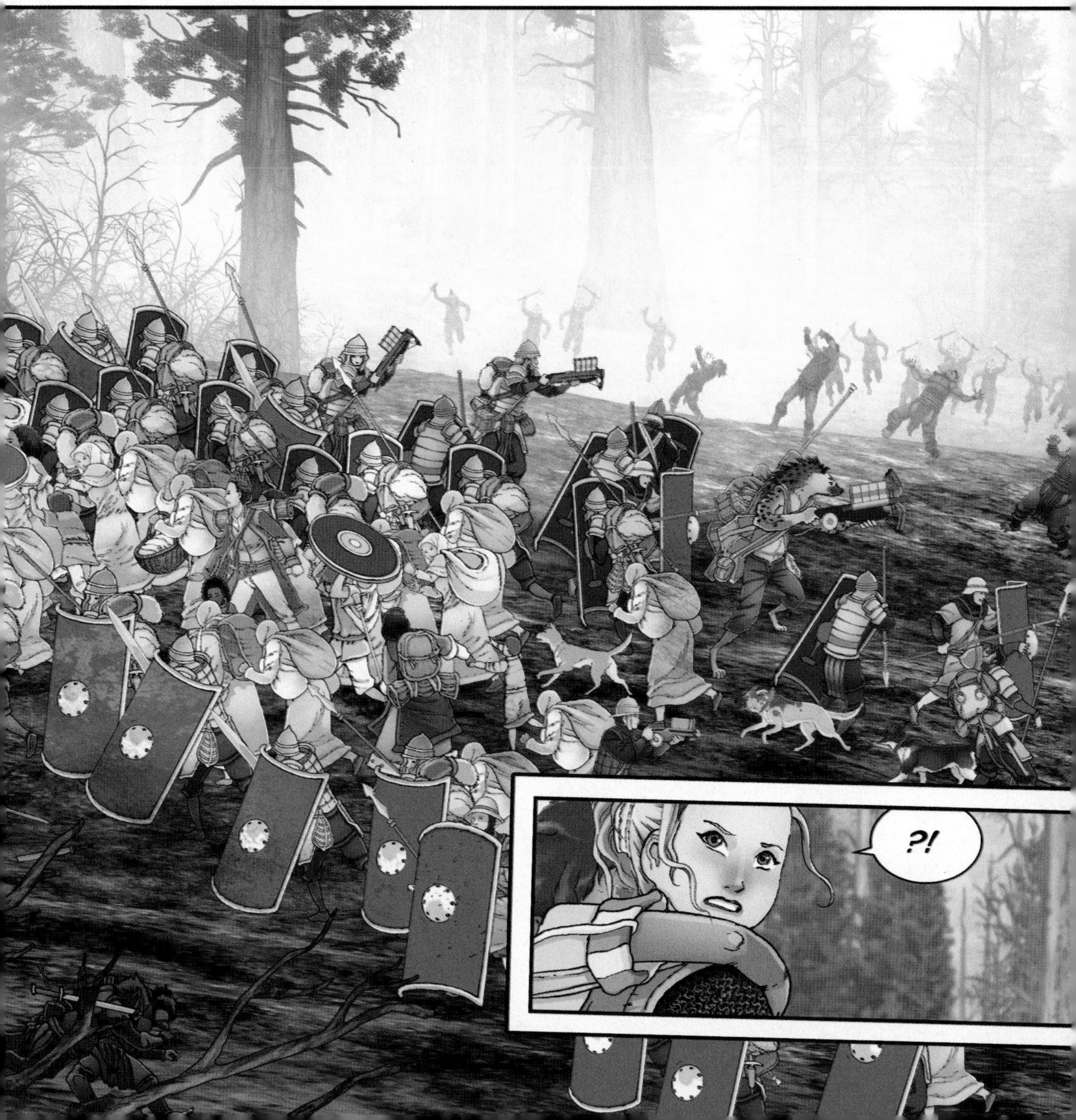

?!

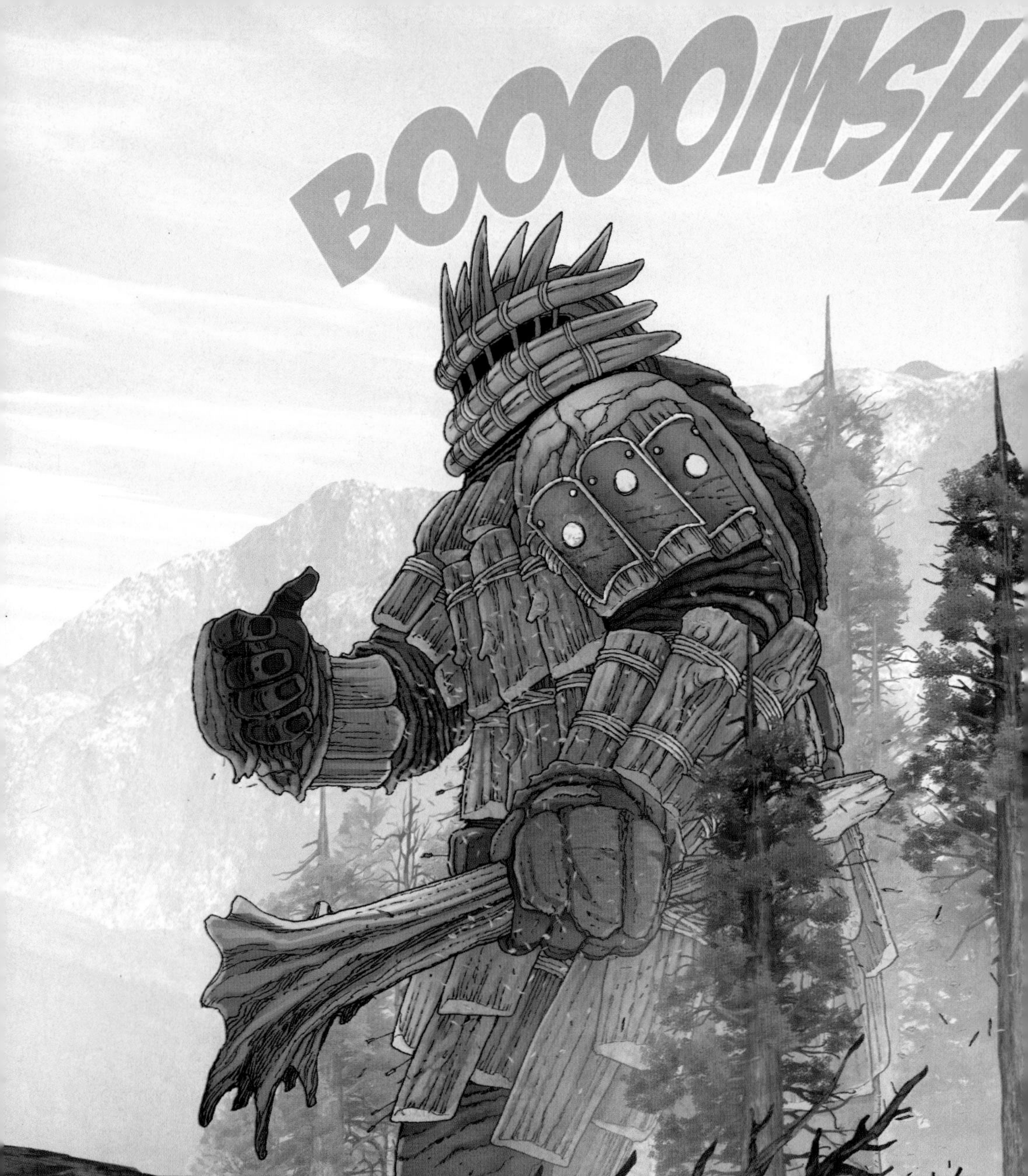
BOOOOMSH!!

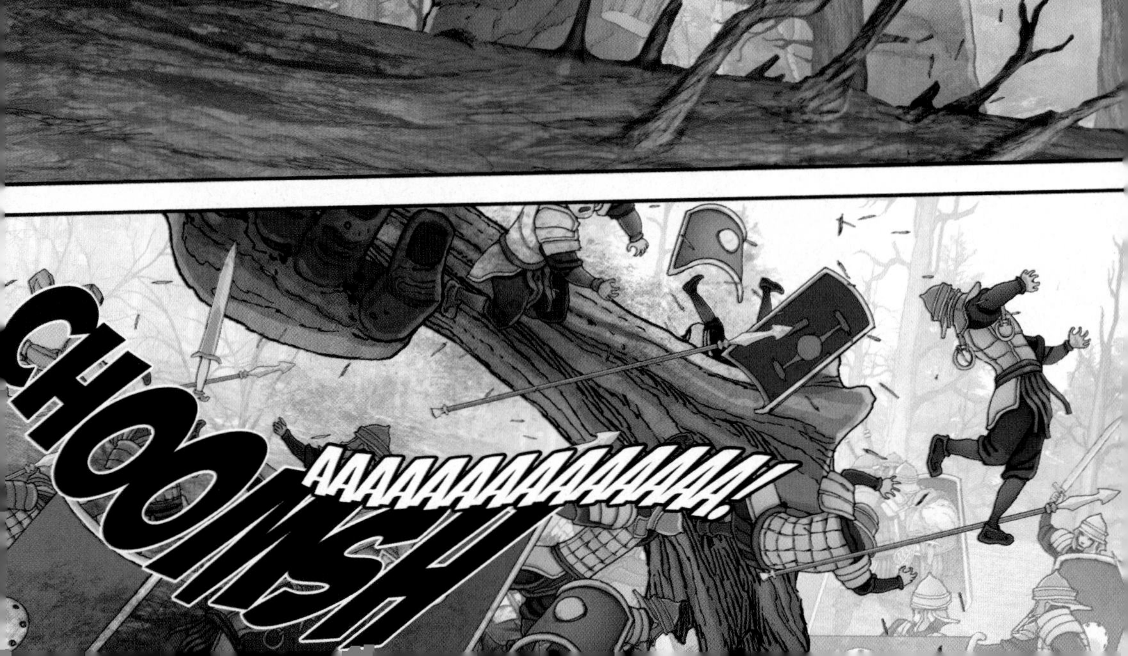
CHOOMSH
AAAAAAAAAAAAA!

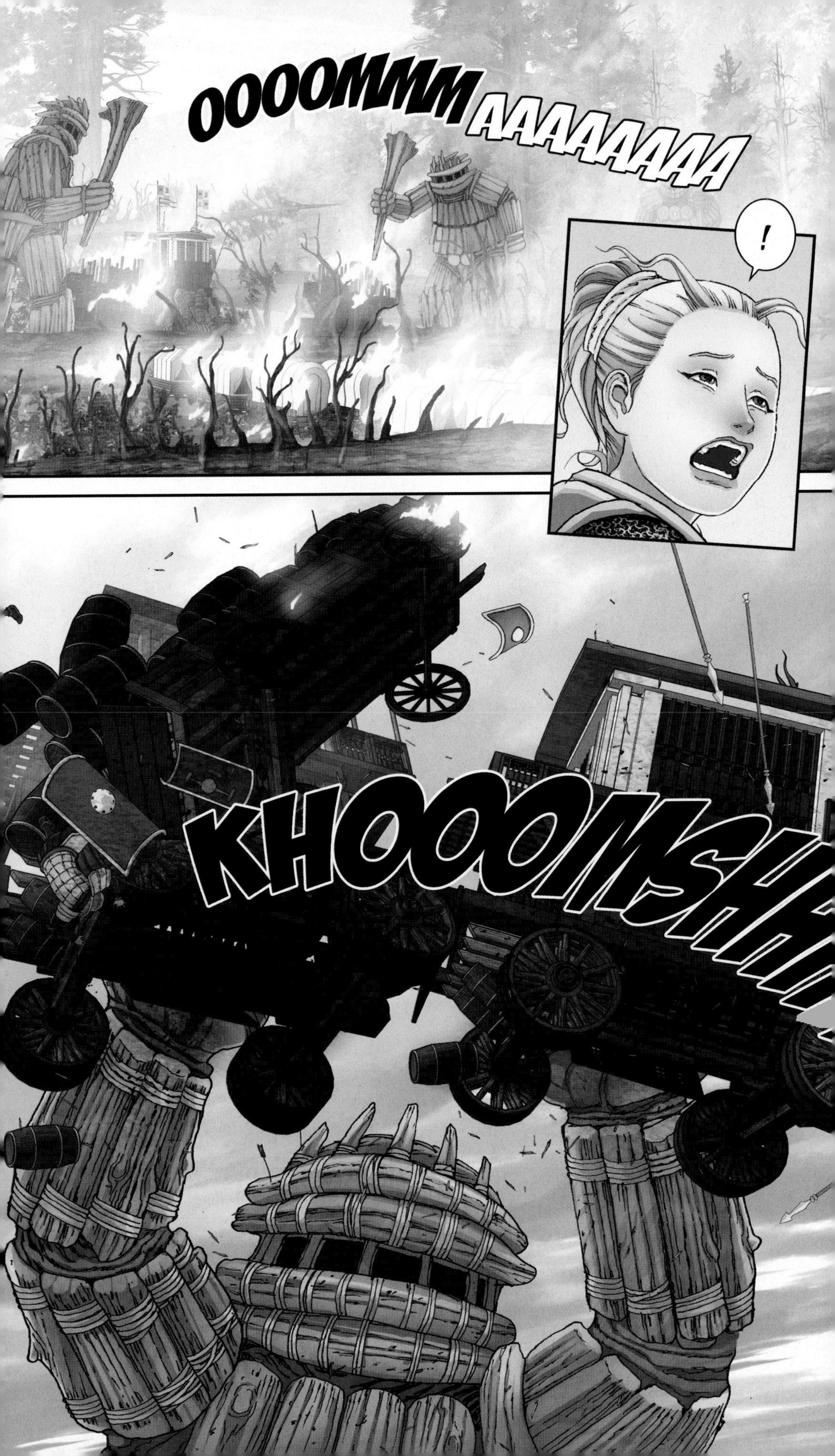

OOOOMMM AAAAAAAA
!
KHOOOMSHH

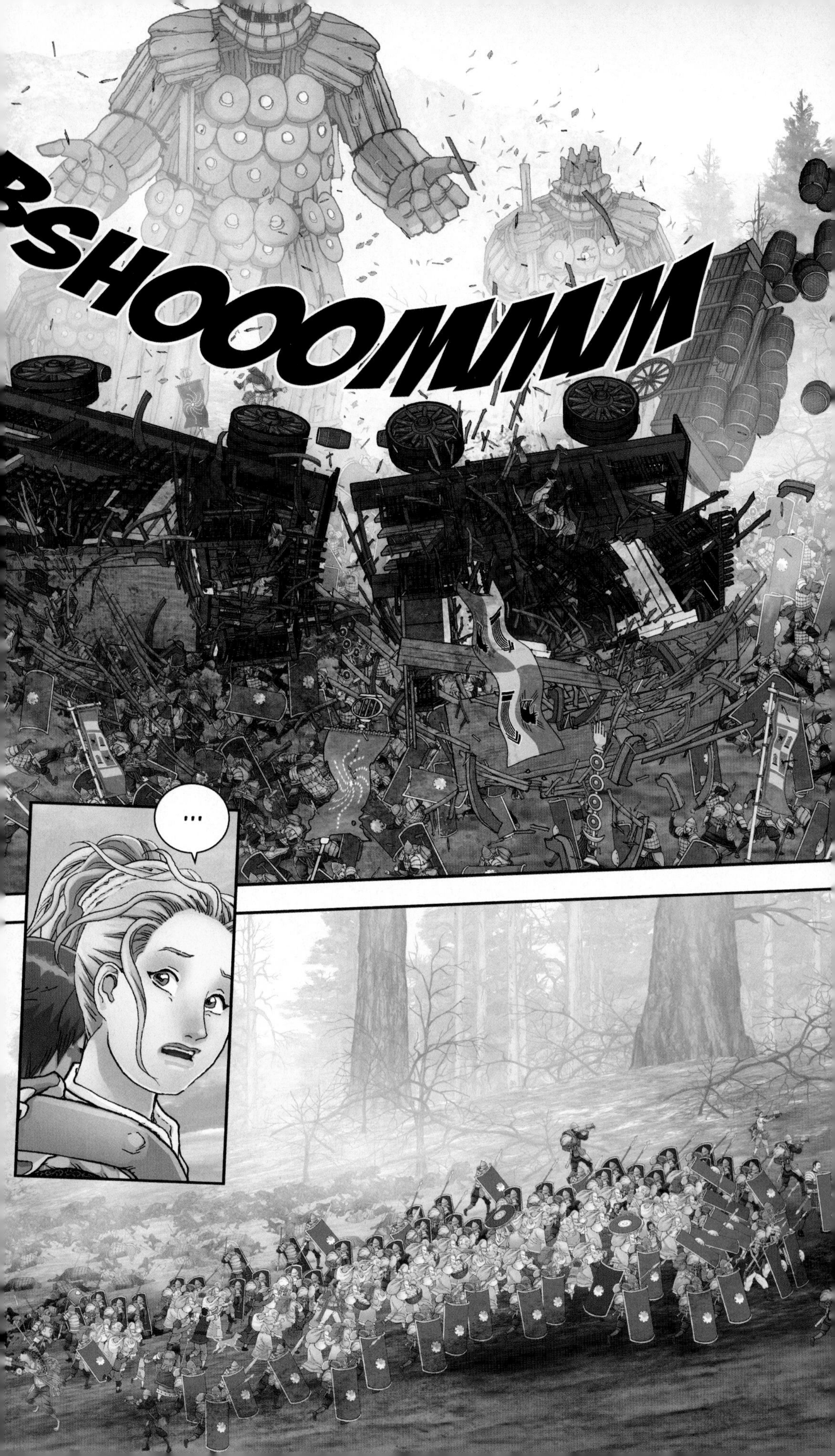
BSHOOOMMM
...

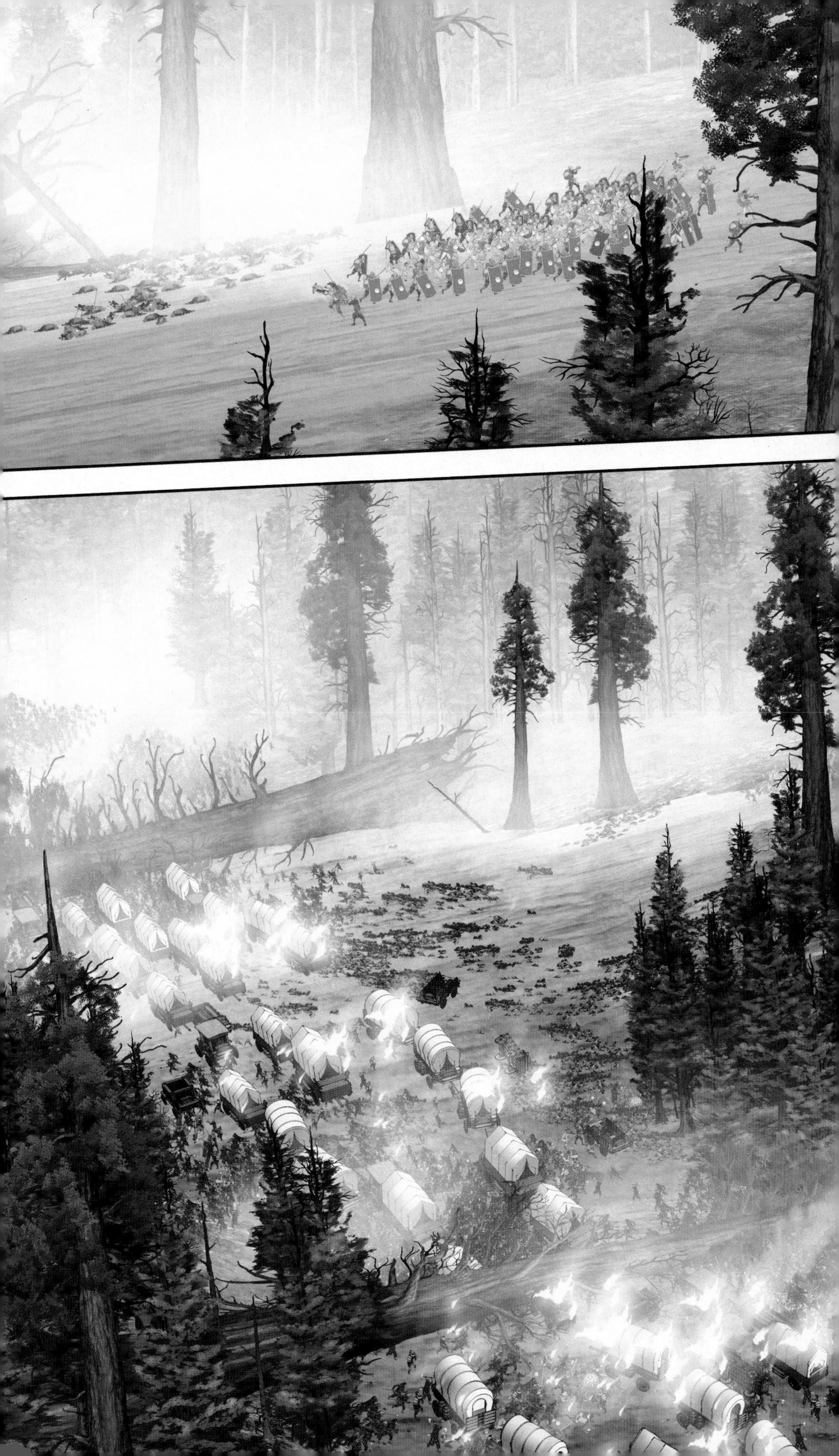

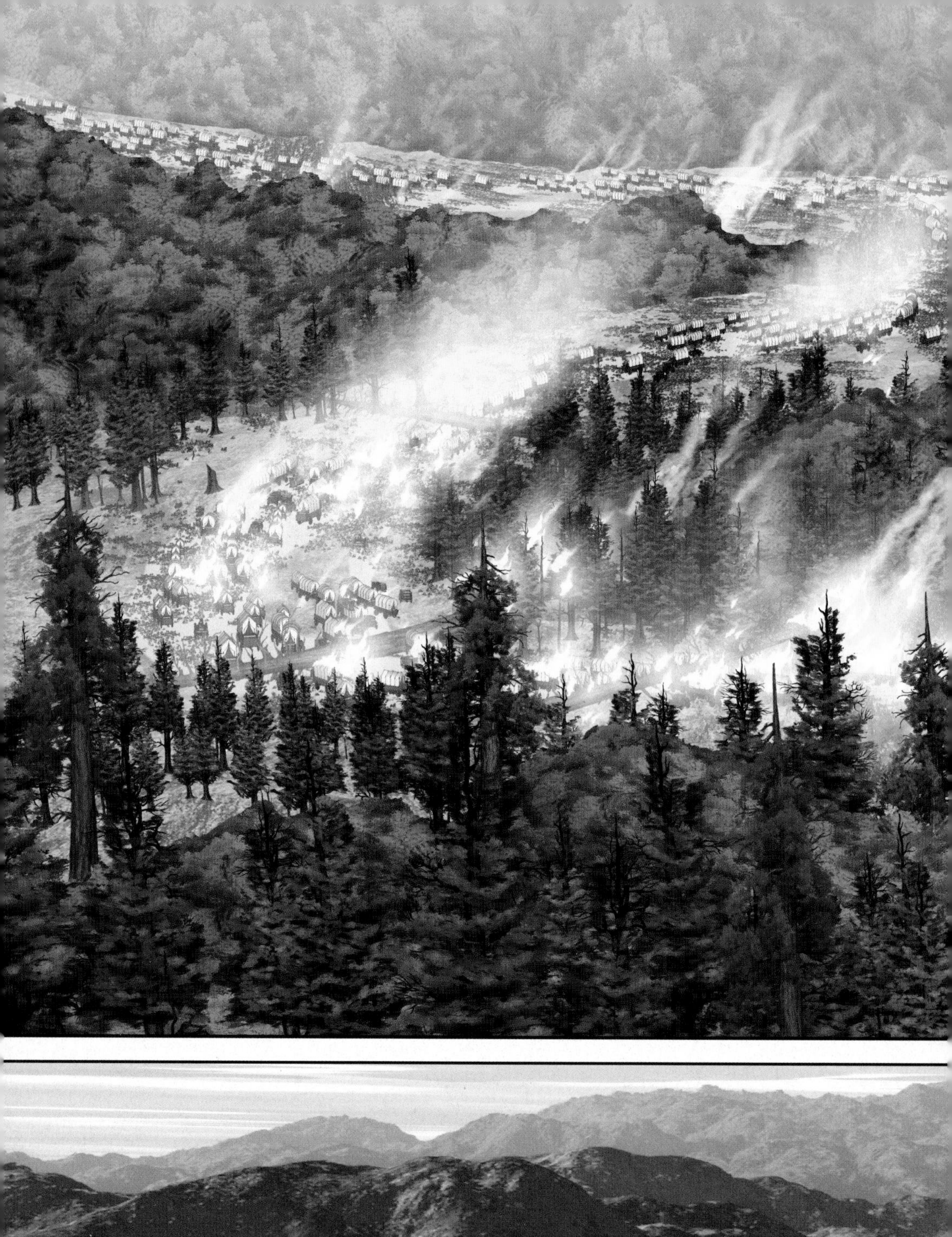
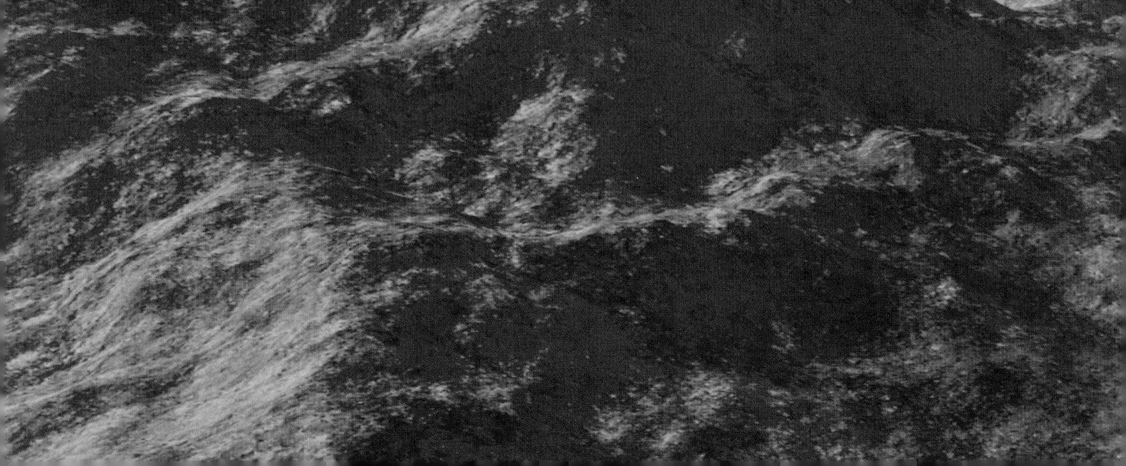

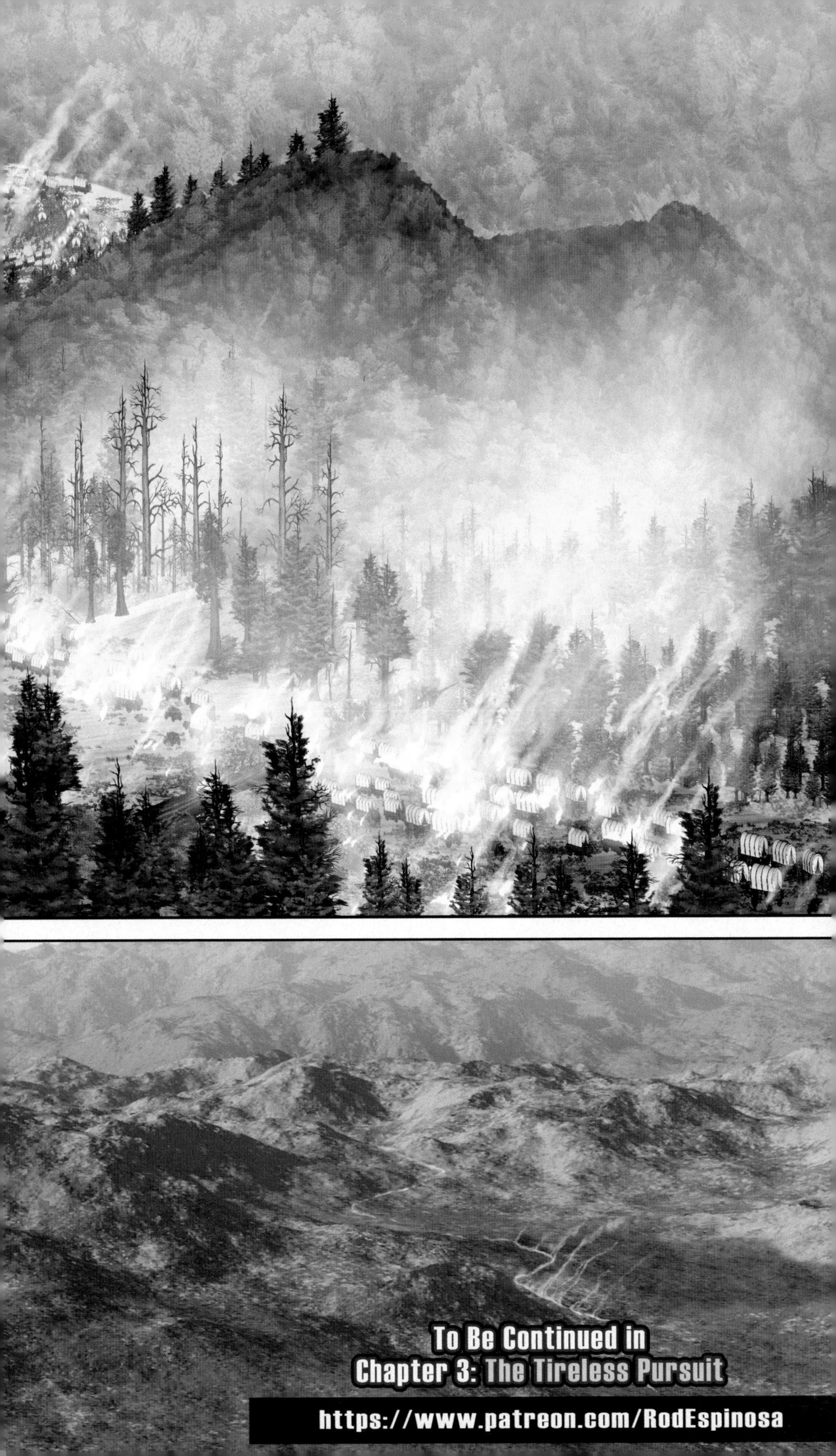
To Be Continued in
Chapter 3: The Tireless Pursuit
https://www.patreon.com/RodEspinosa

ADVENTURE FINDERS
BY ROD ESPINOSA

Her Story Begins

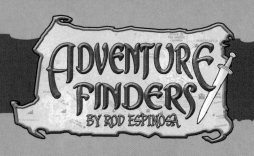

Sometimes our stories begin
in darkness. Alone.
Helpless.

We were
born with life.
But how fragile it
is when nobody is
there for us!

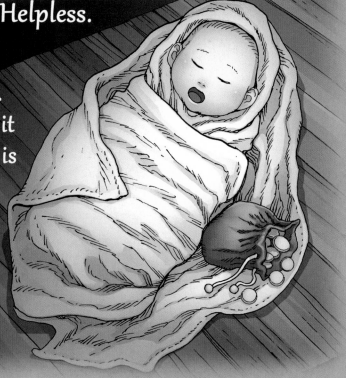

Alone and small, I had no hope.

But someone came.
Someone cared.

That's how I had this
chance at life...

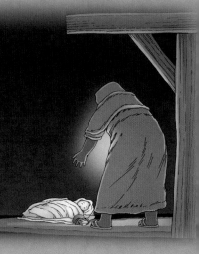

...the chance
to be happy...

...to be loved...

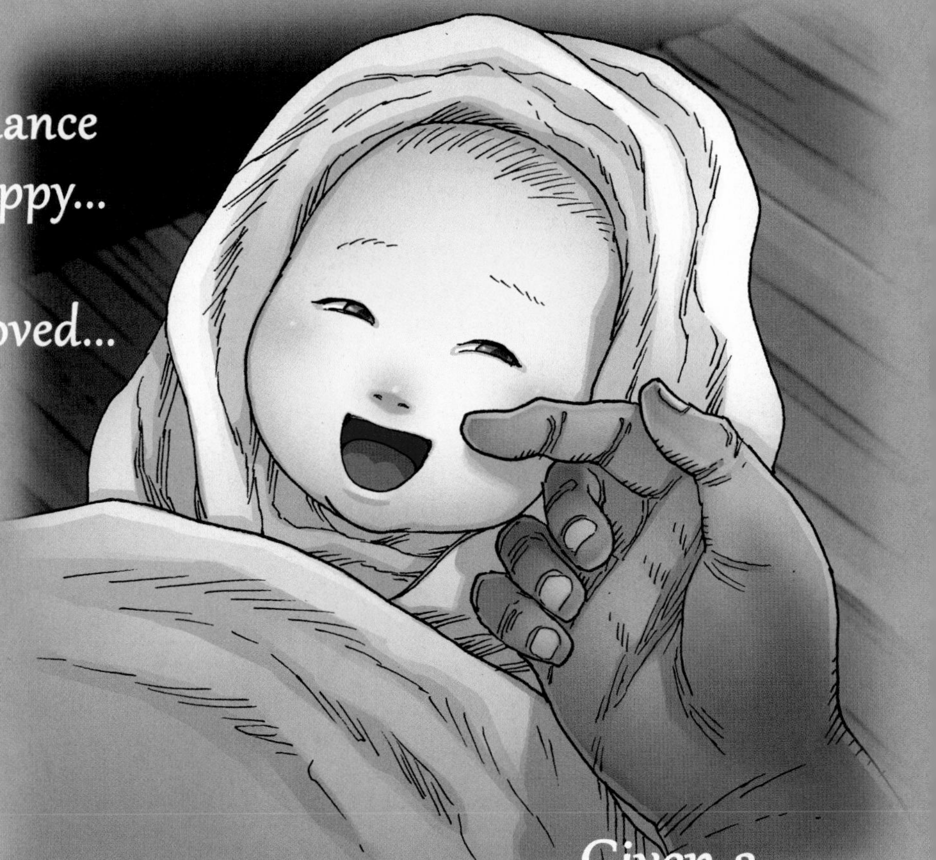

Given a
chance
to grow
up with
kindness and
family...

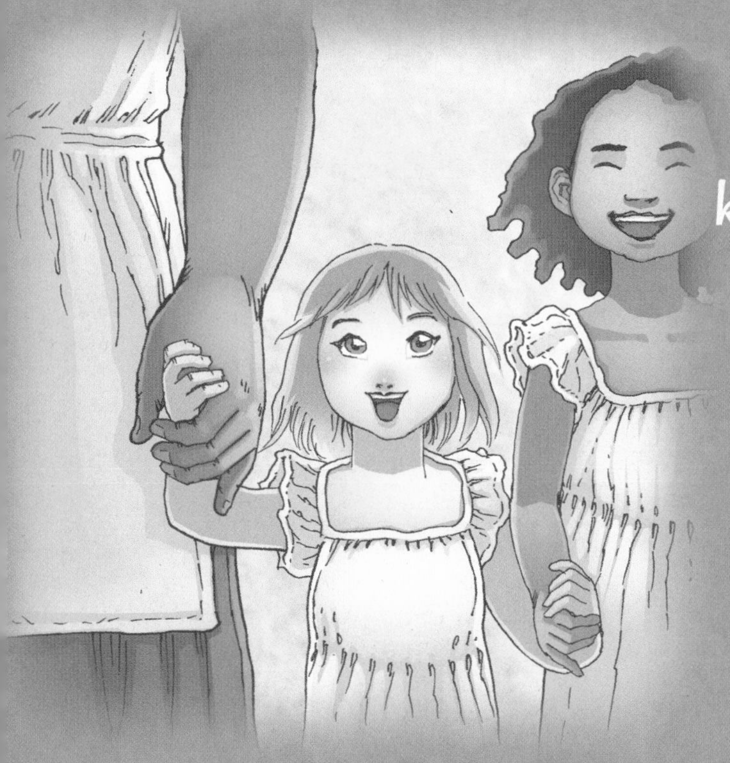

We are given
this rare
gift...

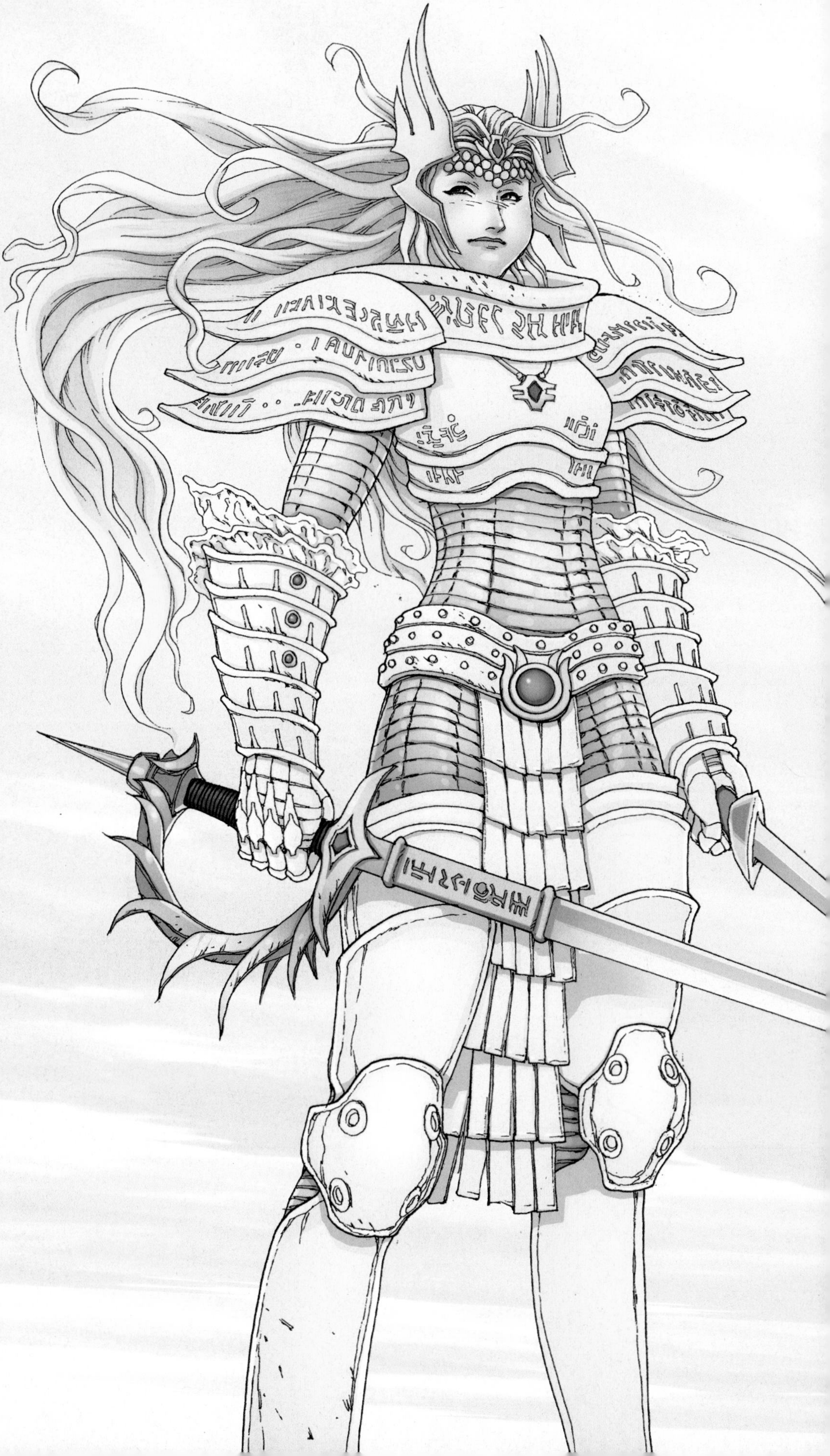

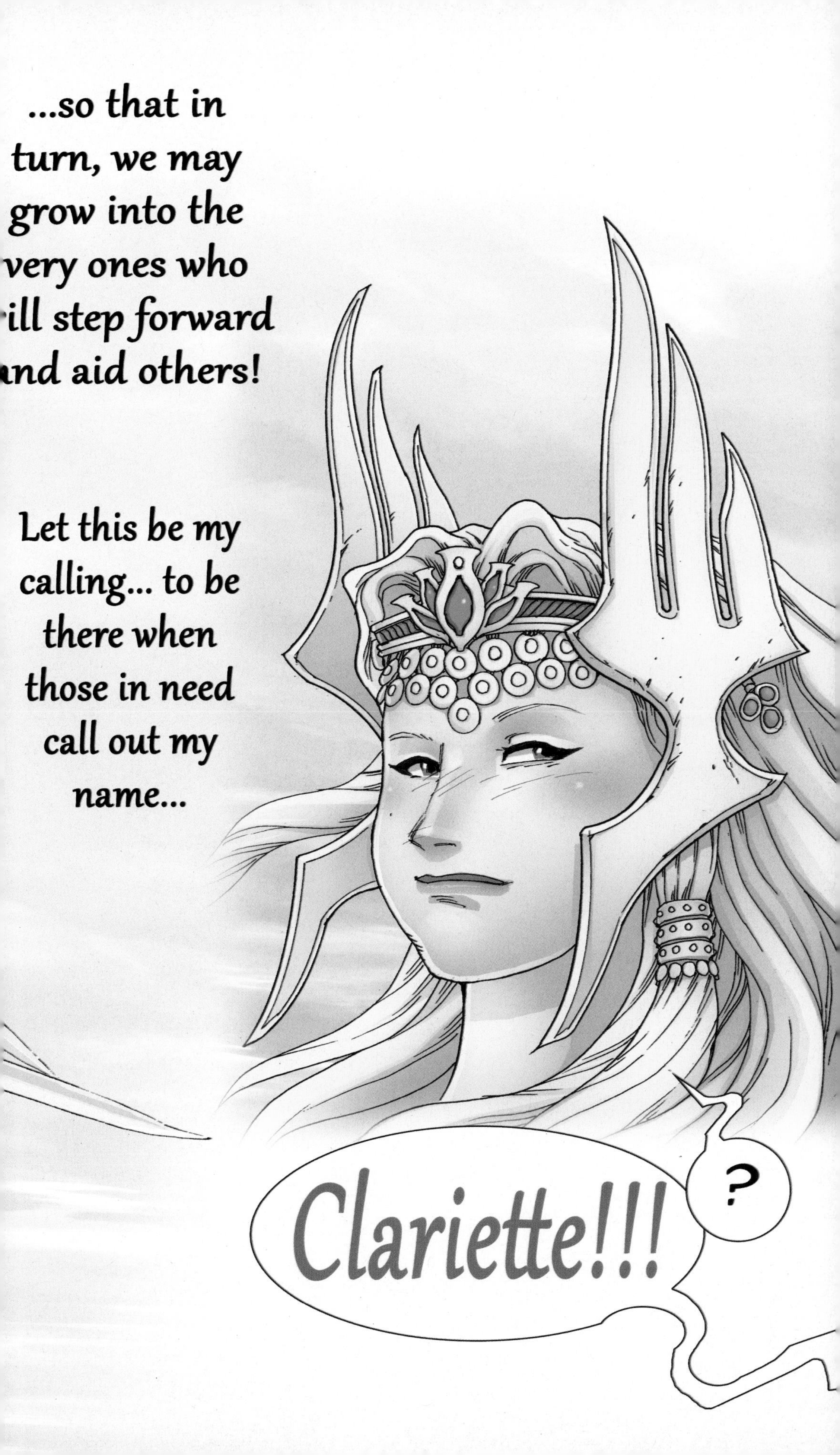
...so that in turn, we may grow into the very ones who ill step forward nd aid others!
Let this be my calling... to be there when those in need call out my name...
Clariette!!!
?

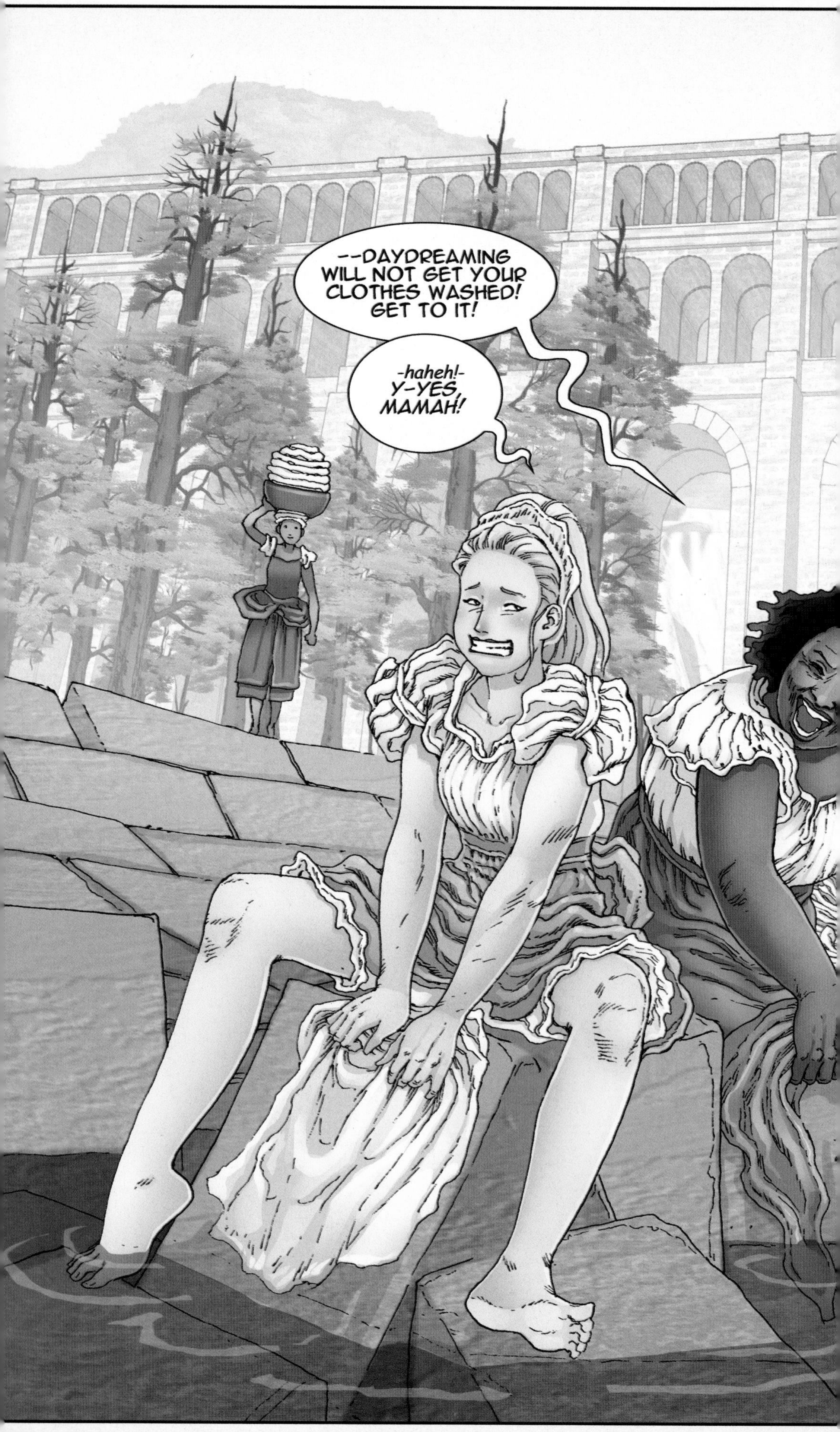
--DAYDREAMING WILL NOT GET YOUR CLOTHES WASHED! GET TO IT!
-haheh!- Y-YES, MAMAH!

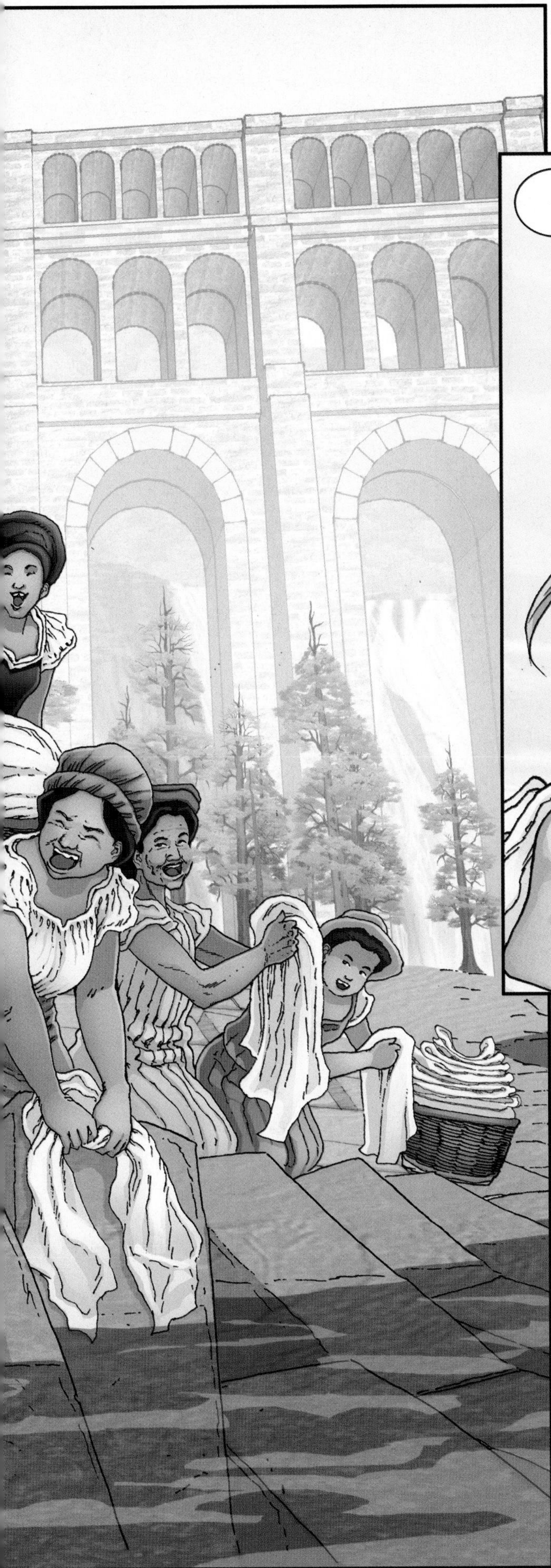

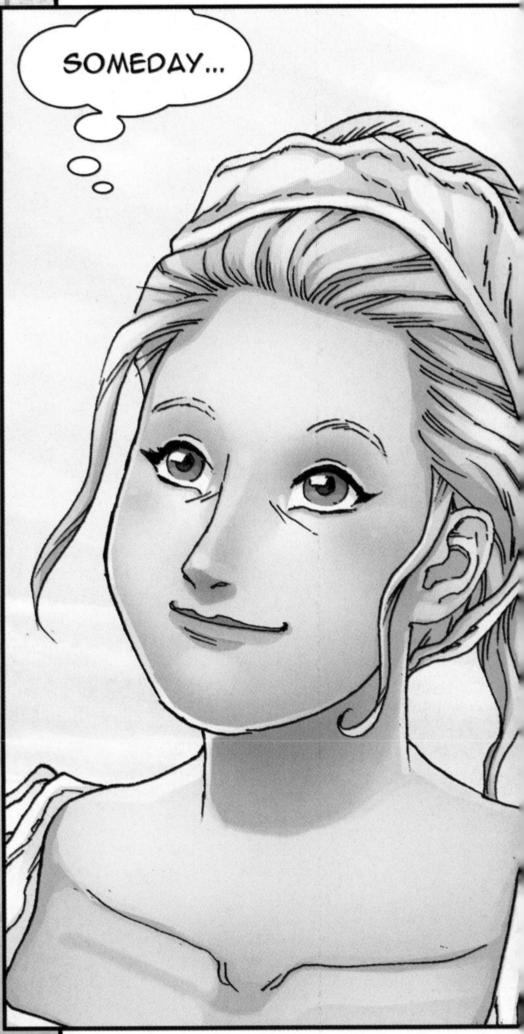
SOMEDAY...

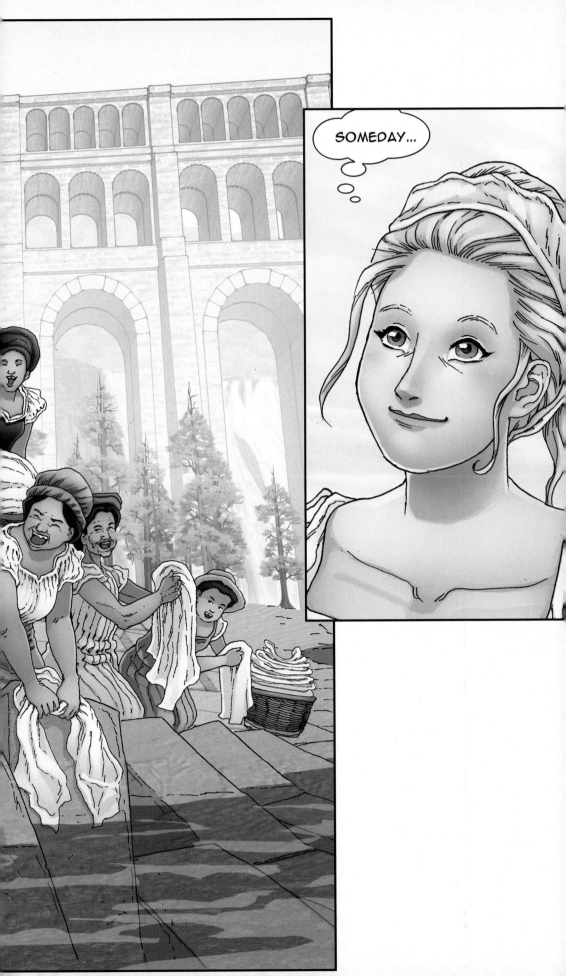

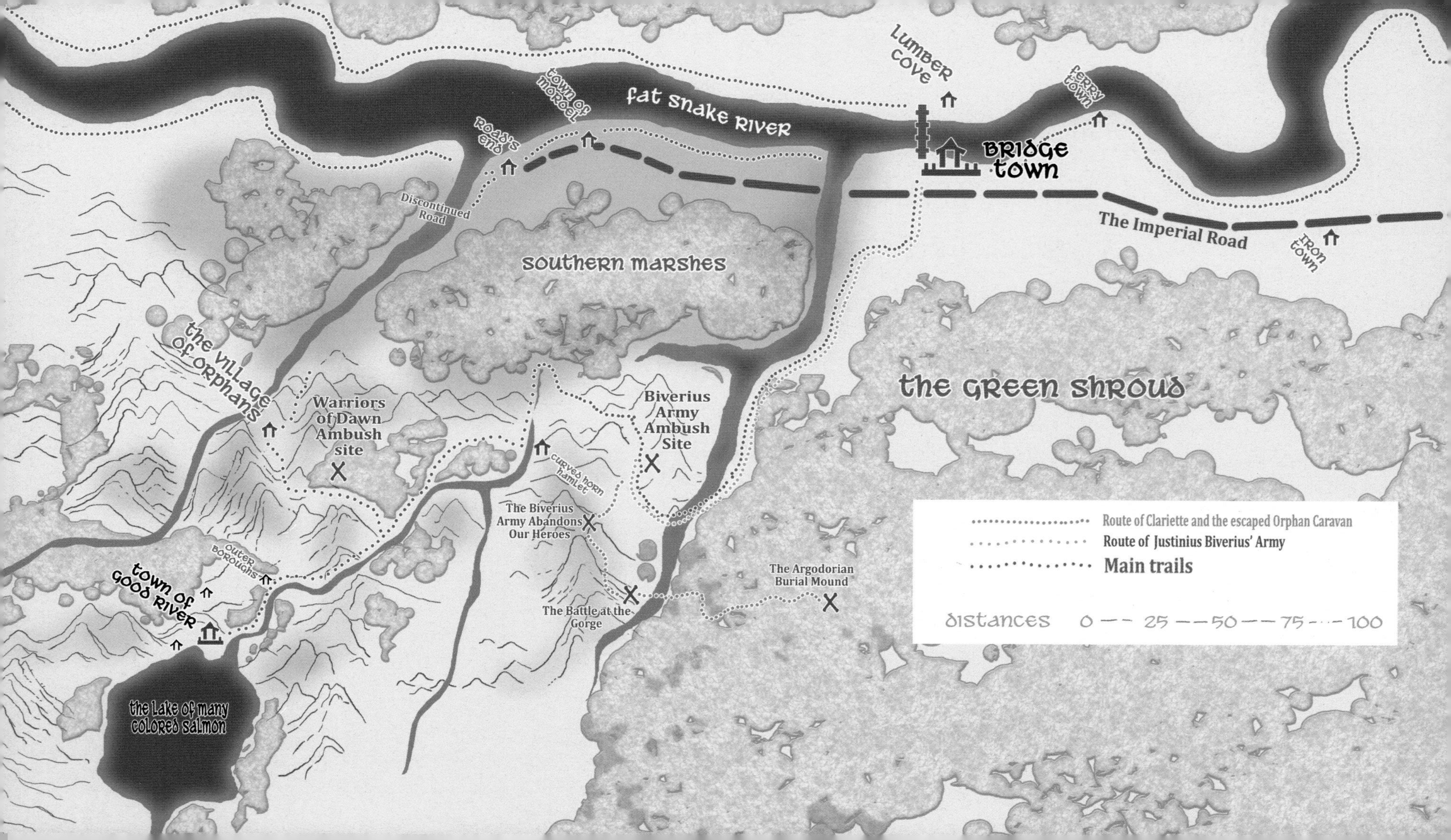
fat snake river
Lumber cove
town of moroel
Road's end
Discontinued Road
Bridge town
ferry town
The Imperial Road
Iron town
southern marshes
the village of orphans
Warriors of Dawn Ambush site
Biverius Army Ambush Site
the green shroud
curved horn hamlet
The Biverius Army Abandons Our Heroes
outer boroughs
town of good river
The Battle at the Gorge
The Argodorian Burial Mound
the Lake of many colored salmon
Route of Clariette and the escaped Orphan Caravan
Route of Justinius Biverius' Army
Main trails
distances 0 25 50 75 100

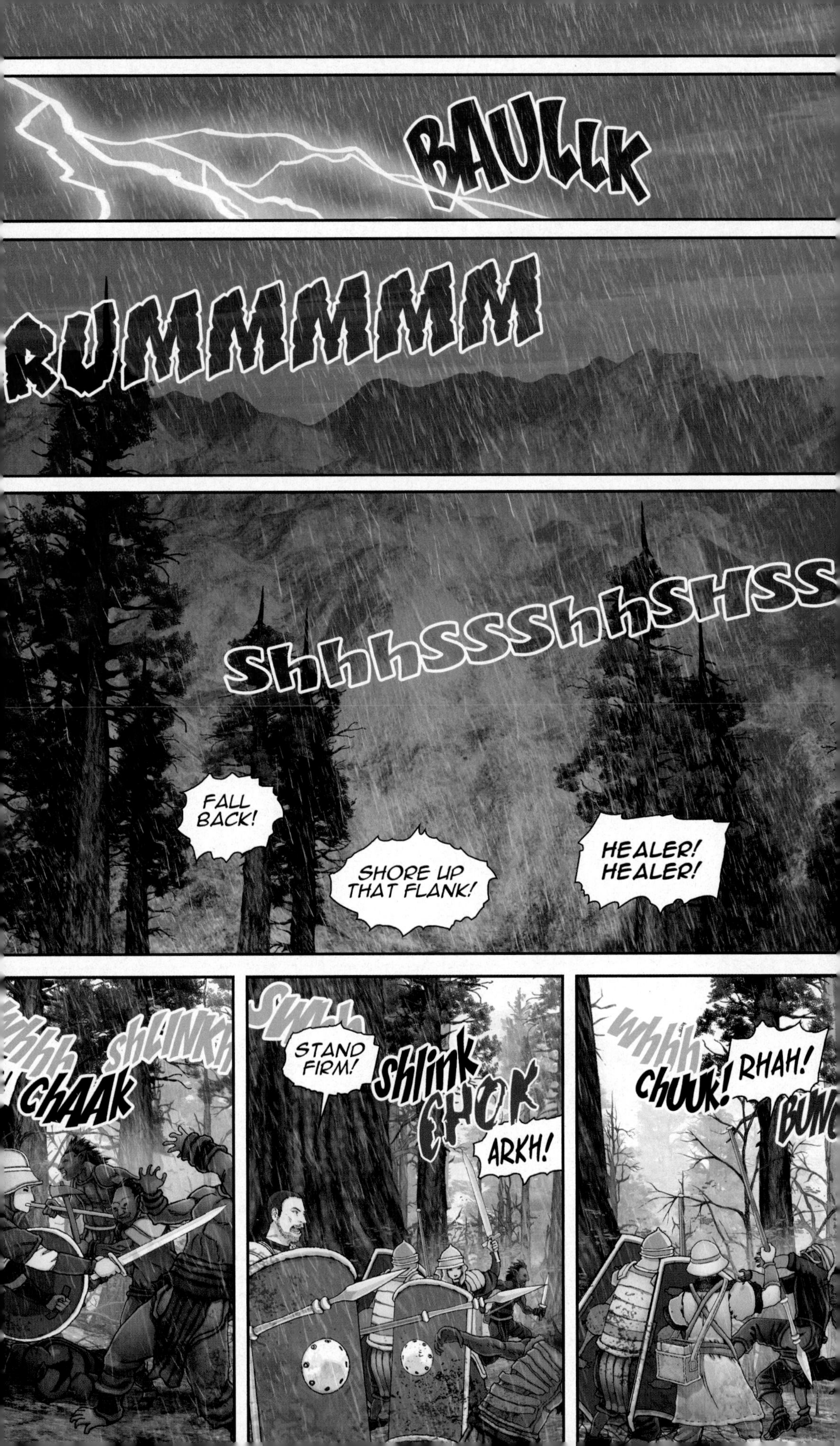
BAULLK
RUMMMMMM
ShhhSSShhSHSS
FALL BACK!
SHORE UP THAT FLANK!
HEALER! HEALER!
CHAAK
STAND FIRM!
shlink
CHOK
ARKH!
whhh
CHUUK!
RHAH!

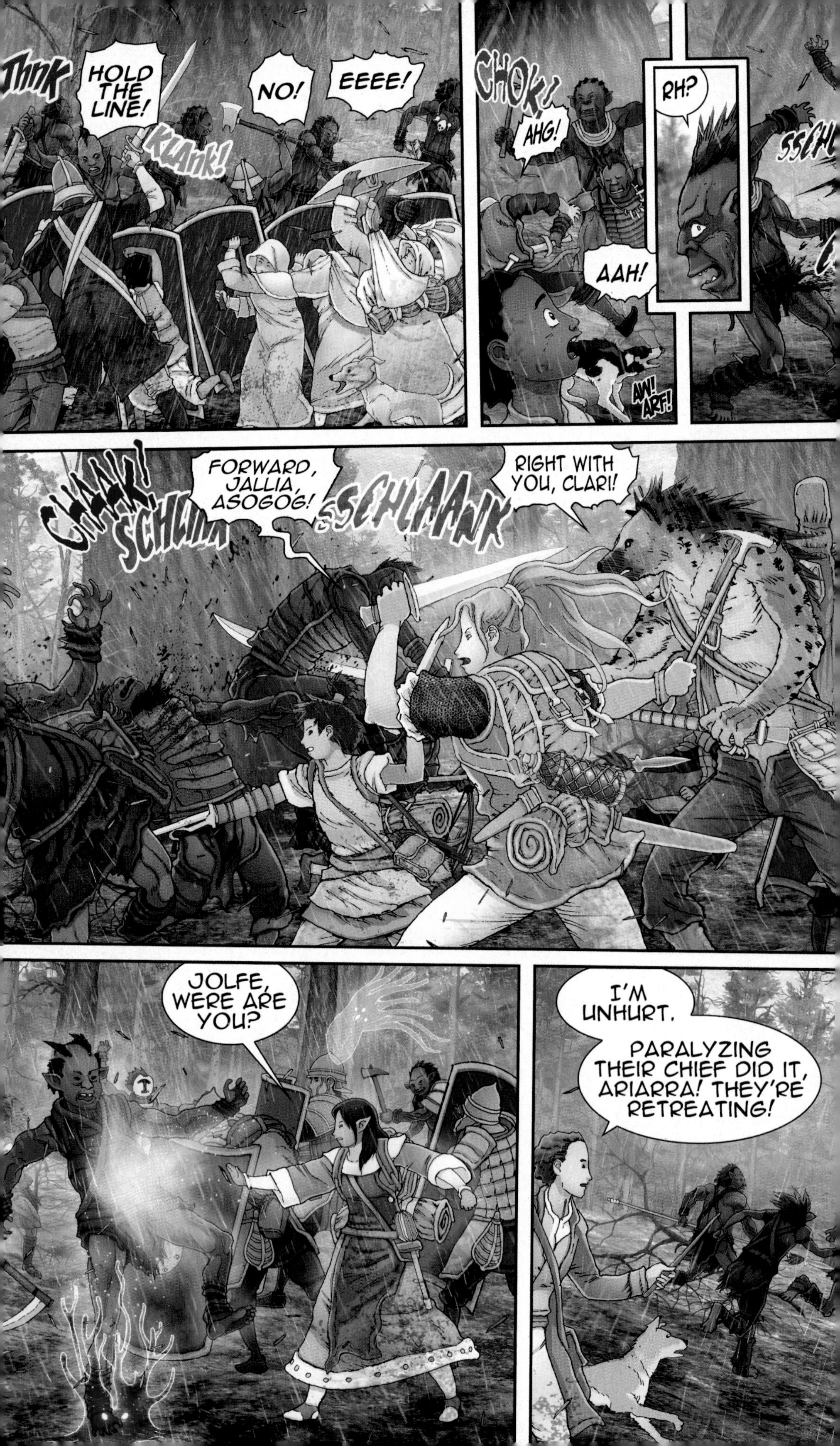
THNK
HOLD THE LINE!
KLANK!
NO!
EEEE!
CHOK!
AHG!
AAH!
AW! ARF!
RH?
SSCHL
CHAAK!
SCHLUNN
FORWARD, JALLIA, ASOGOG!
SSCHLAAANK
RIGHT WITH YOU, CLARI!
JOLFE, WERE ARE YOU?
I'M UNHURT.
PARALYZING THEIR CHIEF DID IT, ARIARRA! THEY'RE RETREATING!

Chapter 3: The Tireless Pursuit

- No Rest for the Harried

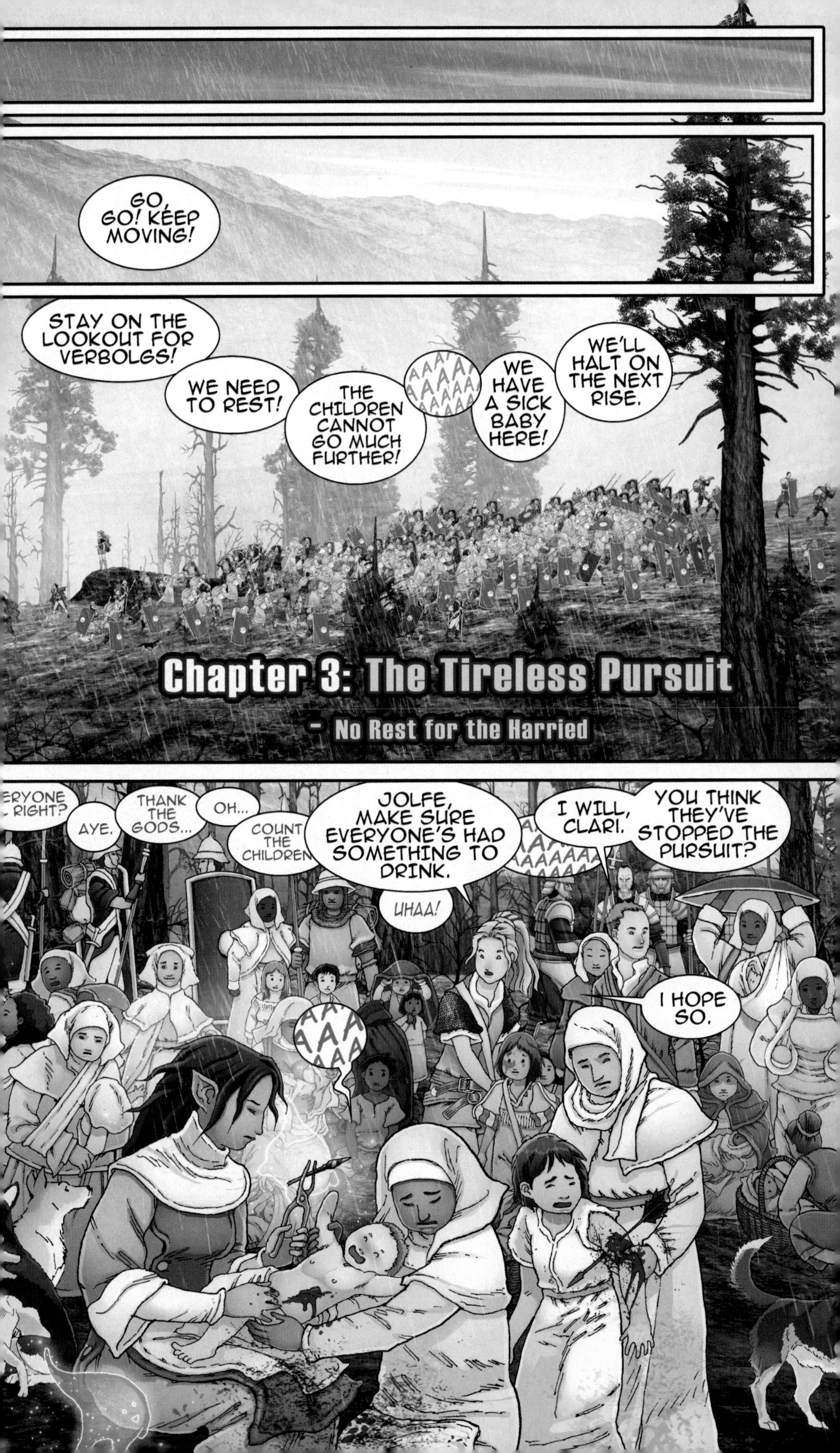
GO, GO! KEEP MOVING!
STAY ON THE LOOKOUT FOR VERBOLGS!
WE NEED TO REST!
THE CHILDREN CANNOT GO MUCH FURTHER!
WE HAVE A SICK BABY HERE!
WE'LL HALT ON THE NEXT RISE.
ERYONE RIGHT?
AYE.
THANK THE GODS...
OH...
COUNT THE CHILDREN
JOLFE, MAKE SURE EVERYONE'S HAD SOMETHING TO DRINK.
UHAA!
I WILL, CLARI.
YOU THINK THEY'VE STOPPED THE PURSUIT?
I HOPE SO.

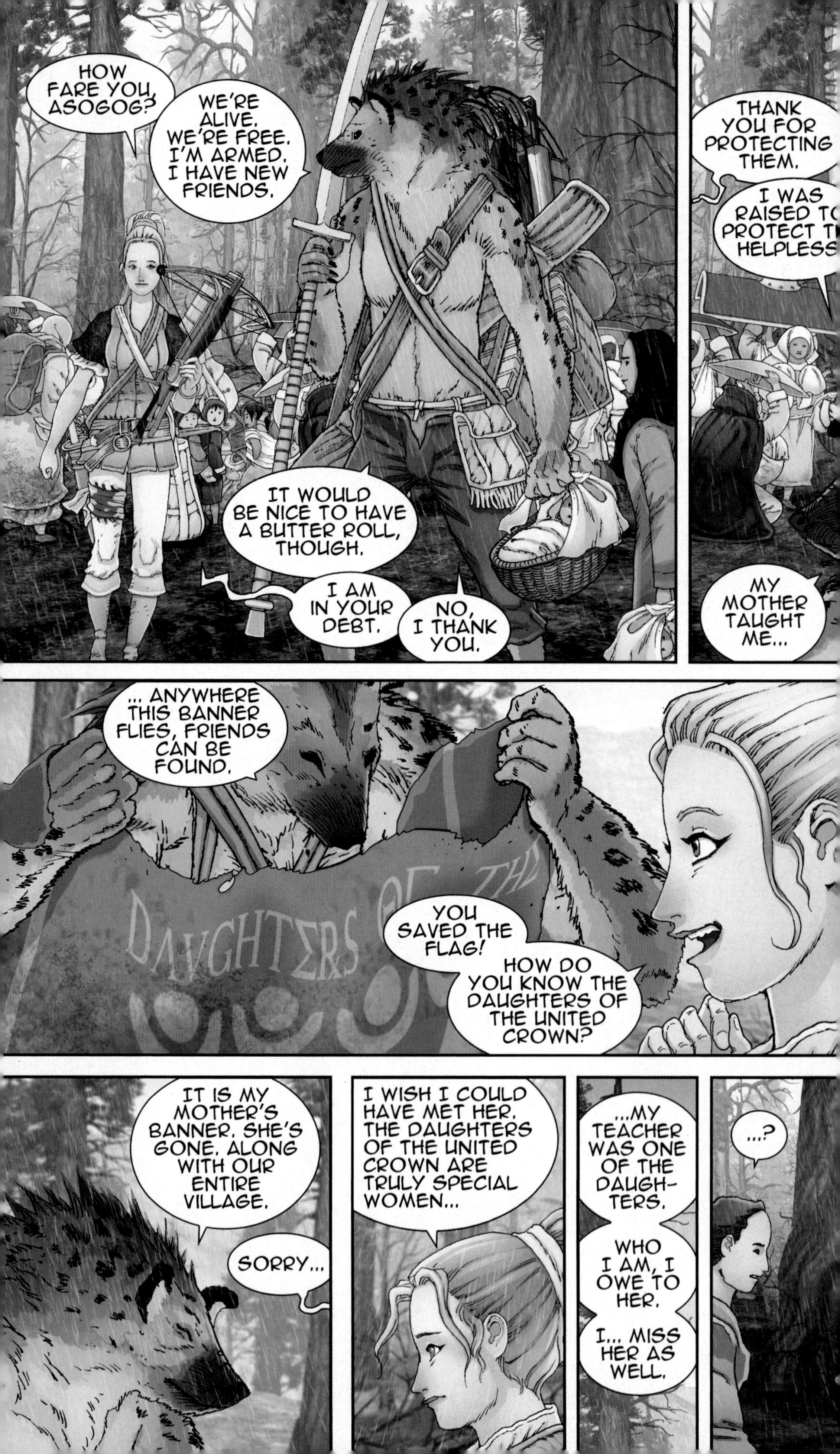
HOW FARE YOU, ASOGOG?
WE'RE ALIVE. WE'RE FREE. I'M ARMED. I HAVE NEW FRIENDS.
IT WOULD BE NICE TO HAVE A BUTTER ROLL, THOUGH.
I AM IN YOUR DEBT.
NO, I THANK YOU.
THANK YOU FOR PROTECTING THEM.
I WAS RAISED TO PROTECT THE HELPLESS.
MY MOTHER TAUGHT ME...
... ANYWHERE THIS BANNER FLIES, FRIENDS CAN BE FOUND.
DAUGHTERS OF THE
YOU SAVED THE FLAG!
HOW DO YOU KNOW THE DAUGHTERS OF THE UNITED CROWN?
IT IS MY MOTHER'S BANNER. SHE'S GONE. ALONG WITH OUR ENTIRE VILLAGE.
SORRY...
I WISH I COULD HAVE MET HER. THE DAUGHTERS OF THE UNITED CROWN ARE TRULY SPECIAL WOMEN...
...MY TEACHER WAS ONE OF THE DAUGH-TERS.
WHO I AM, I OWE TO HER.
I... MISS HER AS WELL.
...?

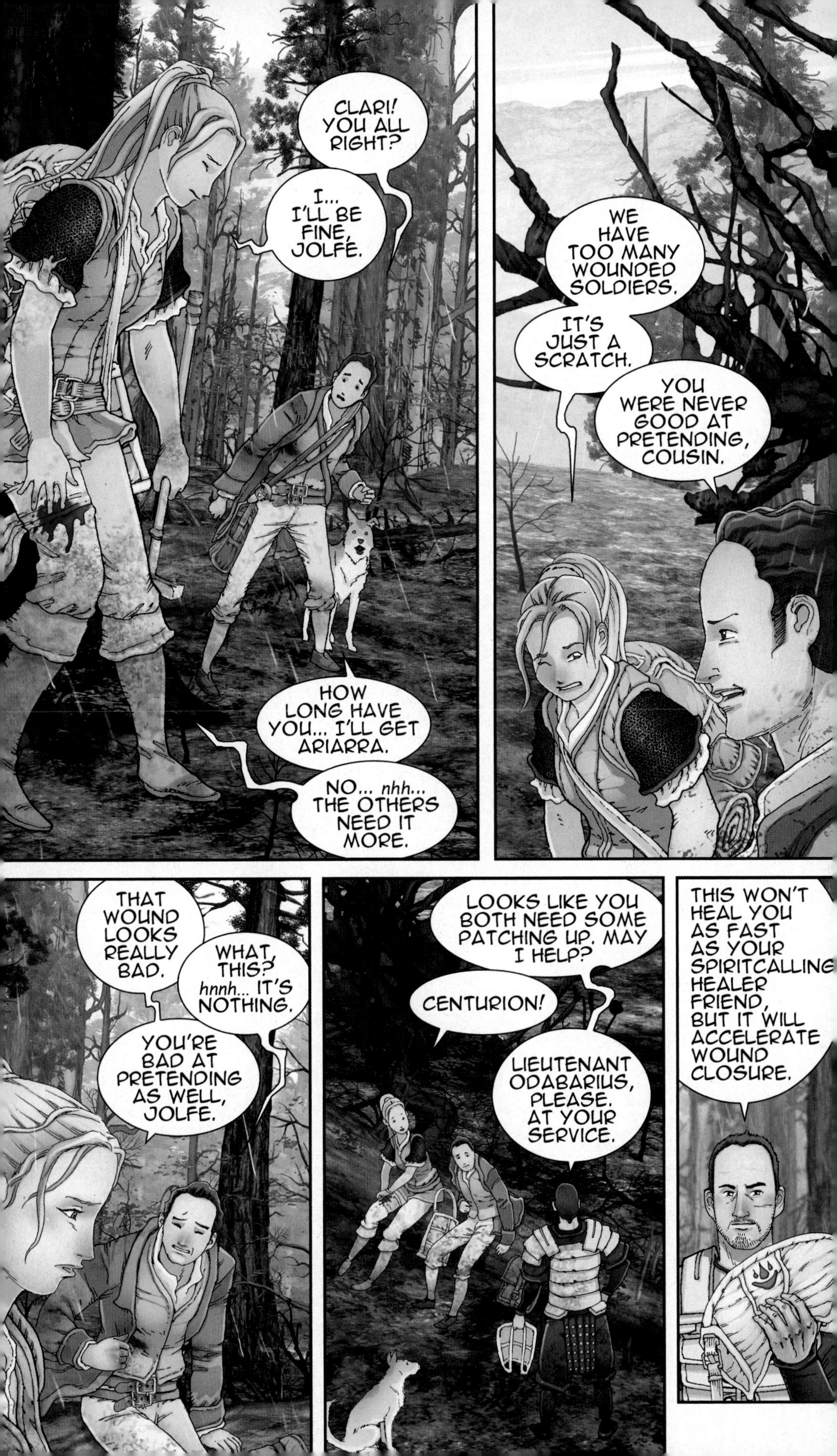
CLARI! YOU ALL RIGHT?
I... I'LL BE FINE, JOLFE.
HOW LONG HAVE YOU... I'LL GET ARIARRA.
NO... nhh... THE OTHERS NEED IT MORE.
WE HAVE TOO MANY WOUNDED SOLDIERS.
IT'S JUST A SCRATCH.
YOU WERE NEVER GOOD AT PRETENDING, COUSIN.
THAT WOUND LOOKS REALLY BAD.
WHAT, THIS? hnnh... IT'S NOTHING.
YOU'RE BAD AT PRETENDING AS WELL, JOLFE.
LOOKS LIKE YOU BOTH NEED SOME PATCHING UP. MAY I HELP?
CENTURION!
LIEUTENANT ODABARIUS, PLEASE. AT YOUR SERVICE.
THIS WON'T HEAL YOU AS FAST AS YOUR SPIRITCALLING HEALER FRIEND, BUT IT WILL ACCELERATE WOUND CLOSURE.

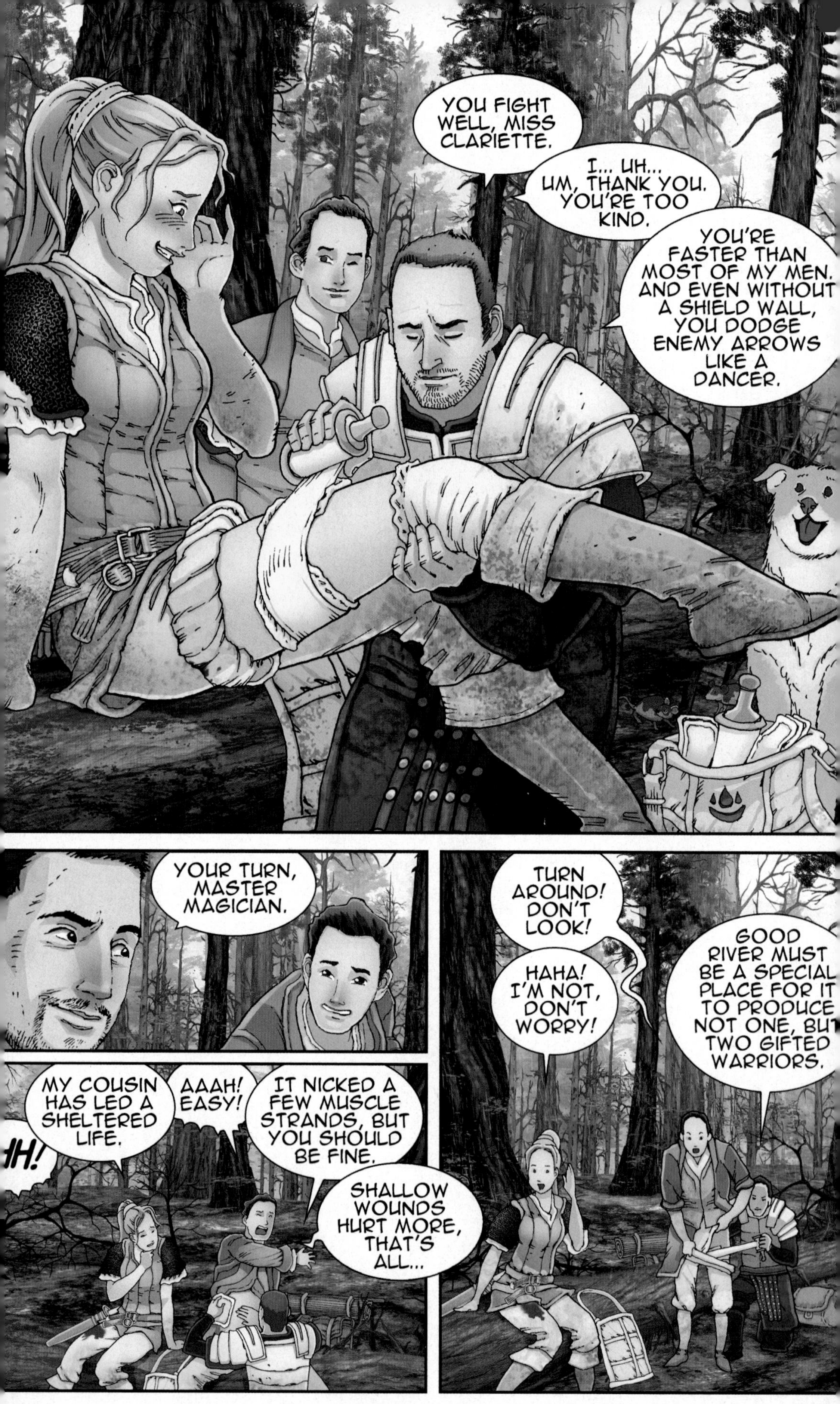
YOU FIGHT WELL, MISS CLARIETTE.
I... UH... UM, THANK YOU. YOU'RE TOO KIND.
YOU'RE FASTER THAN MOST OF MY MEN. AND EVEN WITHOUT A SHIELD WALL, YOU DODGE ENEMY ARROWS LIKE A DANCER.
YOUR TURN, MASTER MAGICIAN.
MY COUSIN HAS LED A SHELTERED LIFE.
AAAH! EASY!
IT NICKED A FEW MUSCLE STRANDS, BUT YOU SHOULD BE FINE.
SHALLOW WOUNDS HURT MORE, THAT'S ALL...
TURN AROUND! DON'T LOOK!
HAHA! I'M NOT, DON'T WORRY!
GOOD RIVER MUST BE A SPECIAL PLACE FOR IT TO PRODUCE NOT ONE, BUT TWO GIFTED WARRIORS.

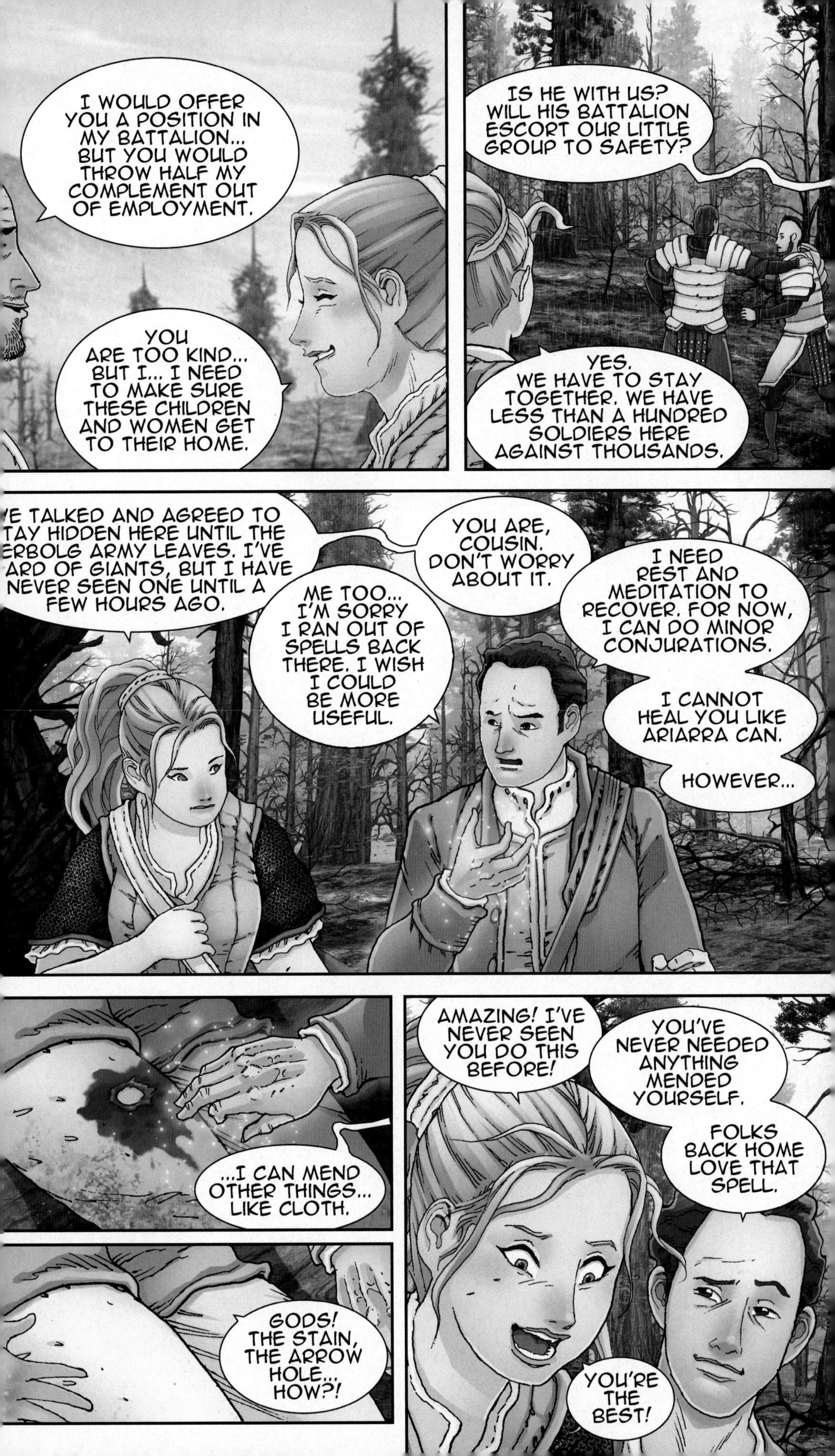
I WOULD OFFER YOU A POSITION IN MY BATTALION... BUT YOU WOULD THROW HALF MY COMPLEMENT OUT OF EMPLOYMENT.
YOU ARE TOO KIND... BUT I... I NEED TO MAKE SURE THESE CHILDREN AND WOMEN GET TO THEIR HOME.
IS HE WITH US? WILL HIS BATTALION ESCORT OUR LITTLE GROUP TO SAFETY?
YES. WE HAVE TO STAY TOGETHER. WE HAVE LESS THAN A HUNDRED SOLDIERS HERE AGAINST THOUSANDS.
'E TALKED AND AGREED TO TAY HIDDEN HERE UNTIL THE ERBOLG ARMY LEAVES. I'VE ARD OF GIANTS, BUT I HAVE NEVER SEEN ONE UNTIL A FEW HOURS AGO.
ME TOO... I'M SORRY I RAN OUT OF SPELLS BACK THERE. I WISH I COULD BE MORE USEFUL.
YOU ARE, COUSIN. DON'T WORRY ABOUT IT.
I NEED REST AND MEDITATION TO RECOVER. FOR NOW, I CAN DO MINOR CONJURATIONS.
I CANNOT HEAL YOU LIKE ARIARRA CAN.
HOWEVER...
...I CAN MEND OTHER THINGS... LIKE CLOTH.
GODS! THE STAIN, THE ARROW HOLE..., HOW?!
AMAZING! I'VE NEVER SEEN YOU DO THIS BEFORE!
YOU'VE NEVER NEEDED ANYTHING MENDED YOURSELF.
FOLKS BACK HOME LOVE THAT SPELL.
YOU'RE THE BEST!

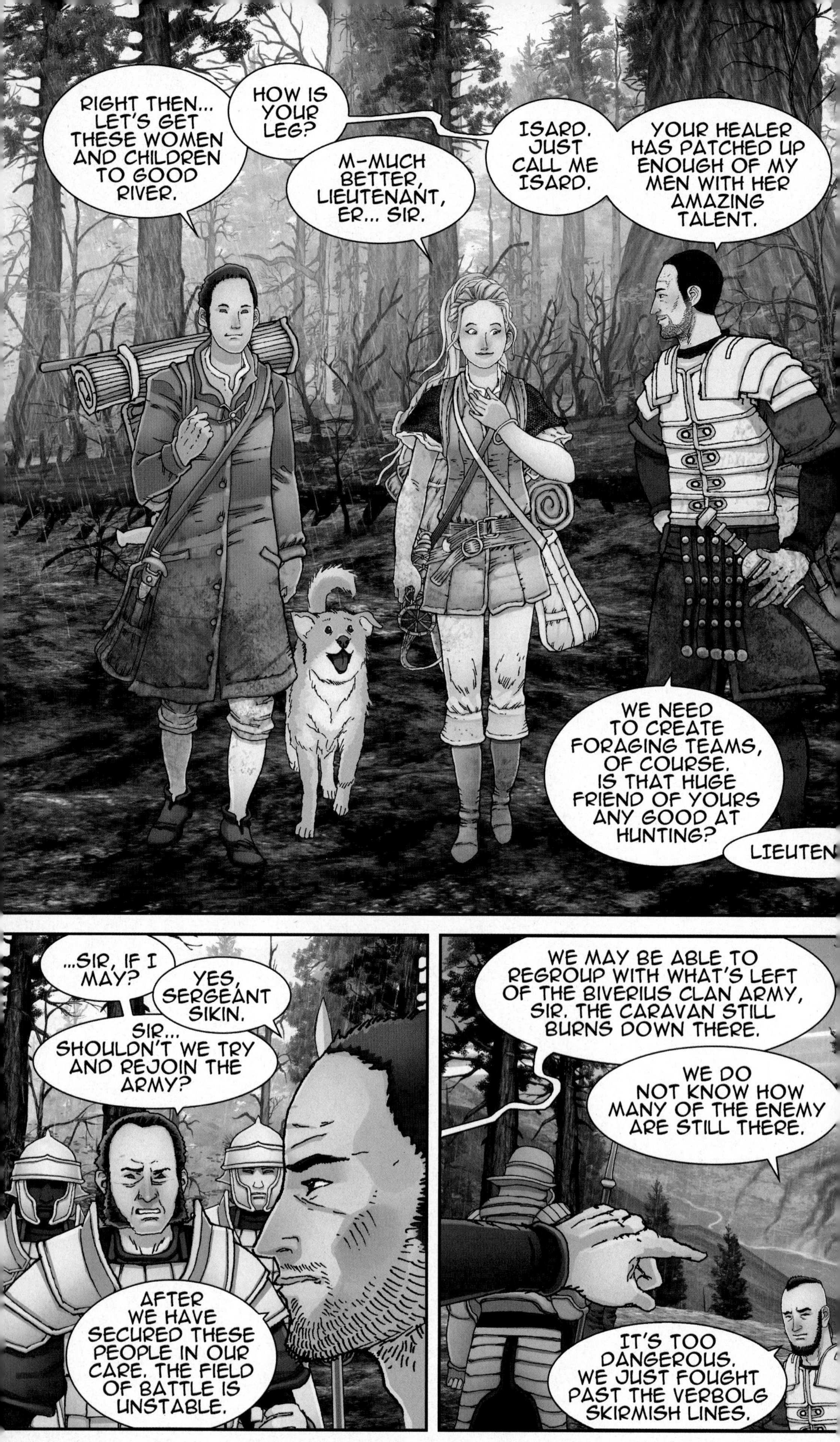
RIGHT THEN... LET'S GET THESE WOMEN AND CHILDREN TO GOOD RIVER.
HOW IS YOUR LEG?
M-MUCH BETTER, LIEUTENANT, ER... SIR.
ISARD. JUST CALL ME ISARD.
YOUR HEALER HAS PATCHED UP ENOUGH OF MY MEN WITH HER AMAZING TALENT.
WE NEED TO CREATE FORAGING TEAMS, OF COURSE. IS THAT HUGE FRIEND OF YOURS ANY GOOD AT HUNTING?
LIEUTEN
...SIR, IF I MAY?
YES, SERGEANT SIKIN.
SIR... SHOULDN'T WE TRY AND REJOIN THE ARMY?
AFTER WE HAVE SECURED THESE PEOPLE IN OUR CARE. THE FIELD OF BATTLE IS UNSTABLE.
WE MAY BE ABLE TO REGROUP WITH WHAT'S LEFT OF THE BIVERIUS CLAN ARMY, SIR. THE CARAVAN STILL BURNS DOWN THERE.
WE DO NOT KNOW HOW MANY OF THE ENEMY ARE STILL THERE.
IT'S TOO DANGEROUS. WE JUST FOUGHT PAST THE VERBOLG SKIRMISH LINES.

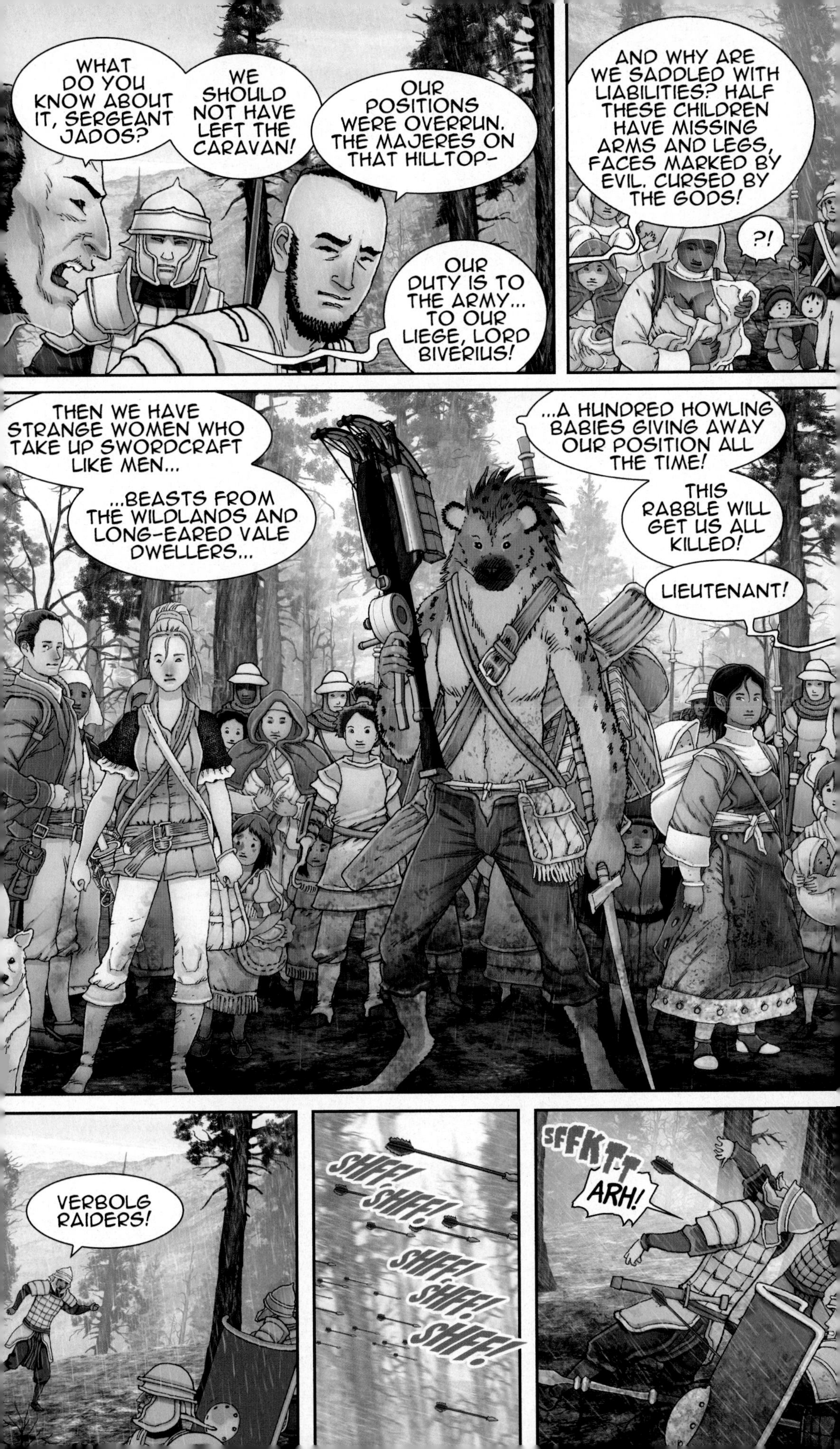
WHAT DO YOU KNOW ABOUT IT, SERGEANT JADOS?
WE SHOULD NOT HAVE LEFT THE CARAVAN!
OUR POSITIONS WERE OVERRUN. THE MAJERES ON THAT HILLTOP-
OUR DUTY IS TO THE ARMY... TO OUR LIEGE, LORD BIVERIUS!
AND WHY ARE WE SADDLED WITH LIABILITIES? HALF THESE CHILDREN HAVE MISSING ARMS AND LEGS, FACES MARKED BY EVIL. CURSED BY THE GODS!
?!
THEN WE HAVE STRANGE WOMEN WHO TAKE UP SWORDCRAFT LIKE MEN...
...BEASTS FROM THE WILDLANDS AND LONG-EARED VALE DWELLERS...
...A HUNDRED HOWLING BABIES GIVING AWAY OUR POSITION ALL THE TIME!
THIS RABBLE WILL GET US ALL KILLED!
LIEUTENANT!
VERBOLG RAIDERS!
SHFF! SHFF!
SHFF! SHFF! SHFF!
SFFKT-T
ARH!

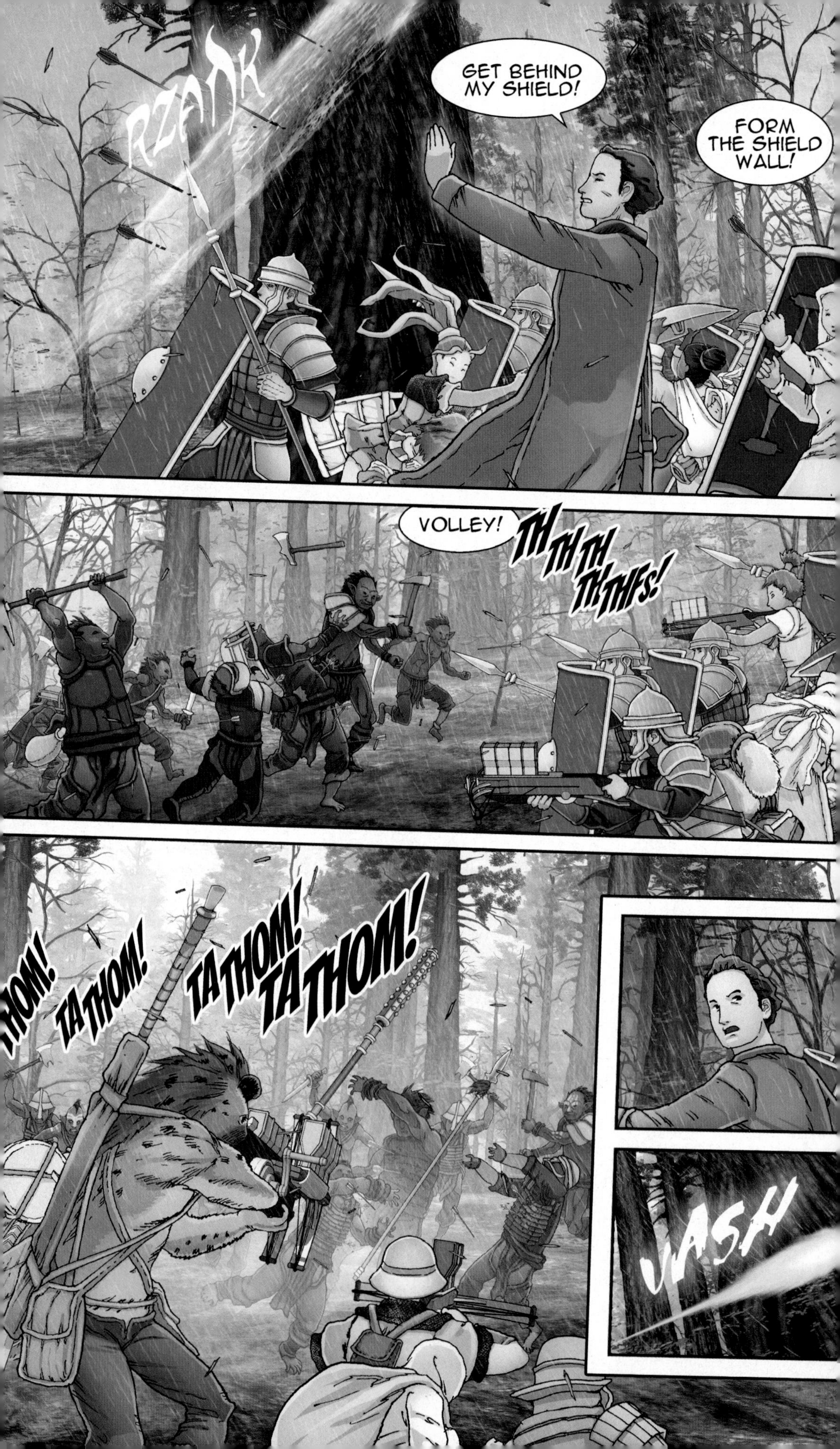
RZAAK
GET BEHIND MY SHIELD!
FORM THE SHIELD WALL!
VOLLEY!
TH TH TH TH THFS!
THOM!
TA THOM!
TA THOM!
TA THOM!
VASH

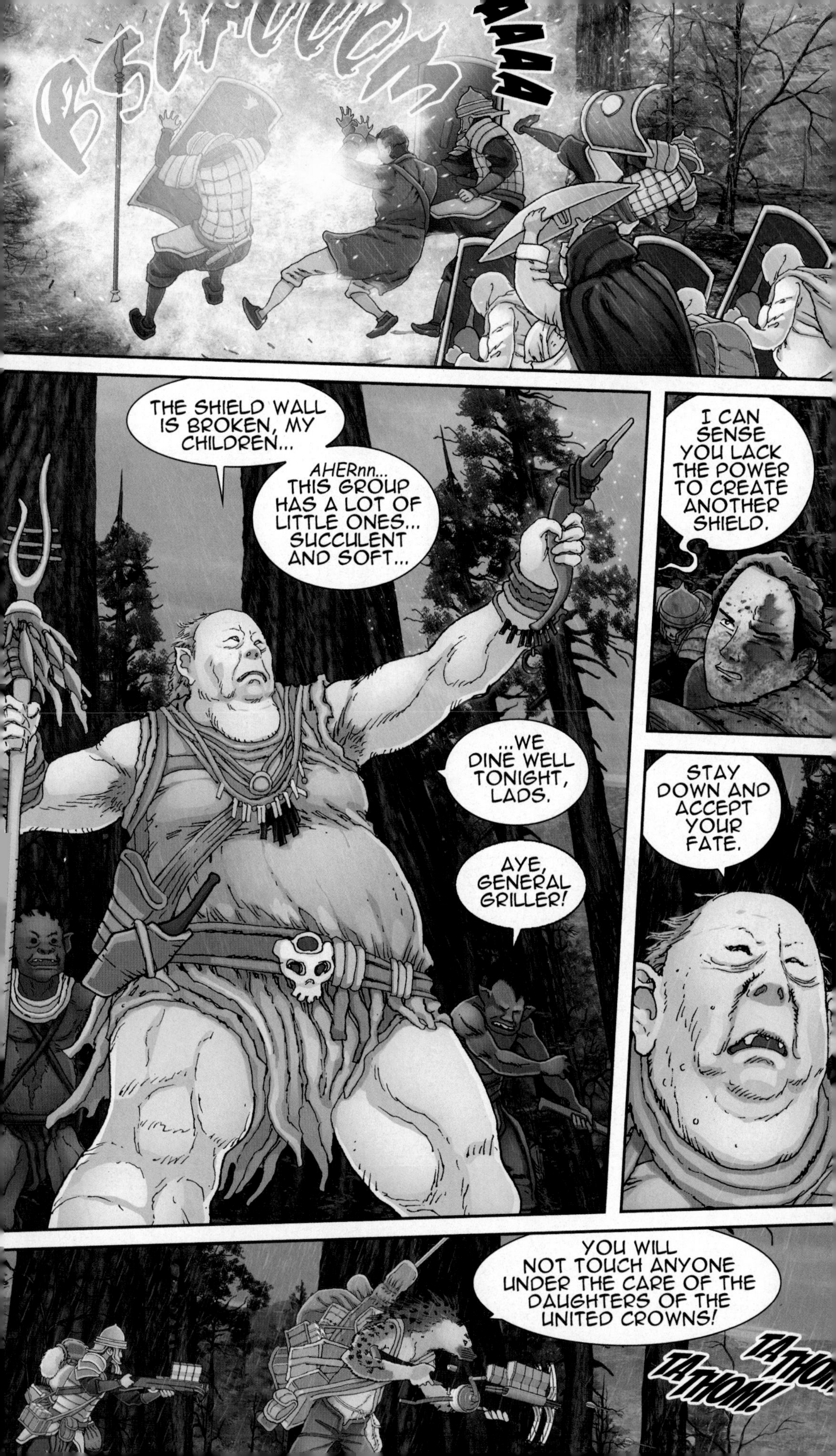
AAAA
THE SHIELD WALL IS BROKEN, MY CHILDREN...
AHERnn... THIS GROUP HAS A LOT OF LITTLE ONES... SUCCULENT AND SOFT...
I CAN SENSE YOU LACK THE POWER TO CREATE ANOTHER SHIELD.
...WE DINE WELL TONIGHT, LADS.
AYE, GENERAL GRILLER!
STAY DOWN AND ACCEPT YOUR FATE.
YOU WILL NOT TOUCH ANYONE UNDER THE CARE OF THE DAUGHTERS OF THE UNITED CROWNS!
TA THOM!

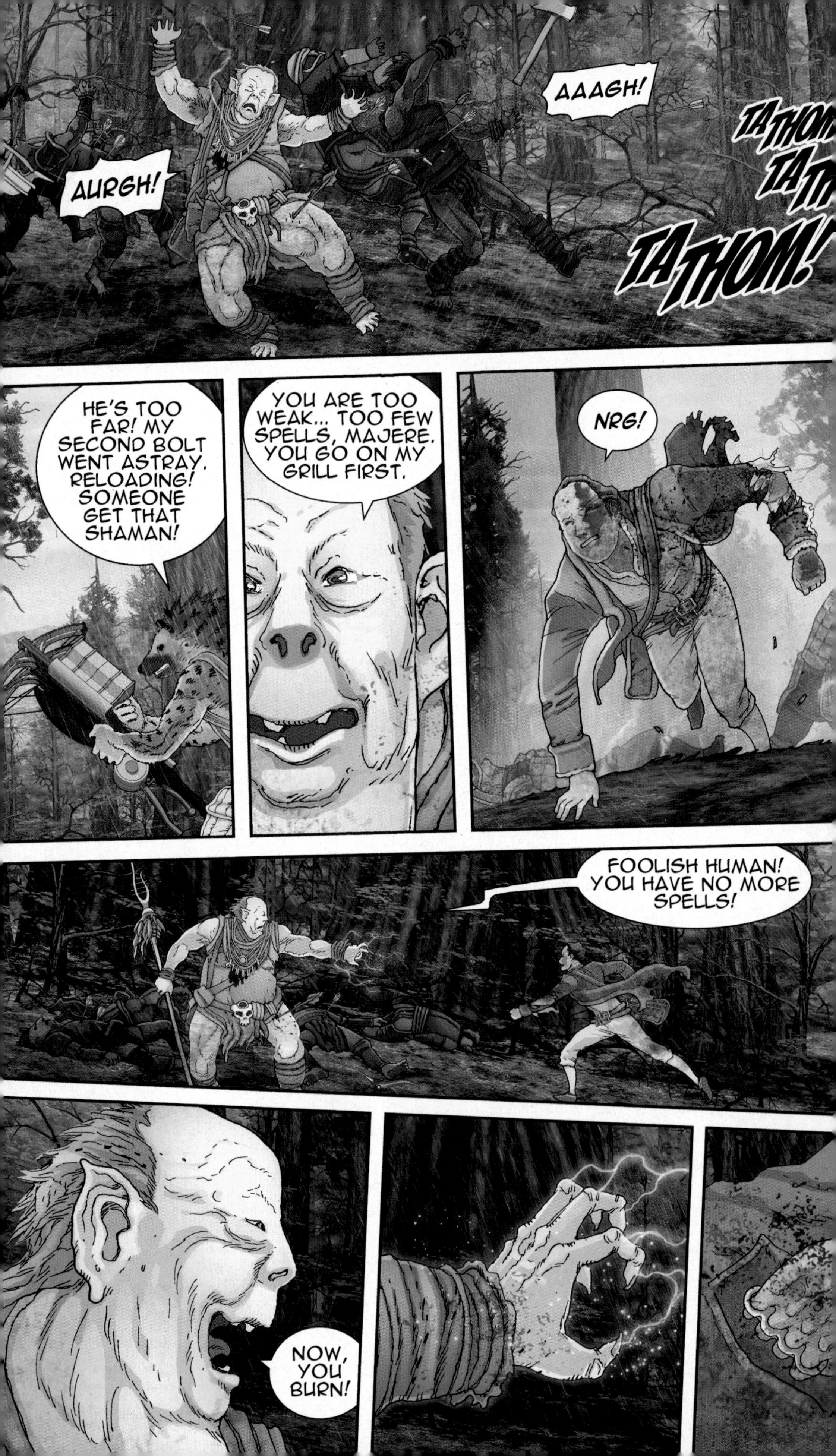
AURGH!
AAAGH!
TA THOM
TA TH
TA THOM!
HE'S TOO FAR! MY SECOND BOLT WENT ASTRAY. RELOADING! SOMEONE GET THAT SHAMAN!
YOU ARE TOO WEAK... TOO FEW SPELLS, MAJERE. YOU GO ON MY GRILL FIRST.
NRG!
FOOLISH HUMAN! YOU HAVE NO MORE SPELLS!
NOW, YOU BURN!

AAAAHHK!

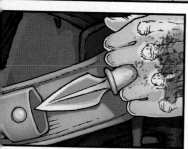

HDHK!

WHGK

RHAAA!

CHUK!

ARKH!

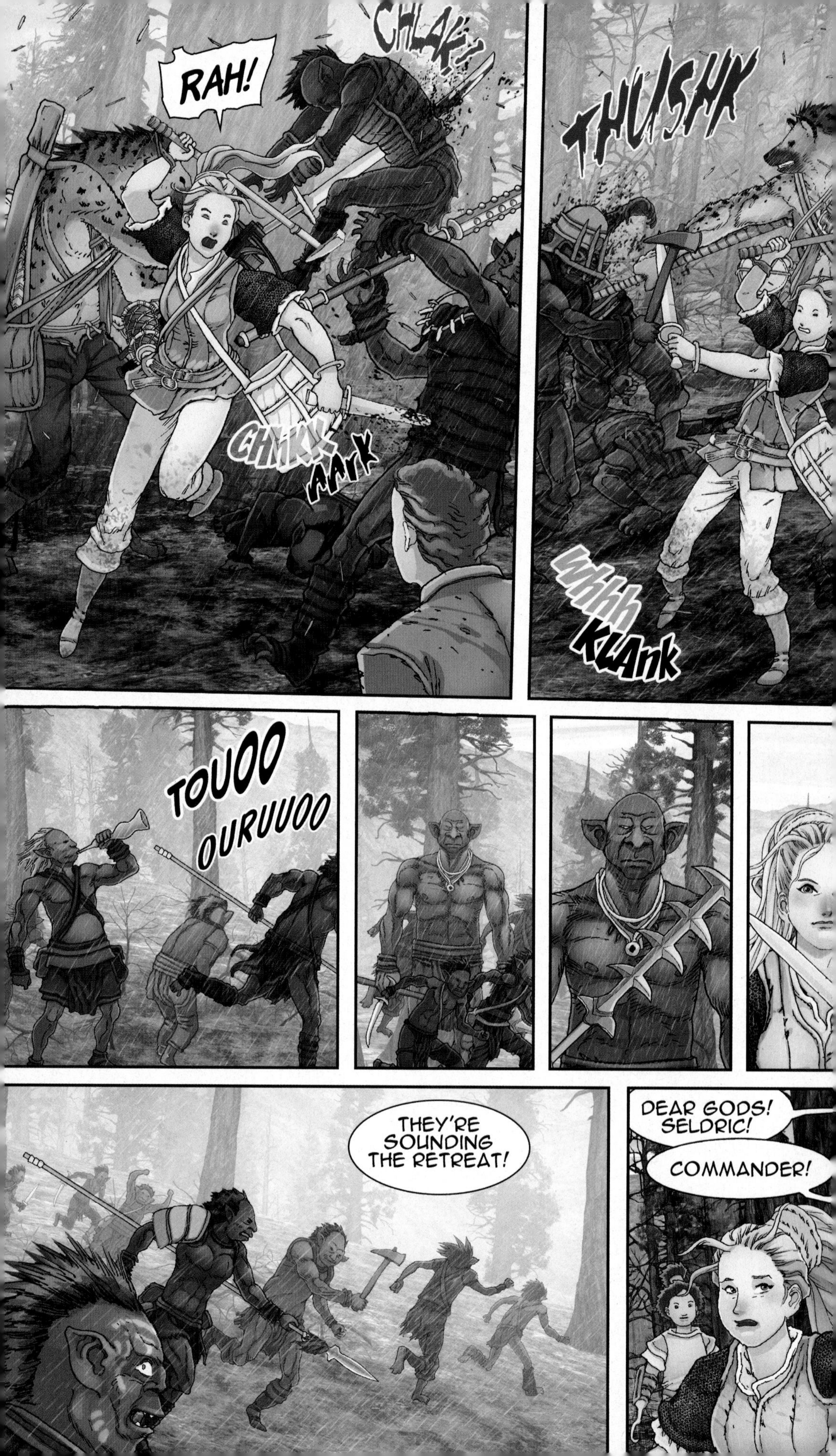
RAH!
CHLAK!!
CHiKK
AArK
THUSHK
WHHH
KLAnk
TOUOO
OURUUOO
THEY'RE SOUNDING THE RETREAT!
DEAR GODS! SELDRIC!
COMMANDER!

THIS IS MY LAST HEALING KEEP. I NEED TO REST.

AHgghguh!

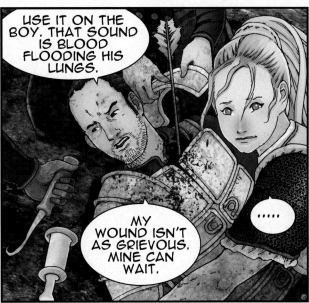

USE IT ON THE BOY. THAT SOUND IS BLOOD FLOODING HIS LUNGS.

MY WOUND ISN'T AS GRIEVOUS. MINE CAN WAIT.

.....

OH, GOD, HE'S GOING TO DIE!

OH NO!

AAAA AAAAA AAAAA AAAA

PLEASE, NO!

.....

GODDESS OF THE HEALING SPIRITS... HEAL THIS CHILD.

LOOK! HE'S BREATHING AGAIN!

THE BLEEDING STOPPED!

THE WOUND... IT'S GONE!

IT'S A MIRACLE! THANK T GODS

WAIT!

WHERE IS THIS BLOOD COMING FROM?

CLOSE IT! CLOSE IT!

HE'S FADING!

NO NO!

MEN... PROTECT THESE PEOPLE... GET THEM TO SAFETY.

MISS... CLARIETTE DE ARTEGNEAN... THE DAUGHTERS OF THE UNITED CROWN HAVE ALWAYS LOOKED AFTER THE WOMEN AND CHILDREN OF THE REALM...

I HAVE... ONE LAST REQUEST OF YOU.

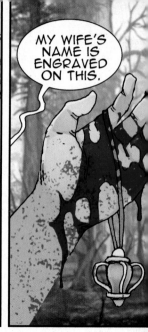

MY WIFE'S NAME IS ENGRAVED ON THIS.

PLEASE... BRING IT BACK TO HER.

TELL HER... I WILL AWAIT HER IN THE GARDENS OF GETHARNIS...

I'M IN COMMAND NOW MEN, PICK UP YOUR GEAR. W ARE REJOININ THE CARAVAN

NOTHING'S HANGED. WE WILL CARRY OUT THE LIEUTENANT'S LAST ORDERS.

OUR BEST CHANCE IS TO STAY TOGETHER!

QUIET, WOMAN! WHAT DO YOU KNOW?

YOU'RE WALKING INTO THOUSANDS OF VERBOLG, FIRE THROWERS AND GIANTS!

GO AWAY! LET ME DO MY JOB!

MAKE READY TO MARCH BACK!

ARREST ANY SOLDIER WHO RESISTS!

STOP THIS!

PUT DOWN THOSE SWOR—

NO!

NO, YOU PUT DO[WN] THAT S[WORD]

THE LIEUTENANT ORDERED—

HE'S DEAD!

YOU'RE STAYING BECAUSE YOU'VE FALLEN FOR ONE OF THOSE MILK MAIDS!

CO[ME] TO YOUR SENSES!

FOR THE LOVE OF GODDESS, STOP!

MEN, TAKE THE ARMS BACK. THEY ARE UNITED CROWN PROPERTY!

RARF! RARF!

ARF!

ARF! N'ARF!

[Y]OU CAN'T DO [TH]AT! WE'LL BE [D]EFENSELESS!

COME AND TAKE THEM, OR BE ON YOUR WAY.

THEY ARE OURS BY RULE OF SALVAGE. ARTICLES OF WAR, SECTION 119. YOU ARE NOT THE ONLY ONES WHO KNOW UNITED CROWN LAW.

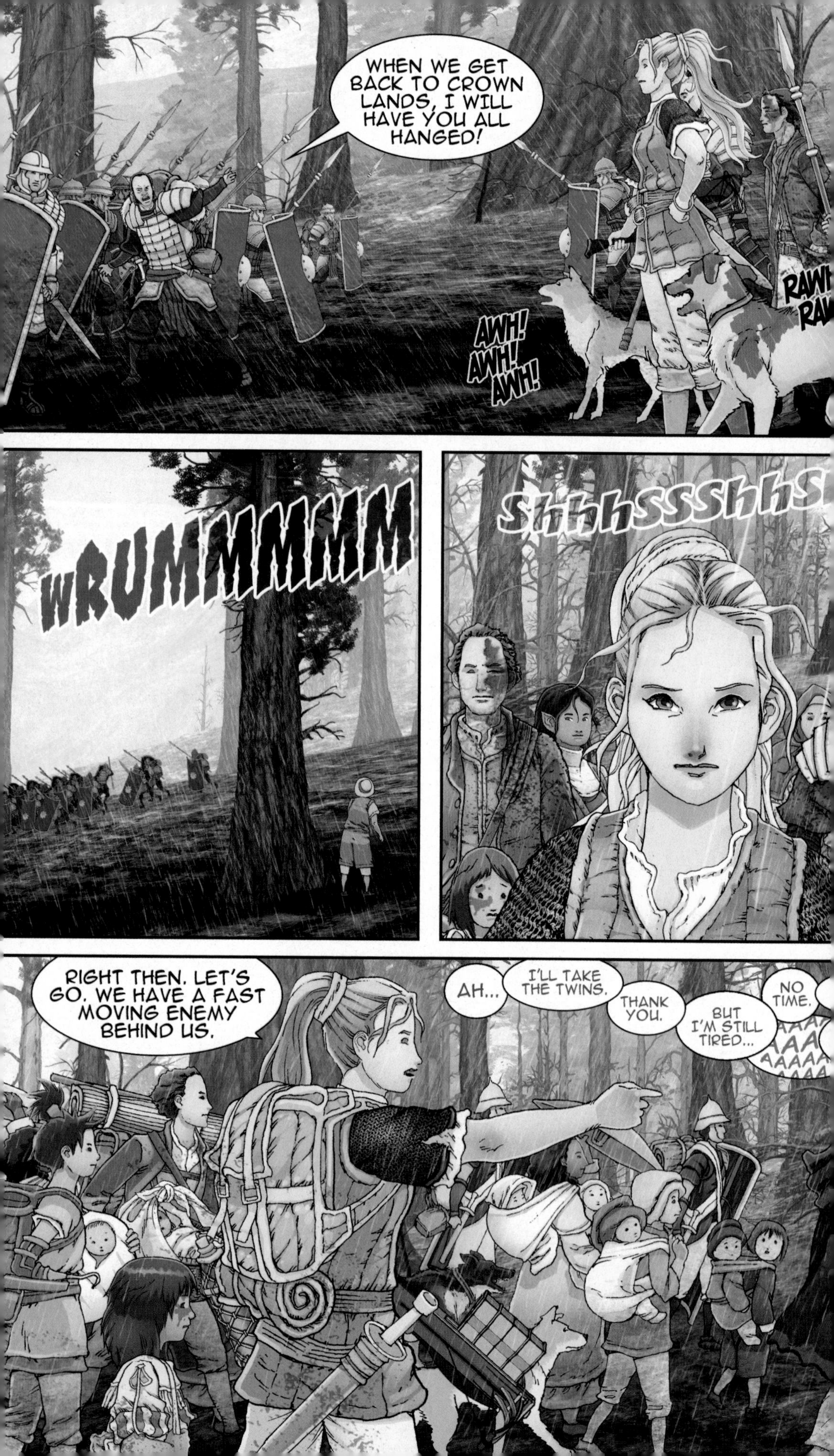
WHEN WE GET BACK TO CROWN LANDS, I WILL HAVE YOU ALL HANGED!
AWH! AWH! AWH!
wRUMMMMMM
RIGHT THEN. LET'S GO. WE HAVE A FAST MOVING ENEMY BEHIND US.
AH...
I'LL TAKE THE TWINS.
THANK YOU.
BUT I'M STILL TIRED...
NO TIME.

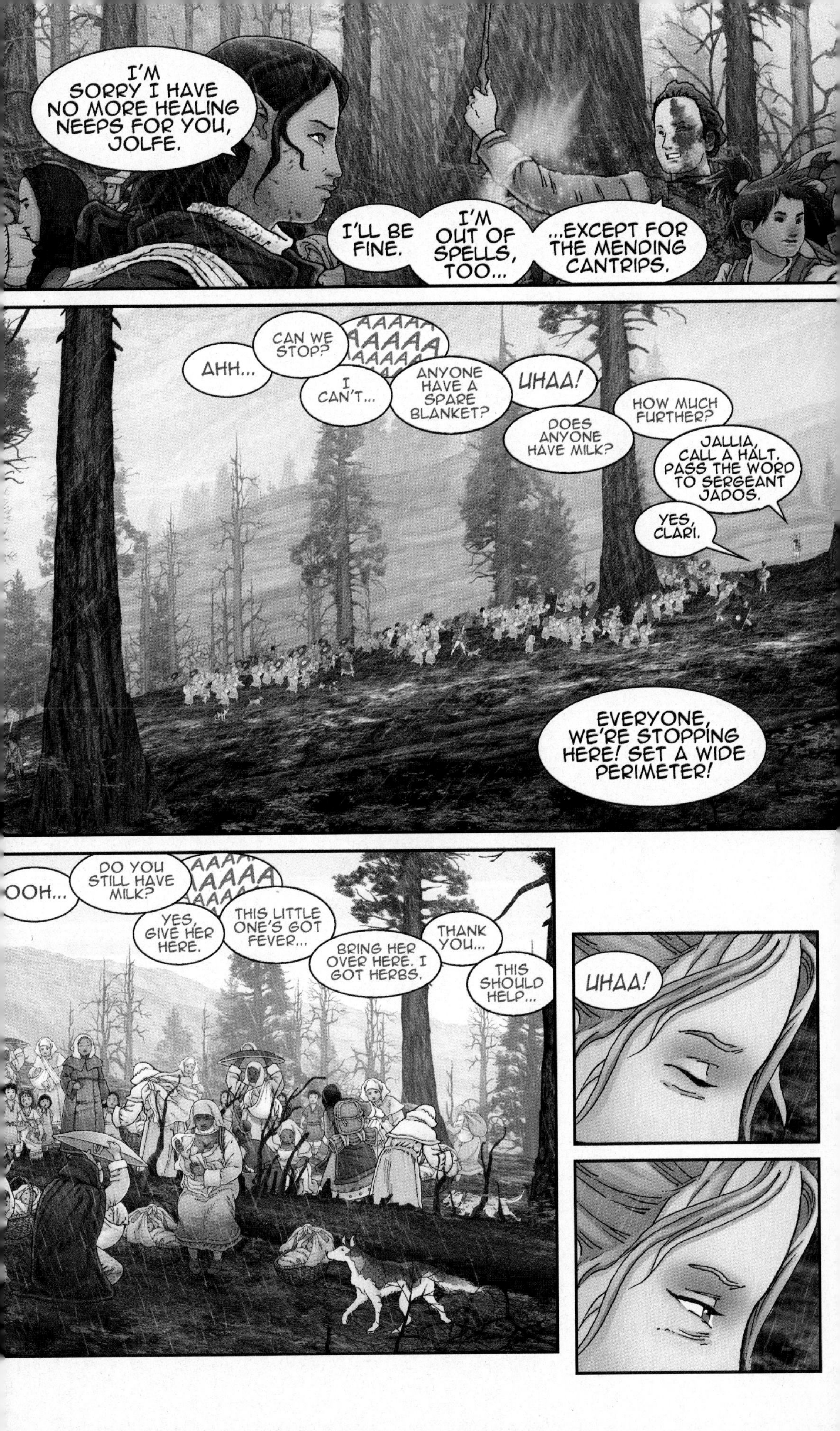
I'M SORRY I HAVE NO MORE HEALING NEEPS FOR YOU, JOLFE.
I'LL BE FINE.
I'M OUT OF SPELLS, TOO...
...EXCEPT FOR THE MENDING CANTRIPS.
AHH...
CAN WE STOP?
AAAAA AAAAA AAAAA
I CAN'T...
ANYONE HAVE A SPARE BLANKET?
UHAA!
DOES ANYONE HAVE MILK?
HOW MUCH FURTHER?
JALLIA, CALL A HALT. PASS THE WORD TO SERGEANT JADOS.
YES, CLARI.
EVERYONE, WE'RE STOPPING HERE! SET A WIDE PERIMETER!
OOH...
DO YOU STILL HAVE MILK?
AAAA AAAAA AAAA
YES, GIVE HER HERE.
THIS LITTLE ONE'S GOT FEVER...
BRING HER OVER HERE. I GOT HERBS.
THANK YOU...
THIS SHOULD HELP...
UHAA!

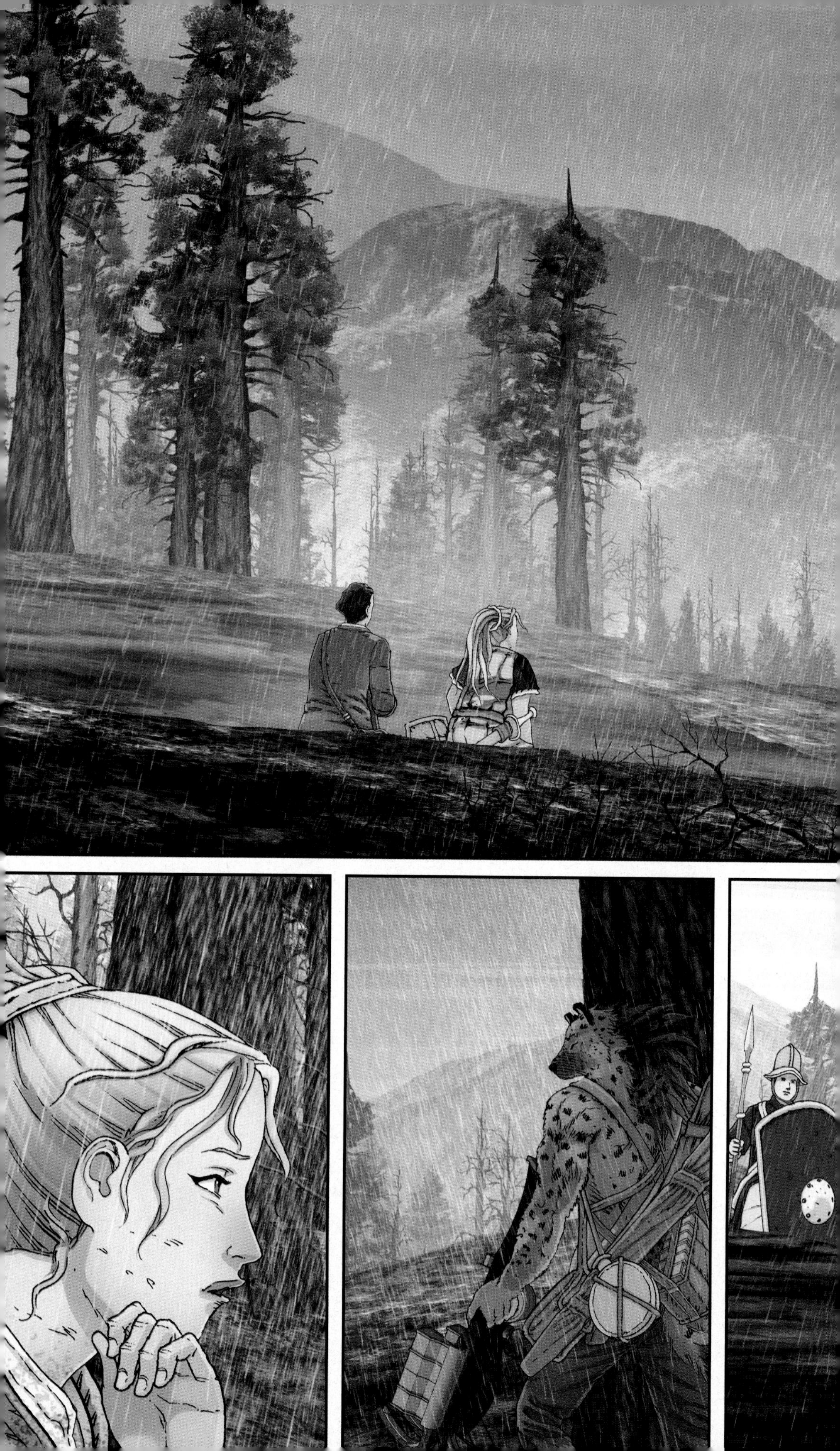

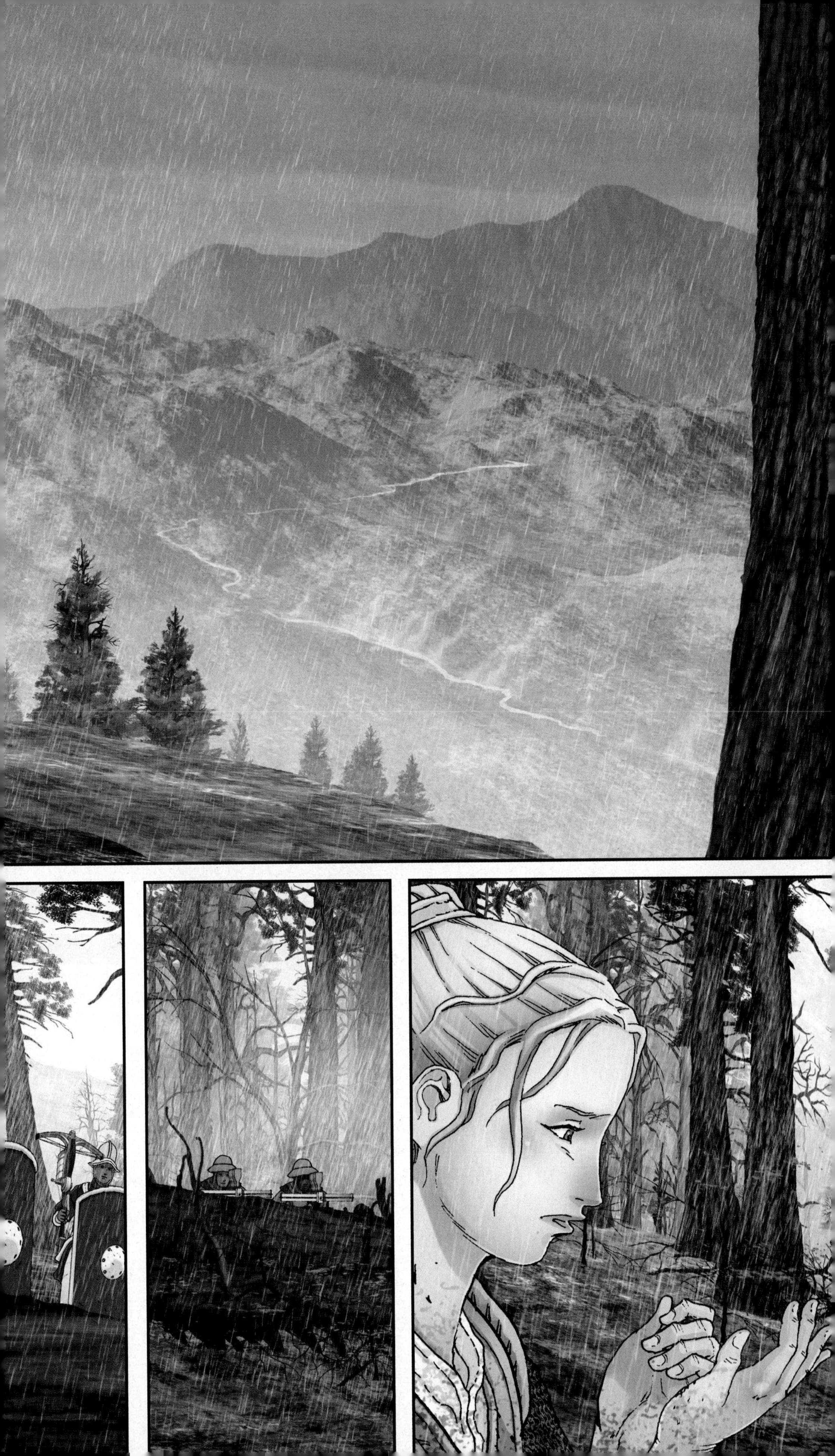

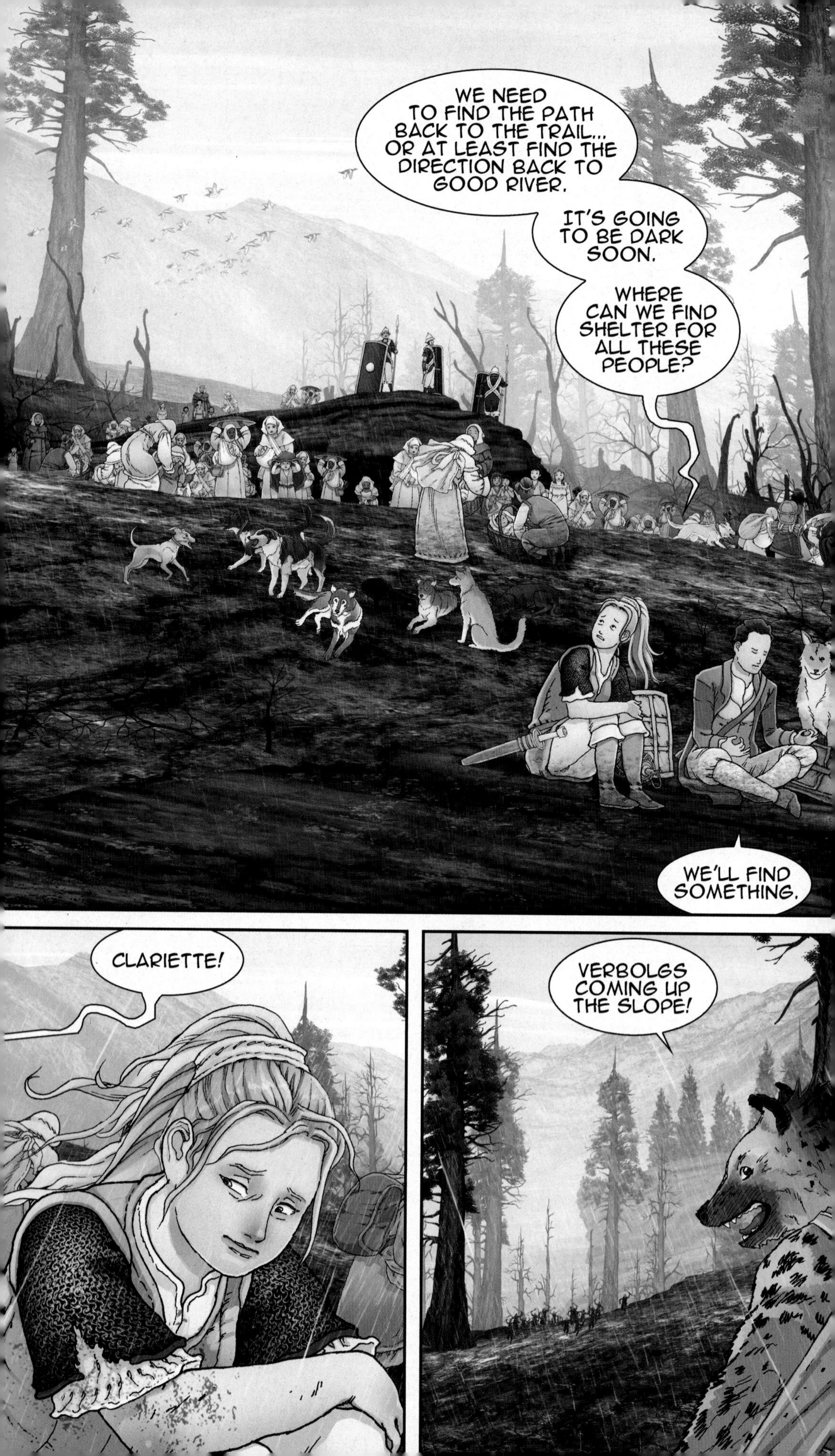
WE NEED TO FIND THE PATH BACK TO THE TRAIL... OR AT LEAST FIND THE DIRECTION BACK TO GOOD RIVER.
IT'S GOING TO BE DARK SOON.
WHERE CAN WE FIND SHELTER FOR ALL THESE PEOPLE?
WE'LL FIND SOMETHING.
CLARIETTE!
VERBOLGS COMING UP THE SLOPE!

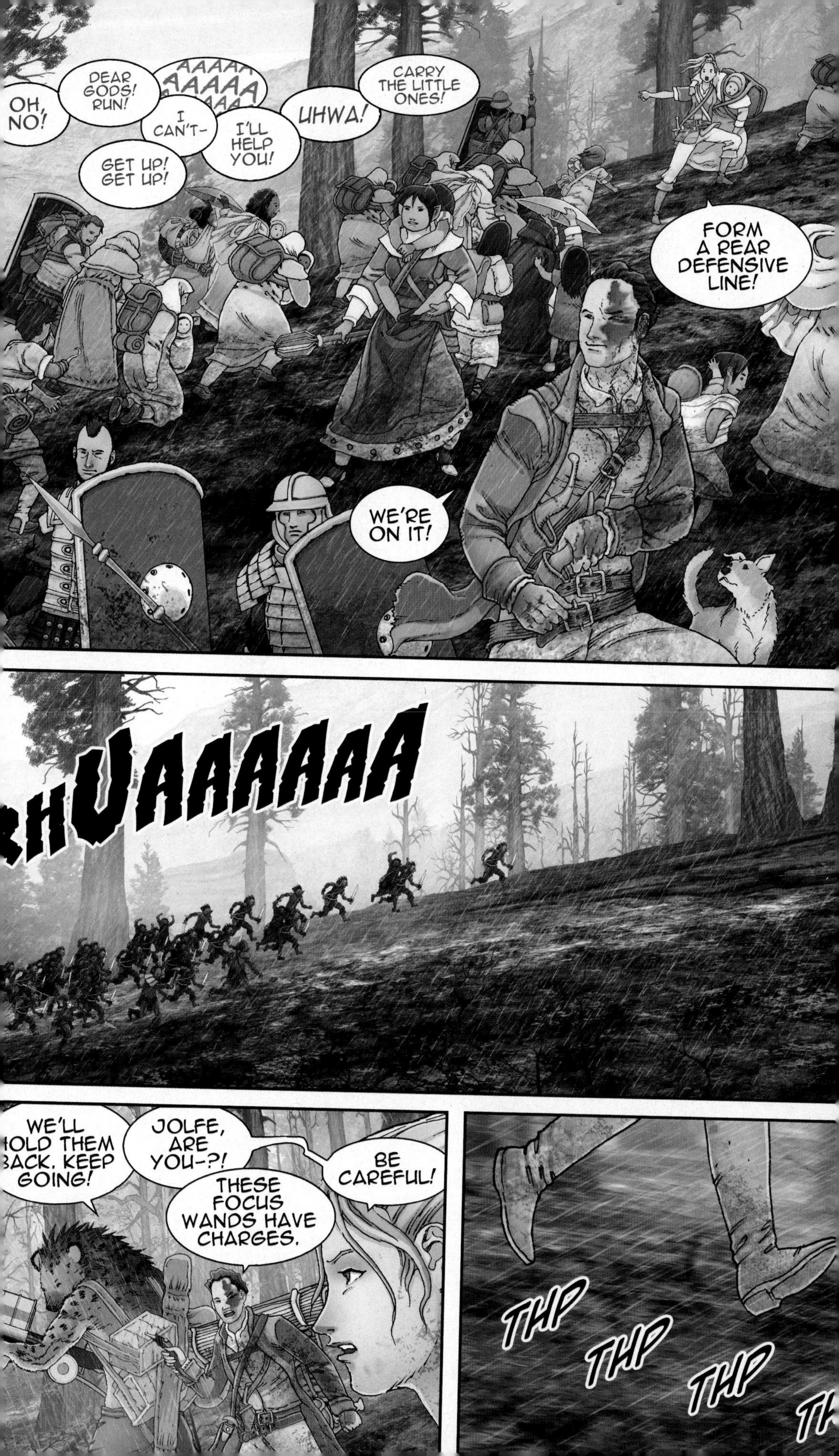

OH, NO!
DEAR GODS! RUN!
AAAAA AAAAA AAAA
I CAN'T-
GET UP! GET UP!
I'LL HELP YOU!
UHWA!
CARRY THE LITTLE ONES!
FORM A REAR DEFENSIVE LINE!
WE'RE ON IT!
RHUAAAAAAA
WE'LL HOLD THEM BACK. KEEP GOING!
JOLFE, ARE YOU-?!
THESE FOCUS WANDS HAVE CHARGES.
BE CAREFUL!
THP
THP
THP

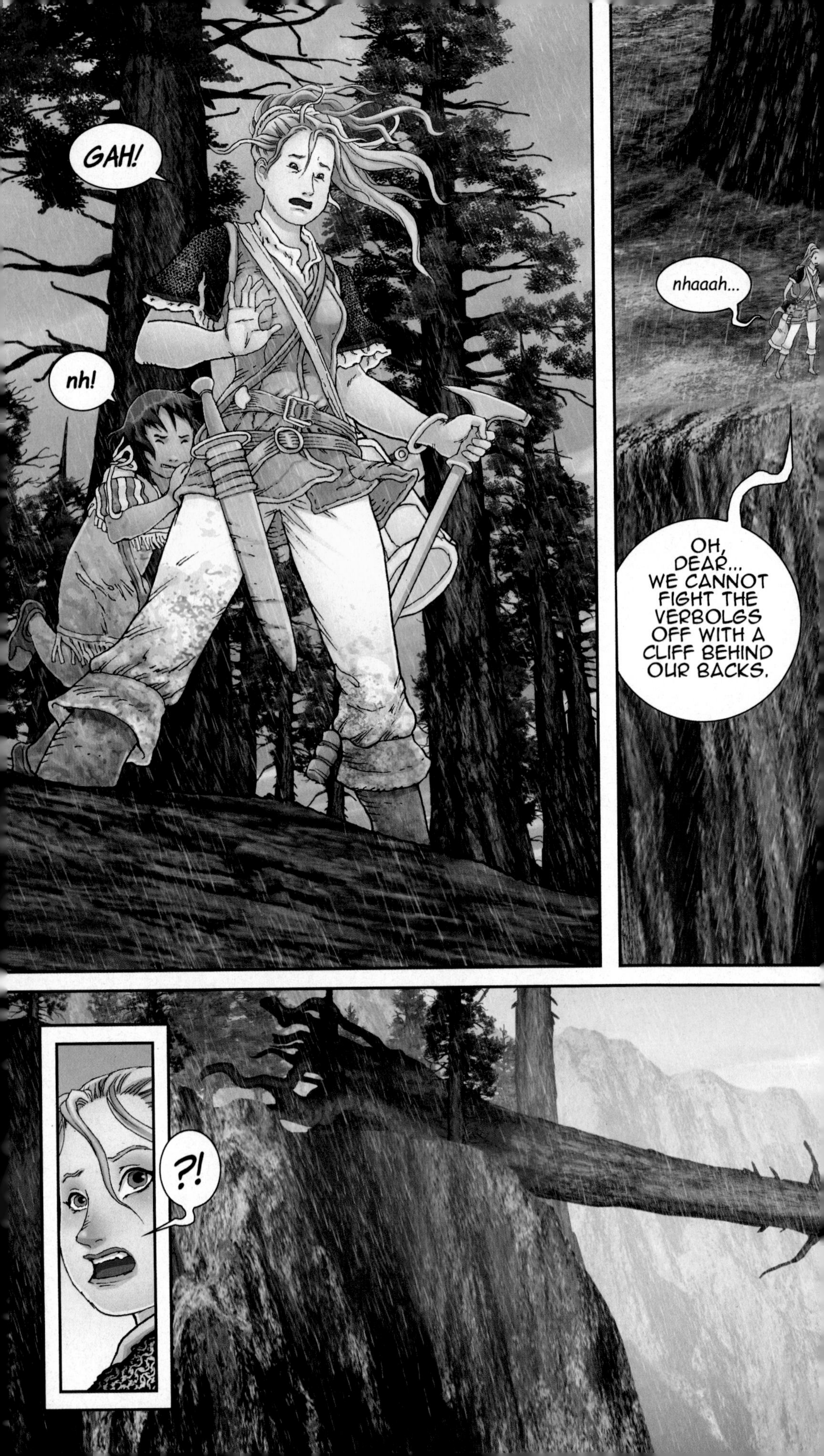
GAH!
nh!
nhaaah...
OH, DEAR... WE CANNOT FIGHT THE VERBOLGS OFF WITH A CLIFF BEHIND OUR BACKS.
?!

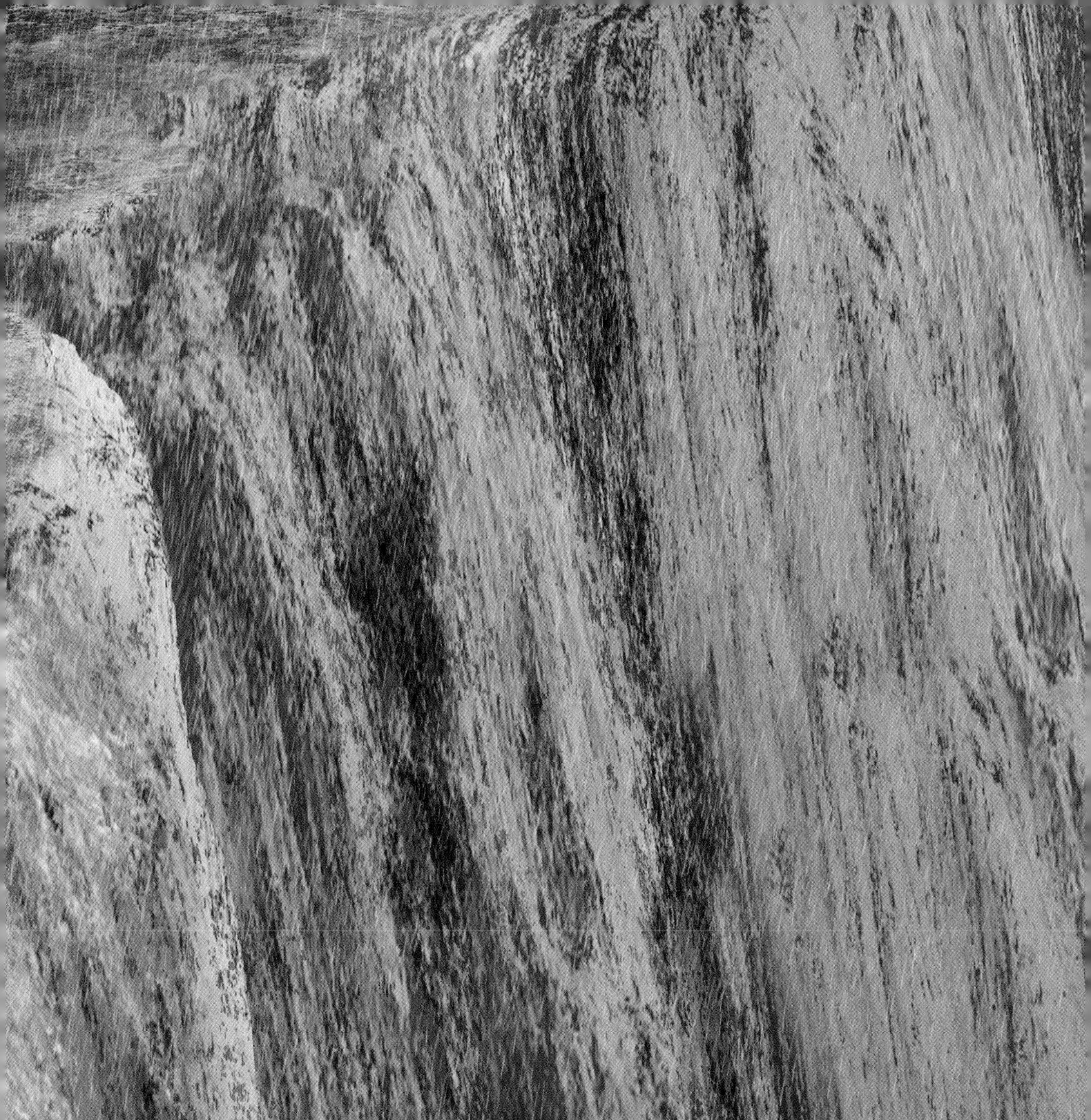

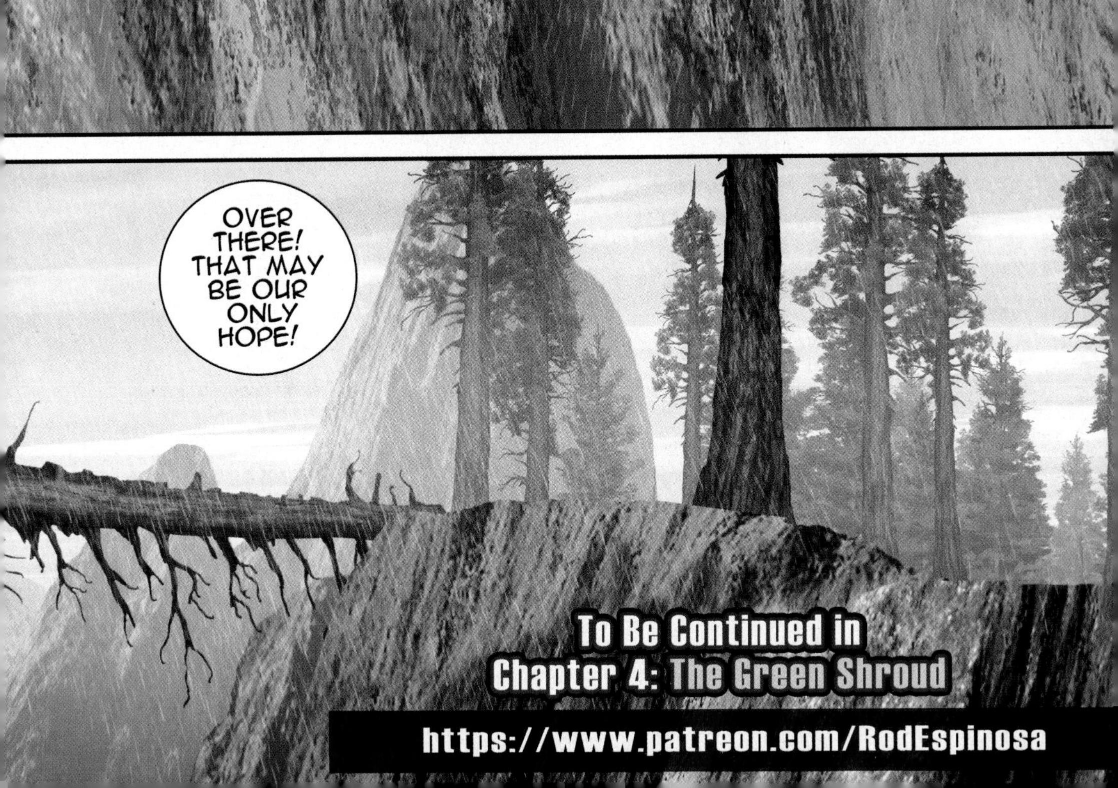
OVER THERE! THAT MAY BE OUR ONLY HOPE!
To Be Continued in
Chapter 4: The Green Shroud
https://www.patreon.com/RodEspinosa

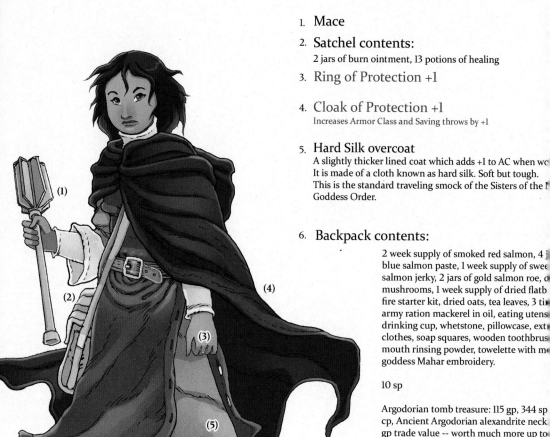

1. **Mace**

2. **Satchel contents:**
   2 jars of burn ointment, 13 potions of healing

3. **Ring of Protection +1**

4. **Cloak of Protection +1**
   Increases Armor Class and Saving throws by +1

5. **Hard Silk overcoat**
   A slightly thicker lined coat which adds +1 to AC when wo
   It is made of a cloth known as hard silk. Soft but tough.
   This is the standard traveling smock of the Sisters of the N
   Goddess Order.

6. **Backpack contents:**

   2 week supply of smoked red salmon, 4 j
   blue salmon paste, 1 week supply of swe
   salmon jerky, 2 jars of gold salmon roe, d
   mushrooms, 1 week supply of dried flatb
   fire starter kit, dried oats, tea leaves, 3 ti
   army ration mackerel in oil, eating utens
   drinking cup, whetstone, pillowcase, ext
   clothes, soap squares, wooden toothbrus
   mouth rinsing powder, towelette with m
   goddess Mahar embroidery.

   10 sp

   Argodorian tomb treasure: 115 gp, 344 sp
   cp, Ancient Argodorian alexandrite neck
   gp trade value -- worth much more up to
   to an antique dealer/art collector in a big
   the Brigand's treasure: 25 gp, 46 sp, 120 c
   lapiz lazuli earrings (30)
   Crude talisman of shielding +1 to all save
   (gotten from General Thunder)

Spirit Summoner Cleric level: 6

STR 12, DEX 10, WIS 19, CHA 11, INT 13, CON 12

HP 38
AC: 13 (10 + 1 hard silk coat / +1 (ring)   base move 30
Melee: +4 (mace d6)

Additional Feats: Potion Creation, Extra Channeling, !
tive Channel
Additional Skills: (6) Religion, (2) Tumble, (1) Scribe,
Heraldry, (2) Animal Handling, (3) Sleight of Hand, (
ception,

SA: Summoning Spirit Spells and Clerical healing

For further information about statistics and terms applied here, please reference the Pathfinder guide 3.0 up to 5th edition Dungeons and Dragons game systems.

Ariarra (Anana) Popplevensie

HALF ELF FEMALE, AGE 23, HEIGHT 5'2

1. **The Blade of the Dark Sun +2**
   * Critical damage on a piercing roll of 18-20 (3x)

2. **Sagodese curved long glaive**
   +1 to damage (high quality masterwork)

3. **Long spear bag**
   Contains 3 spears, Sagodese long glaive and the Blade of the Dark Sun

4. **Military Automatic Heavy Crossbow**
   1d8+1 sm / 1d10+1 med-large

5. **Pendant of dodging**
   20% chance of attacks and projectiles missing target (gained from General Smash).

6. **Necklace of the forest**
   +1 to AC / +10' to movement rating in foliage

7. **Heavy Crossbow munitions satchels**
   6 automatic crossbow ammunition satchels with 2 ammunition cases each (60 bolts).

8. **Satchel bag contents:**
   Regular items: soldier's travel kit (razor, eating utensils, 1 week dried beef jerky, 1 week dried flat bread), spear bag with sharpening stone, military water canteen, towelette 1 extra waterskin

   Argodorian tomb treasure: 115 gp, 344 sp, 900 cp, Small Argodorian treasure chest (well made)
   the Brigand's treasure: 25 gp, 46 sp, 120 cp, 2 finely made silver spoons (20), 3 small daggers, 1 well made dining set, copper necklace (5), jade ring (10)
   A weathered copy of "The Adventures of Field Mouse and Prince Eagle".

9. **Gannalotian style satchel**
   Circus Master's money: 134 gp, 612 sp, and 355 cp
   Orc Chief's wealth: 4 small peridots (30 gp), 78 cp, rough amethyst (20),

10. **Battle Armor of King Belderach the IV +3:**
    * +AC 8 (+3 bonus magical AC), max dex +6, armor check penalty (-1) weight: (25lbs)
    * The armor also gives the wearer a benefit of saving throw bonus of +1 vs fire and lightning.

    Fighter level: 6
    STR 17, DEX 14, WIS 12, CHA 4, INT 12, CON 16
    hp 68   total Initiative bonus: +2
    AC: 26 (10 +2(dex) +11 (Belderach's armor) +2 (gnoll natural hide toughness) +1 (Necklace of the forest))   base move 30'
    Melee: +14/+9 (+6/+1 (+2 training and focus) (+4 STR bonus) +2 Glaive
    Damage: Glaive +2 d10+9 (d10 +2 (+3 training) (+4 STR bonus)

    Missile: +6 (+4 +2(dex))

Asogog the Clanless

GNOLL, MALE, AGE 25, HEIGHT 7'10 Alignment: NG

1. The Beast Slayer Greatsword

* +2 (+3 vs. any beasts/animals with intelligence score lower tha[n]
* Double normal critical threat range (17-20). It also seems to c[hange]
weight from 4 lbs to 8 lbs as necessity requires.
* Cast cure critical wounds (3d8+3) on the wielder once per day
action to trigger).

2. Chain Armor and padded gambeson pan[ts]
and shirt (+5 AC)

3. Ring of Protection +1 AC

4. The Imperial Automatic Crossbow

* Crossbow, light 150 gp 1d6+1 1d8+1 19–20/x2 140 ft. 15 lbs.
Automatic feature
Automatic Mode spits out a lot of bolts at the expense of accuracy.
Each bolt suffers a cumulative -1 to hit with each shot fired per rou[nd]
So that a 5 bolt burst in one round will be -1, -2, -3, -4, -5 to hit res[pec]
tively.
Becoming specialized in this weapon of course removes some of th[e]
penalties of firing.
Multiple shot: 1d8+1
* Winding up the mechanism to ready it for another 12 shots takes 1
round.

5. +1 Short Sword (*+1 vs orc kin)

6. Favorite reinforced water bottle

7. The dagger of Belderach IV +2

8. Backpack contents:

The Folding Portable Chest: This is a rare i[tem]
works as a portable hole but with a bigger capacity. Th[e]
magical chamber that opens up beyond is a gigantic 15[′]
18′ tall and 30′ deep. This is by far her greatest item to [own]
Weight when opened: 1 ton: door cannot be toppled ov[er]
Weight when shrunk: 15 lbs.

Regular items: 2 week supply of smoked red salmon, b[aked]
salmon roe paste, dried and salted green salmon, 1 wee[k]
supply of sweet green salmon jerky, 3 jars of gold salm[on]
dried mushrooms, dried herbs and spices, dried oats, [dried]
milk squares, cocoa squares, tea leaves, 2 loaves of bre[ad]
drinking cup, eating utensils, small soup ladle, small k[nife]
simple bedroll, Shinshin the teddy bear, water bottle, f[ire]
starter kit, pillowcase, extra inner clothes, soap square[s]
wooden toothbrush, mouth rinsing powder, towelette,
hand mirror.

Fighter level: 5

STR 14, DEX 16, WIS 10, CHA 12, INT 15, CON 13
total Initiative bonus: +7   HP 48
AC: 20 (10 +3(dex) +5 (Chain Armor and padded gam[beson]
pants and shirt) +1 (Ring of Protection)) base move [30]
Melee: +10/+11/+11 (+5 (+3 training and focus) (+3 S[TR]
bonus) +1 Short Sword (*+1 vs orc kin)/+2 Great Sword
Dagger/ -2 when weilding two weapons in each hand)

Damage:
Short sword +1 d6+7 (d6 +2 (*+1 vs orc kin) (+3 trainin[g]
STR bonus)
Great Sword +2 d10+5 (d10 +2 (+2 STR bonus) (+1 tra[ining]
Dagger +2 d4+6 (d4 +2 (+3 training) (+2 STR b[onus]

Missile: +6 (+4 +2
Dama

Clariette de Artegnean

HUMAN FEMALE, AGE 19, HEIGHT 5'11

(1)
(2)
(3)
(4)
(5)
(6)

1. Medallion of protection
   +1 AC / +1 to save vs. projectiles/spells

2. Ring of fire
   All fire based spells get an additional +1d4 damage. User is shielded from cold temperatures (functions as a ring of warmth).

3. Wand of fire
   Enhances fire spells by adding +1 for every 2 damage dice in the spell OR launches 1d4 fire bolts (1d6 damage) at the enemy per round [8 of 20 charges]

4. Wand of lightning
   Launches a charged bolt of lightning at one target for 1d6 per user level (26 of 50 charges)

5. Satchel contents:
   2 jars of burn ointment, 13 potions of healing.

6. Hard Silk overcoat
   A slightly thicker lined coat, which adds +1 to AC when worn. It is made of a cloth known as hard silk. Soft but harder to cut and penetrate.

7. Backpack contents:
   2 week supply of smoked red salmon, blue salmon roe paste, dried and salted orange salmon, 1 week supply of sweet green salmon jerky, 3 jars of gold salmon roe, 3 jars of oysters in oil, dried mushrooms , dried flatbread, fire starter kit, dried oats, dried milk squares, cocoa squares, tea leaves, drinking cup, eating utensils, small kettle, padded and knit bedroll, pillow-case, extra inner clothes, soap squares, wooden toothbrush, mouth rinsing powder, towelete, razor, towelette, 5 mono-grammed handkerchiefs, 5 potions of fast recovery (cures 1 hp and accelerates daily healing to +2 hp)

   Weapons: brass knuckles, fist dagger
   Apprentice's wand (his original wand) capable of adding +1 to spell damage and adds +20% to 0 level spell durations.

   460 gp, 77 sp, 23 cp

   Argodorian tomb treasure: 115 gp, 344 sp, 900 cp, Ancient Argodorian ceremonial censer (50 gp value)
   the Brigand's treasure: 25 gp, 46 sp, 120 cp, 2 orange garnets (30)

Mage level: 5
STR 14, DEX 12, WIS 11, CHA 12, INT 18, CON 12
HP 32
Initiative bonus: +7
AC: 13 (17 with mage armor) (10 + 1 hard silk coat / +1 (ring) /+1 dex

base move 30'
Melee: +4 (dagger d4) (+1 pugilist) (+2 strength)

SA: Spells

Jolfe Mhou Endarion

HUMAN MALE, AGE 19, HEIGHT 6'1 Alignment: NG

ADVENTURE FINDERS
BY ROD ESPINOSA

Jallia

Centurion
Isard Odabarius

Naha

Seldric

Sergeant
Sikin

Sergeant
Jados

Shaman
Chim C'nol

Verbolg
Chieftain
"General
Giant"

The unrevealed leaders of the monster army

What we know
so far is they are
giants and are
capable of high
magic.

The Inquisitor Brigade of Arao

Kolos
Thorosius

Rhopul
Thorosius

Commander
Ogre

Orcs and other
humanoid species
are often used as
auxiliary forces
by the United
Crown's colonial
military.

The People of the Orphan Village

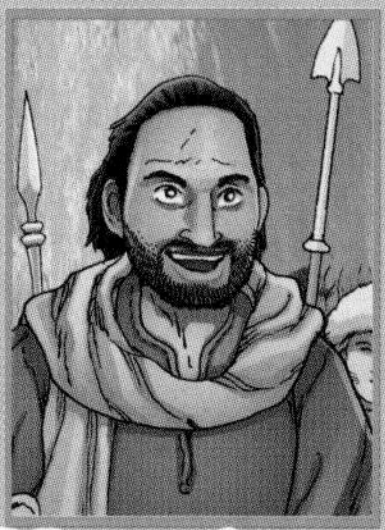
Mayor Anzeri

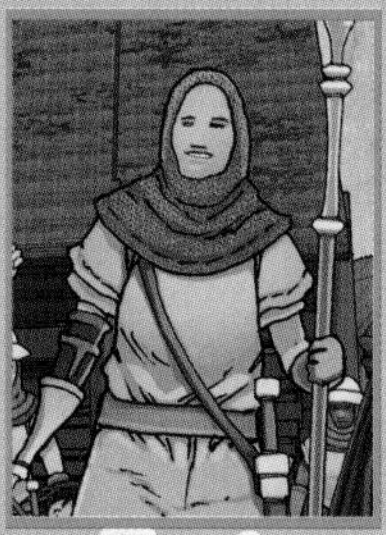
Truvio

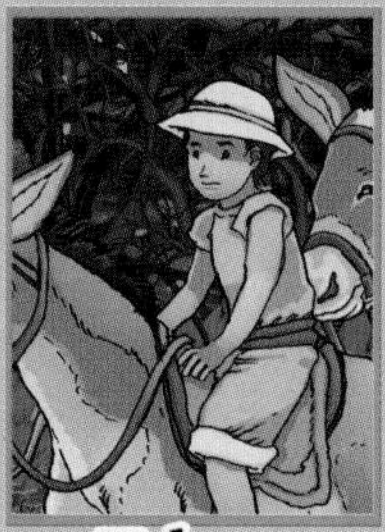
Takou

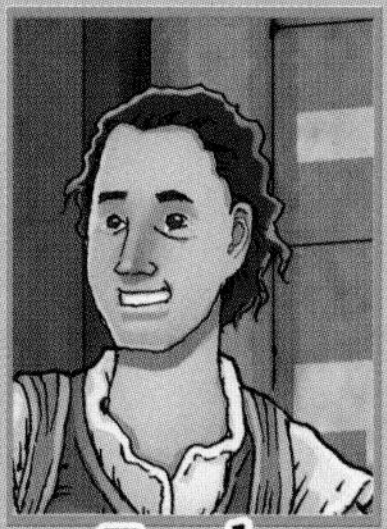
Farole

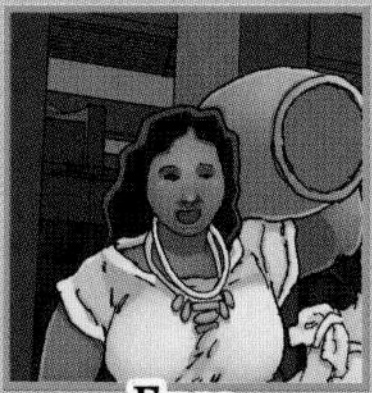
Enca

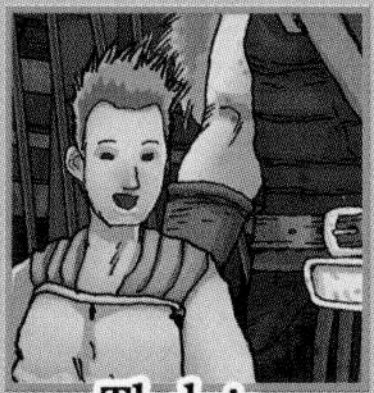
Thelnis

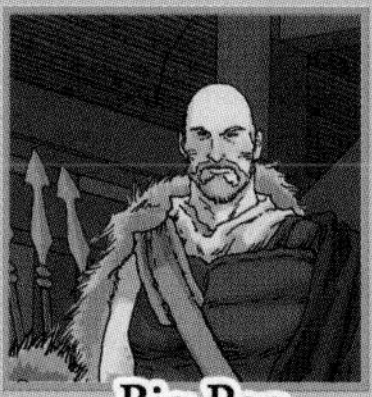
Big Pop

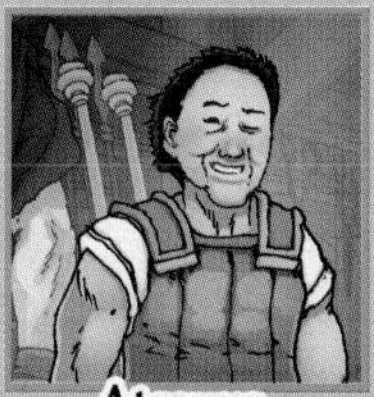
Atreyus

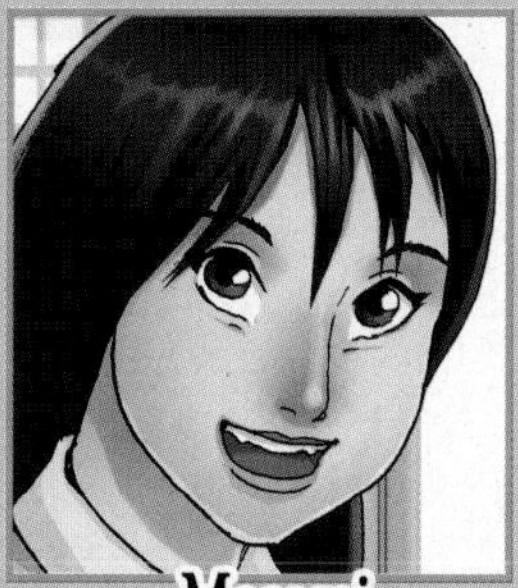
Mecomi
Headmistress of the Children's House

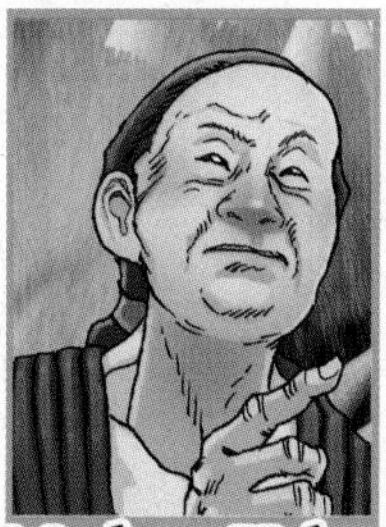
Madam Yabu

The Warriors of Dawn

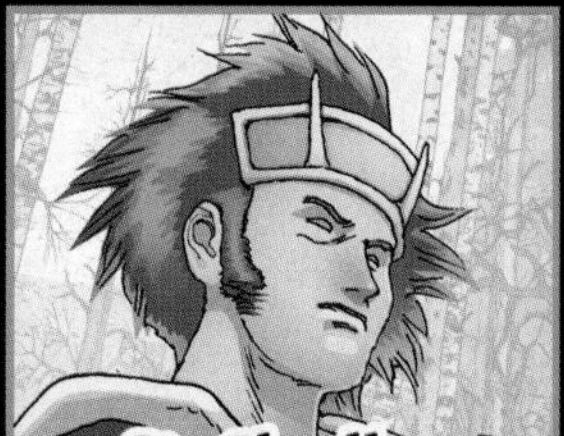
Sir Sharlho

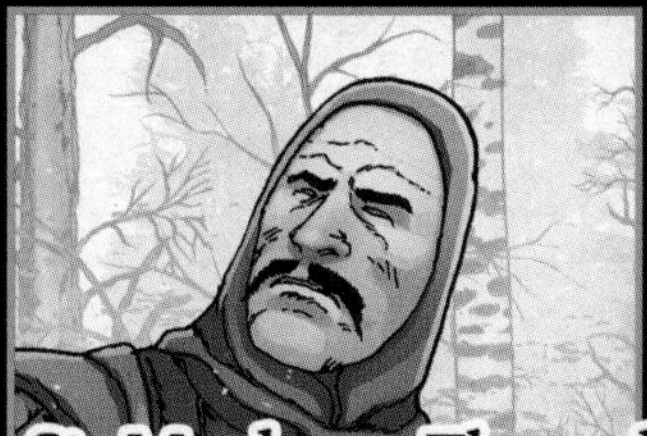
Sir Mardegan Thanard

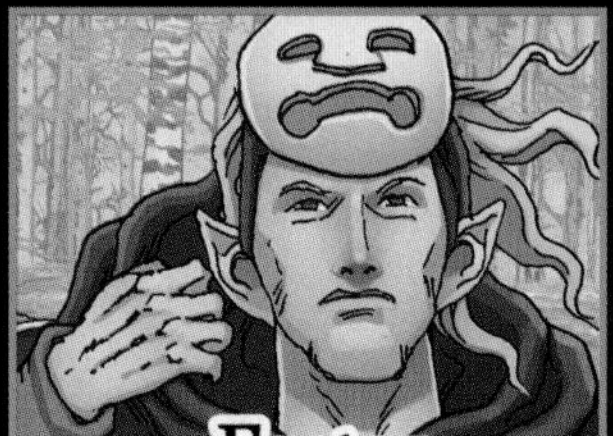
Eretar

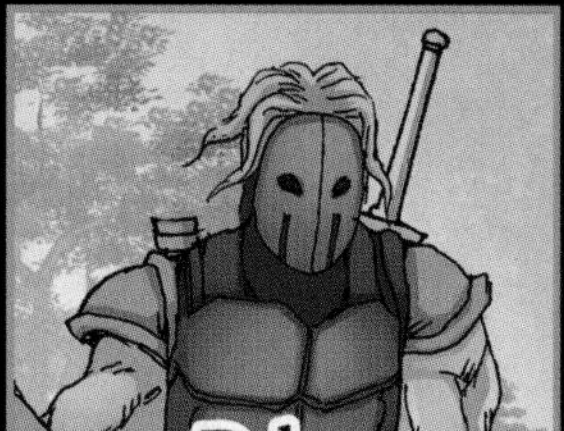
Dehgo

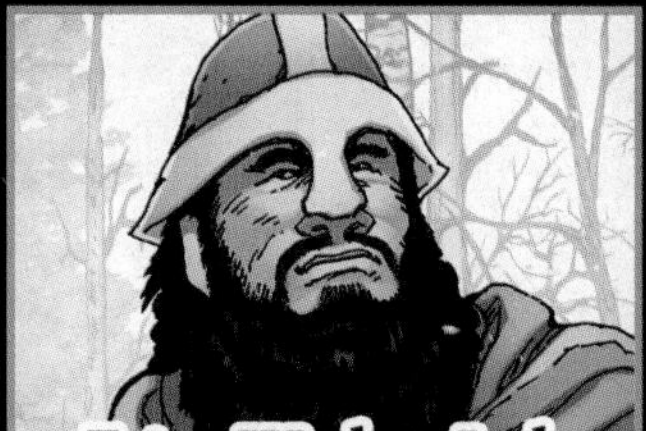
Friar Wadug Jud

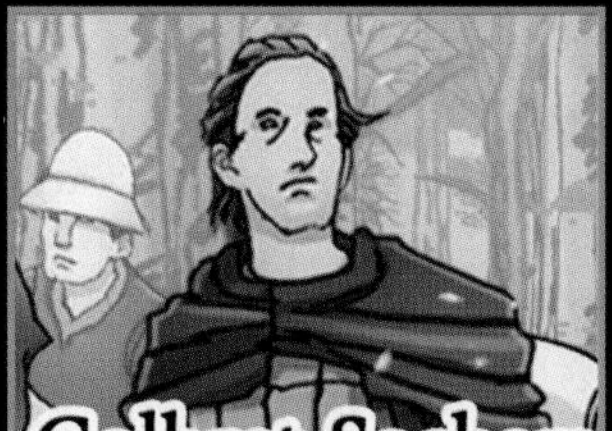
Golbret Sochem

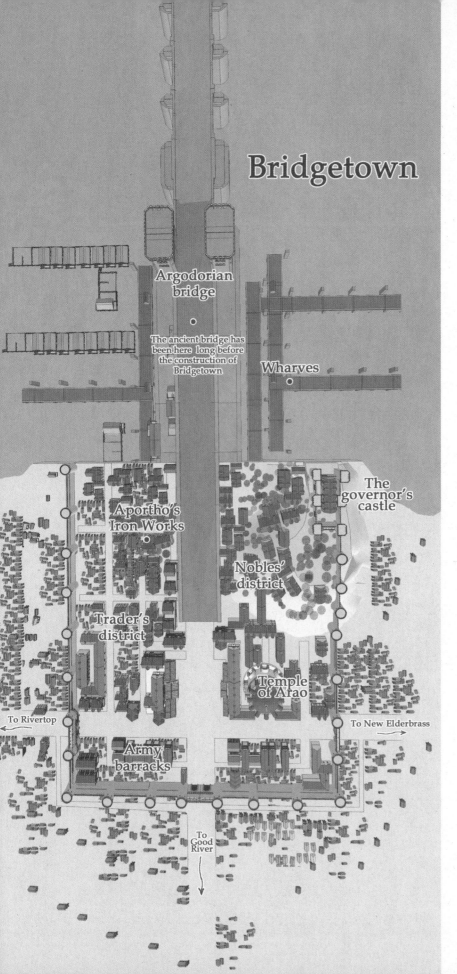

Bridgetown

Argodorian bridge

The ancient bridge has been here long before the construction of Bridgetown

Wharves

Aportho's Iron Works

The governor's castle

Nobles' district

Trader's district

Temple of Arao

To Rivertop

To New Elderbrass

Army barracks

To Good River

In our story, Bridgetown is the furthest Clari and her friends have gone in their large world.

This is a place she is familiar with, as evidenced by her friendship with Maati which she will revisit again in a future time.

When we come upon Bridgetown, it isn't a picture of tranquility as in ages past when Clari visited the city.

Being a crossroads into the upper river lands, it is currently swamped with refugees and all manner of folk fleeing war and monsters upstream.

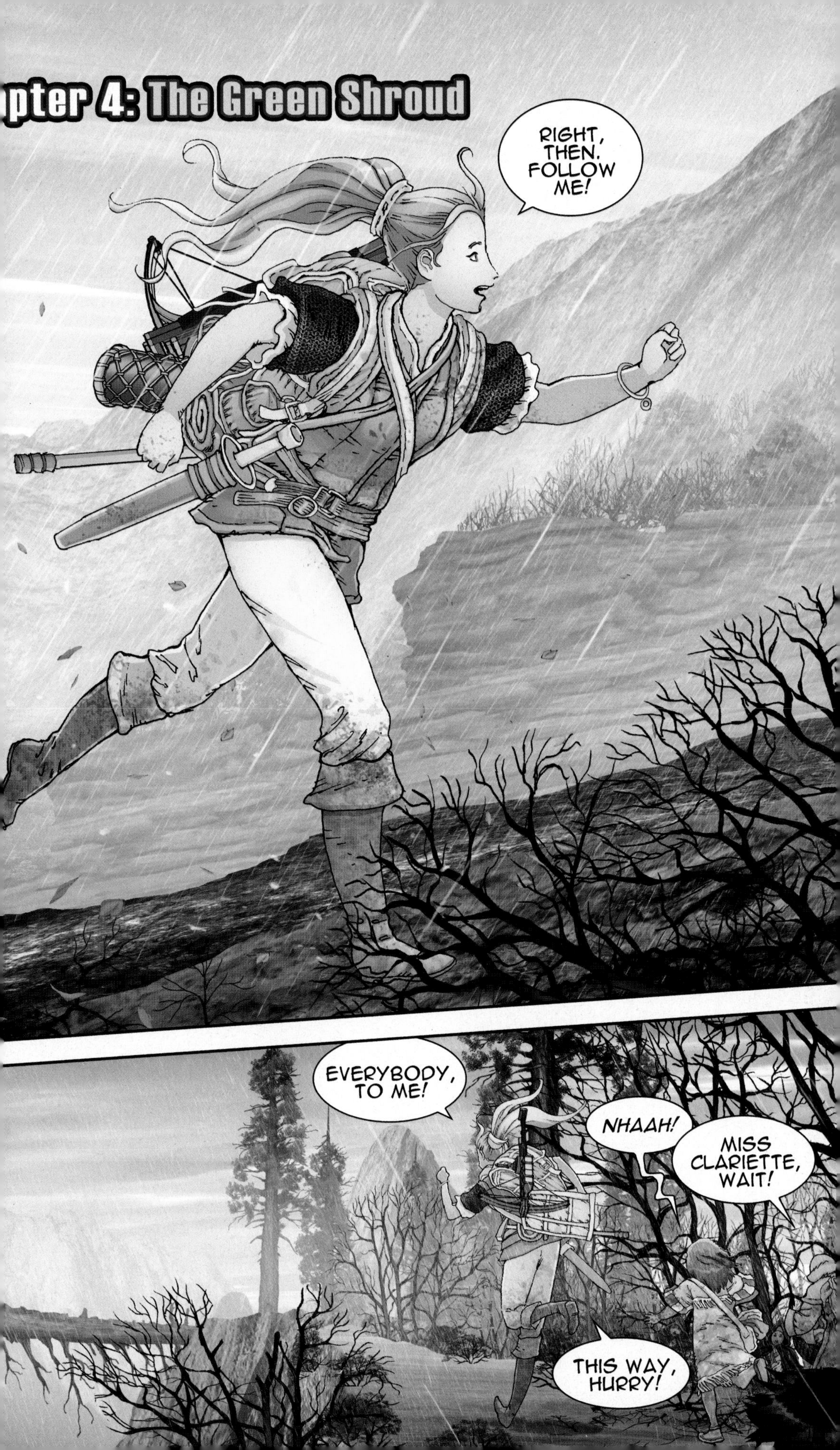
pter 4: The Green Shroud
RIGHT, THEN. FOLLOW ME!
EVERYBODY, TO ME!
NHAAH!
MISS CLARIETTE, WAIT!
THIS WAY, HURRY!

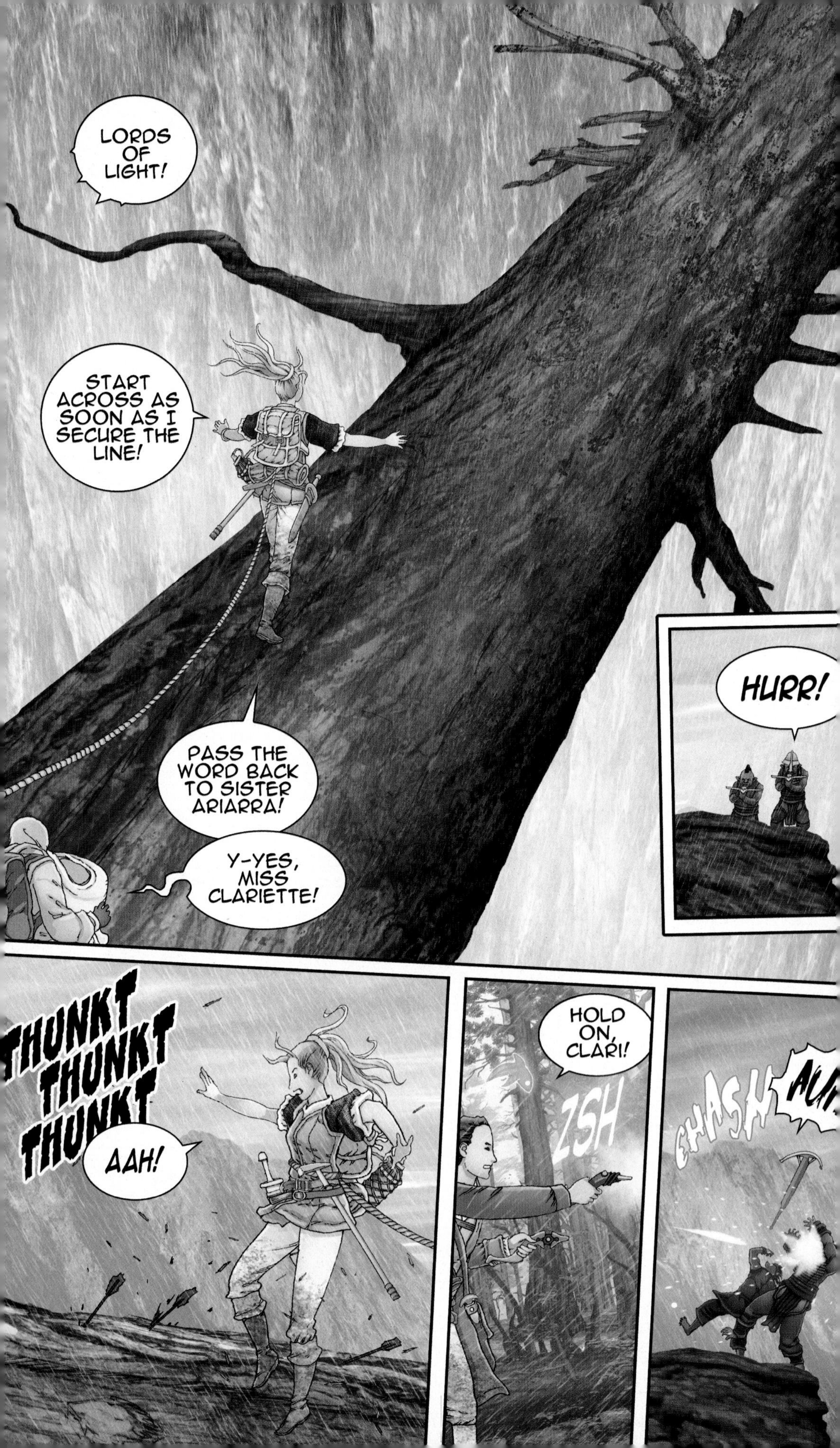
LORDS OF LIGHT!
START ACROSS AS SOON AS I SECURE THE LINE!
PASS THE WORD BACK TO SISTER ARIARRA!
Y-YES, MISS CLARIETTE!
HURR!
THUNKT THUNKT THUNKT
AAH!
HOLD ON, CLARI!
ZSH
CHASH
AUK!

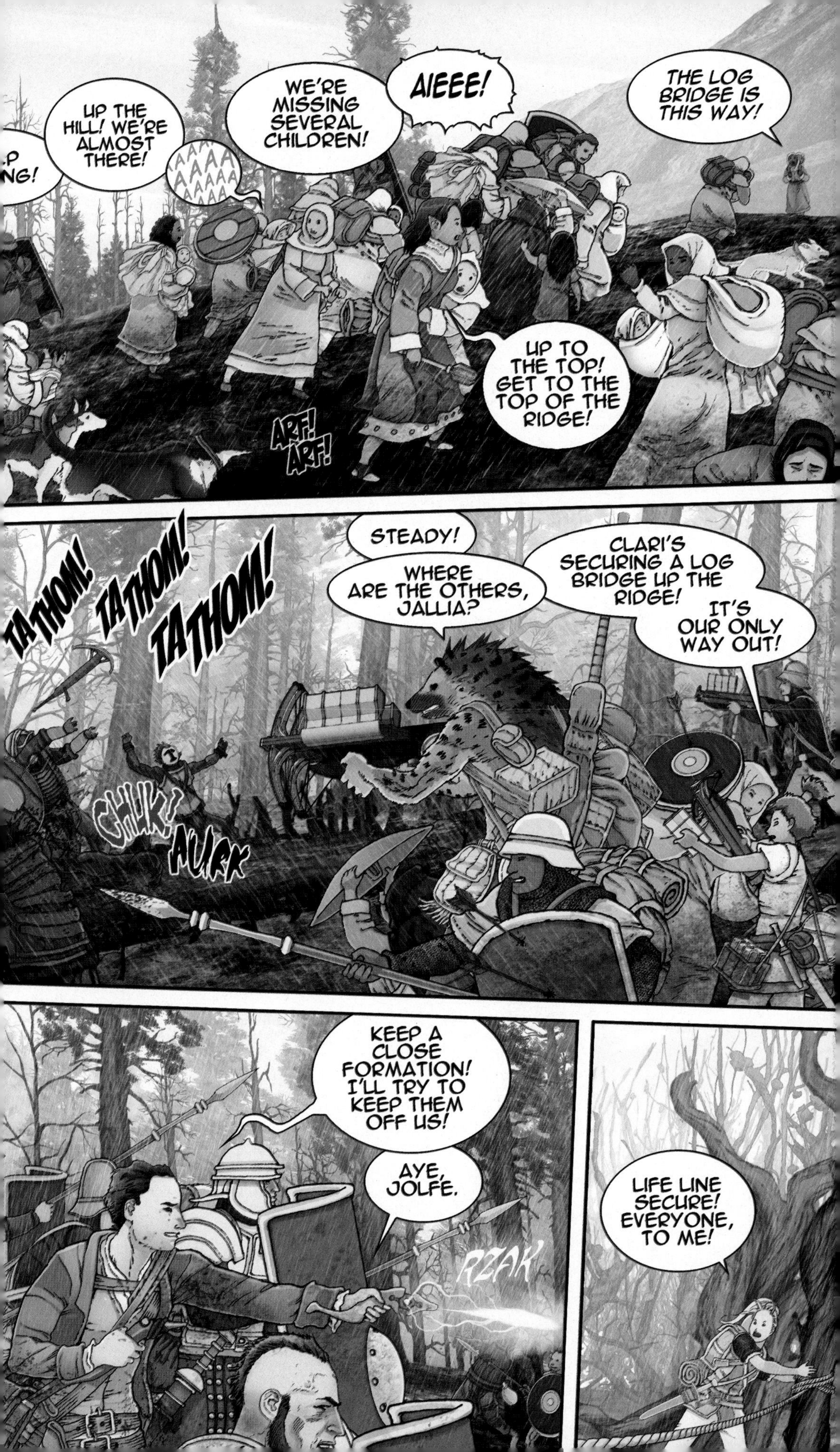
UP THE HILL! WE'RE ALMOST THERE!
AAAAAAAAAAA
WE'RE MISSING SEVERAL CHILDREN!
AIEEE!
THE LOG BRIDGE IS THIS WAY!
UP TO THE TOP! GET TO THE TOP OF THE RIDGE!
ARF! ARF!
TA THOM!
TA THOM!
TA THOM!
STEADY!
WHERE ARE THE OTHERS, JALLIA?
CLARI'S SECURING A LOG BRIDGE UP THE RIDGE!
IT'S OUR ONLY WAY OUT!
CHUK!
AURK
KEEP A CLOSE FORMATION! I'LL TRY TO KEEP THEM OFF US!
AYE, JOLFE.
RZAK
LIFE LINE SECURE! EVERYONE, TO ME!

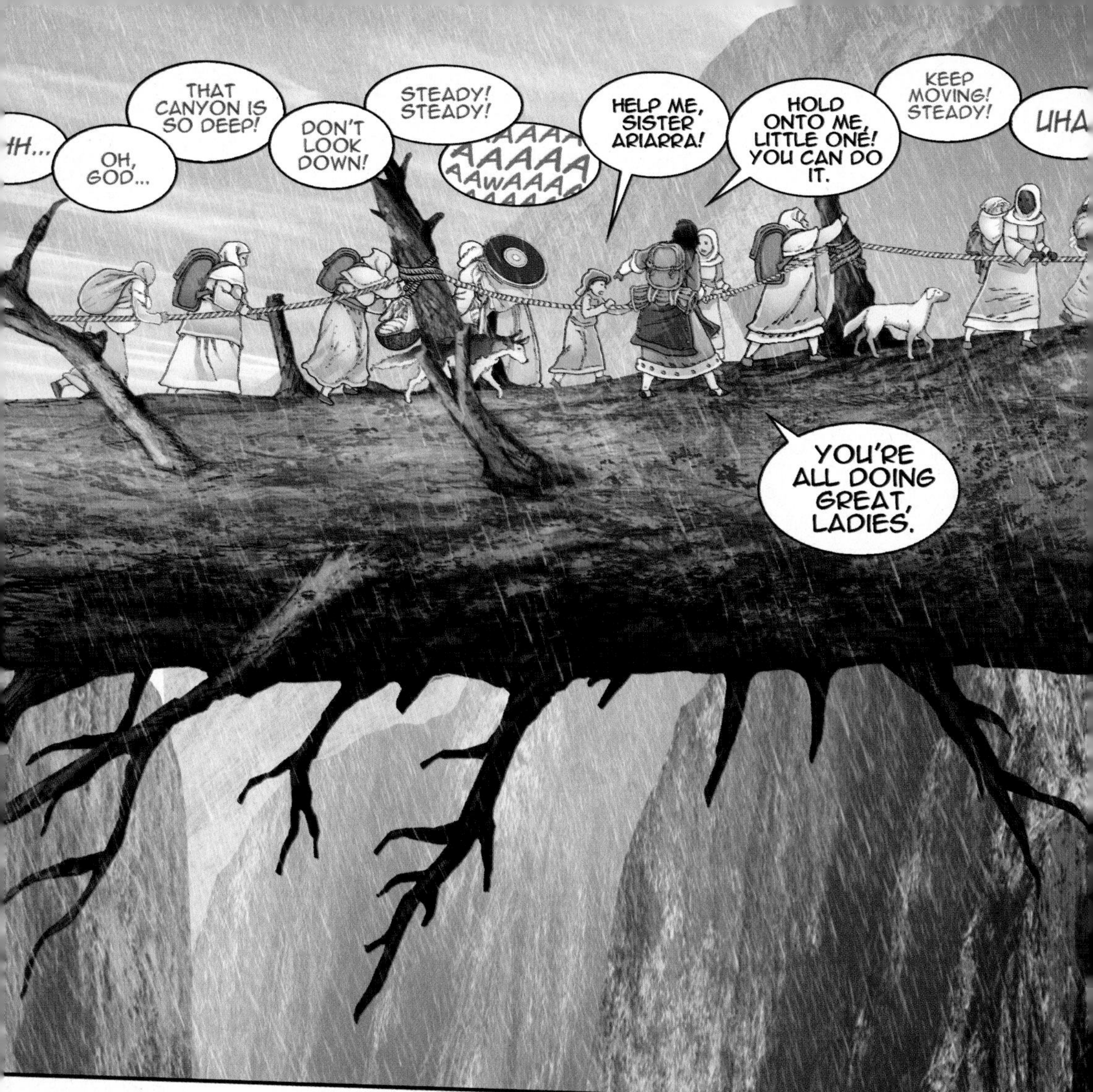
OH, GOD...
THAT CANYON IS SO DEEP!
DON'T LOOK DOWN!
STEADY! STEADY!
HELP ME, SISTER ARIARRA!
HOLD ONTO ME, LITTLE ONE! YOU CAN DO IT.
KEEP MOVING! STEADY!
YOU'RE ALL DOING GREAT, LADIES.

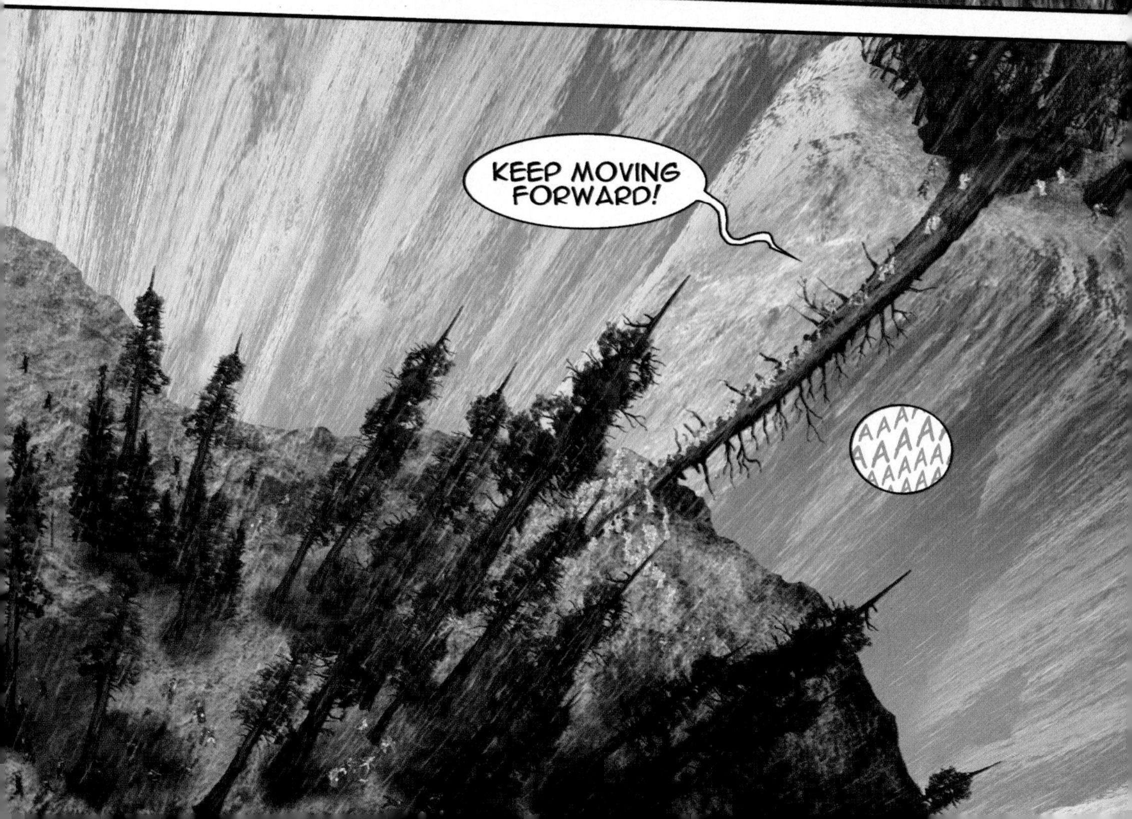
KEEP MOVING FORWARD!

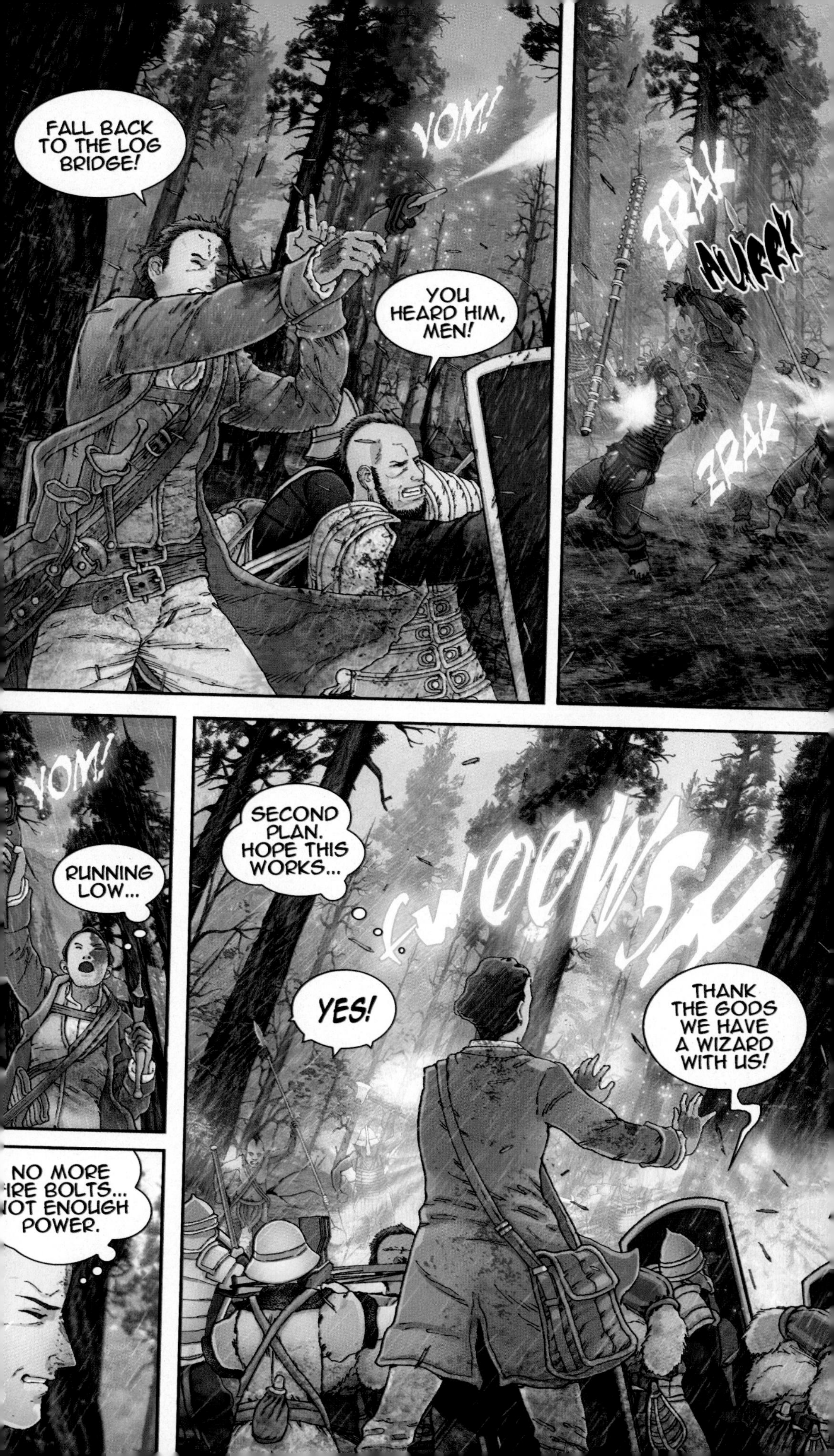
FALL BACK TO THE LOG BRIDGE!
VOM!
YOU HEARD HIM, MEN!
ZRAK
AURRK
ZRAK
VOM!
RUNNING LOW...
NO MORE FIRE BOLTS... NOT ENOUGH POWER.
SECOND PLAN. HOPE THIS WORKS...
FWOOWSH
YES!
THANK THE GODS WE HAVE A WIZARD WITH US!

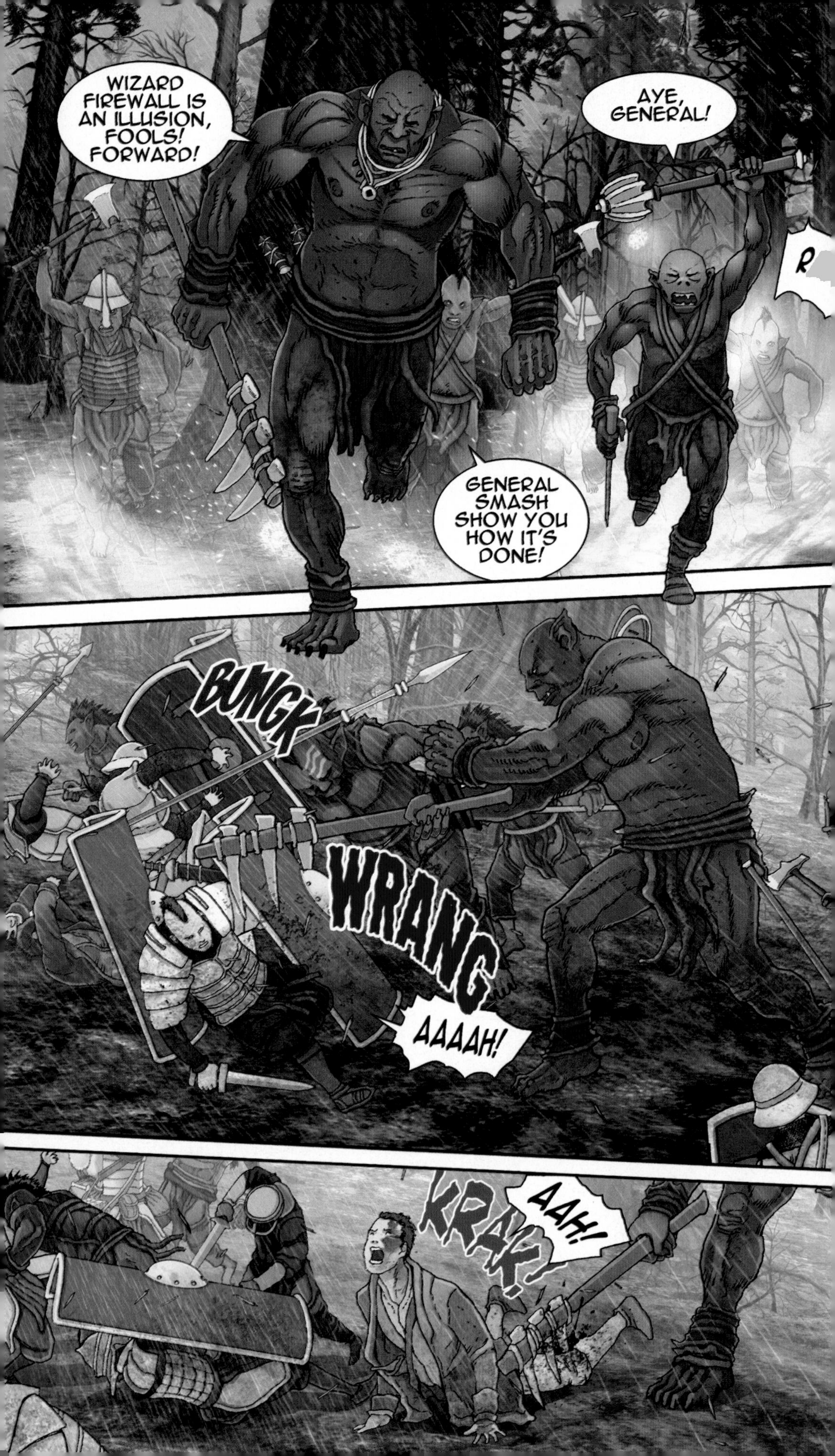
WIZARD FIREWALL IS AN ILLUSION, FOOLS! FORWARD!
AYE, GENERAL!
GENERAL SMASH SHOW YOU HOW IT'S DONE!
BUNGK
WRANG
AAAAH!
KRAK
AAH!

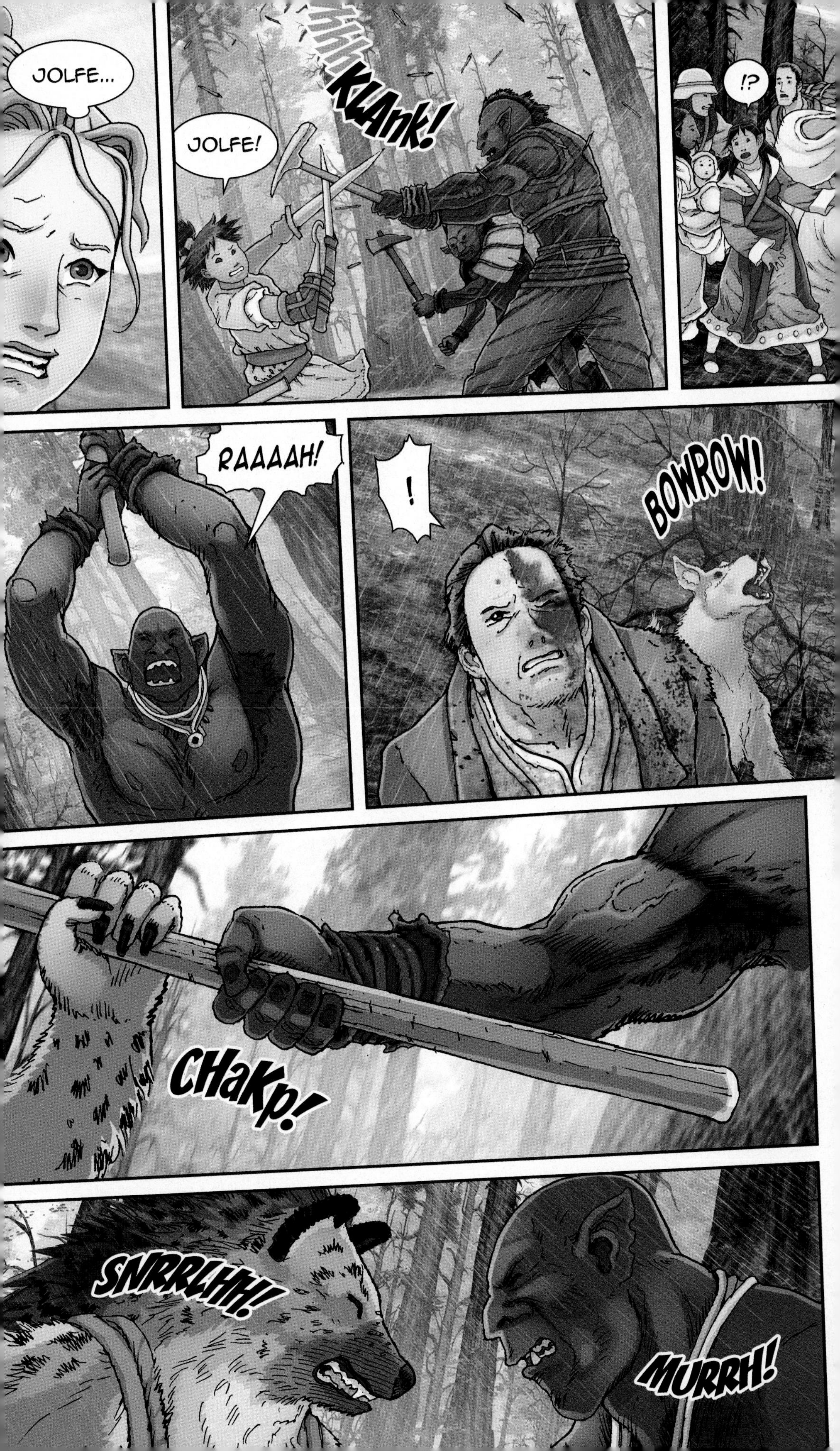
JOLFE...
JOLFE!
KLAnk!
!?
RAAAAH!
!
BOWROW!
CHaKp!
SNRRLHH!
MURRH!

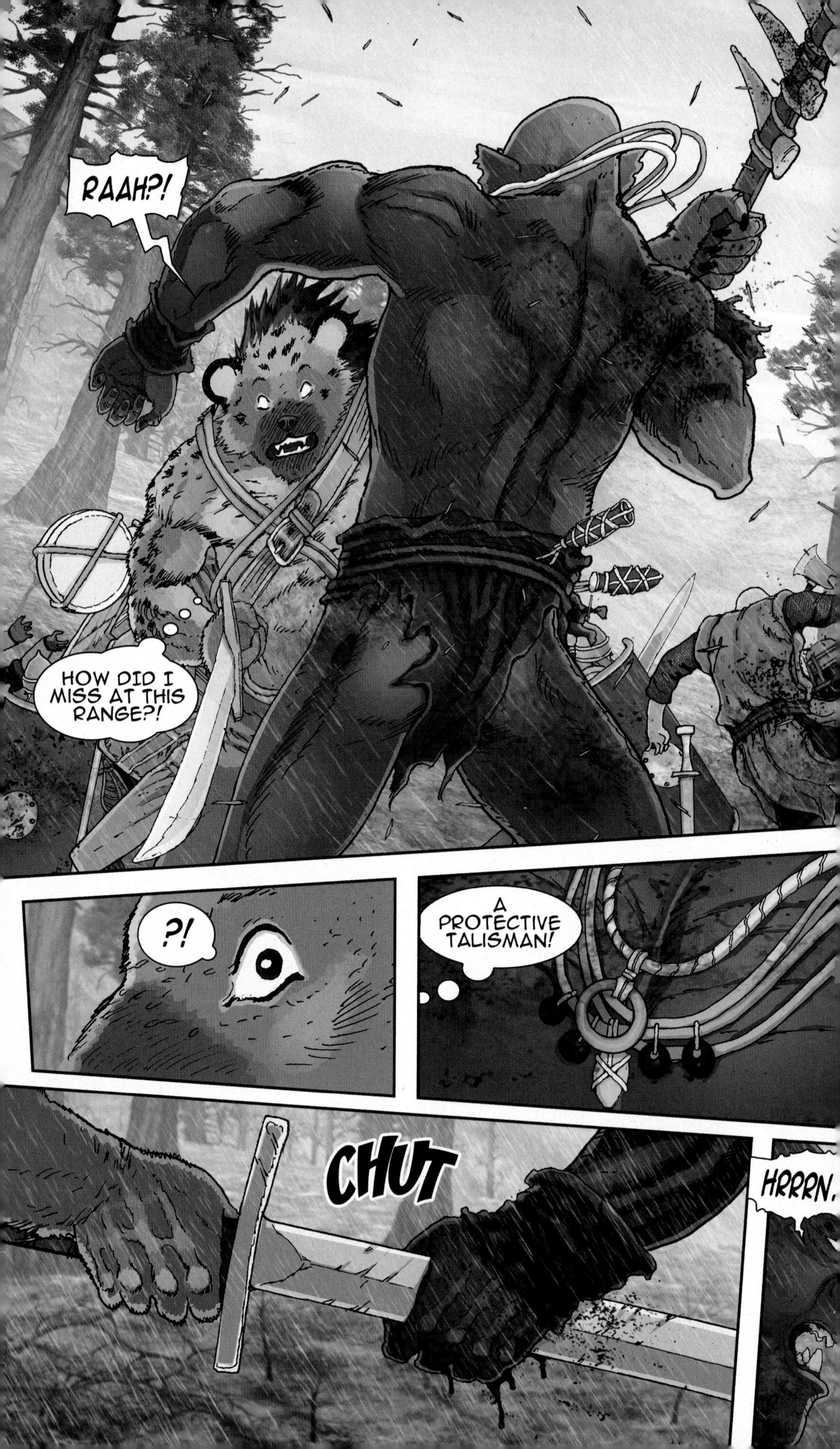
RAAH?!
HOW DID I MISS AT THIS RANGE?!
?!
A PROTECTIVE TALISMAN!
CHUT
HRRRN.

THUDDT AAUF!

ASOGOG!

BLUNK

GLUK
GLUK
GLUK

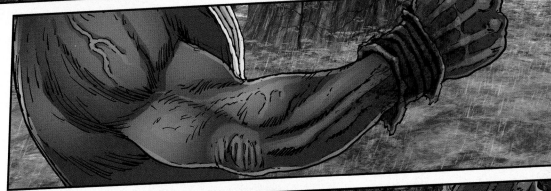

RAAAAH...

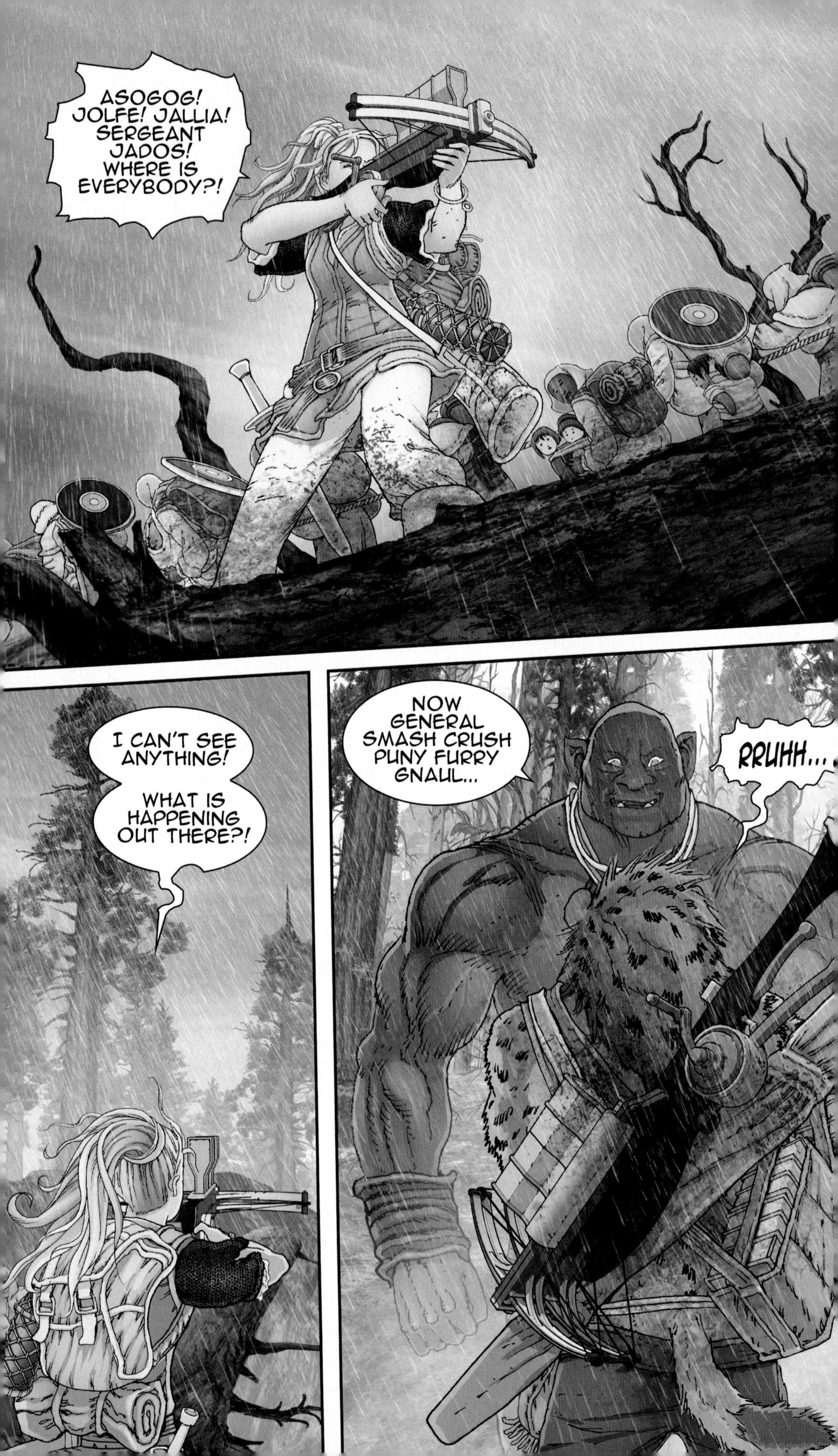
ASOGOG! JOLFE! JALLIA! SERGEANT JADOS! WHERE IS EVERYBODY?!
I CAN'T SEE ANYTHING!
WHAT IS HAPPENING OUT THERE?!
NOW GENERAL SMASH CRUSH PUNY FURRY GNAUL...
RRUHH...

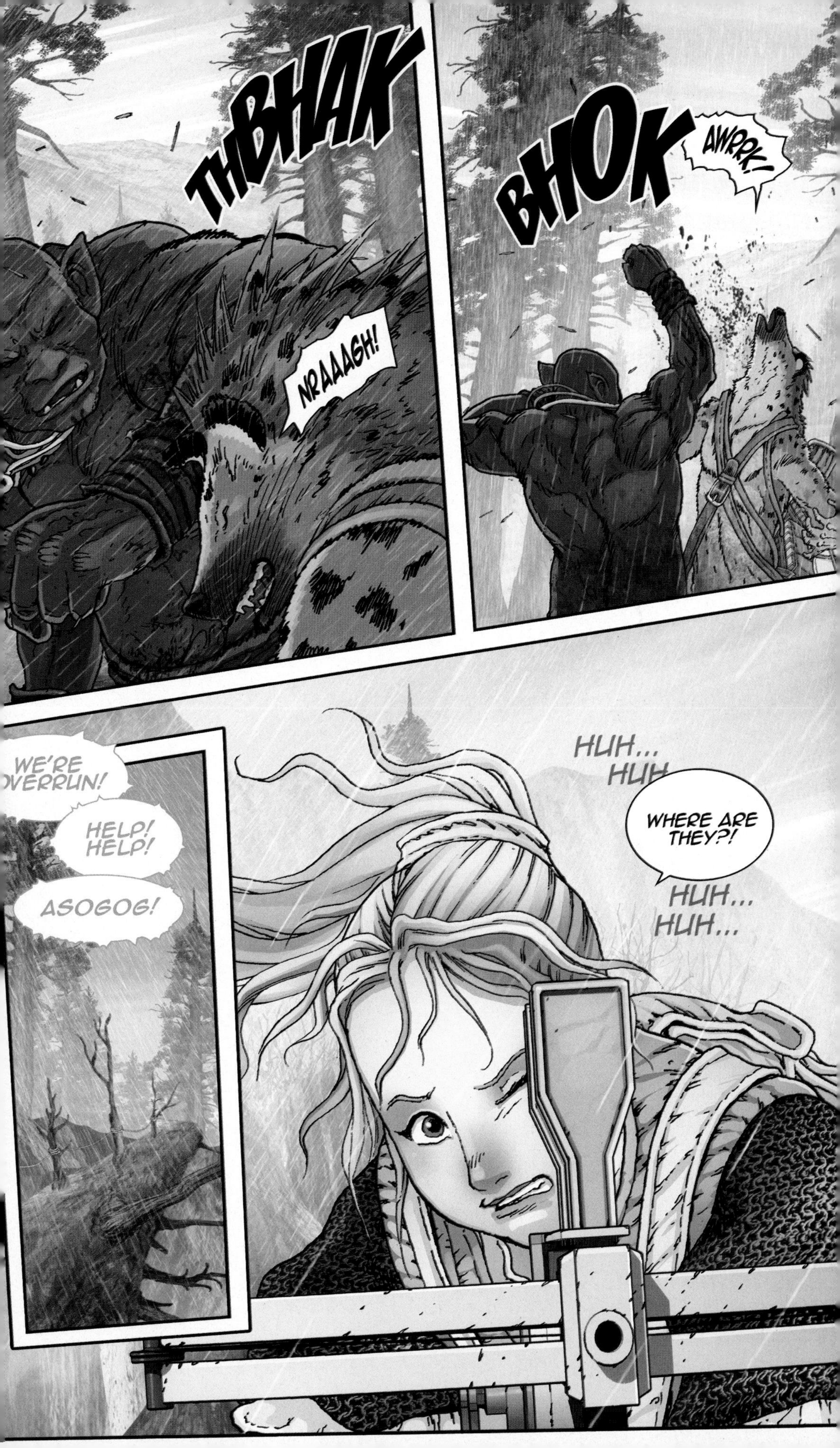
THBHAK
NRAAAGH!
BHOK
AWRRK!
WE'RE OVERRUN!
HELP! HELP!
ASOGOG!
HUH... HUH
WHERE ARE THEY?!
HUH... HUH...

CHASK

URK!

ASOGOG, HELP!

NHURRR...

ARH...

TA THOM!
TA THOM!
TA THOM!

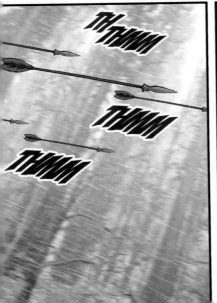

TH THMM
THMM
THMM

SHFK-SHFK SHFK

NAAKK!

KAHK!

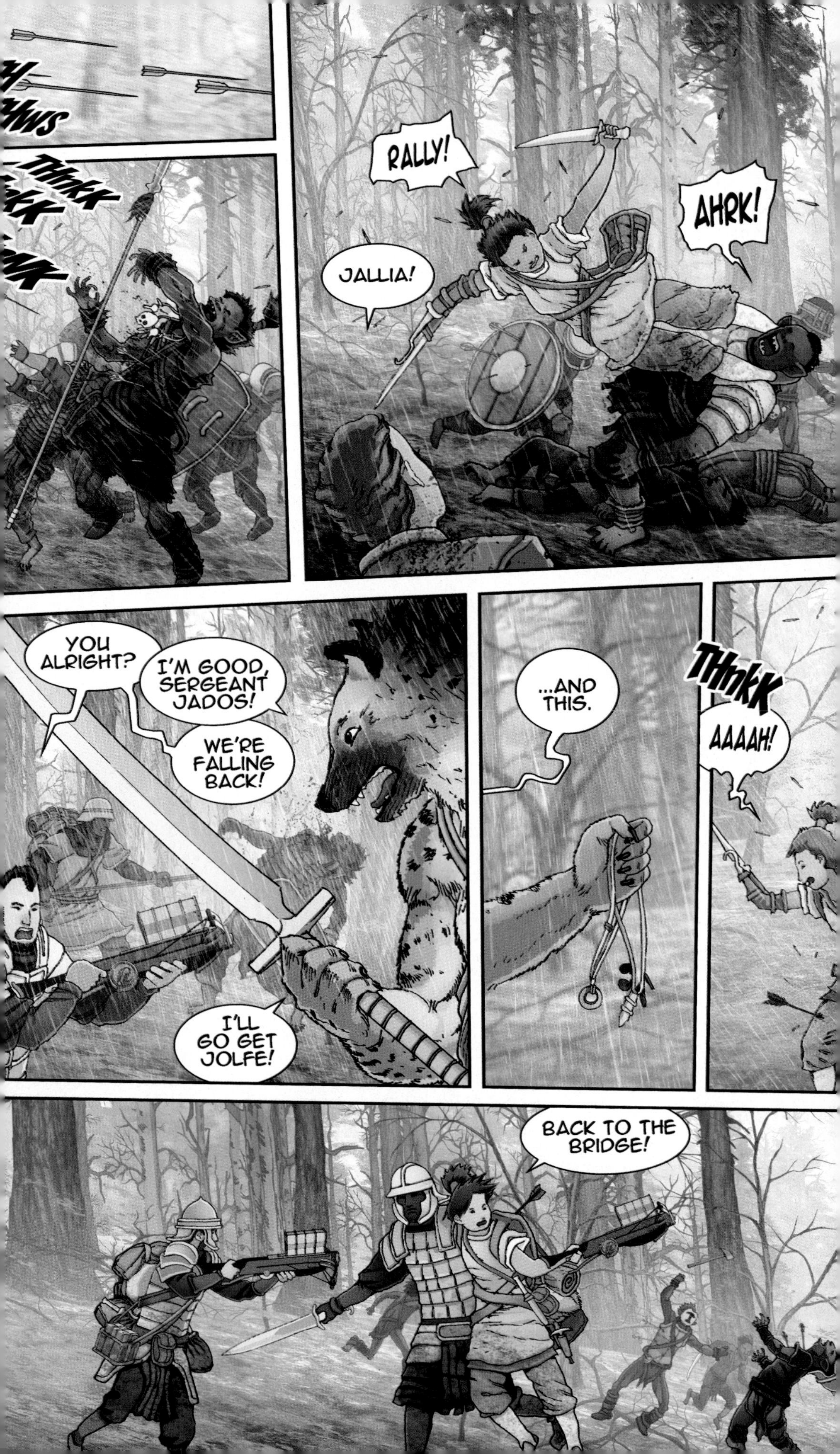
THNKK
RALLY!
JALLIA!
AHRK!
YOU ALRIGHT?
I'M GOOD, SERGEANT JADOS!
WE'RE FALLING BACK!
I'LL GO GET JOLFE!
...AND THIS.
THNKK
AAAAH!
BACK TO THE BRIDGE!

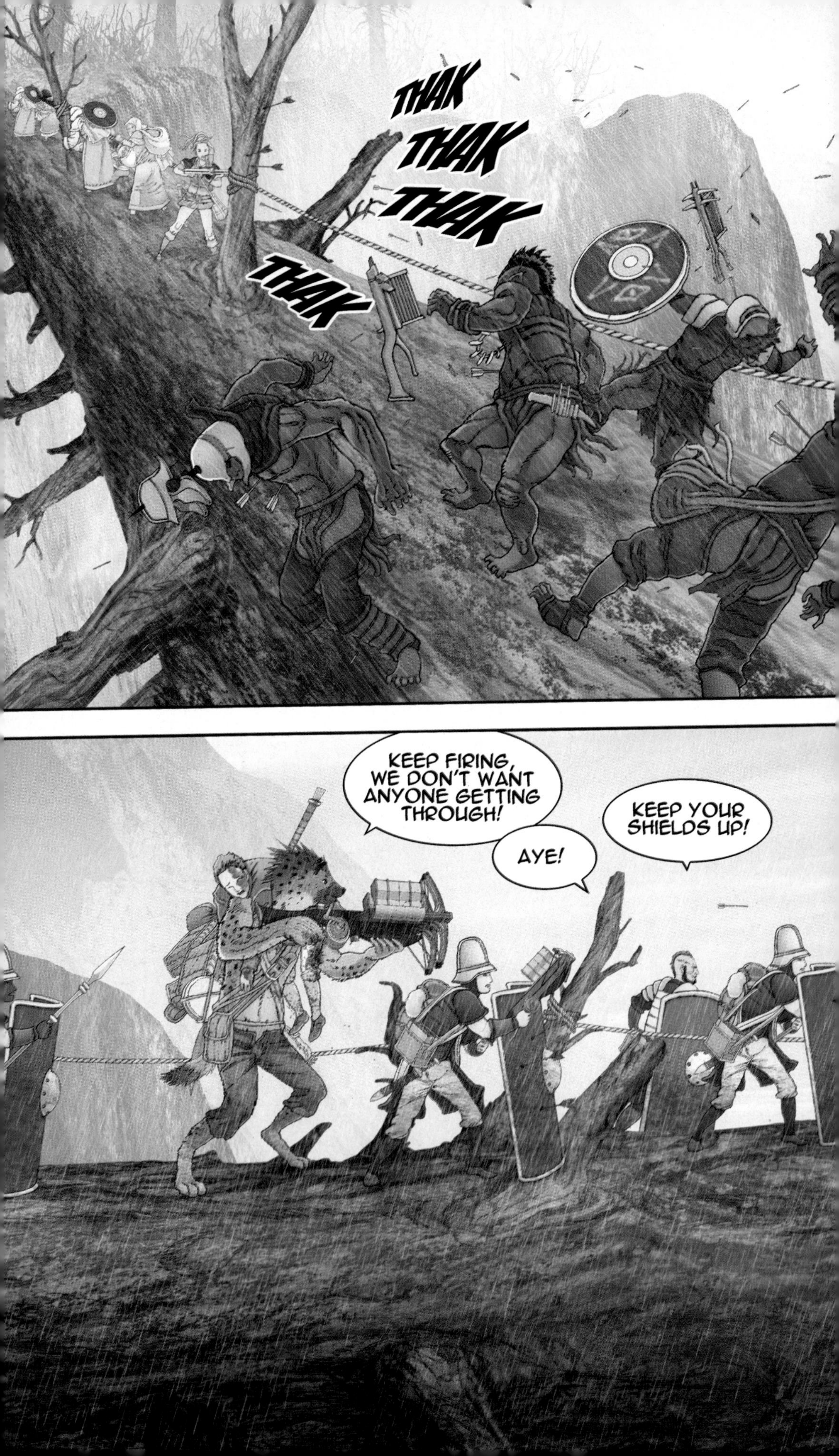
THAK
THAK
THAK
THAK
KEEP FIRING, WE DON'T WANT ANYONE GETTING THROUGH!
AYE!
KEEP YOUR SHIELDS UP!

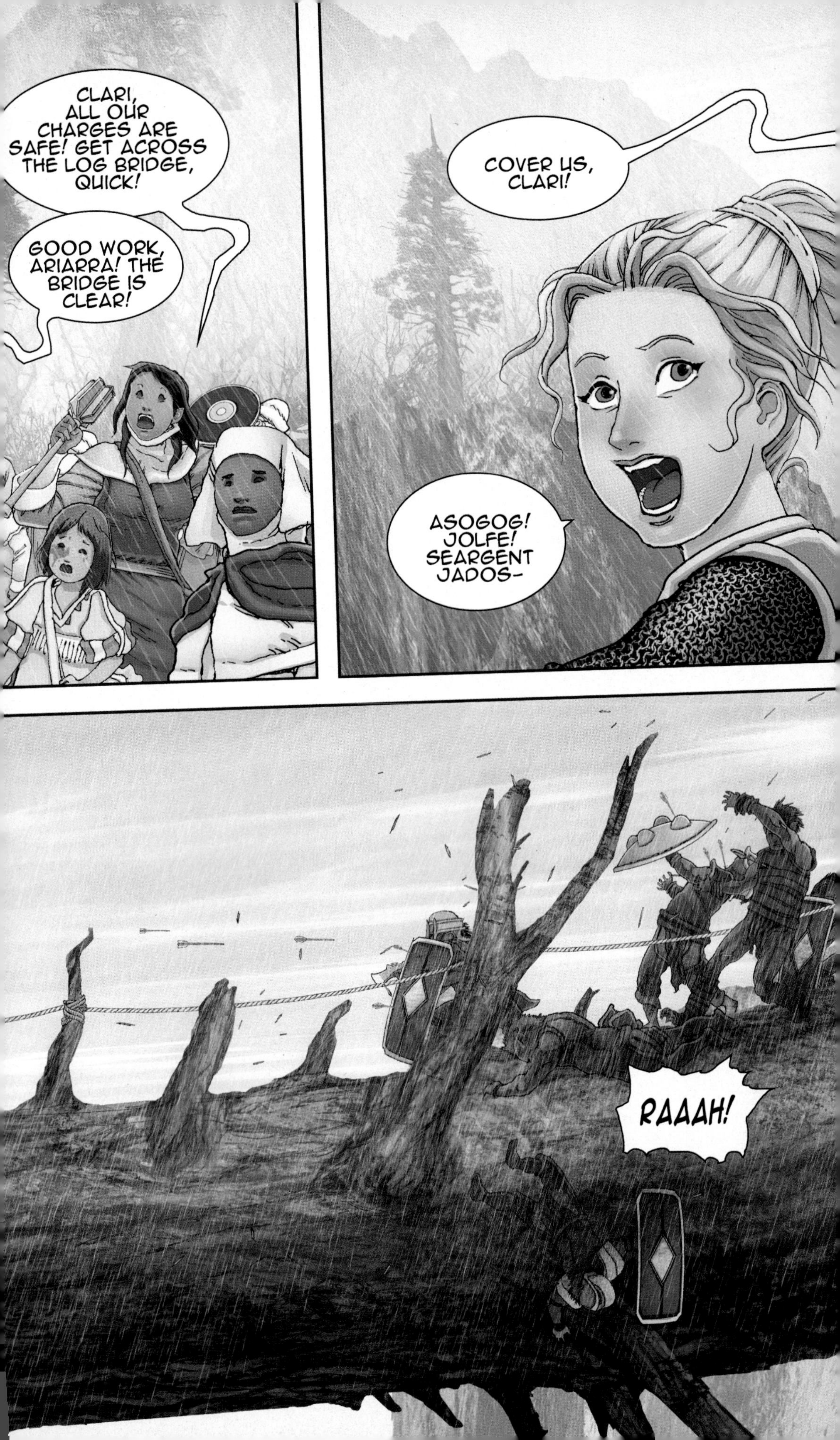
CLARI, ALL OUR CHARGES ARE SAFE! GET ACROSS THE LOG BRIDGE, QUICK!
GOOD WORK, ARIARRA! THE BRIDGE IS CLEAR!
COVER US, CLARI!
ASOGOG! JOLFE! SEARGENT JADOS-
RAAAH!

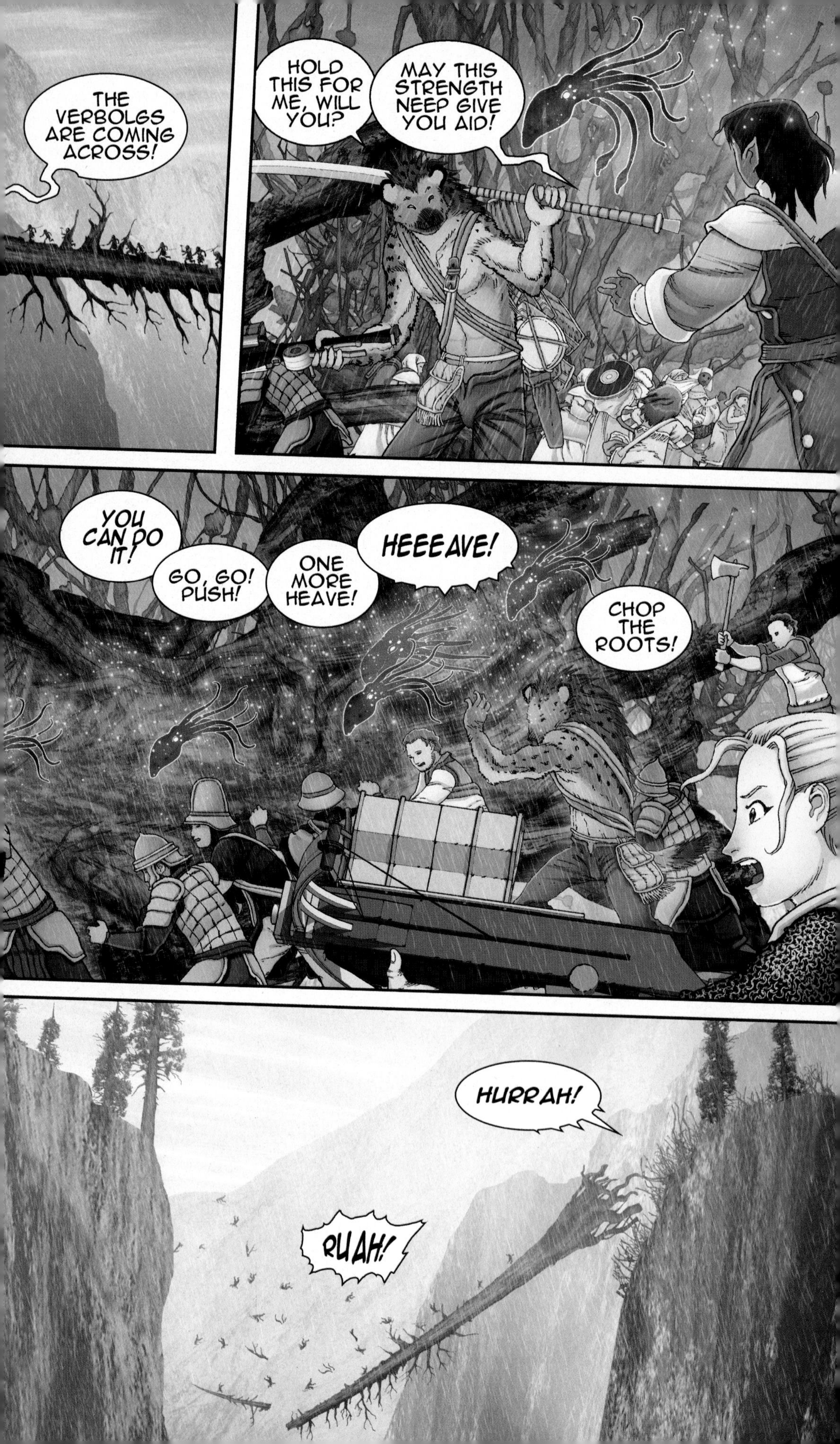
THE VERBOLGS ARE COMING ACROSS!
HOLD THIS FOR ME, WILL YOU?
MAY THIS STRENGTH NEEP GIVE YOU AID!
YOU CAN DO IT!
GO, GO! PUSH!
ONE MORE HEAVE!
HEEEAVE!
CHOP THE ROOTS!
HURRAH!
RUAH!

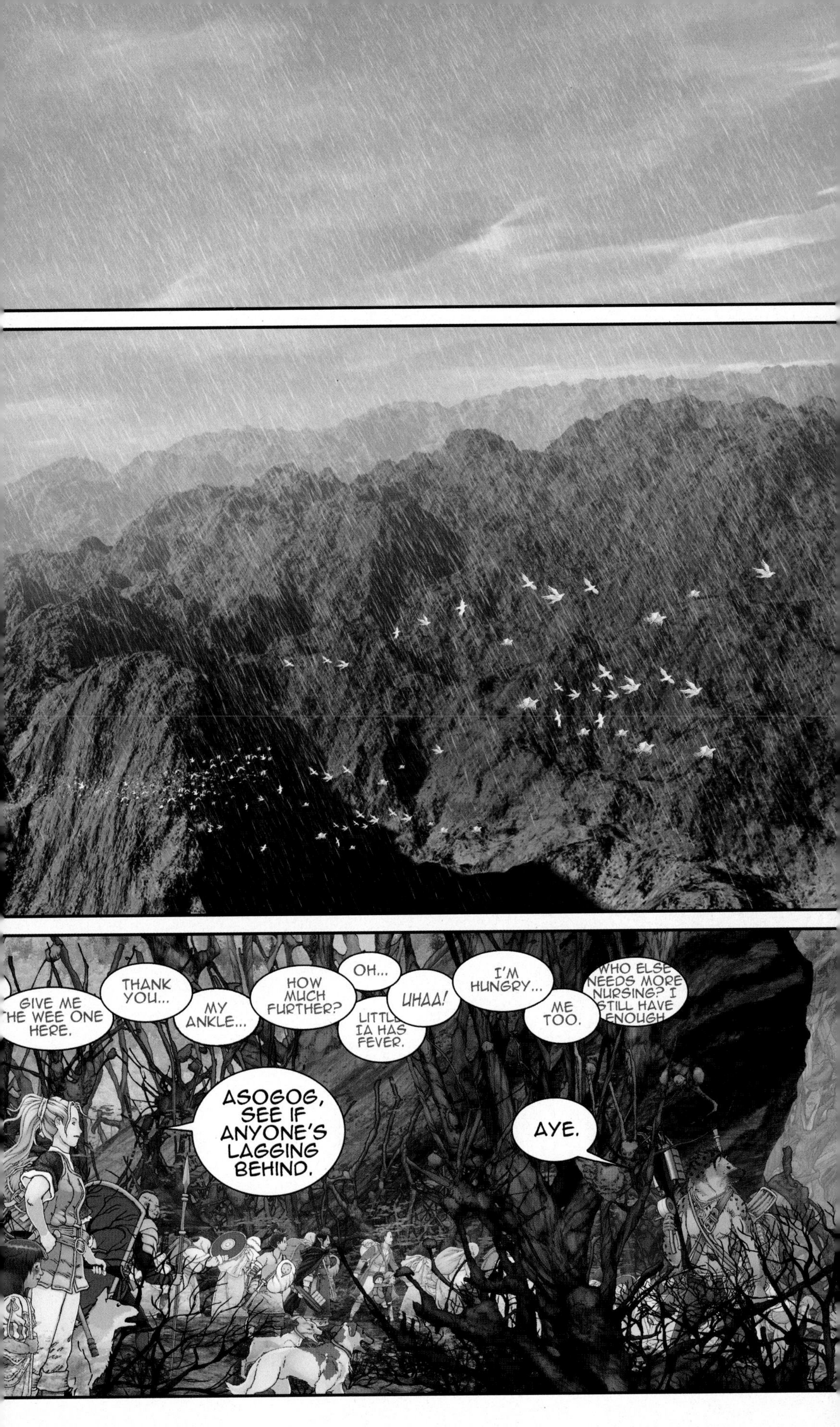
GIVE ME HE WEE ONE HERE.
THANK YOU...
MY ANKLE...
HOW MUCH FURTHER?
OH...
LITTLE IA HAS FEVER.
UHAA!
I'M HUNGRY...
ME TOO.
WHO ELSE NEEDS MORE NURSING? I TILL HAVE ENOUGH.
ASOGOG, SEE IF ANYONE'S LAGGING BEHIND.
AYE.

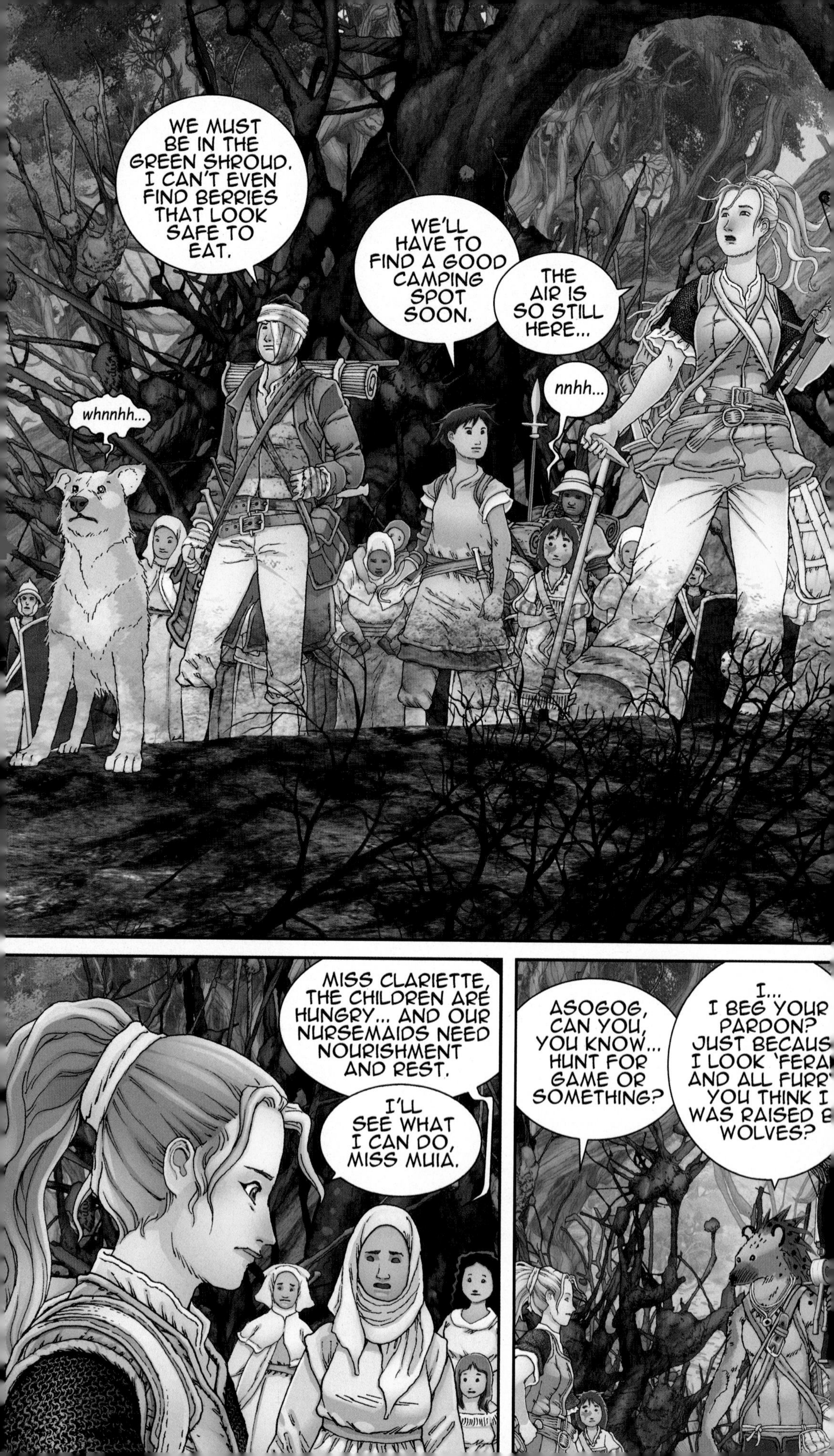
WE MUST BE IN THE GREEN SHROUD. I CAN'T EVEN FIND BERRIES THAT LOOK SAFE TO EAT.
WE'LL HAVE TO FIND A GOOD CAMPING SPOT SOON.
THE AIR IS SO STILL HERE...
whnnhh...
nnhh...
MISS CLARIETTE, THE CHILDREN ARE HUNGRY... AND OUR NURSEMAIDS NEED NOURISHMENT AND REST.
I'LL SEE WHAT I CAN DO, MISS MUIA.
ASOGOG, CAN YOU, YOU KNOW... HUNT FOR GAME OR SOMETHING?
I... I BEG YOUR PARDON? JUST BECAUS I LOOK 'FERA AND ALL FURR YOU THINK I WAS RAISED B WOLVES?

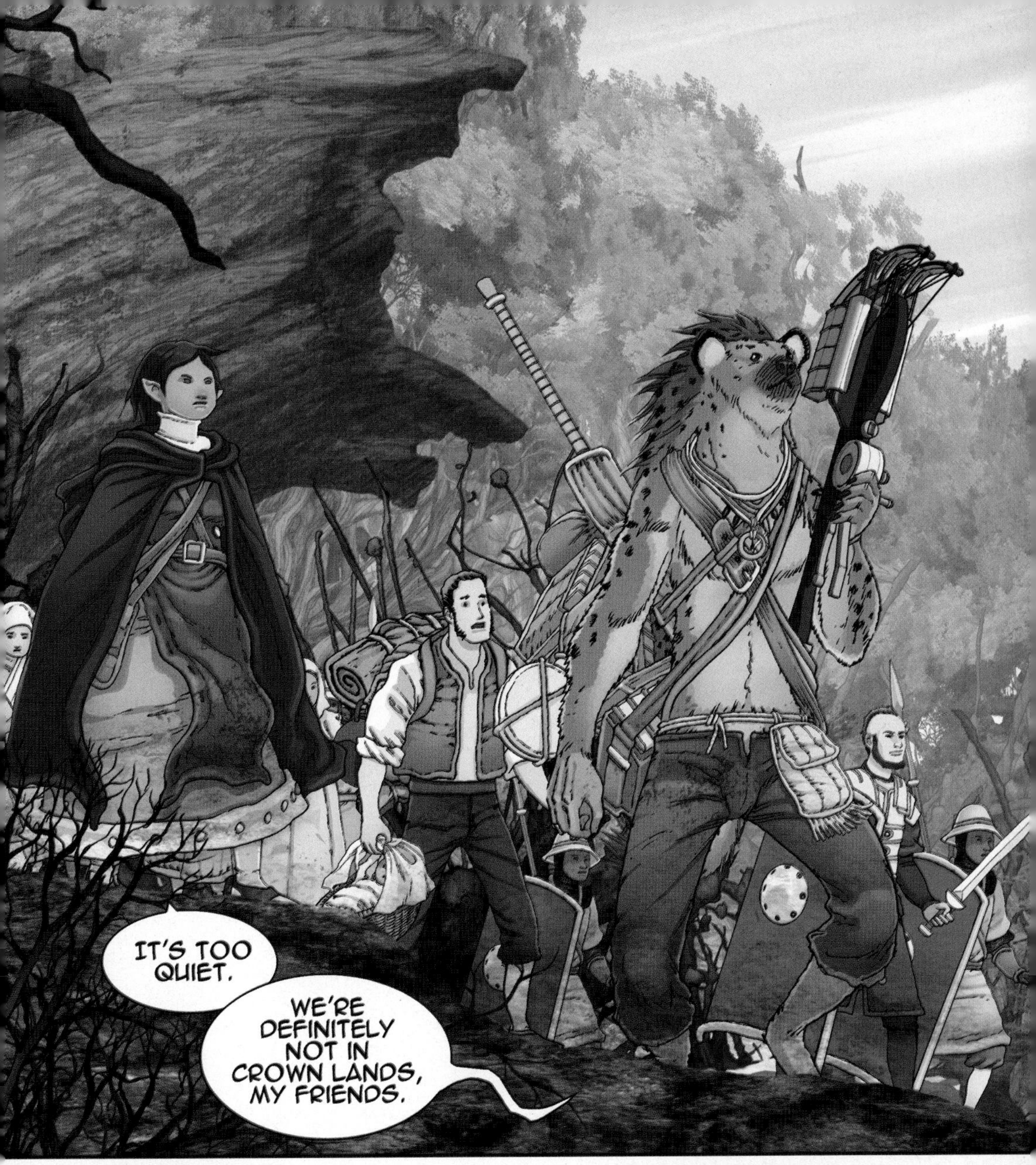
IT'S TOO QUIET.
WE'RE DEFINITELY NOT IN CROWN LANDS, MY FRIENDS.

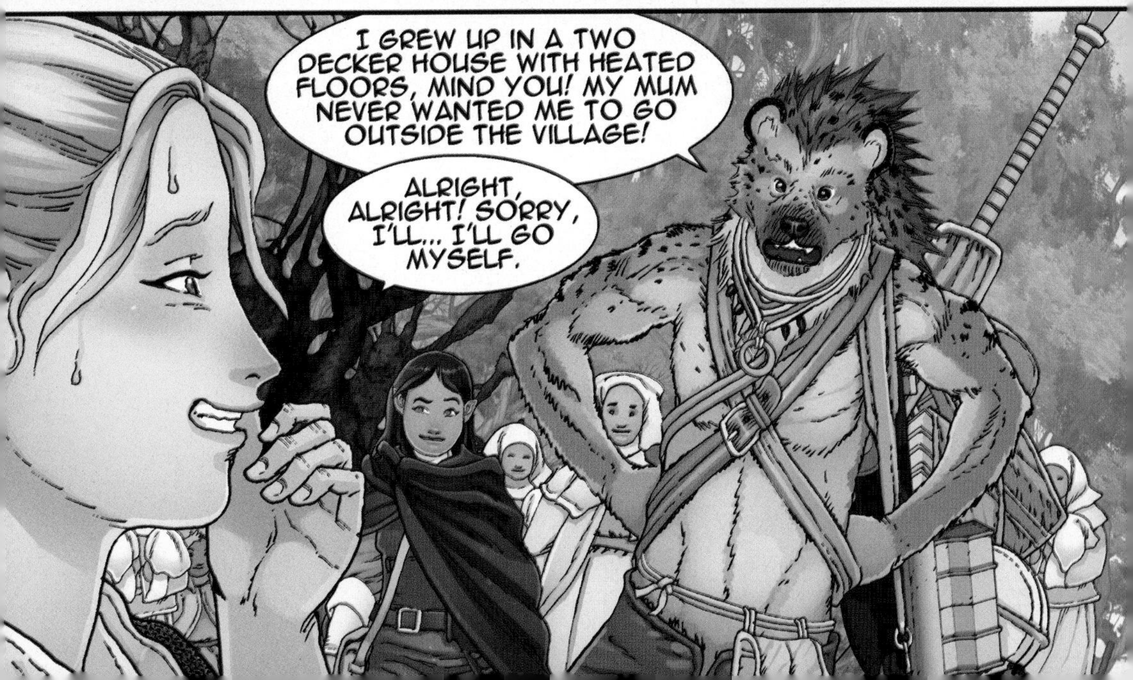
I GREW UP IN A TWO DECKER HOUSE WITH HEATED FLOORS, MIND YOU! MY MUM NEVER WANTED ME TO GO OUTSIDE THE VILLAGE!
ALRIGHT, ALRIGHT! SORRY, I'LL... I'LL GO MYSELF.

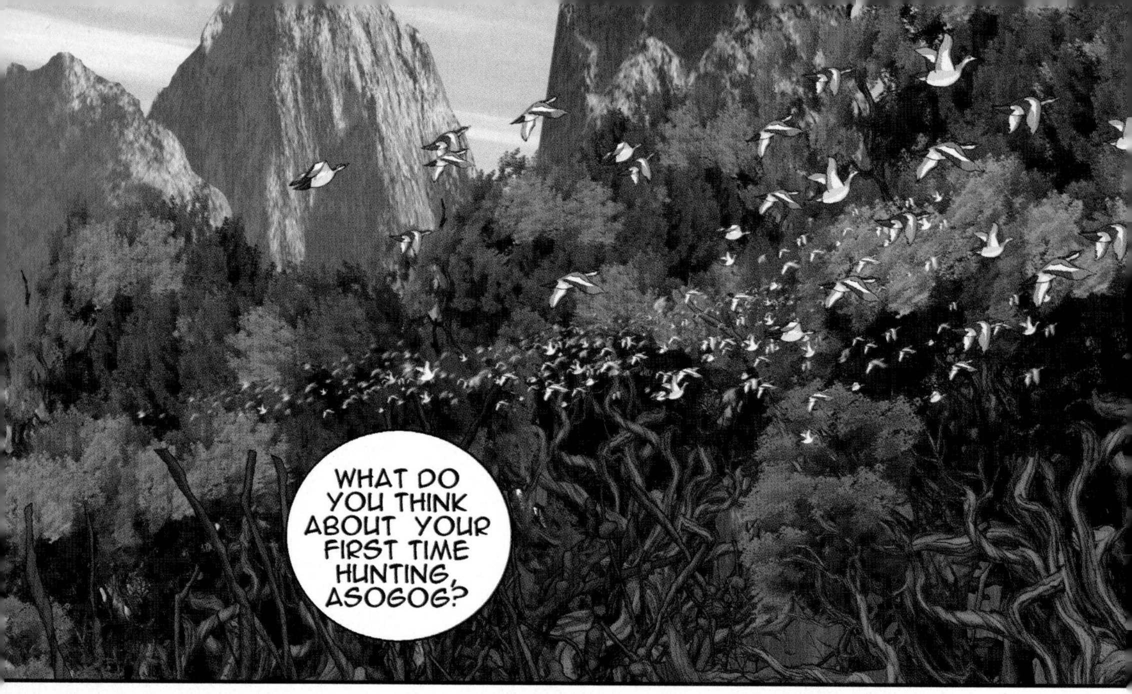
WHAT DO YOU THINK ABOUT YOUR FIRST TIME HUNTING, ASOGOG?

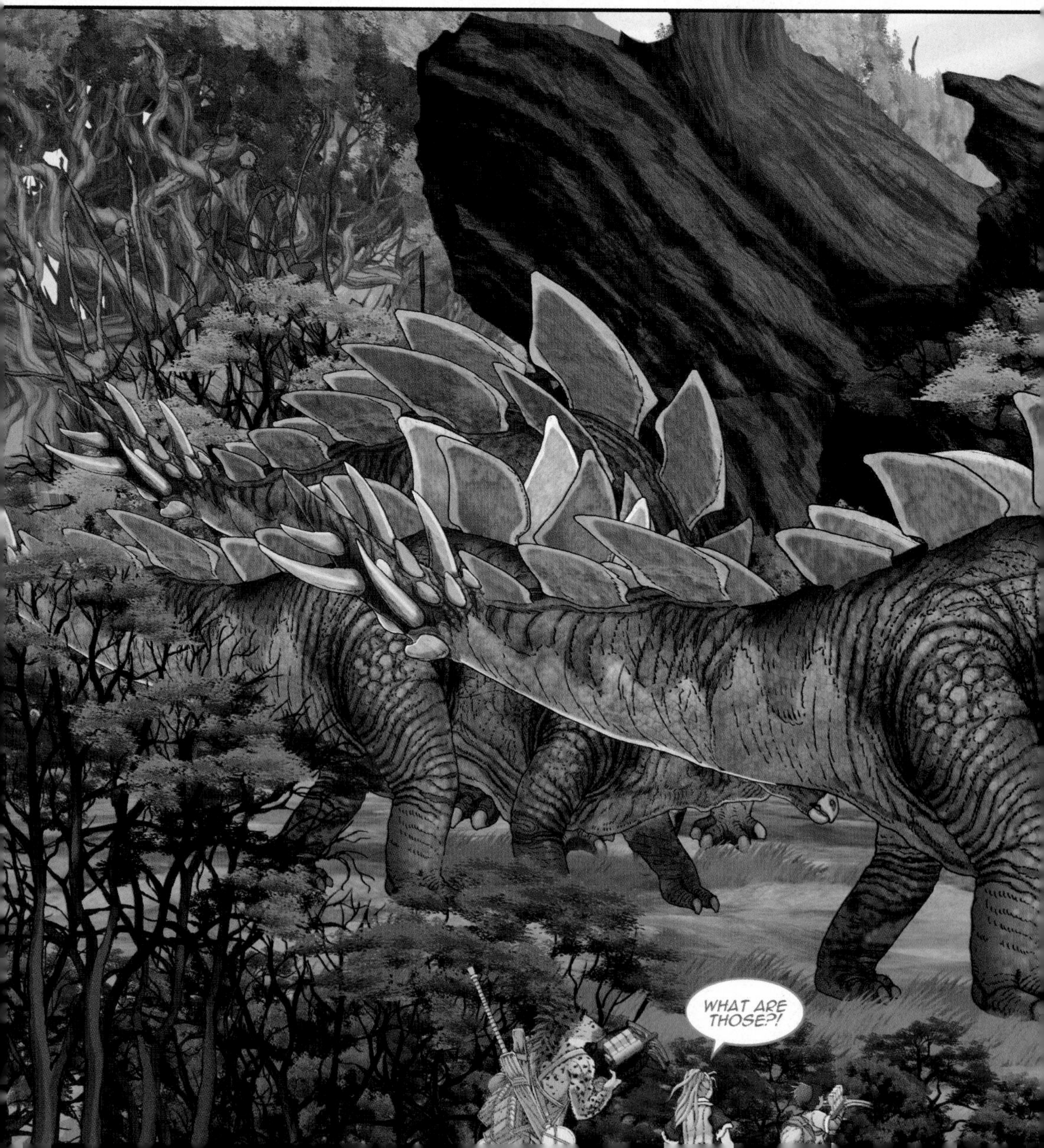
WHAT ARE THOSE?!

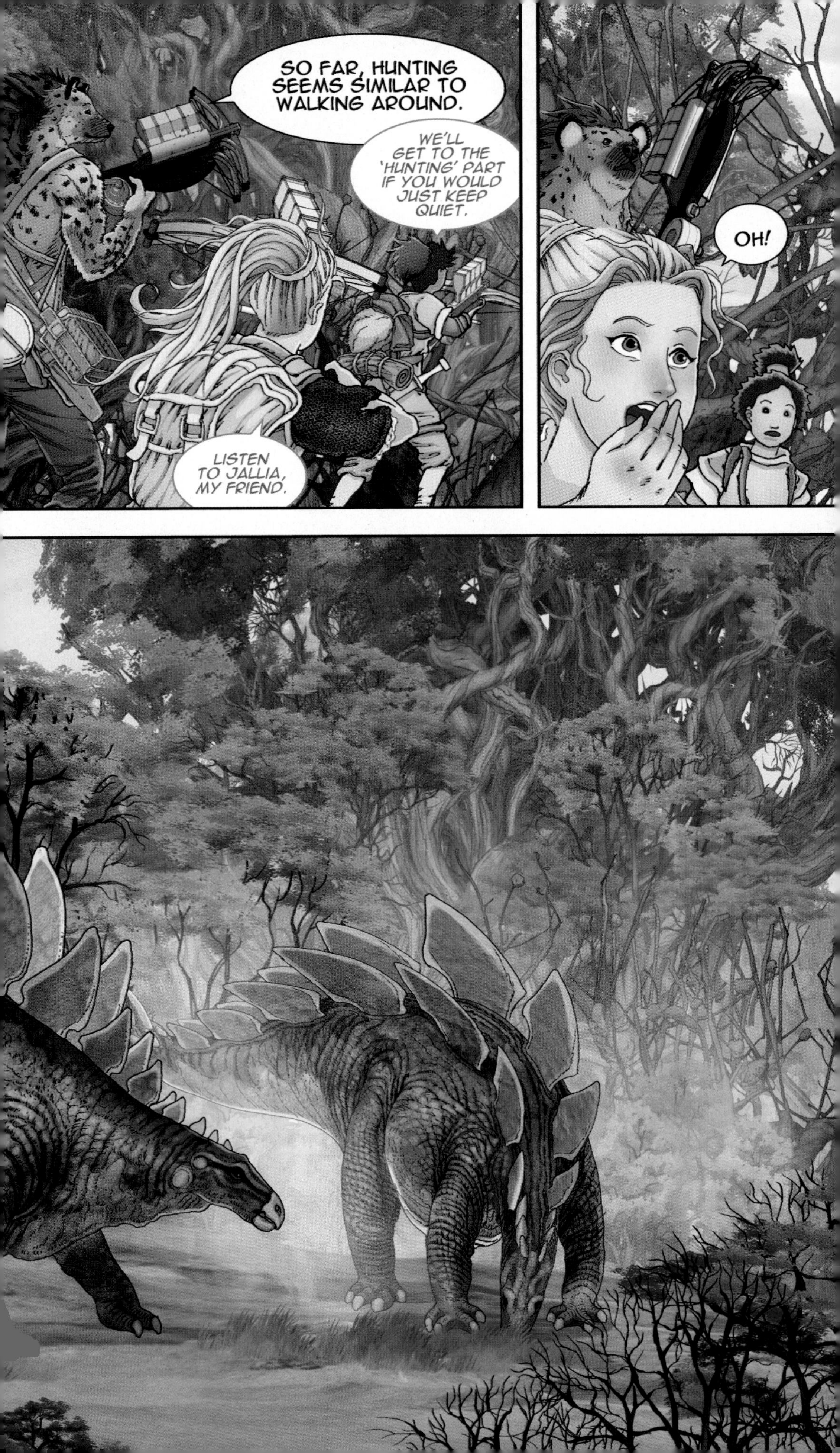
SO FAR, HUNTING SEEMS SIMILAR TO WALKING AROUND.
WE'LL GET TO THE 'HUNTING' PART IF YOU WOULD JUST KEEP QUIET.
LISTEN TO JALLIA, MY FRIEND.
OH!

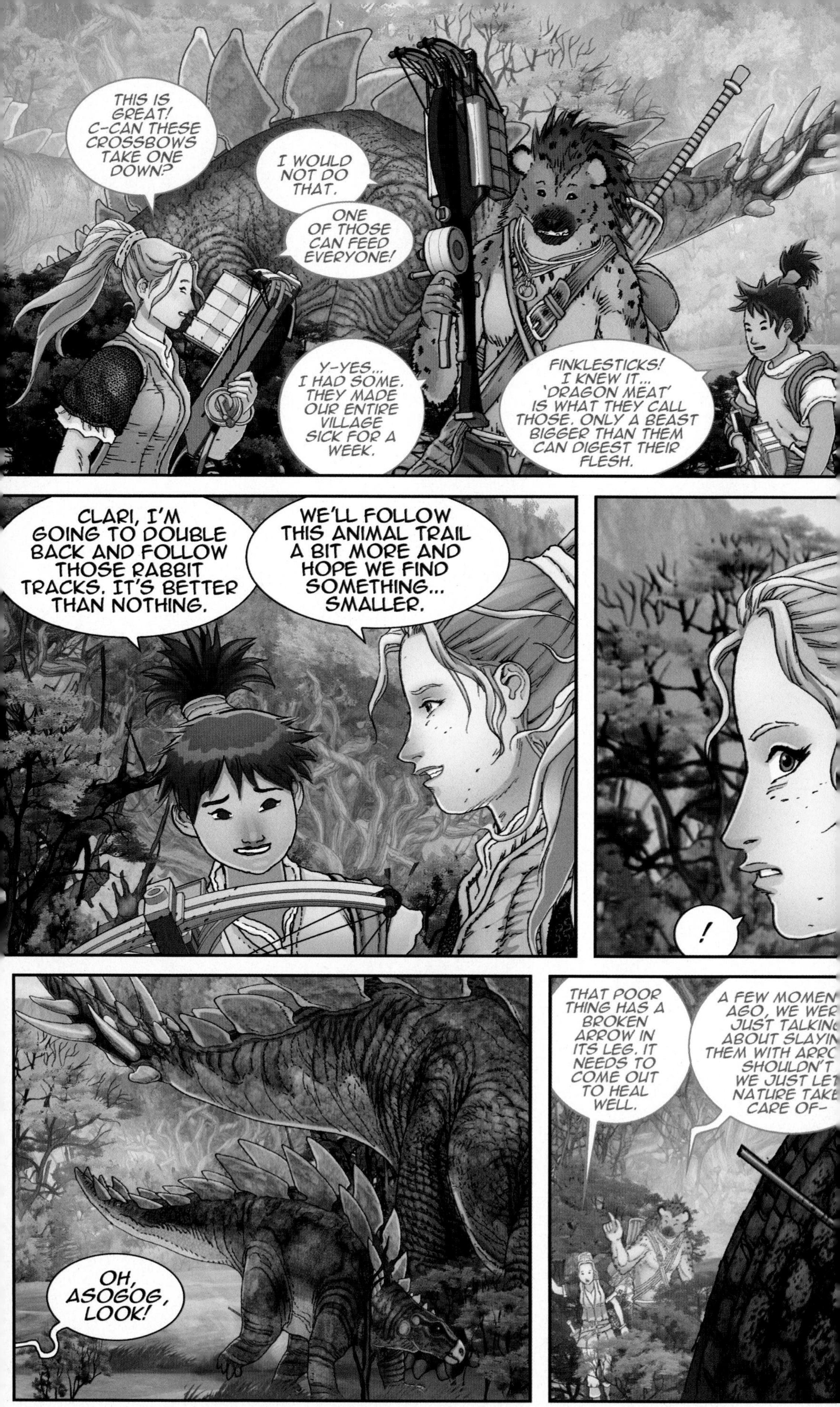
THIS IS GREAT! C-CAN THESE CROSSBOWS TAKE ONE DOWN?
I WOULD NOT DO THAT.
ONE OF THOSE CAN FEED EVERYONE!
Y-YES... I HAD SOME. THEY MADE OUR ENTIRE VILLAGE SICK FOR A WEEK.
FINKLESTICKS! I KNEW IT... 'DRAGON MEAT' IS WHAT THEY CALL THOSE. ONLY A BEAST BIGGER THAN THEM CAN DIGEST THEIR FLESH.
CLARI, I'M GOING TO DOUBLE BACK AND FOLLOW THOSE RABBIT TRACKS. IT'S BETTER THAN NOTHING.
WE'LL FOLLOW THIS ANIMAL TRAIL A BIT MORE AND HOPE WE FIND SOMETHING... SMALLER.
!
OH, ASOGOG, LOOK!
THAT POOR THING HAS A BROKEN ARROW IN ITS LEG. IT NEEDS TO COME OUT TO HEAL WELL.
A FEW MOMEN AGO, WE WER JUST TALKIN ABOUT SLAYIN THEM WITH ARRO SHOULDN'T WE JUST LET NATURE TAKE CARE OF-

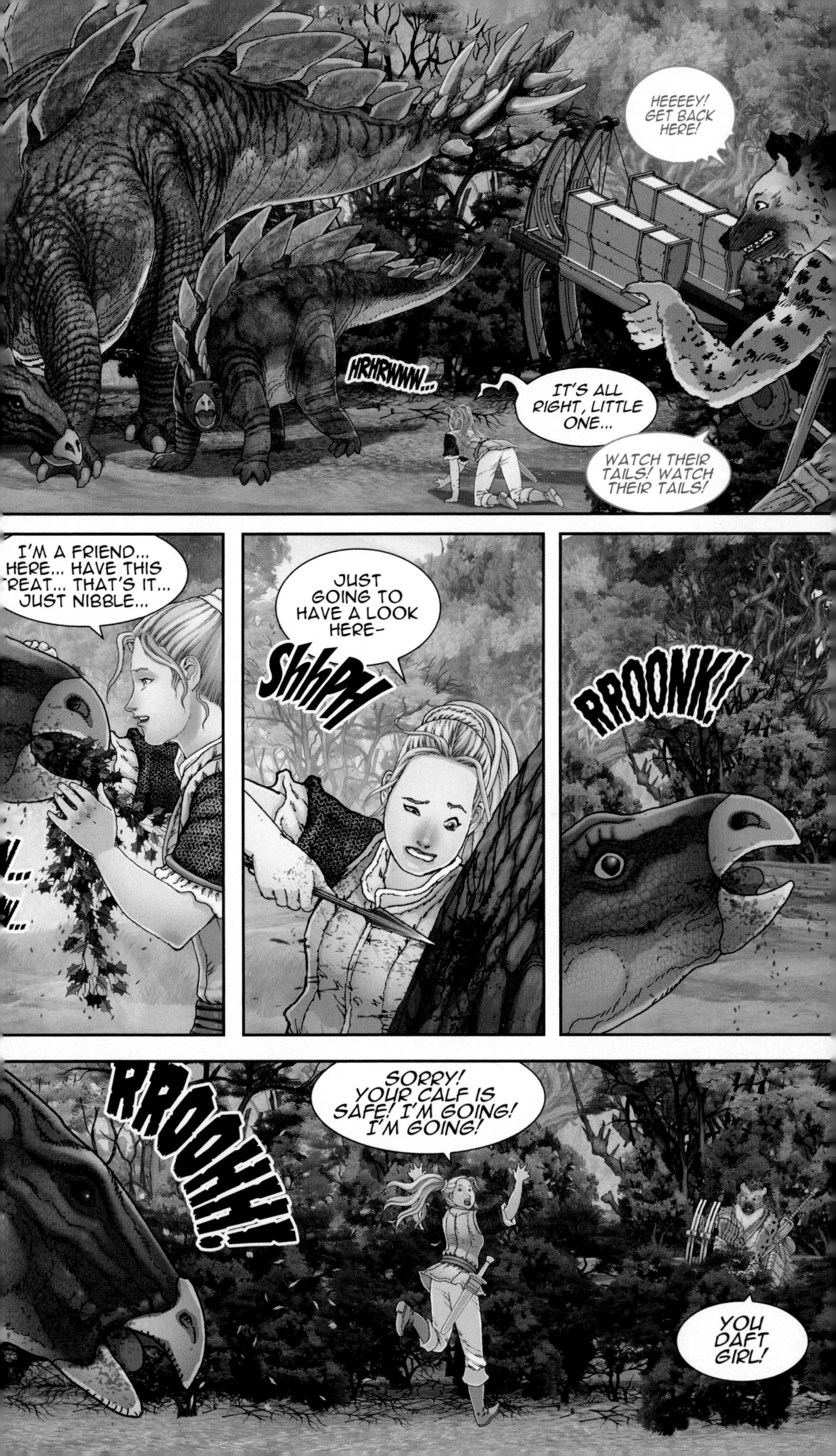
HEEEEY! GET BACK HERE!
HRHRWWW...
IT'S ALL RIGHT, LITTLE ONE...
WATCH THEIR TAILS! WATCH THEIR TAILS!
I'M A FRIEND... HERE... HAVE THIS TREAT... THAT'S IT... JUST NIBBLE...
JUST GOING TO HAVE A LOOK HERE-
ShhPH
RROONK!
RROOHH!
SORRY! YOUR CALF IS SAFE! I'M GOING! I'M GOING!
YOU DAFT GIRL!

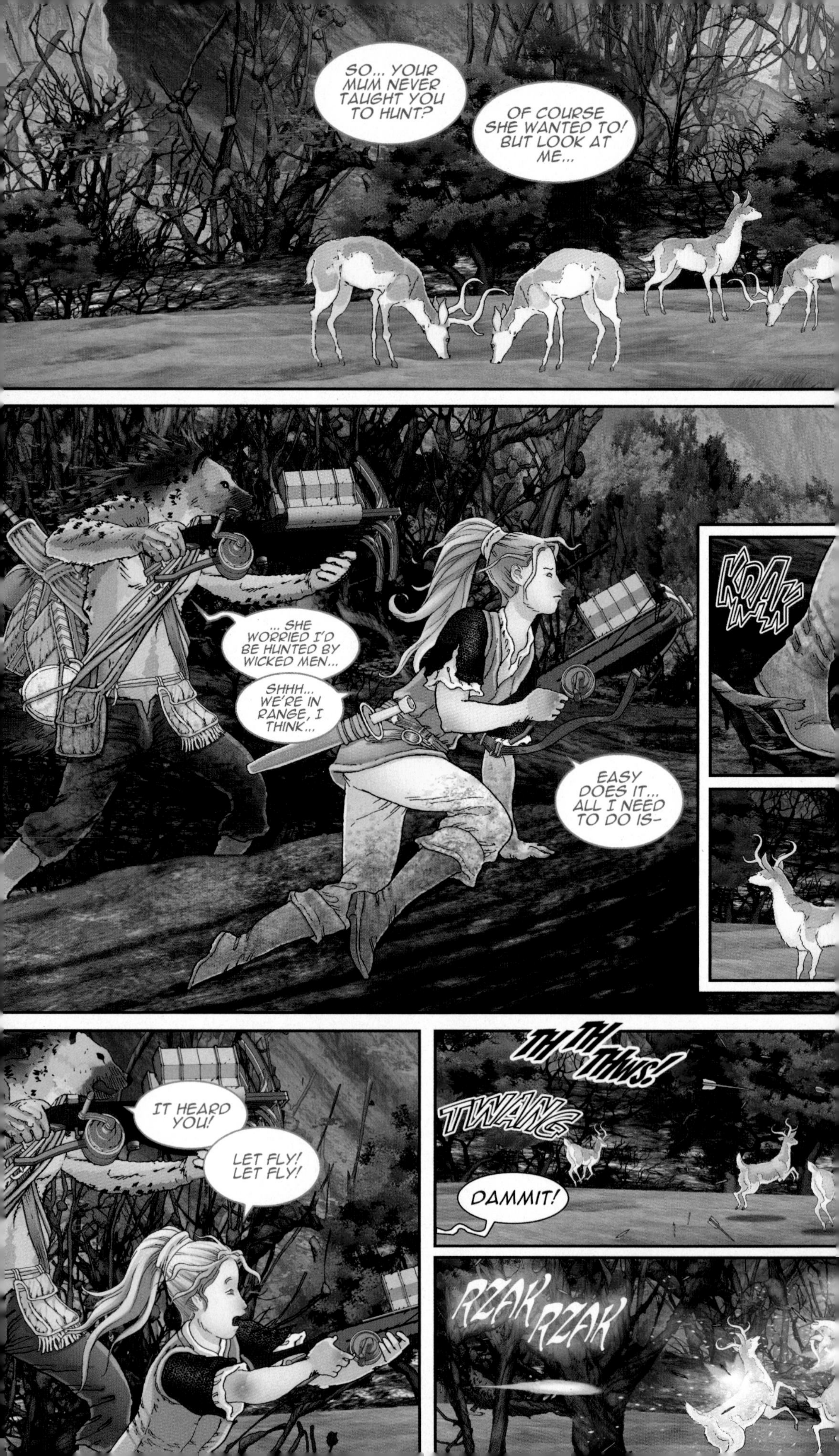
SO... YOUR MUM NEVER TAUGHT YOU TO HUNT?
OF COURSE SHE WANTED TO! BUT LOOK AT ME...
... SHE WORRIED I'D BE HUNTED BY WICKED MEN...
SHHH... WE'RE IN RANGE, I THINK...
EASY DOES IT... ALL I NEED TO DO IS-
KRAK
IT HEARD YOU!
LET FLY! LET FLY!
TH TH THWS!
TWANG
DAMMIT!
RZAK RZAK

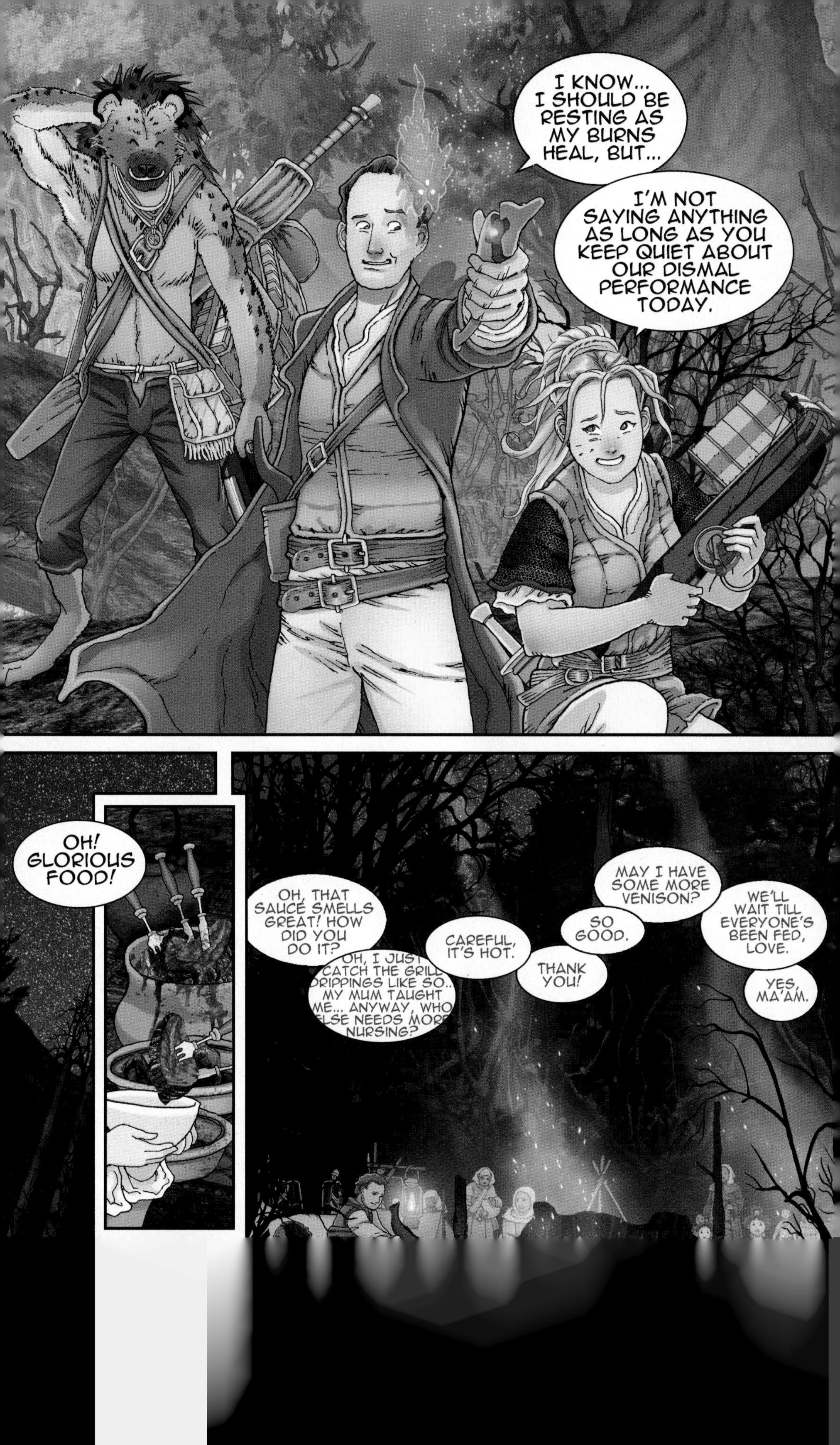
I KNOW... I SHOULD BE RESTING AS MY BURNS HEAL, BUT...
I'M NOT SAYING ANYTHING AS LONG AS YOU KEEP QUIET ABOUT OUR DISMAL PERFORMANCE TODAY.
OH! GLORIOUS FOOD!
OH, THAT SAUCE SMELLS GREAT! HOW DID YOU DO IT?
OH, I JUST CATCH THE GRILL DRIPPINGS LIKE SO.. MY MUM TAUGHT ME... ANYWAY, WHO ELSE NEEDS MORE NURSING?
CAREFUL, IT'S HOT.
THANK YOU!
SO GOOD.
MAY I HAVE SOME MORE VENISON?
WE'LL WAIT TILL EVERYONE'S BEEN FED, LOVE.
YES, MA'AM.

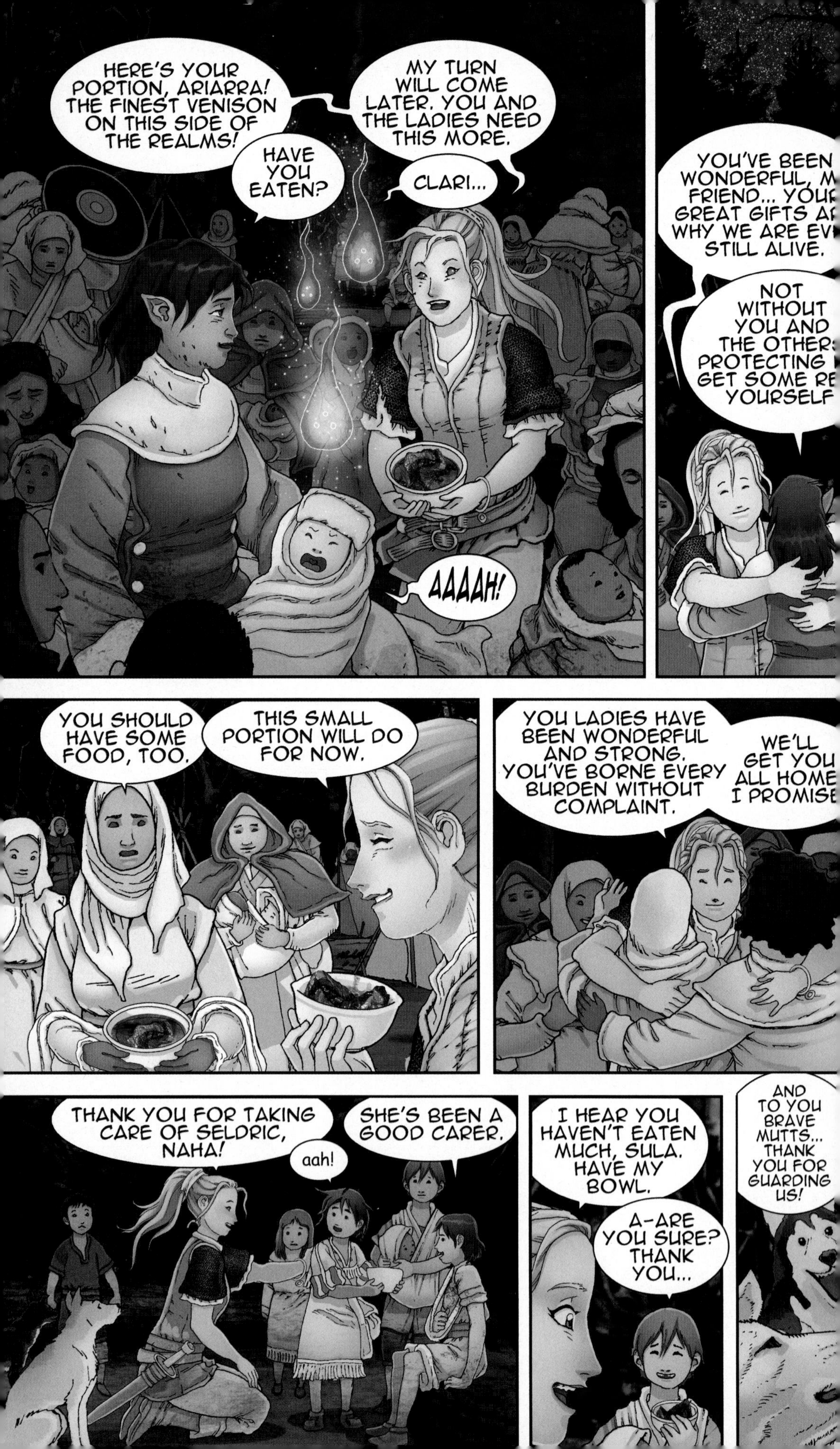
HERE'S YOUR PORTION, ARIARRA! THE FINEST VENISON ON THIS SIDE OF THE REALMS!
HAVE YOU EATEN?
MY TURN WILL COME LATER. YOU AND THE LADIES NEED THIS MORE.
CLARI...
AAAAH!
YOU'VE BEEN WONDERFUL, M FRIEND... YOUR GREAT GIFTS AR WHY WE ARE EV STILL ALIVE.
NOT WITHOUT YOU AND THE OTHERS PROTECTING GET SOME RE YOURSELF
YOU SHOULD HAVE SOME FOOD, TOO.
THIS SMALL PORTION WILL DO FOR NOW.
YOU LADIES HAVE BEEN WONDERFUL AND STRONG. YOU'VE BORNE EVERY BURDEN WITHOUT COMPLAINT.
WE'LL GET YOU ALL HOME I PROMISE
THANK YOU FOR TAKING CARE OF SELDRIC, NAHA!
aah!
SHE'S BEEN A GOOD CARER.
I HEAR YOU HAVEN'T EATEN MUCH, SULA. HAVE MY BOWL.
A-ARE YOU SURE? THANK YOU...
AND TO YOU BRAVE MUTTS... THANK YOU FOR GUARDING US!

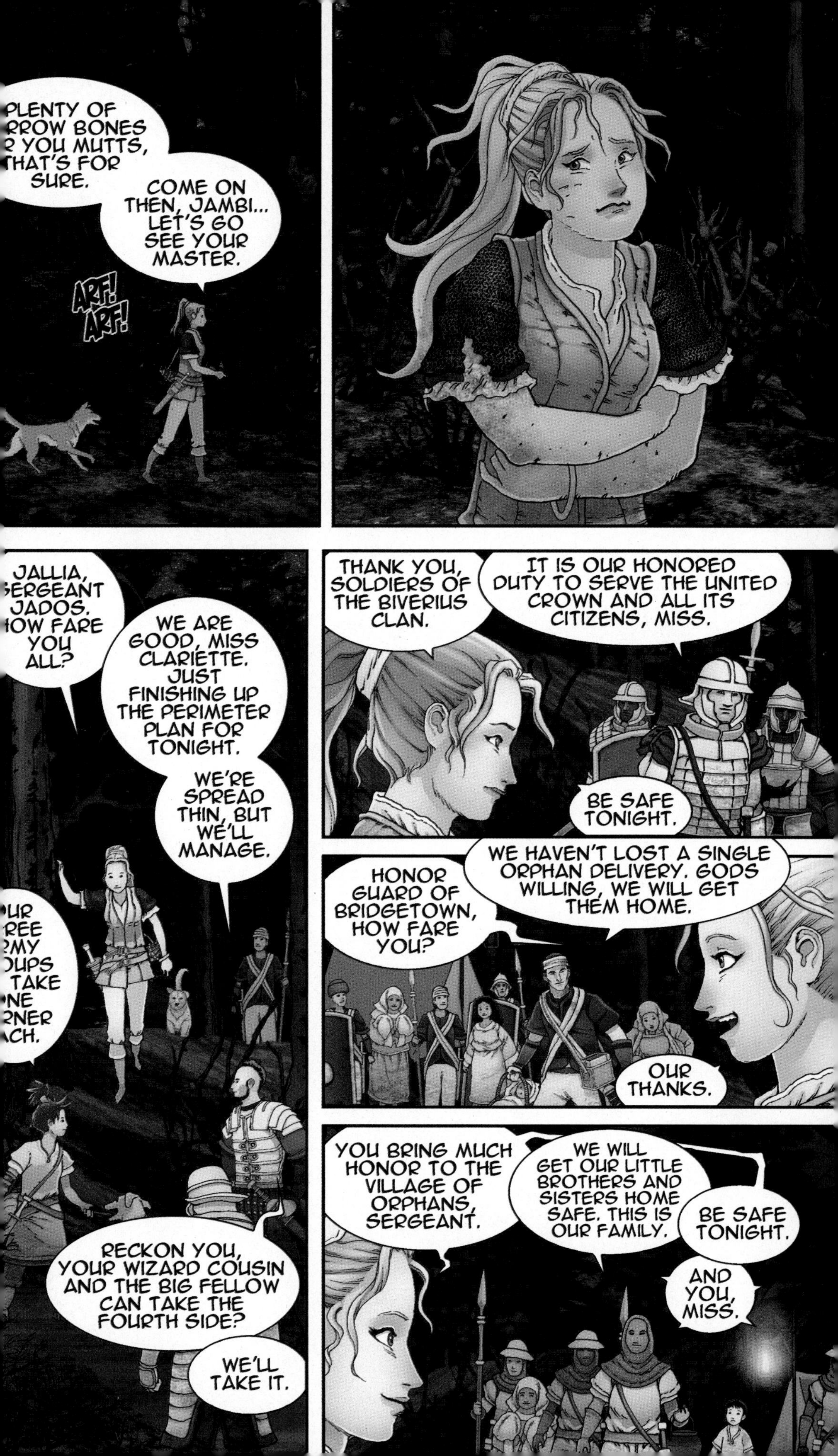
PLENTY OF
RROW BONES
R YOU MUTTS,
THAT'S FOR
SURE.
COME ON THEN, JAMBI... LET'S GO SEE YOUR MASTER.
ARF! ARF!
JALLIA, SERGEANT JADOS. HOW FARE YOU ALL?
WE ARE GOOD, MISS CLARIETTE. JUST FINISHING UP THE PERIMETER PLAN FOR TONIGHT.
WE'RE SPREAD THIN, BUT WE'LL MANAGE.
UR
REE
RMY
OUPS
TAKE
NE
RNER
CH.
RECKON YOU, YOUR WIZARD COUSIN AND THE BIG FELLOW CAN TAKE THE FOURTH SIDE?
WE'LL TAKE IT.
THANK YOU, SOLDIERS OF THE BIVERIUS CLAN.
IT IS OUR HONORED DUTY TO SERVE THE UNITED CROWN AND ALL ITS CITIZENS, MISS.
BE SAFE TONIGHT.
HONOR GUARD OF BRIDGETOWN, HOW FARE YOU?
WE HAVEN'T LOST A SINGLE ORPHAN DELIVERY. GODS WILLING, WE WILL GET THEM HOME.
OUR THANKS.
YOU BRING MUCH HONOR TO THE VILLAGE OF ORPHANS, SERGEANT.
WE WILL GET OUR LITTLE BROTHERS AND SISTERS HOME SAFE. THIS IS OUR FAMILY.
BE SAFE TONIGHT.
AND YOU, MISS.

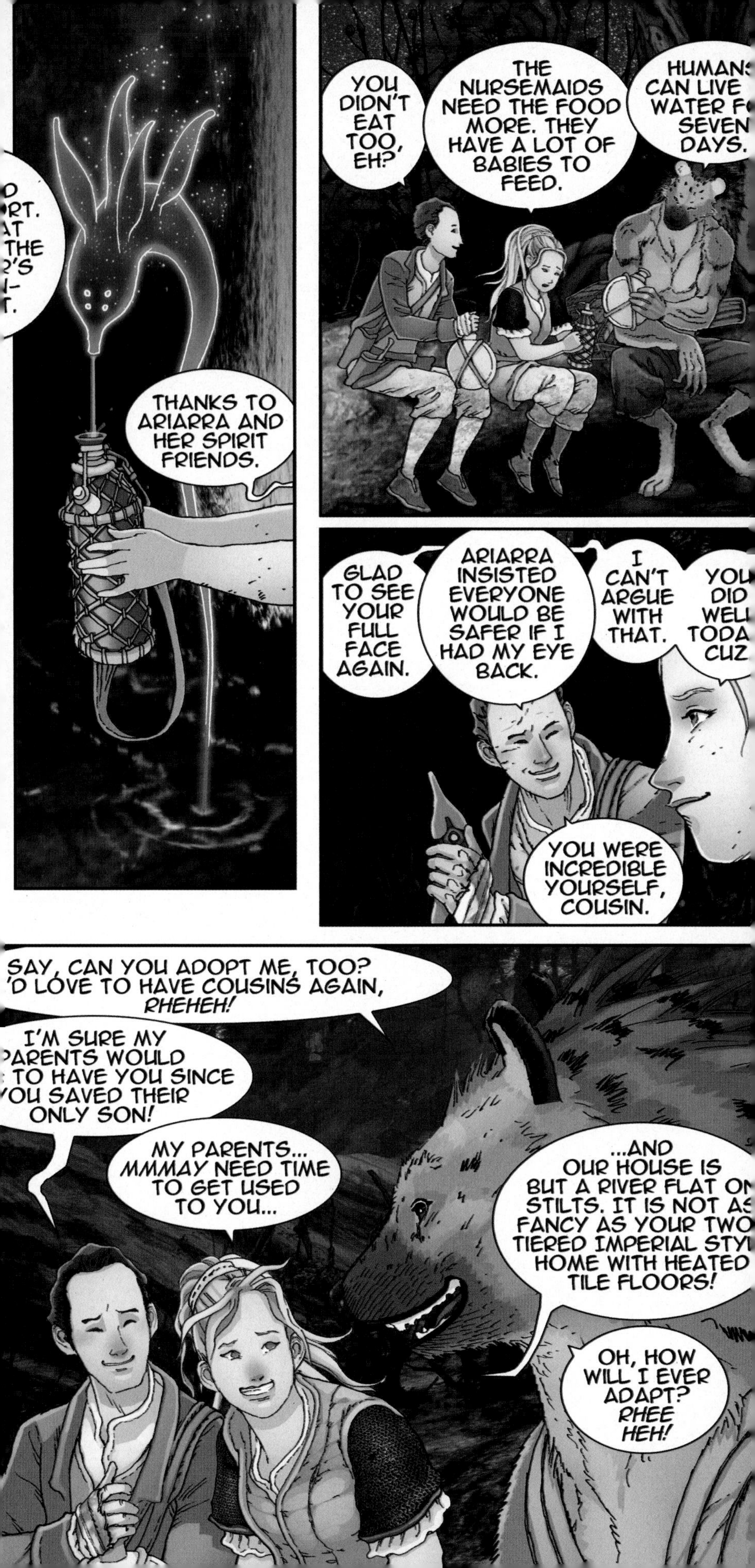
THANKS TO ARIARRA AND HER SPIRIT FRIENDS.
YOU DIDN'T EAT TOO, EH?
THE NURSEMAIDS NEED THE FOOD MORE. THEY HAVE A LOT OF BABIES TO FEED.
HUMANS CAN LIVE WATER F SEVEN DAYS.
GLAD TO SEE YOUR FULL FACE AGAIN.
ARIARRA INSISTED EVERYONE WOULD BE SAFER IF I HAD MY EYE BACK.
I CAN'T ARGUE WITH THAT.
YOU DID WELL TODA CUZ
YOU WERE INCREDIBLE YOURSELF, COUSIN.
SAY, CAN YOU ADOPT ME, TOO? 'D LOVE TO HAVE COUSINS AGAIN, RHEHEH!
I'M SURE MY PARENTS WOULD TO HAVE YOU SINCE YOU SAVED THEIR ONLY SON!
MY PARENTS... MMMAY NEED TIME TO GET USED TO YOU...
...AND OUR HOUSE IS BUT A RIVER FLAT ON STILTS. IT IS NOT AS FANCY AS YOUR TWO TIERED IMPERIAL STY HOME WITH HEATED TILE FLOORS!
OH, HOW WILL I EVER ADAPT? RHEE HEH!

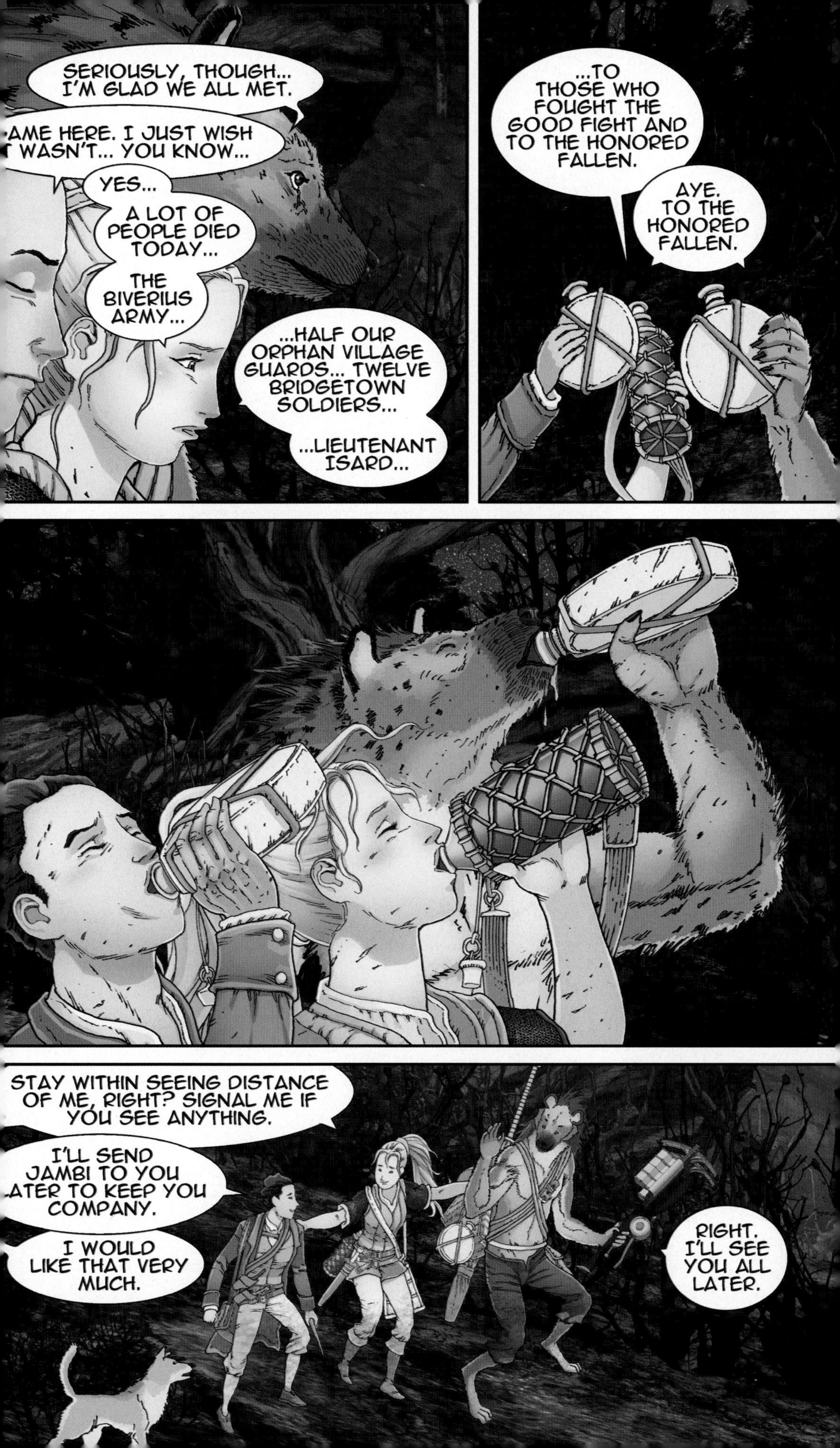
SERIOUSLY, THOUGH... I'M GLAD WE ALL MET.
AME HERE. I JUST WISH T WASN'T... YOU KNOW...
YES...
A LOT OF PEOPLE DIED TODAY...
THE BIVERIUS ARMY...
...HALF OUR ORPHAN VILLAGE GUARDS... TWELVE BRIDGETOWN SOLDIERS...
...LIEUTENANT ISARD...
...TO THOSE WHO FOUGHT THE GOOD FIGHT AND TO THE HONORED FALLEN.
AYE. TO THE HONORED FALLEN.
STAY WITHIN SEEING DISTANCE OF ME, RIGHT? SIGNAL ME IF YOU SEE ANYTHING.
I'LL SEND JAMBI TO YOU LATER TO KEEP YOU COMPANY.
I WOULD LIKE THAT VERY MUCH.
RIGHT. I'LL SEE YOU ALL LATER.

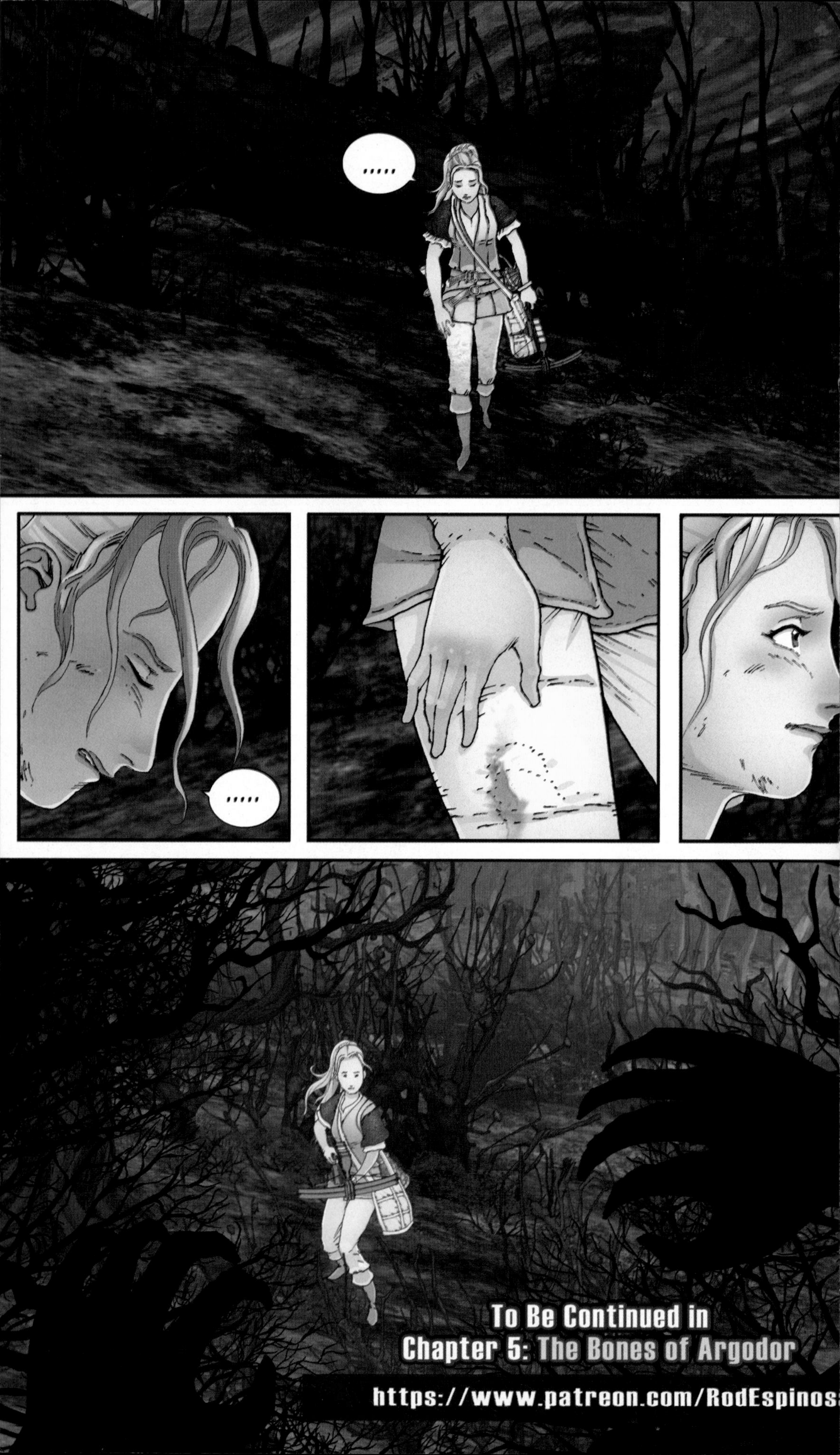
.....
.....
To Be Continued in
Chapter 5: The Bones of Argodor
https://www.patreon.com/RodEspinos

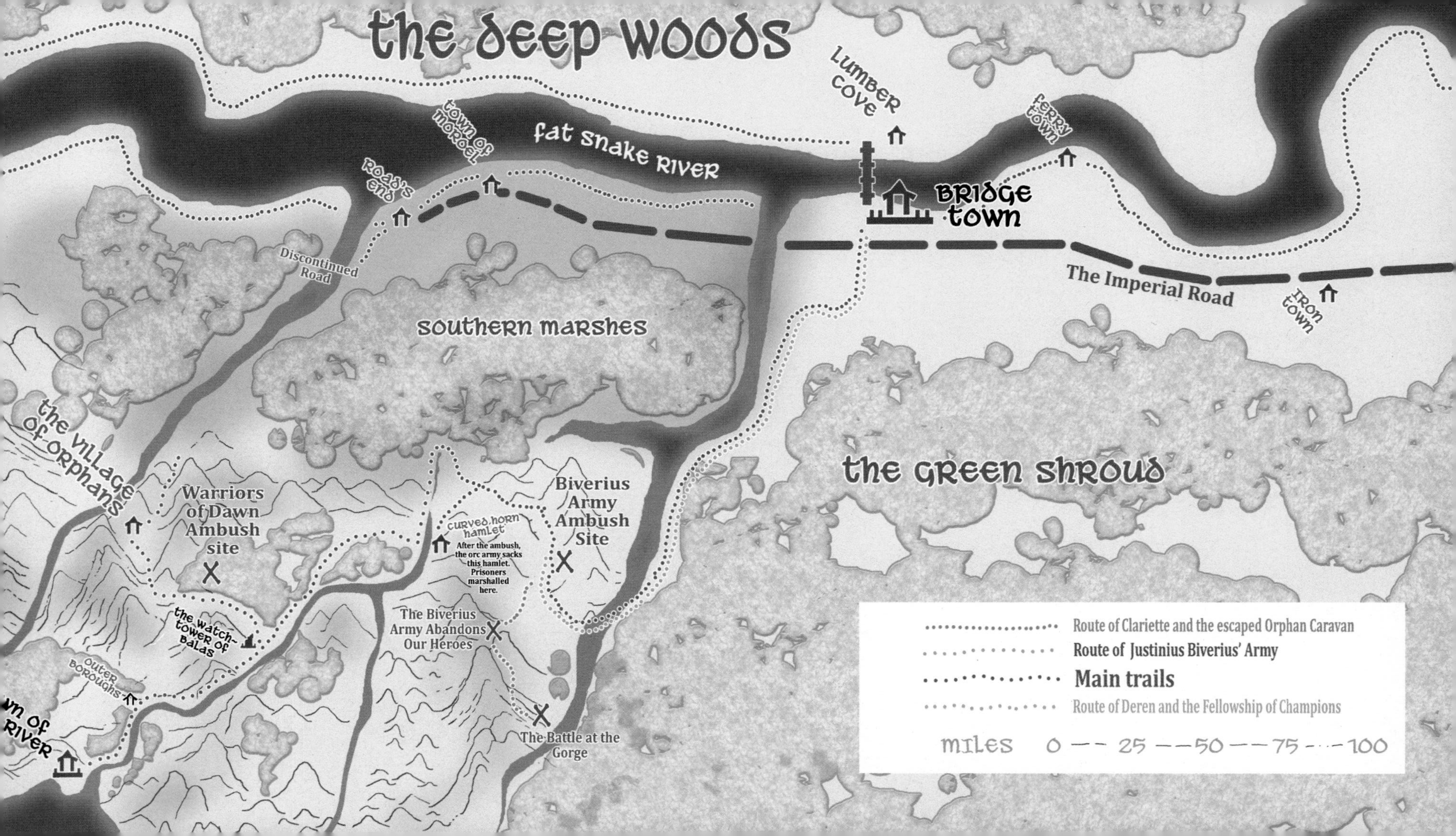
the deep woods
Lumber Cove
ferry town
fat snake River
town of Moroel
Road's end
Bridge town
The Imperial Road
Iron town
Discontinued Road
southern marshes
the green shroud
the village of orphans
Warriors of Dawn Ambush site
curved horn hamlet
After the ambush, the orc army sacks this hamlet. Prisoners marshalled here.
Biverius Army Ambush Site
The Biverius Army Abandons Our Heroes
the watch-tower of Balas
outer boroughs
The Battle at the Gorge
Route of Clariette and the escaped Orphan Caravan
Route of Justinius Biverius' Army
Main trails
Route of Deren and the Fellowship of Champions
miles 0 25 50 75 100

Clariette de Artegnean

Jolfe Endarion
(related on the Mhou side)

Jambi

Ariarra Popplevensie

Asogog
(former captive
of the Circus of
Wild Wonders)

Deren Muml

Justinius
Biverius

Herminia
Biverius

Maati

Jallia

Centurion Isard

Naha

Nheri

Tyrene

Aporto the blacksmith

Seldric

Fisley

Tuug

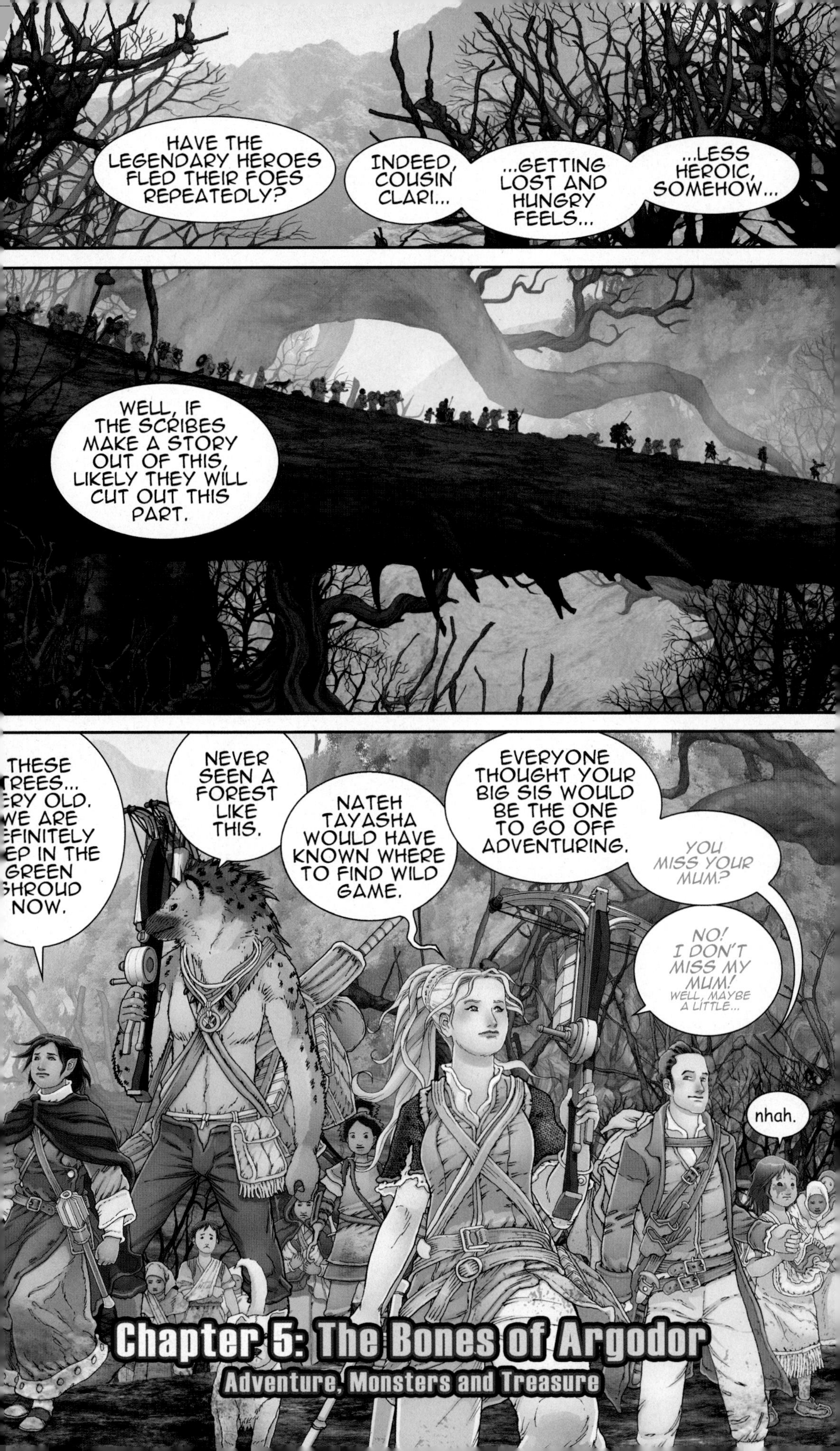
HAVE THE LEGENDARY HEROES FLED THEIR FOES REPEATEDLY?
INDEED, COUSIN CLARI...
...GETTING LOST AND HUNGRY FEELS...
...LESS HEROIC, SOMEHOW...
WELL, IF THE SCRIBES MAKE A STORY OUT OF THIS, LIKELY THEY WILL CUT OUT THIS PART.
THESE REES... ERY OLD. WE ARE EFINITELY EP IN THE GREEN HROUD NOW.
NEVER SEEN A FOREST LIKE THIS.
NATEH TAYASHA WOULD HAVE KNOWN WHERE TO FIND WILD GAME.
EVERYONE THOUGHT YOUR BIG SIS WOULD BE THE ONE TO GO OFF ADVENTURING.
YOU MISS YOUR MUM?
NO! I DON'T MISS MY MUM! WELL, MAYBE A LITTLE...
nhah.
Chapter 5: The Bones of Argodor
Adventure, Monsters and Treasure

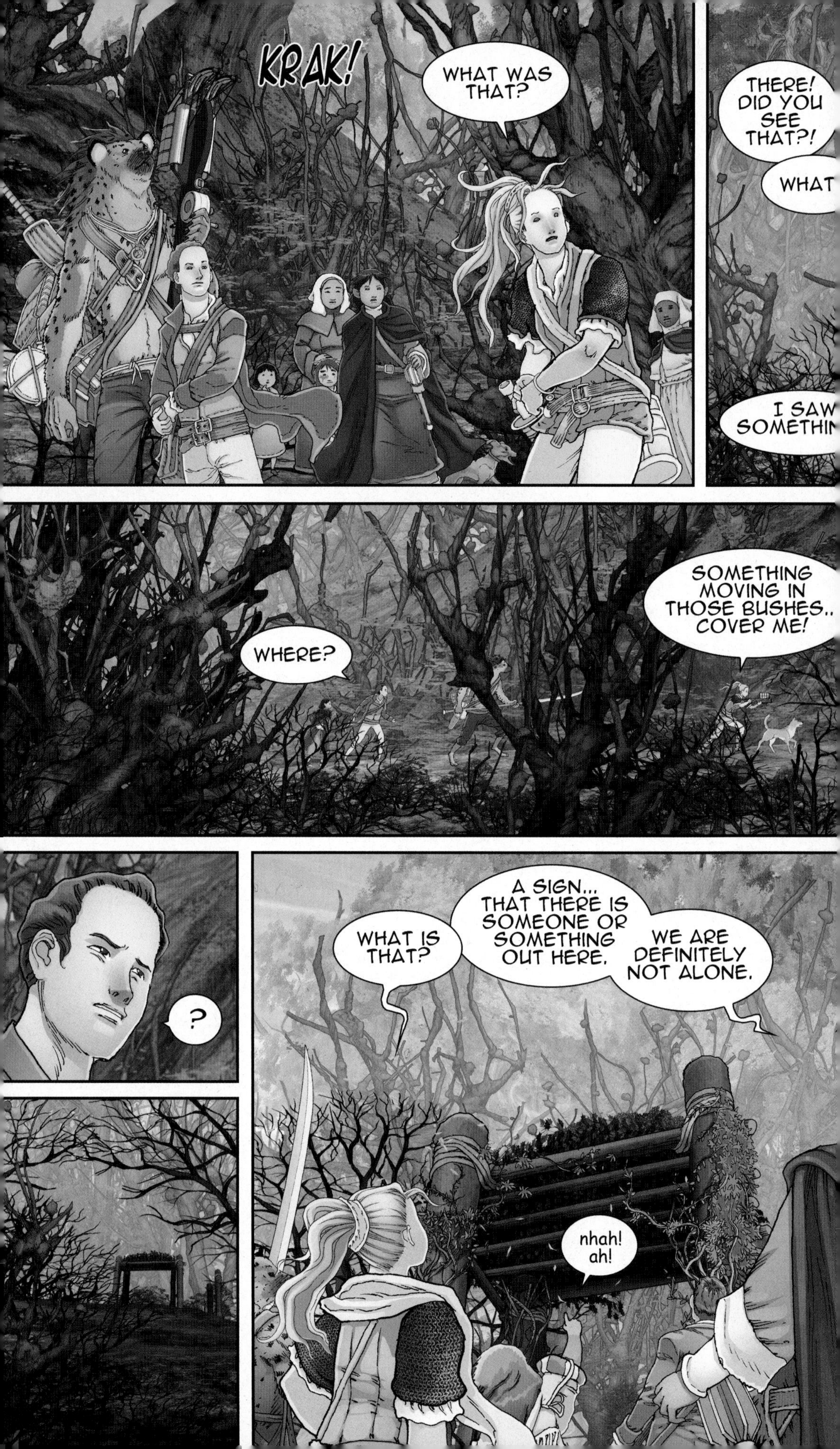
KRAK!
WHAT WAS THAT?
THERE! DID YOU SEE THAT?!
WHAT
I SAW SOMETHIN
WHERE?
SOMETHING MOVING IN THOSE BUSHES.. COVER ME!
?
WHAT IS THAT?
A SIGN... THAT THERE IS SOMEONE OR SOMETHING OUT HERE.
WE ARE DEFINITELY NOT ALONE.
nhah! ah!

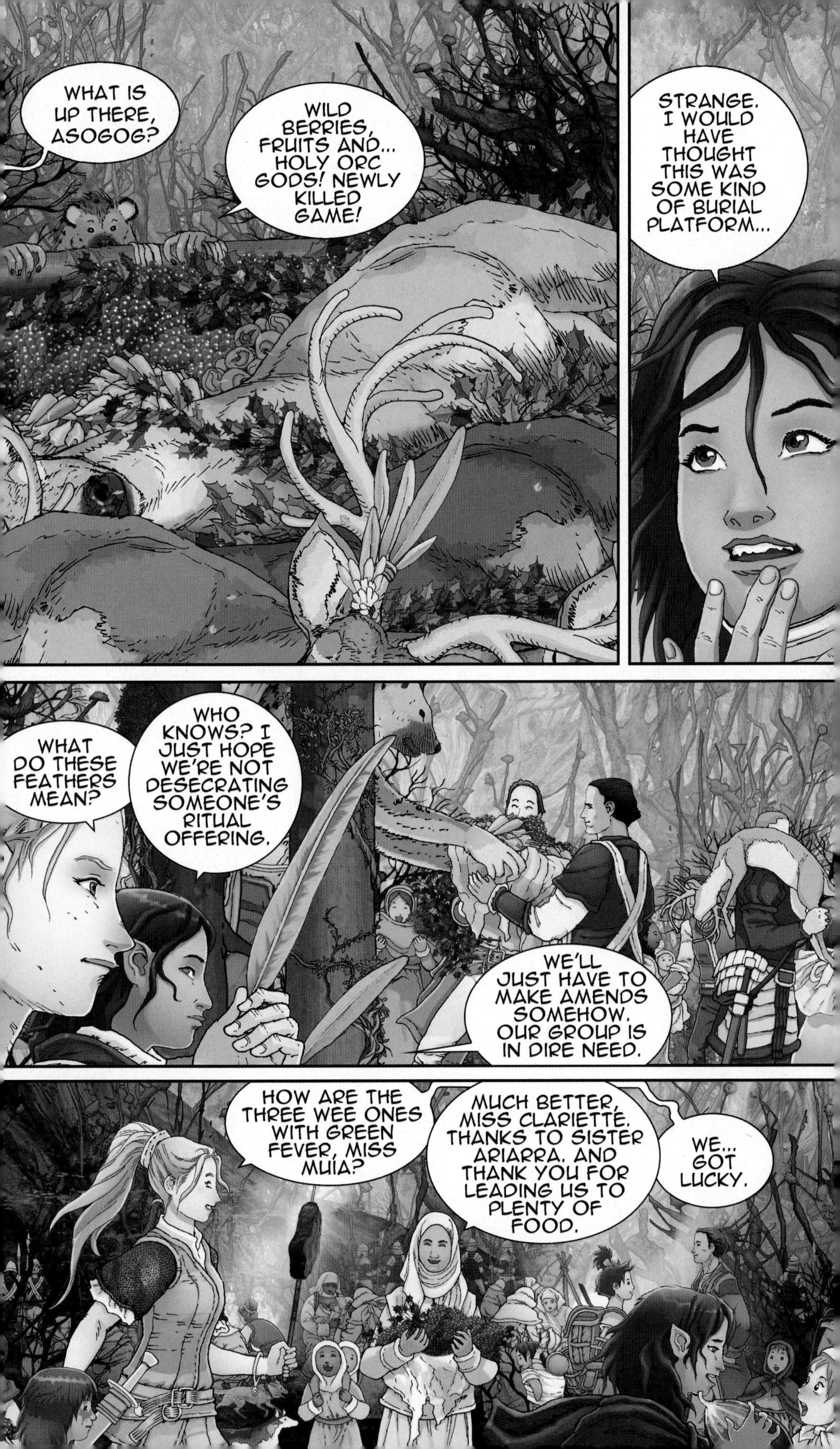
WHAT IS UP THERE, ASOGOG?
WILD BERRIES, FRUITS AND... HOLY ORC GODS! NEWLY KILLED GAME!
STRANGE. I WOULD HAVE THOUGHT THIS WAS SOME KIND OF BURIAL PLATFORM...
WHAT DO THESE FEATHERS MEAN?
WHO KNOWS? I JUST HOPE WE'RE NOT DESECRATING SOMEONE'S RITUAL OFFERING.
WE'LL JUST HAVE TO MAKE AMENDS SOMEHOW. OUR GROUP IS IN DIRE NEED.
HOW ARE THE THREE WEE ONES WITH GREEN FEVER, MISS MUIA?
MUCH BETTER, MISS CLARIETTE. THANKS TO SISTER ARIARRA. AND THANK YOU FOR LEADING US TO PLENTY OF FOOD.
WE... GOT LUCKY.

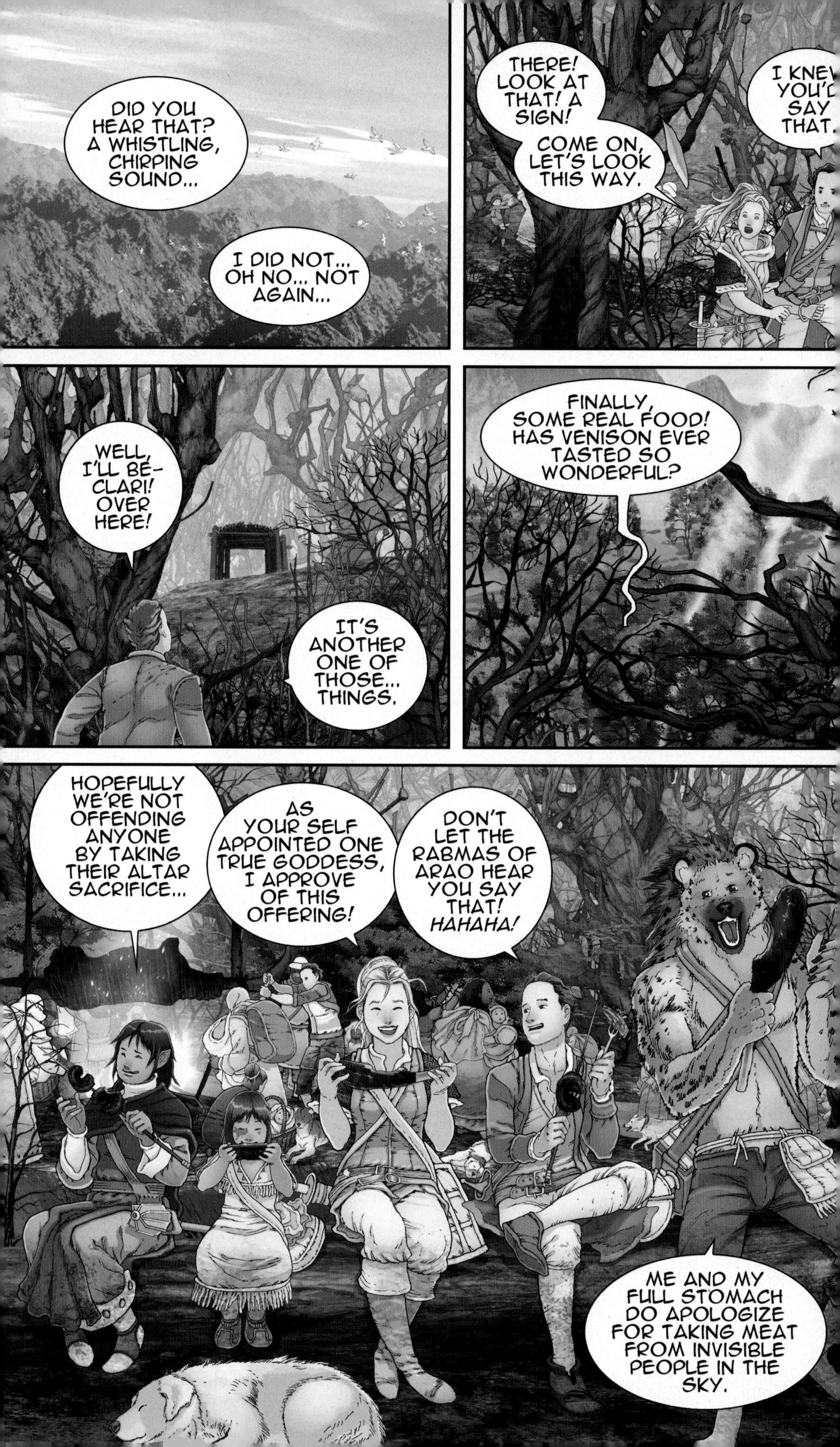
DID YOU HEAR THAT? A WHISTLING, CHIRPING SOUND...
I DID NOT... OH NO... NOT AGAIN...
THERE! LOOK AT THAT! A SIGN!
COME ON, LET'S LOOK THIS WAY.
I KNEW YOU'D SAY THAT.
WELL, I'LL BE- CLARI! OVER HERE!
IT'S ANOTHER ONE OF THOSE... THINGS.
FINALLY, SOME REAL FOOD! HAS VENISON EVER TASTED SO WONDERFUL?
HOPEFULLY WE'RE NOT OFFENDING ANYONE BY TAKING THEIR ALTAR SACRIFICE...
AS YOUR SELF APPOINTED ONE TRUE GODDESS, I APPROVE OF THIS OFFERING!
DON'T LET THE RABMAS OF ARAO HEAR YOU SAY THAT! *HAHAHA!*
ME AND MY FULL STOMACH DO APOLOGIZE FOR TAKING MEAT FROM INVISIBLE PEOPLE IN THE SKY.

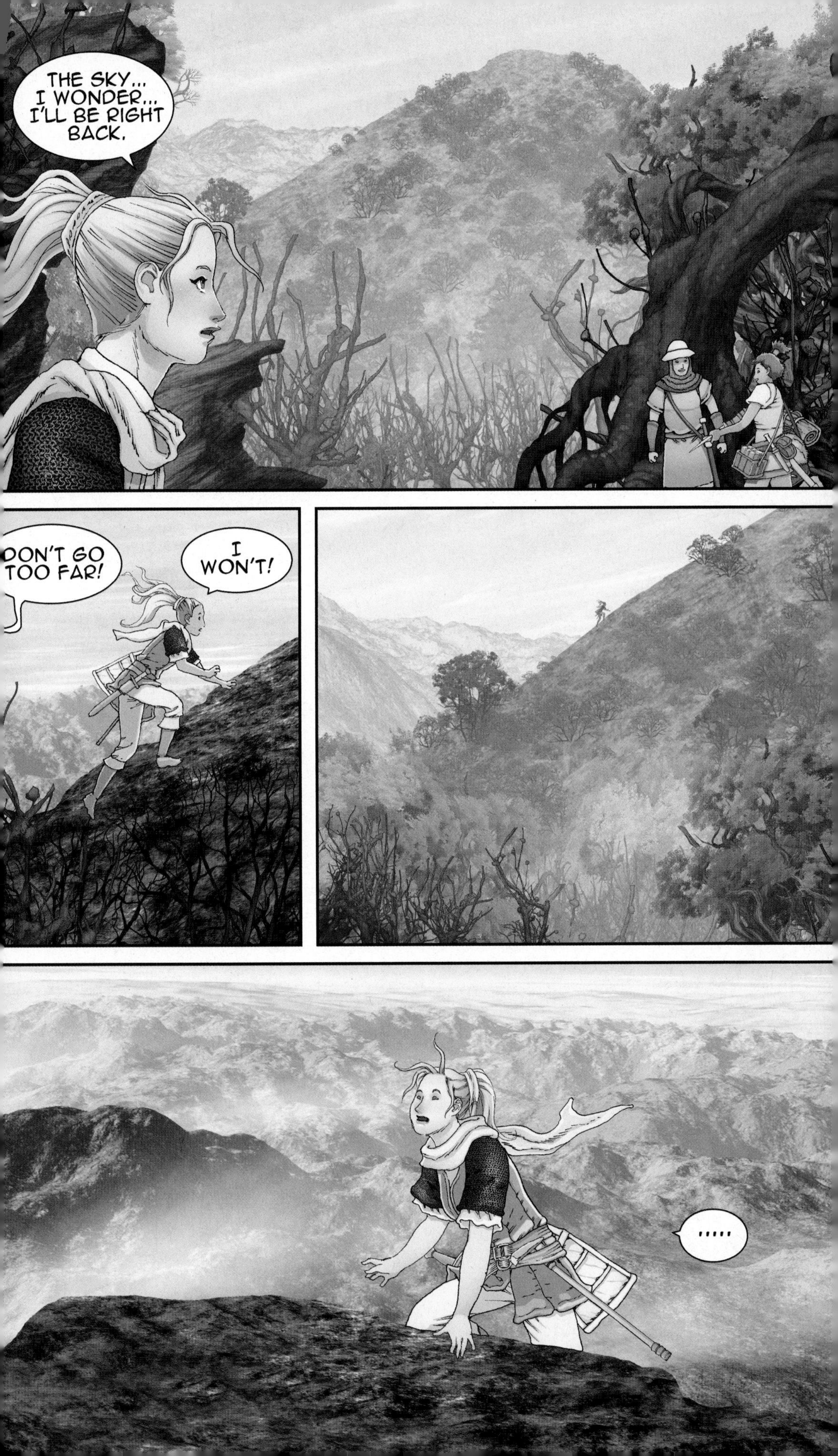
THE SKY... I WONDER... I'LL BE RIGHT BACK.
DON'T GO TOO FAR!
I WON'T!
.....

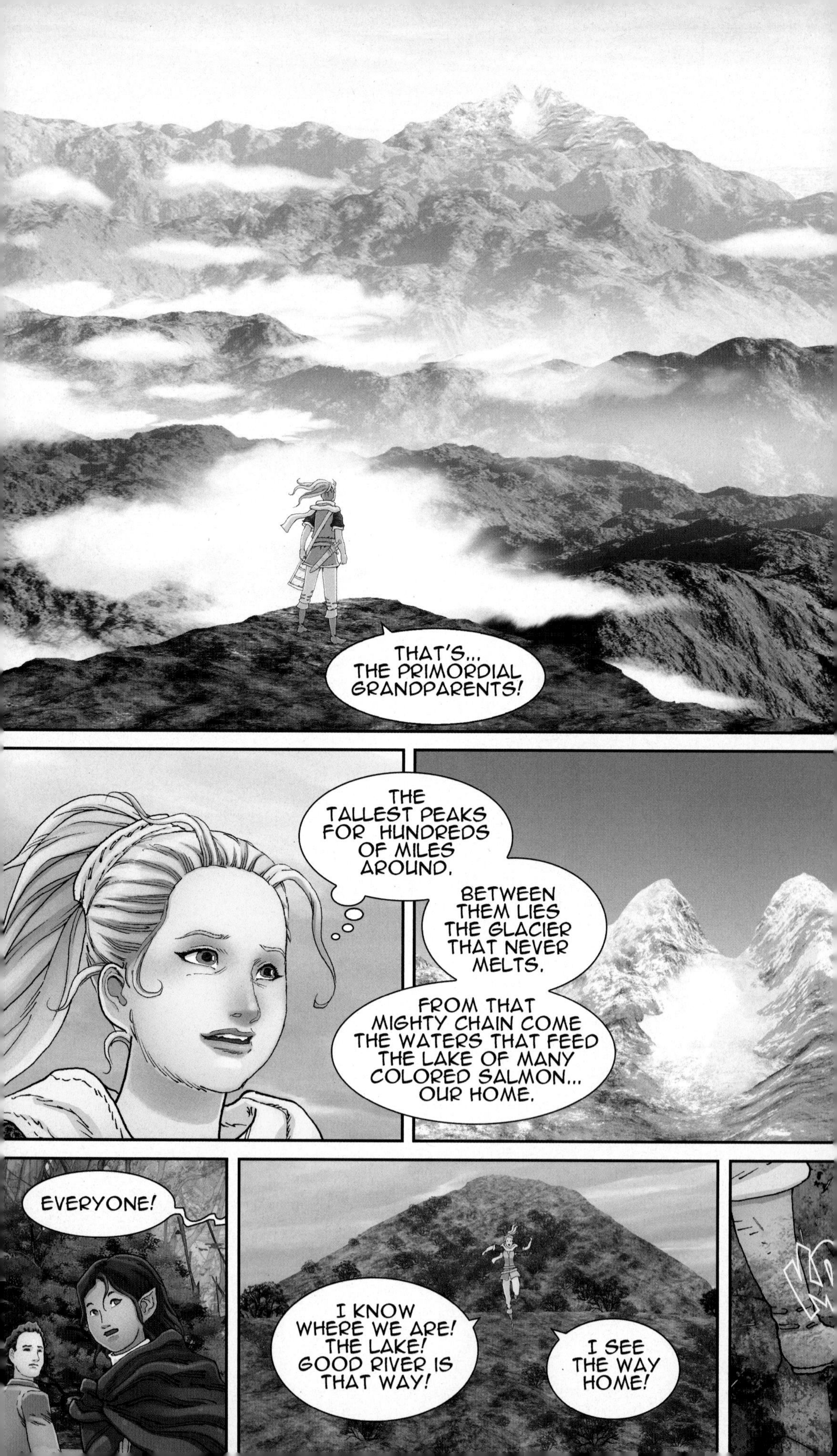
THAT'S... THE PRIMORDIAL GRANDPARENTS!
THE TALLEST PEAKS FOR HUNDREDS OF MILES AROUND.
BETWEEN THEM LIES THE GLACIER THAT NEVER MELTS.
FROM THAT MIGHTY CHAIN COME THE WATERS THAT FEED THE LAKE OF MANY COLORED SALMON... OUR HOME.
EVERYONE!
I KNOW WHERE WE ARE! THE LAKE! GOOD RIVER IS THAT WAY!
I SEE THE WAY HOME!

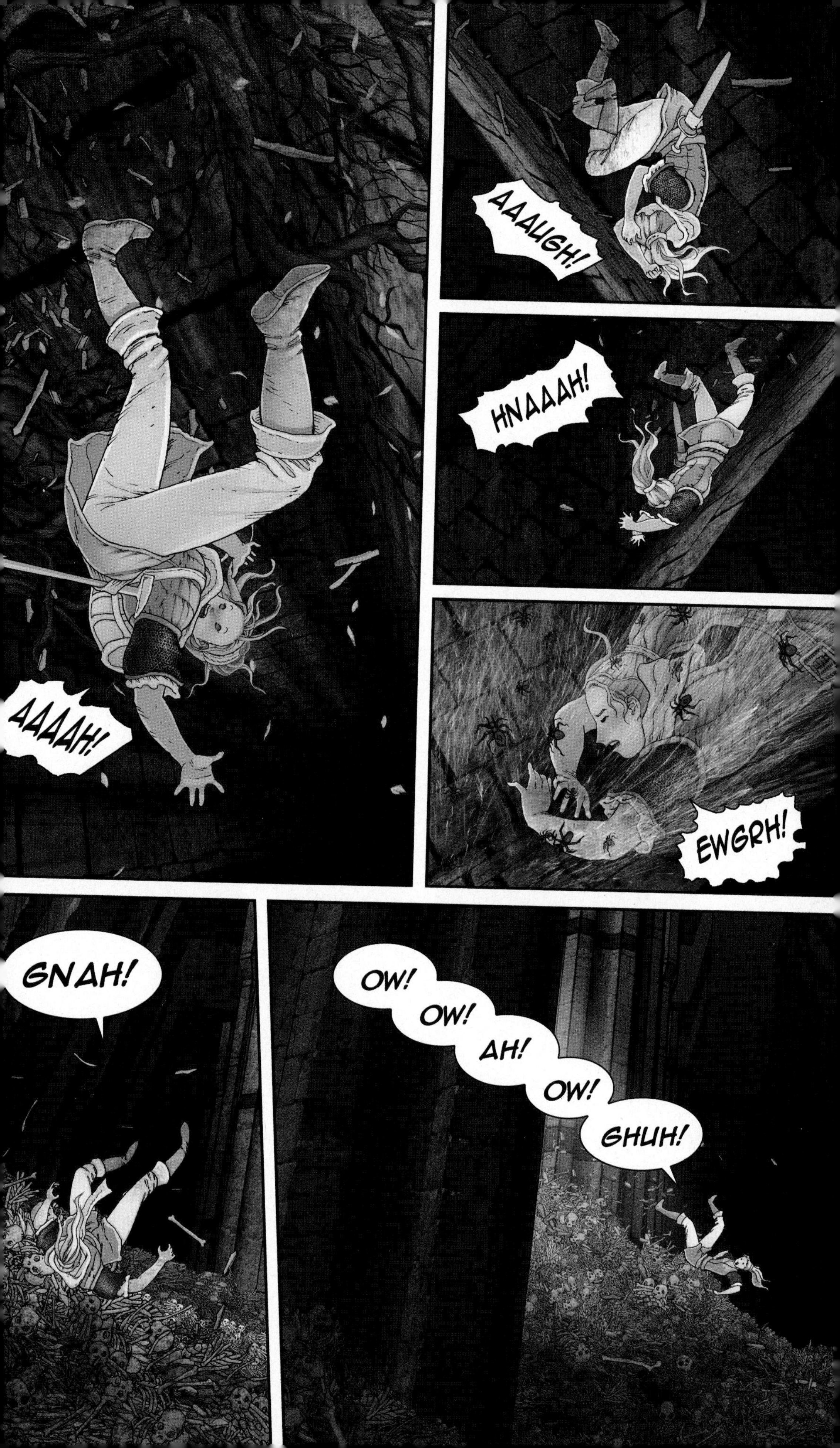
AAAAH!
AAAUGH!
HNAAAH!
EWGRH!
GNAH!
OW!
OW!
AH!
OW!
GHUH!

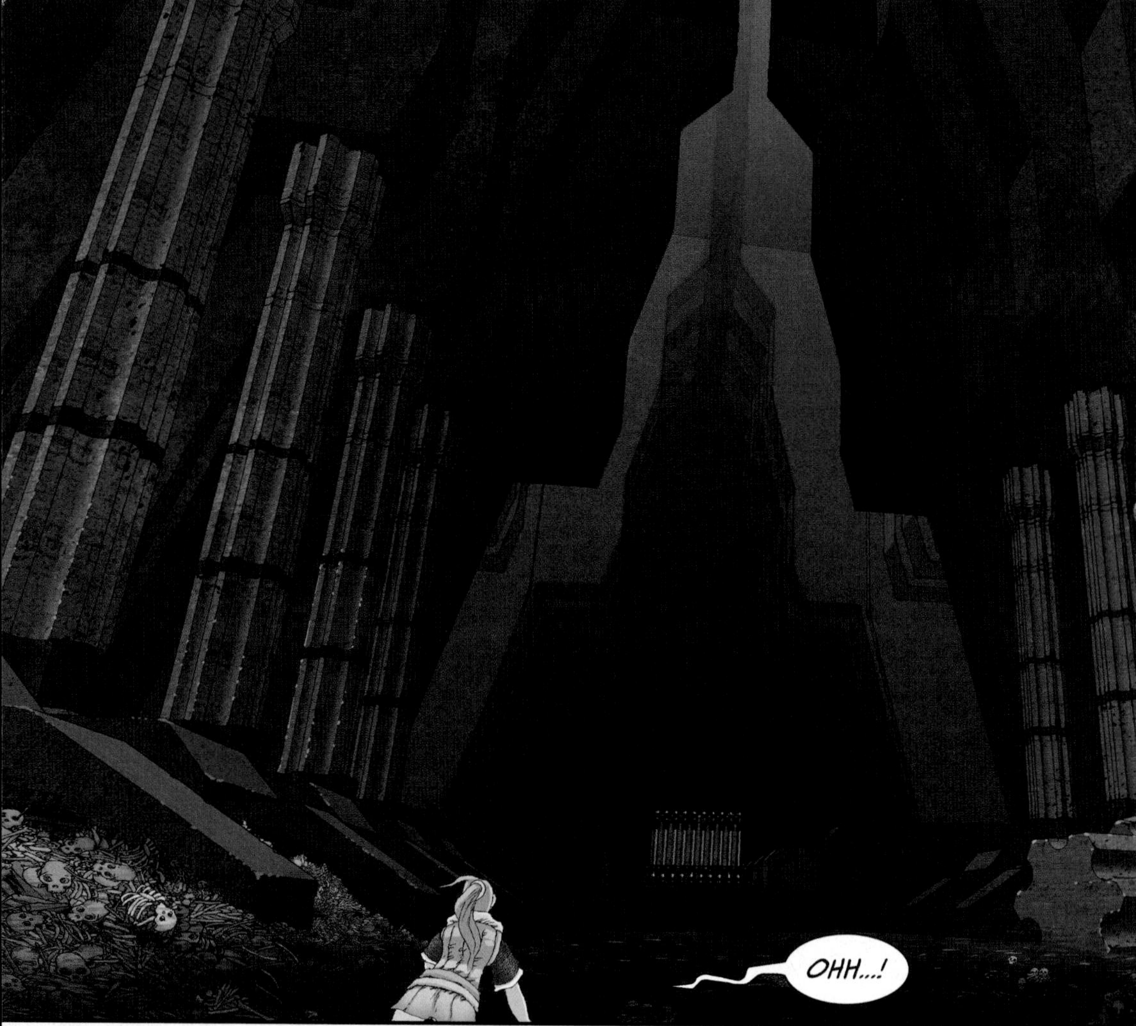
OHH...!

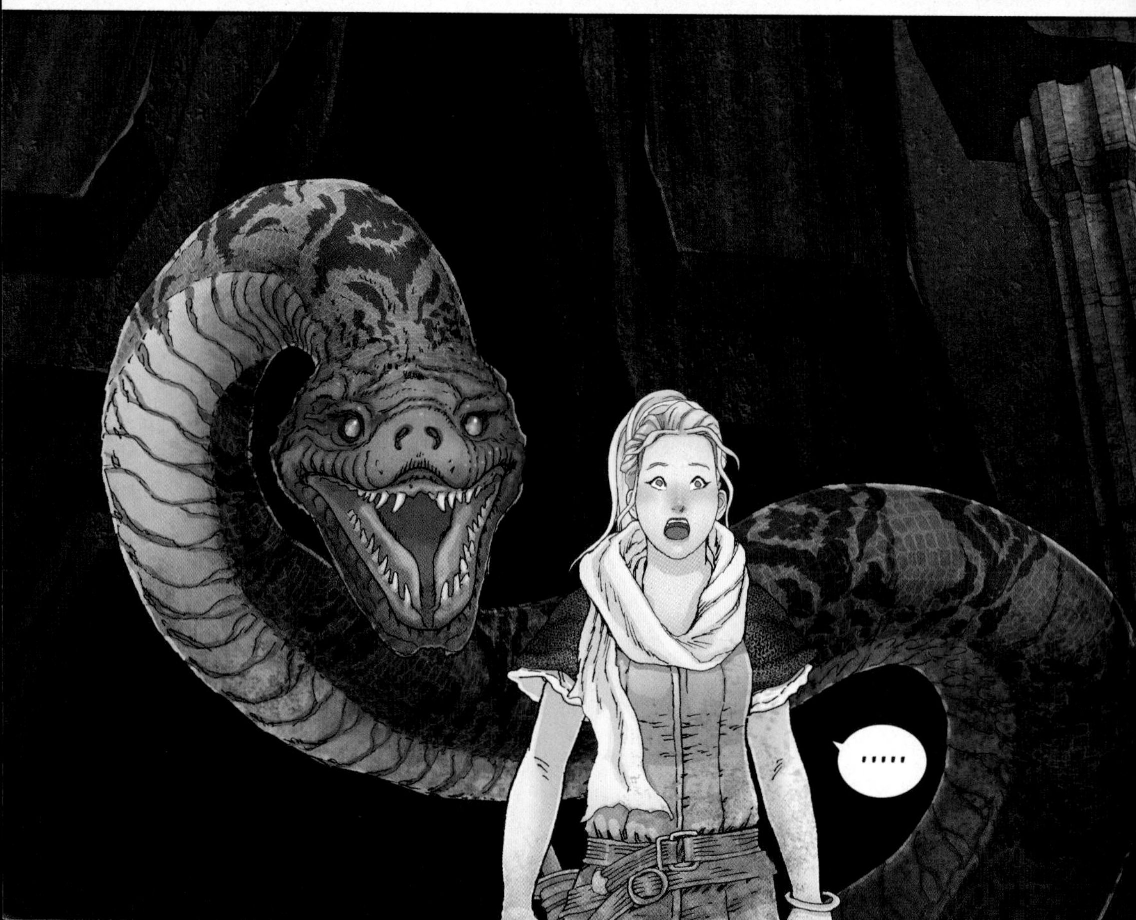
......

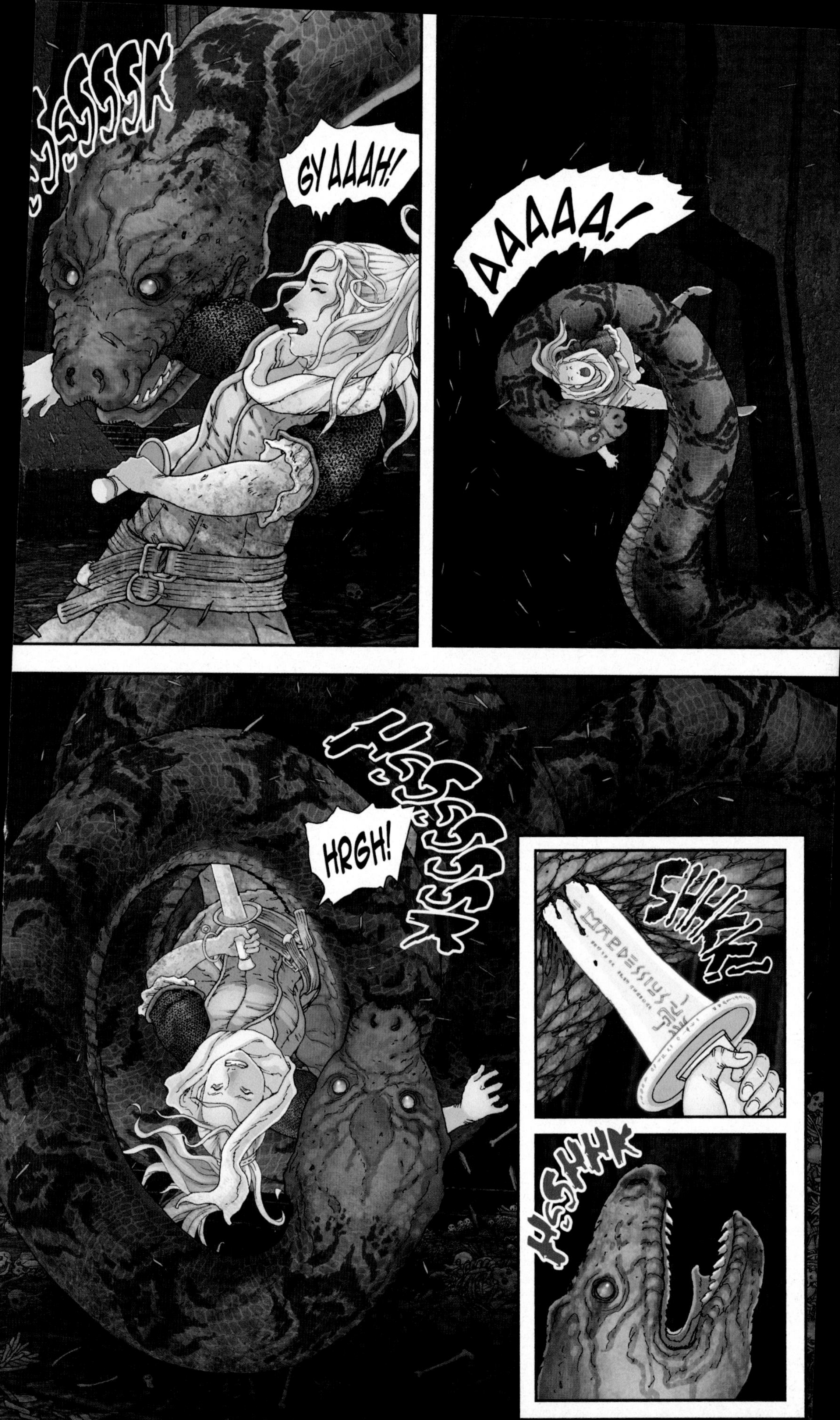
SSSSSK
GYAAAH!
AAAAA!
HSSSSSK
HRGH!
SHHK!
HSSHHK

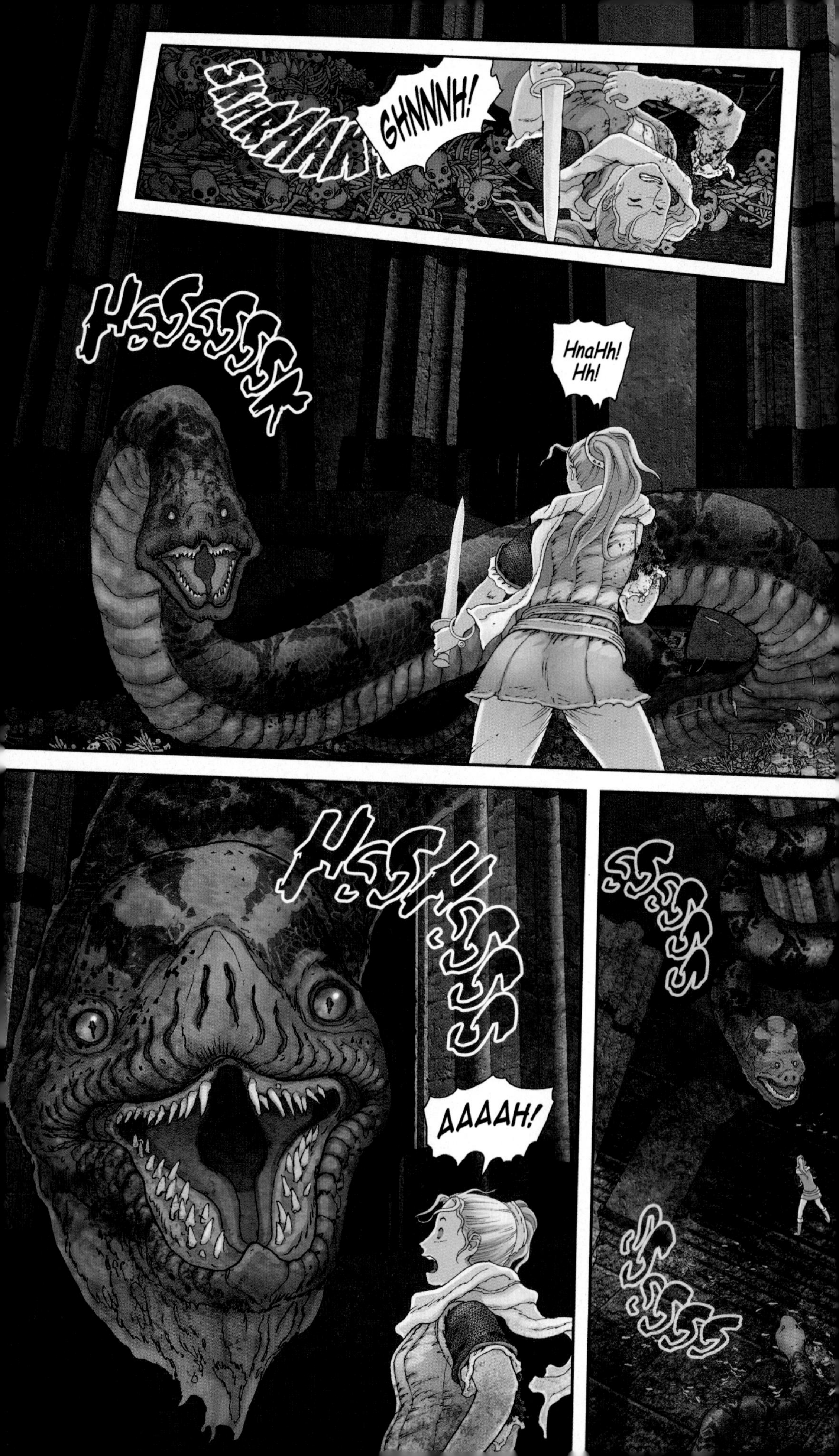
GHNNNH!
HnaHh! Hh!
AAAAH!

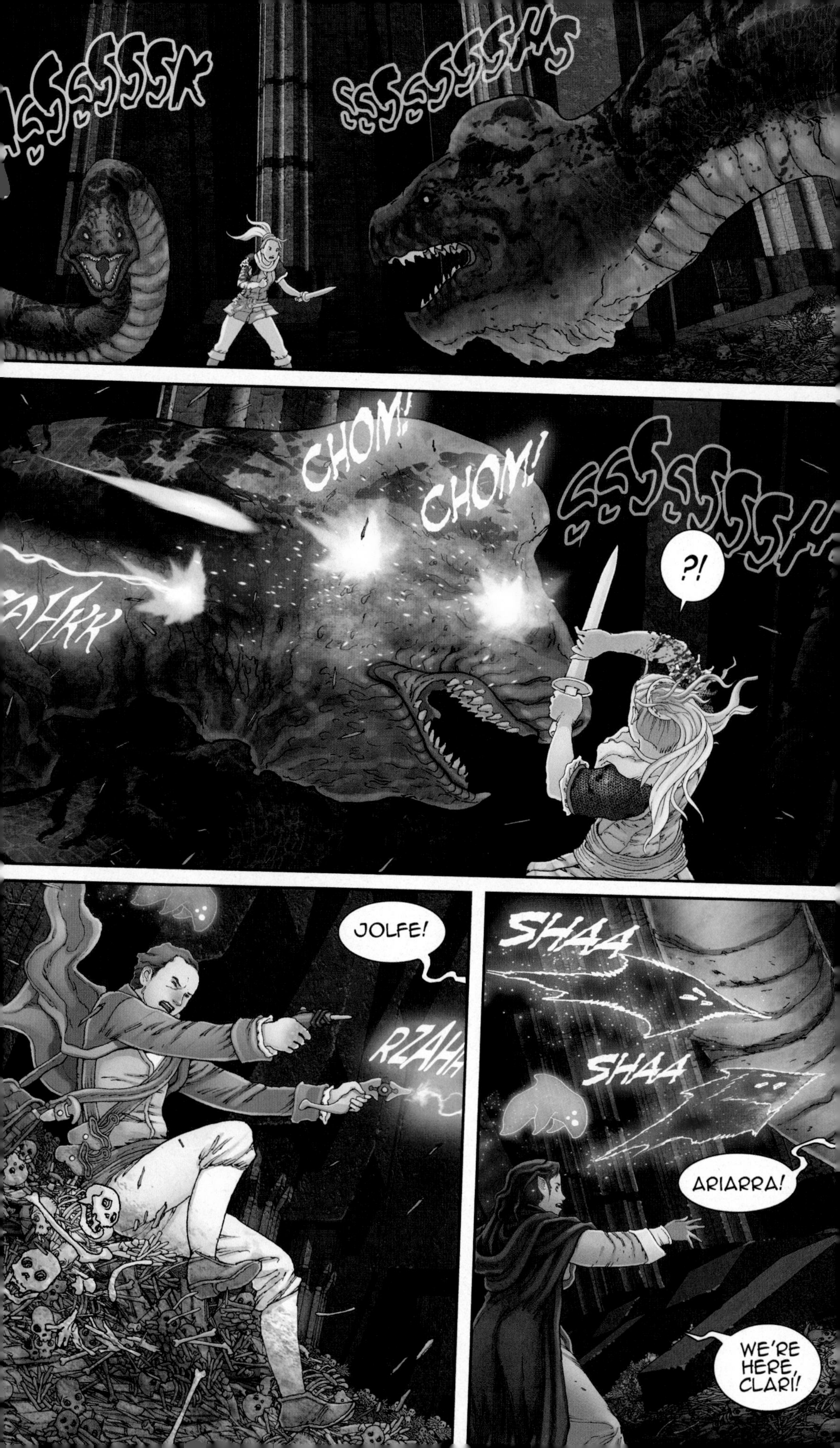
SSSSSSSK
SSSSSSSSHS
CHOM!
CHOM!
SSSSSSSSH
?!
JOLFE!
RZAHH
SHAA
SHAA
ARIARRA!
WE'RE HERE, CLARI!

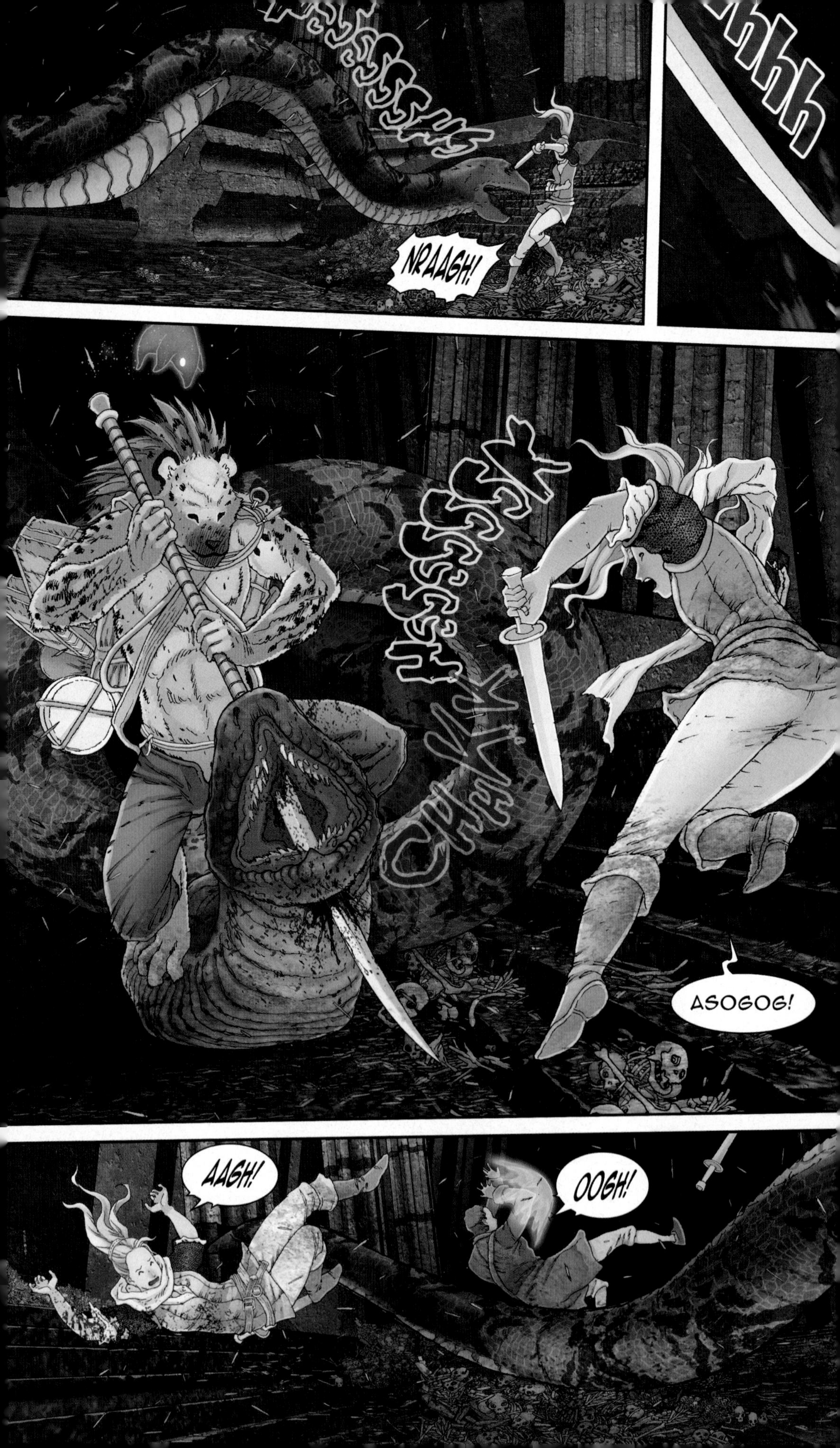
NRAAGH!
ASOGOG!
AAGH!
OOGH!

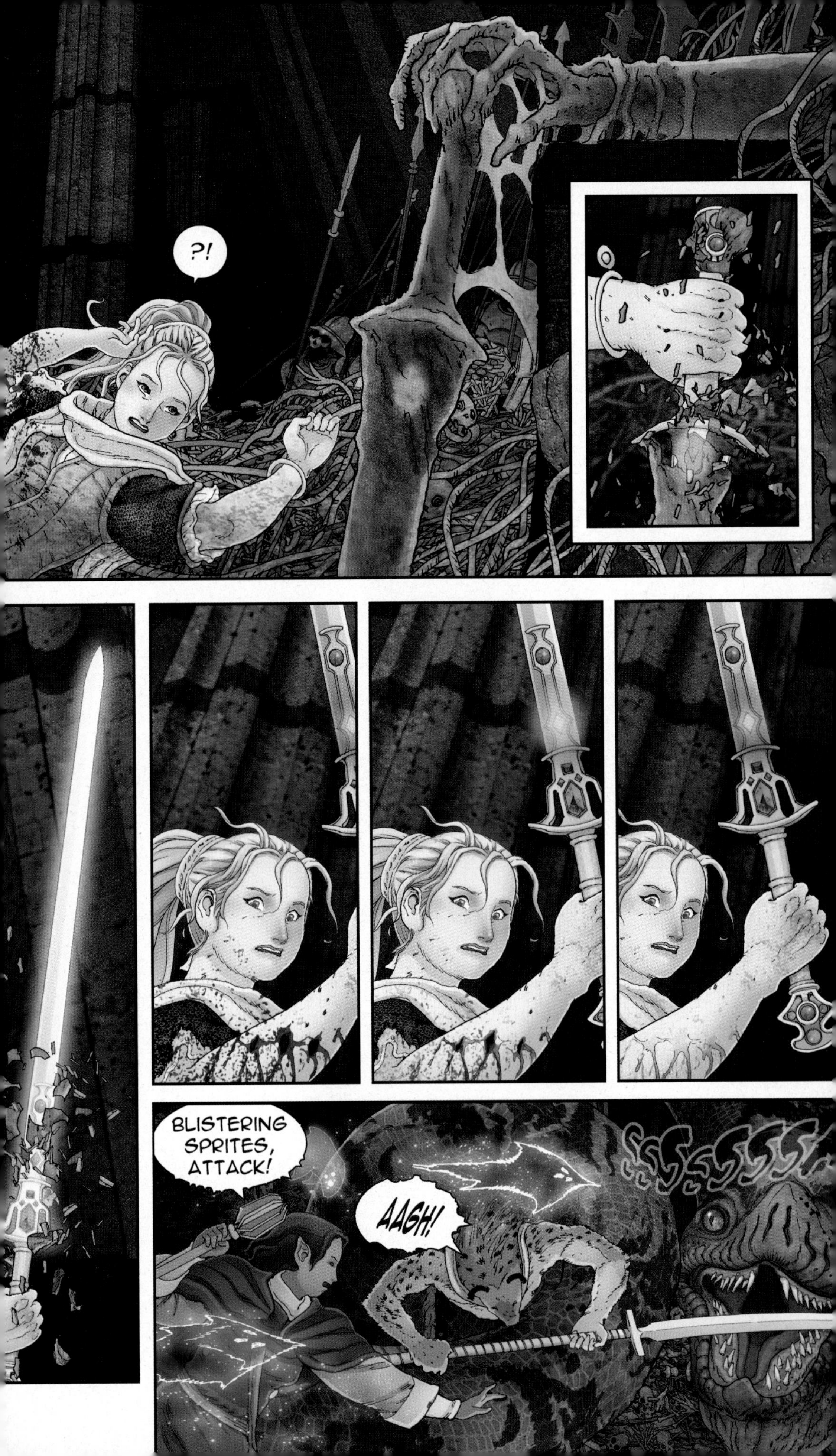
?!
BLISTERING SPRITES, ATTACK!
AAGH!

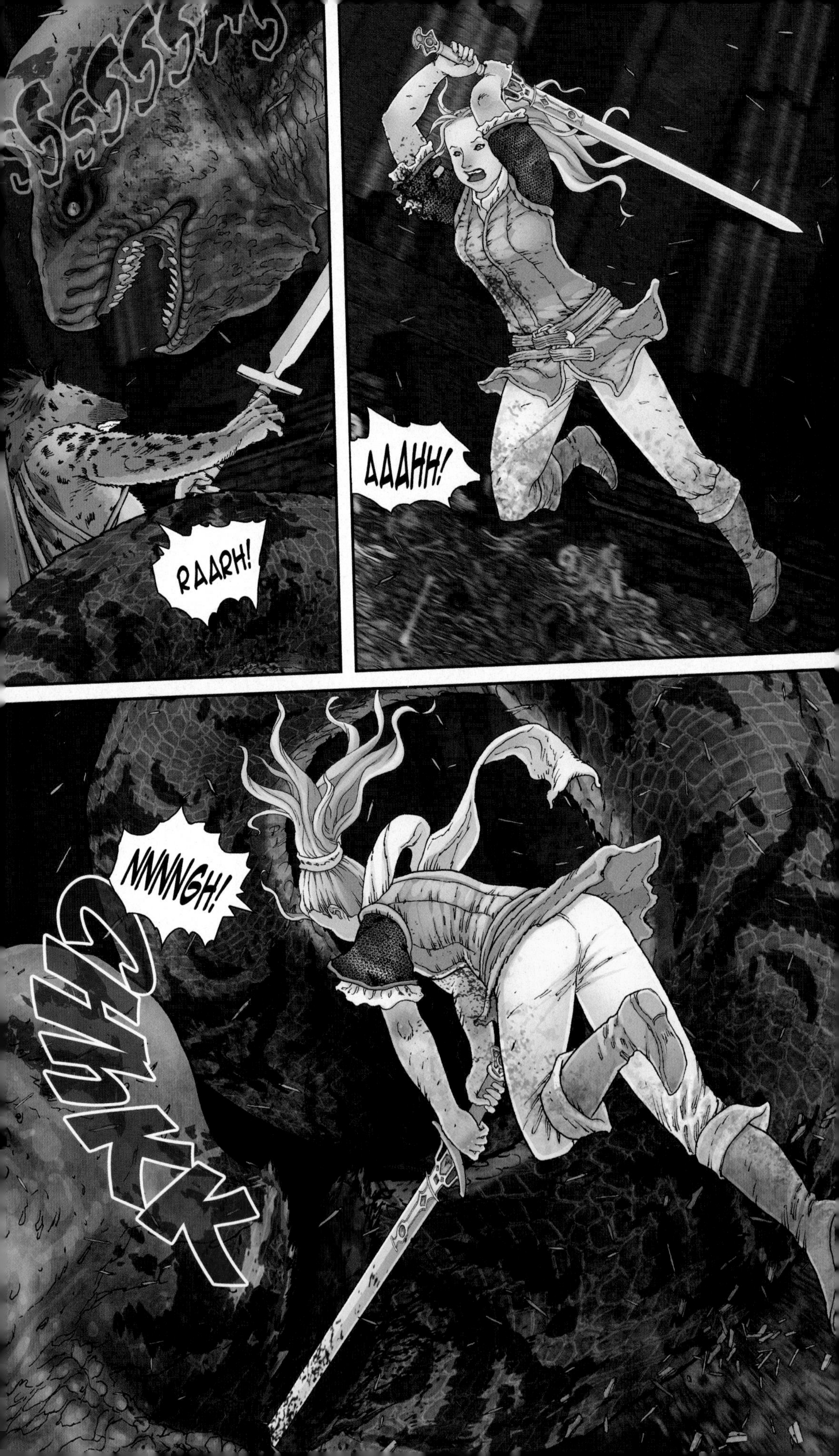
RAARH!
AAAHH!
NNNNGH!

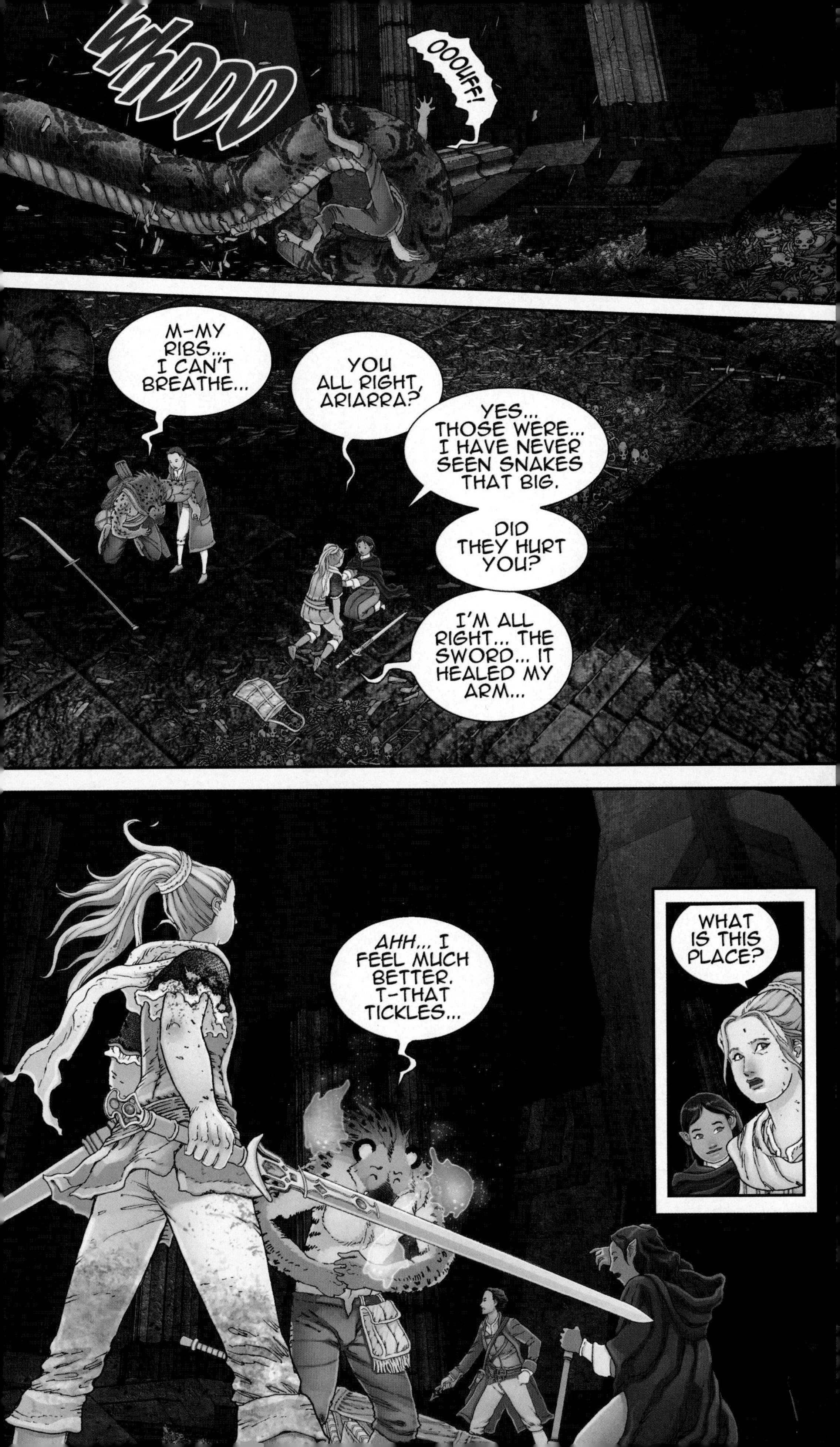
WHOOO
OOOUFF!
M-MY RIBS... I CAN'T BREATHE...
YOU ALL RIGHT, ARIARRA?
YES... THOSE WERE... I HAVE NEVER SEEN SNAKES THAT BIG.
DID THEY HURT YOU?
I'M ALL RIGHT... THE SWORD... IT HEALED MY ARM...
AHH... I FEEL MUCH BETTER. T-THAT TICKLES...
WHAT IS THIS PLACE?

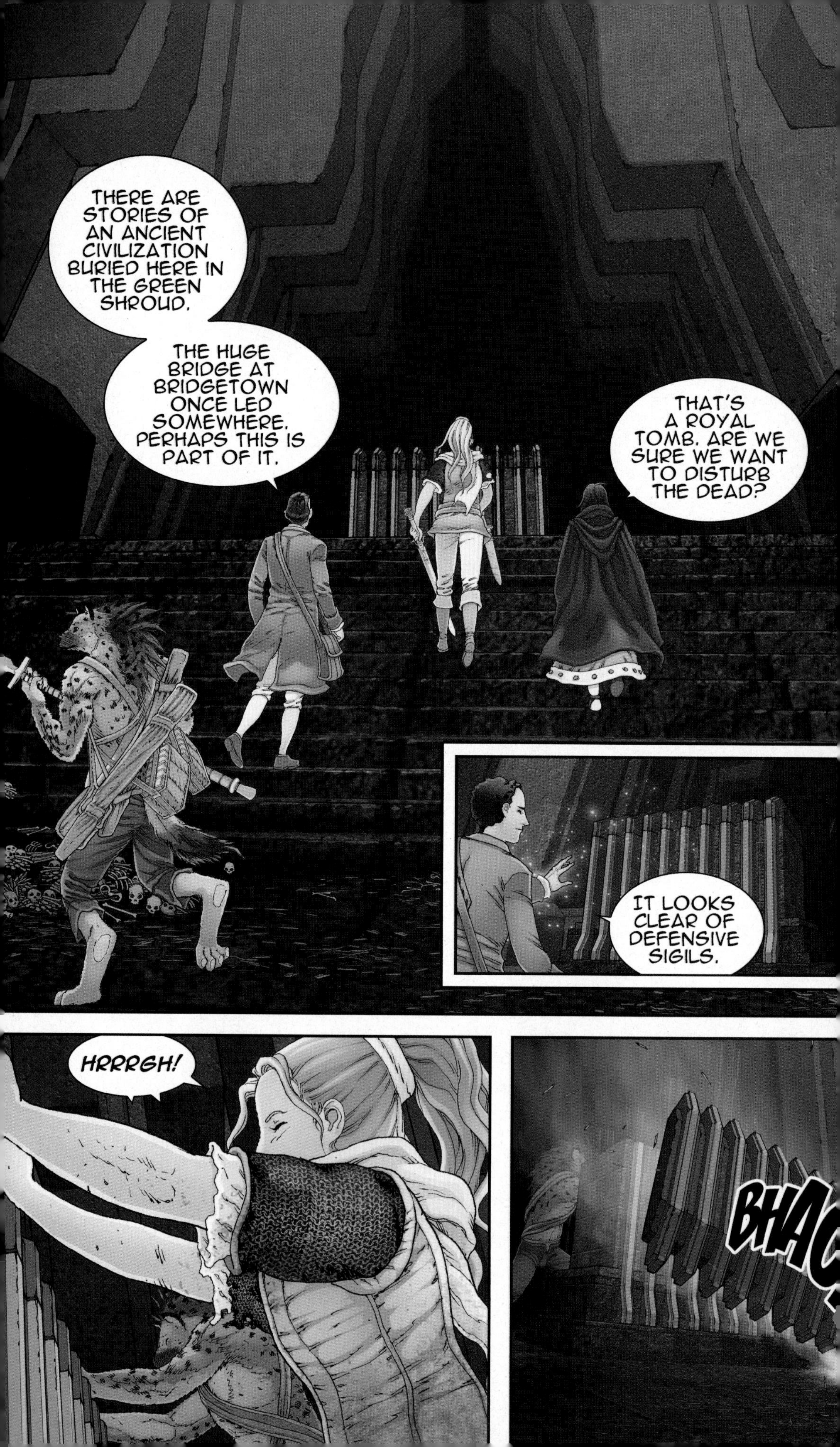
THERE ARE STORIES OF AN ANCIENT CIVILIZATION BURIED HERE IN THE GREEN SHROUD.
THE HUGE BRIDGE AT BRIDGETOWN ONCE LED SOMEWHERE. PERHAPS THIS IS PART OF IT.
THAT'S A ROYAL TOMB. ARE WE SURE WE WANT TO DISTURB THE DEAD?
IT LOOKS CLEAR OF DEFENSIVE SIGILS.
HRRRGH!

SO BEAUTIFUL. THIS PLACE LOOKS LIKE IT'S A THOUSAND YEARS OLD.

YET THIS LOOKS AS IF THIS CLOTH WAS LAID DOWN YESTERDAY.

IT'S NOT CLOTH... THIS IS VELURILE. THEY SAY IT TAKES A HUNDRED THOUSAND YEARS TO ROT...

TOUGHER THAN FIREBULL LEATHER, LIGHTER THAN PADDED ARMOR. SOFT AS SILK.

AND THIS HARD PLATE. IT'S NOT IRON, UNLESS I AM MISTAKEN, THAT'S KAVELNAR.

TEN TIMES LIGHTER AND HARDER THAN STEEL... SLIGHLY FLEXIBLE TO DEFLECT PROJECTILES.

HOW DO YOU KNOW ABOUT VELURILE AND KAVELNAR?

MY MOTHER HAD A CAP MADE OF THEM.

YOU TAKE THE ARMOR.

A-ARE YOU SURE?

YES. I WILL HAVE THIS.

"BELDERACH THE FOURTH... SEVENTEENTH EMPEROR OF ARGODOR."

I'VE READ ABOUT THE BELDERACH LINE OF EMPERORS. THEY WERE THE BUILDERS OF EMPIRES DURING THE GRAND ANCIENT AGE.

MANY FINE WEAPONS WERE FORGED UNDER THEIR RULE.

IT IS SAID THAT THE GREAT DRAGONS FLED AND SLEPT IN THEIR SECRET LAIRS FOR THOUSANDS OF YEARS AFTER.

COUSIN CLARI...

...SPLIT FIVE WAYS? WHAT DO YOU THINK?

ARGODORIAN SILVER CROWNS! OH... RINGS!

OH MY!

A-ARE THOSE...?!

MAYBE... I DON'T KNOW... CAN YOU TELL?

THEY ARE! LOOK AT THE EMBEDDED GEMS!

THE ART OF JEWEL MELDING IS ANOTHER FEATURE OF THE ARGODORIAN MAJERES' PROWESS.

HOW DID THEY EMBED A JEWEL INSIDE ANOTHER JEWEL?

THIS HAS FIRE SIGILS ON IT. I MUST STUDY THIS FURTHER.

OUR VERY FIRST RINGS!

WHAT DO THEY DO, AIARRA?

BOTH OF THEM HAVE THE SHIELD SIGILS ON THE INSIDE, SO THESE SHOULD PROTECT US WELL.

ALL THE COINS BAGGED

WE'LL COUNT THEM LATER.

EVERYTHIN TAKEN?

KING BELDERACH'S ARMOR SUITS YOU WELL.

I THOUGHT IT WOULD NOT FIT, THEN IT JUST... EXPANDED.

COME ON, WE'VE LEFT THE OTHERS LONG ENOUGH.

IT'S TIME WE LEFT THIS FOUL PLACE.

.....

.....

...?

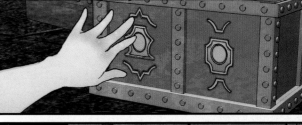

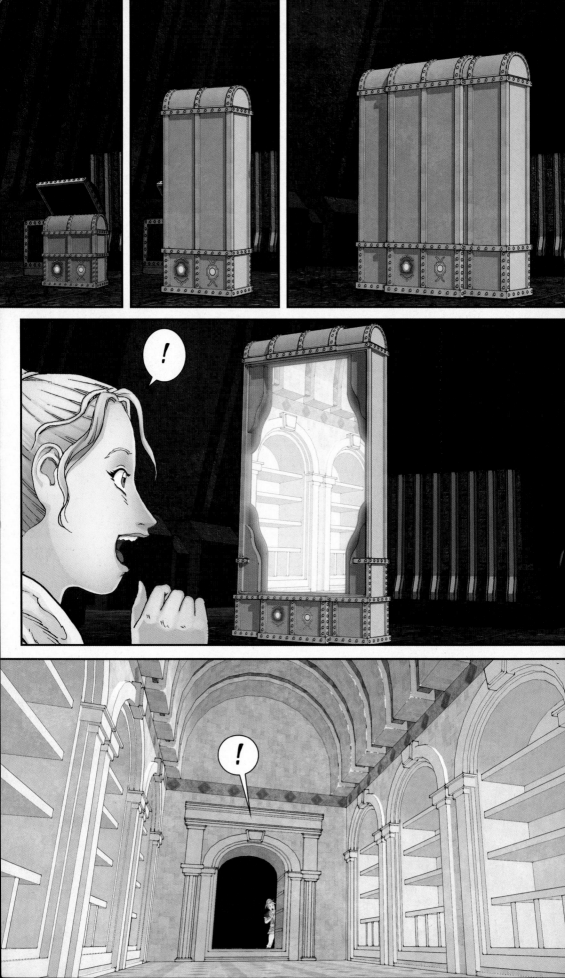

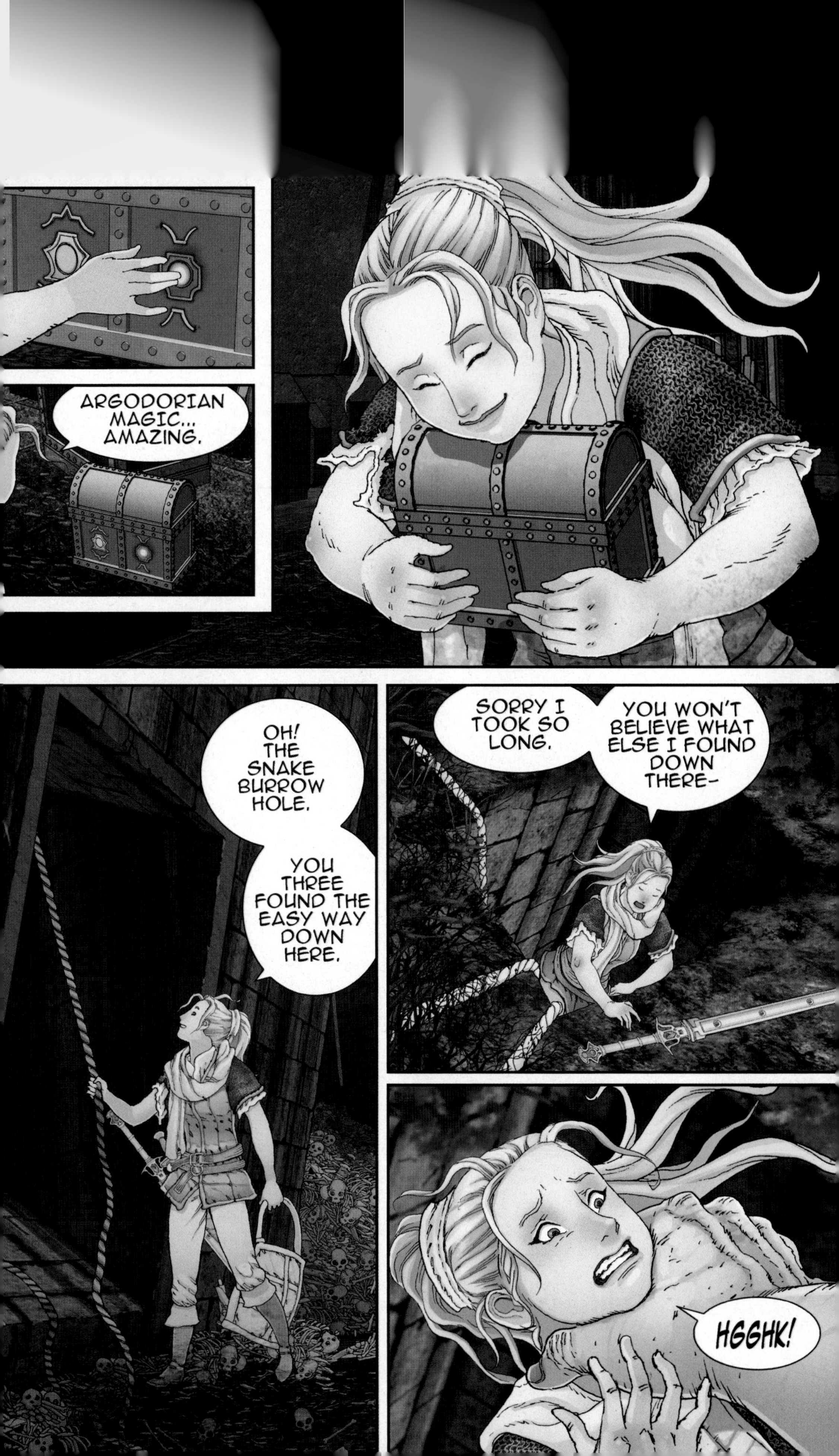
ARGODORIAN MAGIC... AMAZING.
OH! THE SNAKE BURROW HOLE.
YOU THREE FOUND THE EASY WAY DOWN HERE.
SORRY I TOOK SO LONG.
YOU WON'T BELIEVE WHAT ELSE I FOUND DOWN THERE-
HGGHK!

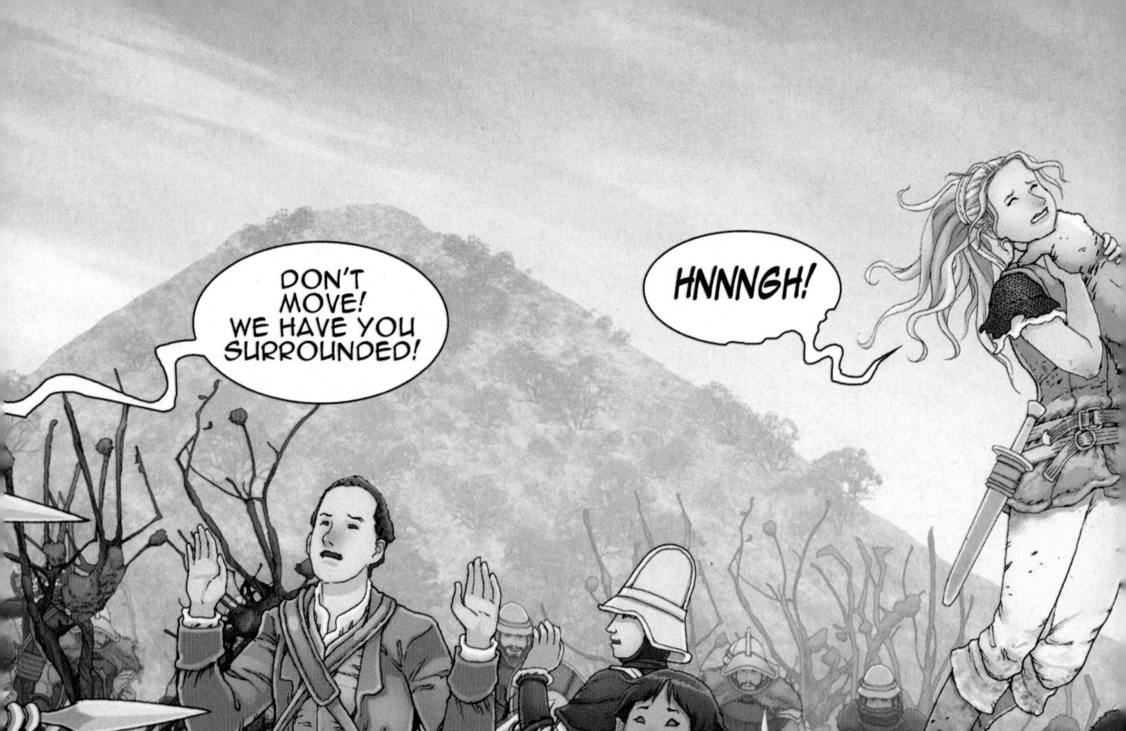
DON'T MOVE! WE HAVE YOU SURROUNDED!
HNNNGH!
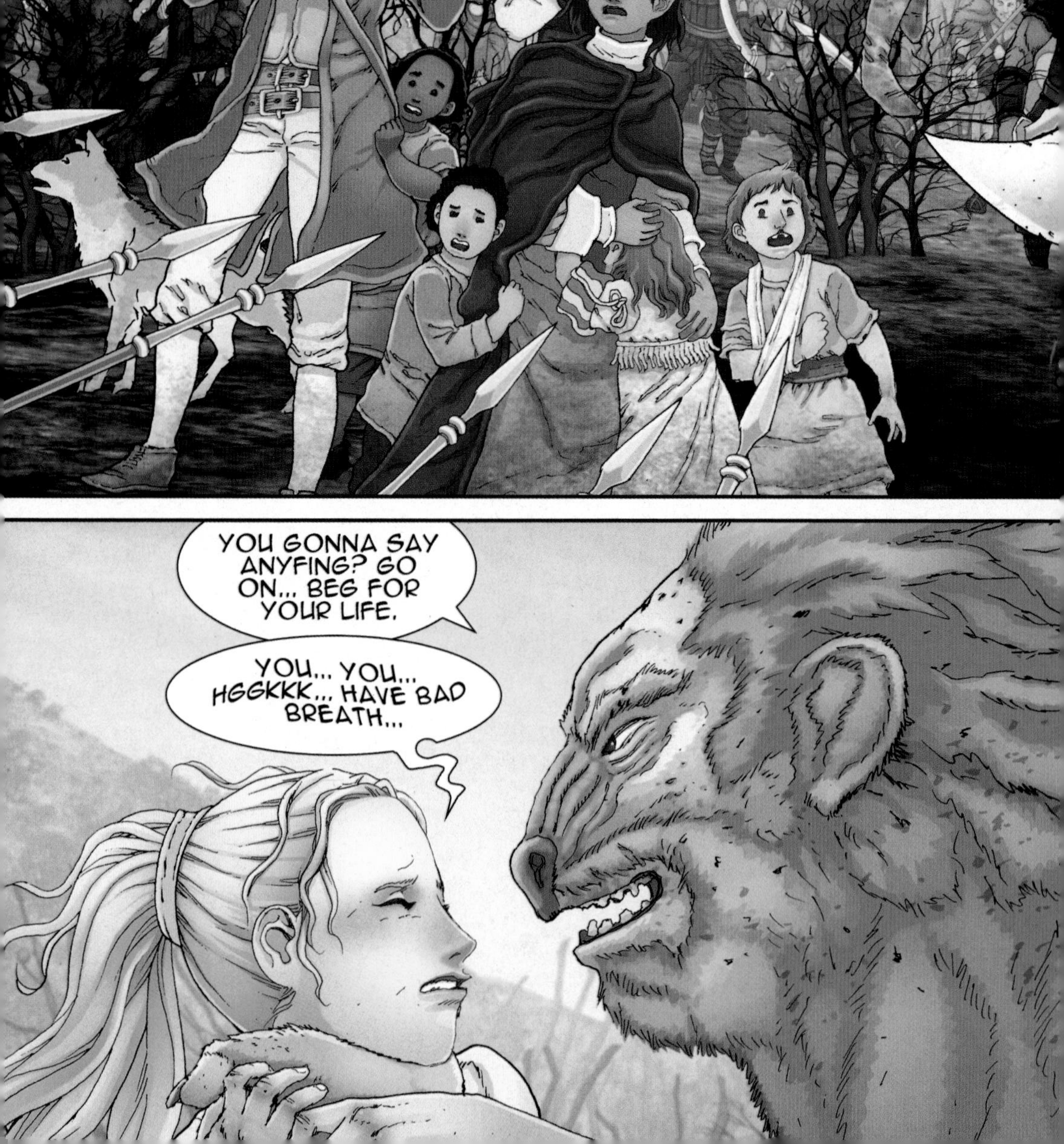
YOU GONNA SAY ANYFING? GO ON... BEG FOR YOUR LIFE.
YOU... YOU... HGGKKK... HAVE BAD BREATH...

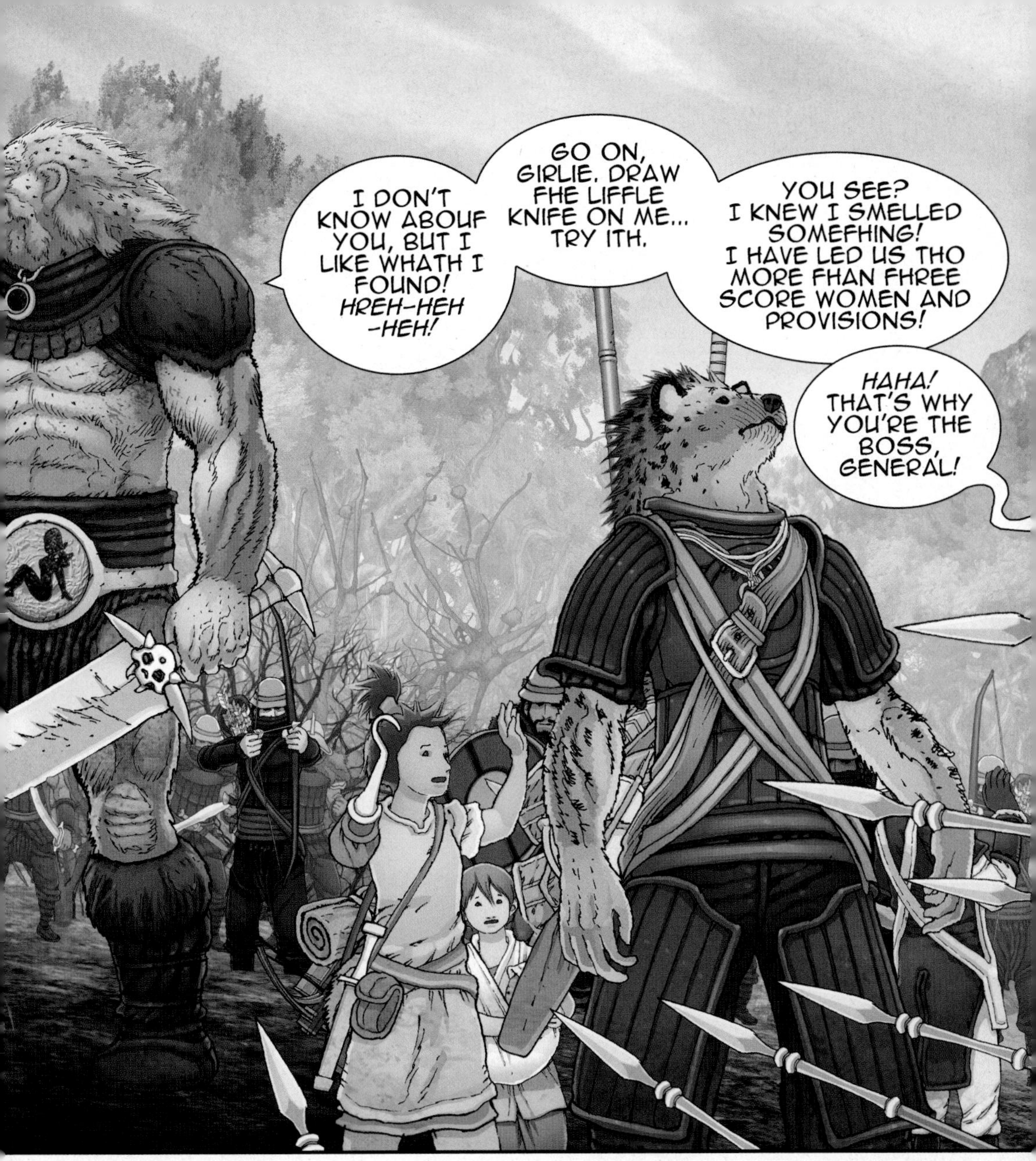
I DON'T KNOW ABOUF YOU, BUT I LIKE WHATH I FOUND! HREH-HEH -HEH!
GO ON, GIRLIE. DRAW FHE LIFFLE KNIFE ON ME... TRY ITH.
YOU SEE? I KNEW I SMELLED SOMEFHING! I HAVE LED US THO MORE FHAN FHREE SCORE WOMEN AND PROVISIONS!
HAHA! THAT'S WHY YOU'RE THE BOSS, GENERAL!

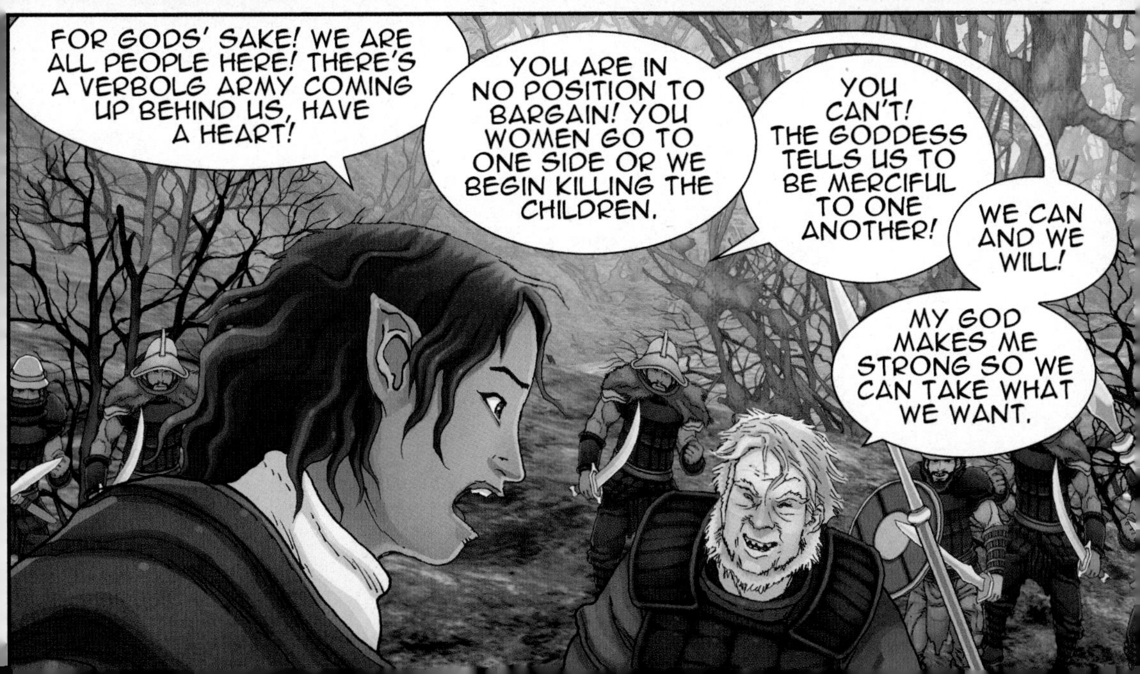
FOR GODS' SAKE! WE ARE ALL PEOPLE HERE! THERE'S A VERBOLG ARMY COMING UP BEHIND US, HAVE A HEART!
YOU ARE IN NO POSITION TO BARGAIN! YOU WOMEN GO TO ONE SIDE OR WE BEGIN KILLING THE CHILDREN.
YOU CAN'T! THE GODDESS TELLS US TO BE MERCIFUL TO ONE ANOTHER!
WE CAN AND WE WILL!
MY GOD MAKES ME STRONG SO WE CAN TAKE WHAT WE WANT.

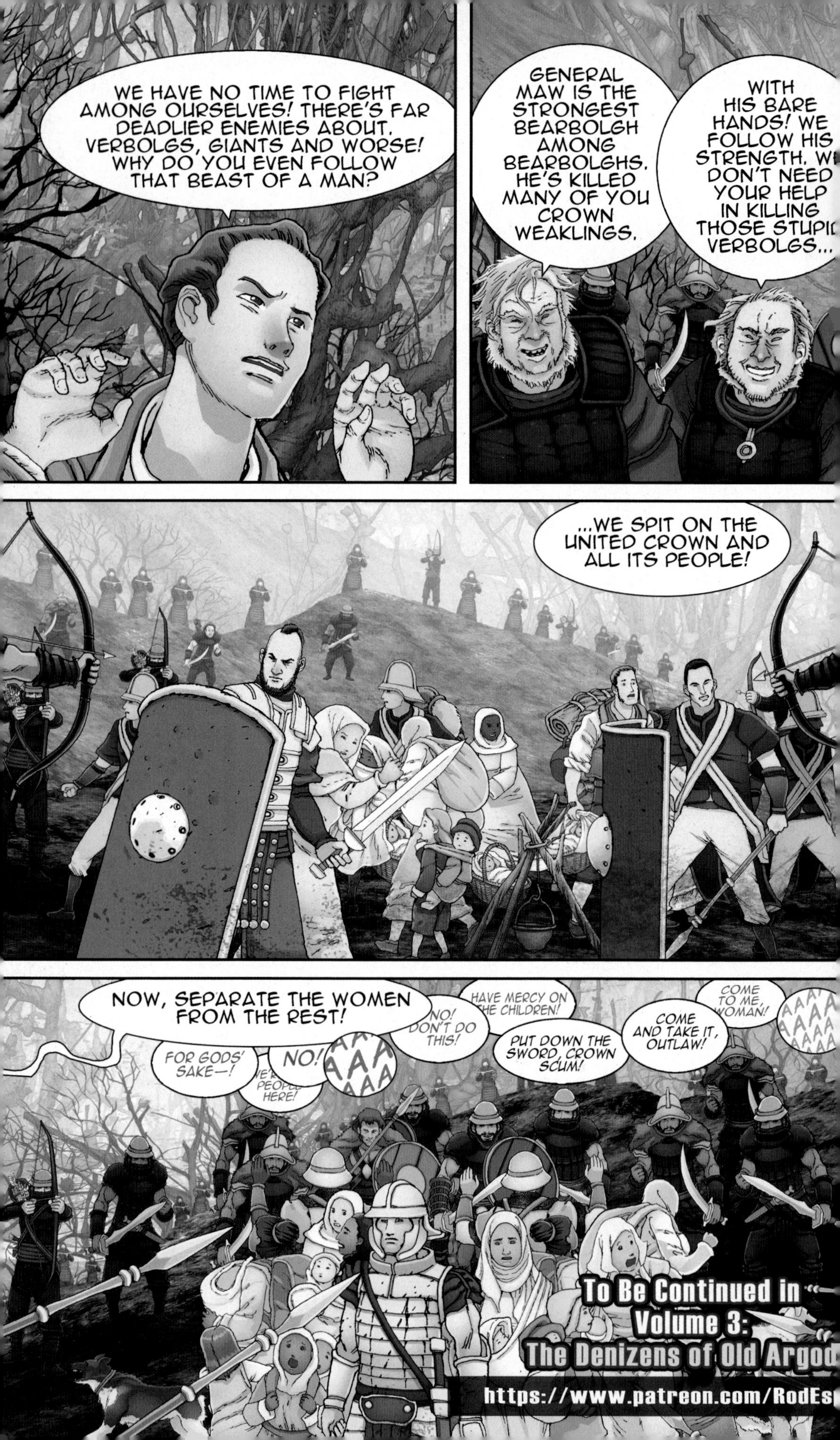

WE HAVE NO TIME TO FIGHT AMONG OURSELVES! THERE'S FAR DEADLIER ENEMIES ABOUT. VERBOLGS, GIANTS AND WORSE! WHY DO YOU EVEN FOLLOW THAT BEAST OF A MAN?
GENERAL MAW IS THE STRONGEST BEARBOLGH AMONG BEARBOLGHS. HE'S KILLED MANY OF YOU CROWN WEAKLINGS.
WITH HIS BARE HANDS! WE FOLLOW HIS STRENGTH. W DON'T NEED YOUR HELP IN KILLING THOSE STUPI VERBOLGS...
...WE SPIT ON THE UNITED CROWN AND ALL ITS PEOPLE!
NOW, SEPARATE THE WOMEN FROM THE REST!
FOR GODS' SAKE—!
NO!
AAAAAAA
NO! DON'T DO THIS!
HAVE MERCY ON HE CHILDREN!
PUT DOWN THE SWORD, CROWN SCUM!
COME AND TAKE IT, OUTLAW!
COME TO ME, WOMAN!
AAAAAAAAA
To Be Continued in Volume 3: The Denizens of Old Argod
https://www.patreon.com/RodEs